MASTER
of
FIRE

ANGELA KNIGHT

B

BERKLEY SENSATION, NEW YORK

PROM
Knight

THE BERKLEY PUBLISHING GROUP
Published by the Penguin Group
Penguin Group (USA) Inc.
375 Hudson Street, New York, New York 10014, USA
Penguin Group (Canada), 90 Eglinton Avenue East, Suite 700, Toronto, Ontario M4P 2Y3, Canada
(a division of Pearson Penguin Canada Inc.)
Penguin Books Ltd., 80 Strand, London WC2R 0RL, England
Penguin Group Ireland, 25 St. Stephen's Green, Dublin 2, Ireland (a division of Penguin Books Ltd.)
Penguin Group (Australia), 250 Camberwell Road, Camberwell, Victoria 3124, Australia
(a division of Pearson Australia Group Pty. Ltd.)
Penguin Books India Pvt. Ltd., 11 Community Centre, Panchsheel Park, New Delhi—110 017, India
Penguin Group (NZ), 67 Apollo Drive, Rosedale, North Shore 0632, New Zealand
(a division of Pearson New Zealand Ltd.)
Penguin Books (South Africa) (Pty.) Ltd., 24 Sturdee Avenue, Rosebank, Johannesburg 2196,
South Africa

Penguin Books Ltd., Registered Offices: 80 Strand, London WC2R 0RL, England

This is a work of fiction. Names, characters, places, and incidents either are the product of the author's imagination or are used fictitiously, and any resemblance to actual persons, living or dead, business establishments, events, or locales is entirely coincidental. The publisher does not have any control over and does not assume any responsibility for author or third-party websites or their content.

MASTER OF FIRE

A Berkley Sensation Book / published by arrangement with the author

PRINTING HISTORY
Berkley Sensation mass-market edition / March 2010

Copyright © 2010 by Angela Knight.
Excerpt from *Master of Smoke* by Angela Knight copyright © by Angela Knight.
Cover art by Phil Heffernan.
Cover design by George Long.

ISBN: 978-0-425-23335-1

BERKLEY® SENSATION
Berkley Sensation Books are published by The Berkley Publishing Group,
a division of Penguin Group (USA) Inc.,
375 Hudson Street, New York, New York 10014.
BERKLEY® SENSATION and the "B" design are trademarks of Penguin Group (USA) Inc.

PRINTED IN THE UNITED STATES OF AMERICA

10   9   8   7   6   5   4   3   2   1

ACKNOWLEDGMENTS

I would like to dedicate this book to the men and women of the Spartanburg County Sheriff's Office. In particular, I want to thank Lieutenant Ashley Harris, forensic chemist, arson investigator, bomb tech, and all-around cool human being. He let me follow him around for a week, watching him do his job, including the bomb squad parts. Ashley is positively brilliant, and we are lucky he only uses his powers for good, since he's the one who helped me come up with the evil stuff the bomber does in this book. He did design sketches, patiently answered all my questions, and told me how my hero could get out of the messes I put him in. Much of Logan's technical dialogue originally came out of Ashley's mouth.

By the way, he actually owns the toy monkey described in Chapter Eight.

I also want to mention my cop buddies in the Lunch Bunch, especially my friend Robert Rosenberg, evidence tech and skin diver. I want to thank my personal pit crew, who helped me cope with some serious back issues that nagged me while I was trying to write this book. Personal trainer Bethany

Morton-Rhye, masseuse Christine Cox, and acupuncture specialist Shawn Jacobs kept my pain to manageable levels.

More thanks are owed to my beta readers, Diane Whiteside, Kate Douglas, Linda Kusiolek, Margaret Riley, and my wonderful Bookdragon, Virginia Ettel. Diane and Virginia also moderate my Yahoo Group at http://groups.yahoo.com/group/angelaknight/. And they do a wonderful job of herding cats, too.

Most of all, I want to thank the two people who inspire all my heroes and heroines. My sister, Angela Patterson, is one of the strongest, kindest people I have ever met. Whenever I wonder what a heroine would do, I just think of Angela.

Then there's my husband of twenty-five years, Mike Woodcock. Mike's endless patience and romantic heart form the sweet and sexy core of every hero I write. Love you, babe.

For more about my work, check out my web page at www .angelasknights.com, where you will find excerpts and blurbs for upcoming books, along with desktop wallpaper, book videos, and other goodies.

MASTER
of
FIRE

ONE

The truck bounced down the snaking gravel driveway that led to the dead man's house. It was a huge armored box of a vehicle, gleaming black, with "Greendale County Sheriff's Office Bomb Disposal Team" painted on the side in white lettering.

Terrence John Anderson watched through his binoculars as the truck rolled up to the old white farmhouse. He lay hidden in a leafy clump of bushes at the edge of the woods, camouflage paint smearing his face, ice gray eyes narrow and watchful amid the writhing patterns of green and black. A sniper rifle lay beside him, but it was just for insurance.

He had something more dramatic in mind than a bullet.

The truck rolled to a stop, and a woman climbed out of the passenger side. He focused the binocs on her. Tall, dressed in wide-legged navy pants that swirled around her long legs. A flowing pale blue blouse draped over lush breasts and nipped in around her narrow waist, cinched by a wide navy belt. Her blond hair was pulled into a twist on the back of her head, but the severe hairstyle only empha-sized her sensual beauty. She scanned the area, her expres-sion watchful and wary. He wondered how she'd look after

the bomb got done with that pretty face. Almost a shame, really.

On the other hand, there was nothing quite like the feeling he got from watching someone die.

Lieutenant Logan MacRoy walked around the truck to join the blonde. He was a big man, broad-shouldered in the black knit shirt of the bomb squad, with his military-style uniform pants tucked into combat boots. Terrence felt his muscles coil in anticipation. His sheriff's department contact had been right. The e-mail from i4ni@zoomcom.com had said MacRoy was the bomb squad tech on call today. Sure enough, here he was.

Terrence did love a reliable informant.

The file the client had provided said MacRoy was thirty-one years old, six-foot-four, two hundred ten pounds, Caucasian, brown and brown. A lieutenant with the Greendale County Sheriff's Office, he'd graduated at the top of his class at the South Carolina law enforcement academy. No surprise, considering he also had a master's degree in chemistry.

MacRoy had a long list of other certifications as well, including arson investigator and, of course, bomb squad tech. An unusual set of qualifications for a forensic chemist, according to Terrence's research.

Actually, it was pretty rare for a Southern sheriff's office to have a lab at all; those that did kept their chemists busy testing seized cocaine, pot, crack, and methamphetamine. Logan had evidently talked his sheriff into letting him do a lot more, maybe on the strength of his nine years in law enforcement. He'd been one of the first forensic chemists in South Carolina.

Somewhere along the line, he'd also pissed somebody off. Really, really bad. Terrence John Anderson bad.

Terrence lifted his cell phone and thumbed 119. Listened to the beep that signaled his booby trap was armed. And smiled in anticipation.

The blonde's head snapped up as if she'd somehow heard that tiny beep. She stared into the woods, right at Terrence,

eyes narrow. The assassin froze, except for the slight movement of his hand finding the rifle. He could snatch it up and fire before the little bitch got the shout of warning out of her mouth.

The metal bracelet the client had given him suddenly blazed hot around his wrist, a ferocious burning bite so intense he could almost smell his skin sizzle. He bit back a snarled curse. The blonde's gaze turned uncertain, and she scanned the woods around him in confusion.

And then she looked away.

The pounding of his heart began to slow, and his hand slid away from the rifle. Seems she hadn't seen him after all.

He could let the chemist go find his little surprise.

"Something wrong?" Logan asked in his deep rumble of a voice.

Giada Shepherd wiped the wary frown off her face and turned toward him. "Thought I saw something moving in the woods." She shrugged and lied. "Just a squirrel."

She wasn't sure what it had been, but it hadn't been a squirrel. Overactive bodyguard imagination, maybe. Furry and four-legged, no.

But for a moment there, she'd felt such a sense of chill menace, she'd been unable to breathe. Then it was just gone. Had to be her imagination, especially since she'd done a scanning spell and found nothing.

On the other hand, it was daylight, and her magic wasn't all that reliable when the sun was up. Maybe somebody in those woods was eyeing Logan MacRoy's handsome head through a sniper scope.

That thought sent ice creeping down her spine on razor claws. She had to protect Logan. That was the whole point of this charade.

Gravel crunched with the sound of running feet. Giada wheeled, only to relax as a small boy darted around the bulk of the bomb truck, his eyes wide as an anime character's under a mop of fine blond hair. She was no expert when

it came to judging a child's age, but she figured he was no more than six or so.

"Hi!" He slid to a stop to study Logan with breathless excitement. "Are you a real cop?" His blue gaze darted to the weapons belt with its nine-millimeter automatic and handcuffs. "Is that a real gun?"

"Yep, and yep." Logan dropped to one black-clad knee and offered the kid a handshake, his smile broad and easy in a way Giada could only envy. She had never been that comfortable with children. *Probably because I never was one.*

Her shoulder blades started itching again. She threw another look at the woods. It was almost sunset, and the trees swayed in a spring breeze, whispering secrets to the shadows.

Somebody out there might be getting ready to blow Logan's head off.

"Can we get this show on the road?" Giada demanded, interrupting Logan's earnest discussion of cop stuff with the kid. "It's been a long day, and I'd like to get back to my hotel."

Logan shot her a cool, disapproving look. Her cheeks heated. She really hated sounding like such a bitch, but he didn't know the situation. And she couldn't tell him what was going on, or his mother would turn her into a frog.

Or not. The woman had probably been joking. On the other hand, Giada had no desire to spend the rest of her life cooling her butt on a lily pad. Like it or not, she had to keep MacRoy in the dark and feed him nothing but bullshit. *Though he'd make an awfully big mushroom . . .*

Her eyes lingered on the breadth of muscular shoulders displayed by that black knit shirt. *Definitely not a mushroom. More like a truffle. Chocolate, not fungus. I'd sure like to give him a nice, long lick . . .*

Stop that. Giada gave her wayward libido a mental swat.

"Josh! Josh, where did you . . ." A plump young woman rounded the truck at a pace just short of a run. She blew out a breath in relief as she spotted the boy. "There you are! Don't

scare me like that." Hurrying over, she snatched the kid's hand. He pouted at having his hero worship interrupted.

Logan rose to his feet and gave the woman his warm, lethal smile. She blinked and looked a bit stunned—a reaction Giada could sympathize with. The lieutenant had a face an Armani model would envy: dramatic cheekbones, slashing brows, and a square, angular jaw. He wore his thick mink brown hair cut ruthlessly short, his long-lashed eyes were richly dark, and his wide mouth was both intensely masculine and nakedly sensual. And every time he turned around, her libido sang arias in praise of his ass.

"I'm Lieutenant Logan MacRoy of the Greendale County Bomb Squad," Logan said, offering a big, tanned hand. He nodded at Giada, who extended her own paler palm. "Dr. Giada Shepherd. She's the new civilian forensic chemist for Tayanita County. I'm showing her the ropes this month."

"Nice to meet you," Giada murmured.

"Karen Harper." The woman gave Giada's hand a limp, unenthusiastic squeeze, looking miserably self-conscious in her dusty jeans and SpongeBob T-shirt. "Thanks for coming."

"Hey, that's why the taxpayers pay us the big money," Logan said easily. "I'm saving up for a Happy Meal."

Karen gave the joke a very faint smile as she turned, gesturing them to follow. "My great-grandfather apparently collected an interesting souvenir during World War II." She grimaced. "The kind that goes boom-yow. I found it while I was cleaning." Hazel eyes darkened in grief. "Great-granddad passed last month—heart failure—and we're getting his house ready to sell."

"He put a mortar in his footlocker," Josh announced earnestly. "It's explosive. It could blow us all up."

"It sure could," Logan agreed. "Which is why I'm going to get rid of it while you two stay outside at a nice, safe distance."

"Oh." Karen paused to frown thoughtfully up at him. "Yeah, I guess you're right." She gestured at the house. "Front door's unlocked. The stairs to the attic are at the end

of the hall. The mortar is in a footlocker in the middle of the floor." Herding the boy ahead of her, she moved off to wait in the front yard, next to a cluster of pink azaleas.

"What about me?" Giada asked in a low voice. She might be a civilian, too, but mortar or no mortar, she wasn't crazy about leaving Logan alone.

"Actually, handling a mortar is pretty safe if you know what you're doing, which I do," he told her. "I just don't want that boy bouncing around me while I do it. But if you're not comfortable . . ."

"No, no, I'm fine. Like I said, I want to watch you do your job. Even the non-chemist parts. You get many cases like this?"

He nodded as he led the way along a set of paving stones toward the front door. "A lot of World War II soldiers brought home explosive souvenirs. Plus, we had a World War II training camp in the county, and we're still digging up all kinds of vintage ammo. The bomb squad gets called out to take care of old grenades and mortars about once a month."

The screen door banged closed behind them, and Giada heaved a breath of relief. Safe. At least until they went back outside.

Her heart lightening, she followed Logan down the hallway. The scent of Lemon Pledge did valiant battle with the smell of musty old house. The carpet was worn underfoot, its red flowered pattern faded and crushed from years of padding feet. A passing doorway revealed stacks of boxes sitting on elderly furniture and crowding the scarred wooden floor.

They climbed one flight of stairs and rounded the corner to ascend steps so narrow, Logan had to angle his broad shoulders sideways to fit between the walls.

Finally they reached a door that creaked on rusting hinges as Logan pushed it open. Cardboard boxes hulked in the dim light cast by a tiny attic window. A lightbulb festooned with spiderwebs dangled overhead. He gave its chain a tug, spilling a dim yellow glow just bright enough

to reveal the words scrawled on the sides of those dusty boxes: "Christmas Decorations," "Winter Clothing," and "Charlie's Toys," whoever Charlie was.

"There it is," Giada said, moving toward the open footlocker that lay just beyond an enormous brown teddy bear that looked like a depressed grizzly.

The mortar lay on top of a stack of folded uniforms, among a battered green helmet, a pair of cracked leather combat boots, and an ancient pack of Lucky Strikes.

Logan had shown Giada a training mortar the previous day, so she was familiar with the long metal tube with its nosecone and fins. But unlike the one she'd seen yesterday, the Bakelite cone on this one was pointed. It was definitely a live mortar. "Is it stable?"

"Oh, yeah. As long as the button on the tip of the cone doesn't get depressed, it won't go boom." Logan sank to one knee to take a closer look.

Curious, Giada followed suit. For a moment, she felt hyperaware of him, his warmth, his sheer size. Their eyes met. His were very dark. Very . . . male . . .

Don't go there, Giada. I do not want to spend the rest of my life catching flies with my tongue.

Logan cleared his throat. "I think we need to take it out to the field in back of the house, dig a nice big hole, put it in with a bursting charge, and blow it the hell up."

"Uh-huh." She forced a grin. "I think you just want to watch it go boom."

He grinned back, and her heart gave a helpless little thump at the pure charm in that white smile. "There is no problem that can't be solved by a suitable application of high explosives."

She eyed him. "You've been on the bomb squad way too long."

"Nope, I'm just male," he informed her, as if she hadn't noticed. "The blow-stuff-up gene is located on the Y chromosome."

Giada snickered as he started to reach into the box.

The vision rolled over her in a silent detonation of blood

and terror. *His hand closed over the mortar, started to lift it. Mercury rolled inside a tiny tube, triggering an explosion that bloomed in vicious slow motion. The fireball ripped into his hand and seared the skin off his face, shattering his skull, sending his body tumbling across the attic to lie smoking. Right hand blasted away, head and torso a burned and bloody ruin. Dead.*

Oh, God, Giada thought in sick horror. *Not a sniper. A bomber. He booby-trapped the mortar.* "Logan!"

He jerked and looked up at her, alarmed at her tone. "What?" Frowning, he studied her face. To her relief, his hand stopped short of the mortar in favor of steadying her elbow. "You okay? You look pale."

She opened her mouth and promptly closed it again. What the hell was she going to tell him? *I had a vision?*

He'd know I'm a witch. And then he'd throw me right out of the house.

His mother had been adamant. *"You can't let Logan know what you are. He'll insist he can take care of himself, and he won't have a prayer."*

On the other hand, she certainly couldn't let him trigger the booby trap. Her only option was to disarm the bomb with a spell before he could touch it.

Giada shot a desperate look at the attic window. Judging by the reddening light, the sun was setting, but was definitely still up. Since she wasn't the strongest witch around, she had to struggle to work a spell on mortal Earth during the day. Could she even disarm the thing this early? "Don't you think we should X-ray it first? Or something?" *Yeah. Go downstairs after the portable X-ray machine in the truck. Leave me alone with this thing long enough to think of something.*

Logan gave her an *Are you nuts?* look. "We already know it's explosive. It's a *mortar,* Giada. And mortars are built to be handled by eighteen-year-old boys with people shooting at them. It'll be fine." He started to reach for it again.

So Giada, sweat breaking out on her forehead, shot out a hand and closed her fingers around the deadly tube.

How much movement would it take to set off the booby trap? Giada had no idea, but she sure didn't want to be the booby it trapped.

"Giada . . ." Suspicion darkened his voice.

"Give me a minute!" *Work fast, girl.* Closing her eyes, she opened her senses to probe the bomb. The assassin had removed the propellant in the shaft of the mortar, replacing it with a cell phone trigger, battery, and mercury switch, all wired to the explosive in the mortar's cone. She saw instantly that if the angle of the mortar changed more than fifteen degrees, the mercury would flow forward in its tiny tube and complete the circuit, setting off the explosion.

Standing as close as they were, the blast would kill both of them deader than Elvis.

There were a number of magical ways to disable the bomb, but she didn't have the time or power for anything fancy. *So go for simple.* Giada reached deep inside herself, seeking that core connection to the alternate universe that was the Mageverse, drawing on the forces there, then sending that alien magical energy down her arm to reshape reality.

But sweet God, it was hard, the magic a feeble trickle instead of the fire-hose stream she was used to. Giada gritted her teeth, sweat breaking out on her forehead, desperation clawing at her mind as she forced the energy to obey.

More. *More*, dammit . . .

And . . . done. Her shoulders sagged in a combination of relief and exhaustion, and she dared open her eyes.

"Giada, what the hell are you doing?" Logan studied her, dark gaze cool and narrow with suspicion.

Oh, heck. She gave him a deliberately cocky grin, picked the mortar up, and handed it to him. "Sometimes you've just got to face your fear."

He blinked, the suspicion fading. "Yeah, but next time, don't do that. If we'd been dealing with a different kind of bomb, you'd have blown your head off."

Giada closed her palm around the tiny glass tube of the mercury switch she'd magically transported out of the

bomb. She was going to have to find a safe way to dispose of it. "I'll keep that in mind."

Was Giada Shepherd a Maja?

The handles of the posthole digger he'd gotten out of the bomb truck felt cool and smooth in Logan's hands as he drove it into the rich, red clay. Luckily, it had just rained, and the dirt gave easily as he dug. He'd picked a spot well out in the field, two hundred feet away from the white farmhouse, to ensure no windows would be broken by the blast.

As he worked, he was entirely too aware of his pretty partner, who was busy reeling out the wire for the electronic detonation.

What had she been up to in that long pause when she'd first laid hands on the mortar? That expression of intense concentration on her face—if she'd been a Maja, he'd have thought she was casting a spell.

Or maybe she really had been wrestling with a perfectly natural fear of things that blew up.

Logan glanced up at her as she picked her way through the lush meadow with the long-legged grace of a thoroughbred. White wildflowers bobbed around her as she worked with the yellow reel, obviously paying great attention to making sure the wire didn't kink or break. The setting sun gilded her upswept blond hair and cast highlights over the silky blue shirt that draped her full breasts. Her face had a sort of delicate strength, with wide, high cheekbones, an elegant nose that just missed being too long, and a square, jutting little chin. Her eyes were wide and serious, as gray as storm clouds, with a thick fringe of honey blond lashes.

But it was those full lips that teased his erotic imagination. God, he could think of all kinds of things he'd love to do to that mouth. And have it do to him in return.

He had never seen her at court. He'd have remembered that striking face if he had.

Yet she definitely had that same maddening whatever-it-

was that made his body sit up and notice Majae. He knew from personal experience that it was damned hard for a Latent to resist a witch. Especially one bent on seduction.

Take Clea, for instance—which he almost had. If he hadn't realized she was a Maja before she'd gotten his clothes off, he'd probably have fangs by now. And he just wasn't ready for that yet.

Thing was, Giada didn't seem to be playing the same kind of game. When he'd given her The Look when they'd met yesterday—only as a test, mind you—she'd blushed brighter than a cherry tomato as her gaze skittered away in panic. If she hadn't been twenty-five, he'd have sworn she was a virgin.

Which didn't sound like somebody Morgana Le Fay would send to relieve him of his mortality. Clea was much more Morgana's style—all legs and tits and carnivorous sexuality. He'd seen her coming a mile off, even though he'd been seriously tempted.

Dad, now . . . Dad knew him well enough to know exactly what bait would have him jumping. Dad would send a Maja who blushed.

But he'd also sworn to let Logan decide when and where to become a Magus, and he would never break a vow. Dad treated oaths like his heart's blood—never lightly given.

Of course, that left Mom, who didn't break oaths either, but was a hell of a lot more ruthless if she thought something was for Logan's own good.

Trouble was, he couldn't imagine what would inspire his mother to that kind of ruthlessness.

Terrence ground his teeth, focusing his binoculars on Mac-Roy as the chemist worked on disposing of the mortar.

The mortar that had fucking failed to go off.

Maybe there'd been something wrong with the mercury switch. He'd tested it three times before he'd installed it in the bomb, and it had passed all three times. Still, something must have gone wrong.

Thing is, he'd anticipated that possibility and included a fail-safe—the cell phone detonator. He'd called it as he'd watched Logan carry the mortar from the house.

No boom.

Hell, the cell hadn't even beeped. It was as if something had fried the damn thing.

Furious all over again, Terrence lifted the rifle and drew a bead on MacRoy's dark head. His finger started to tighten on the trigger . . .

No. No, dammit. The little fucker wasn't going to beat him into using the easy way. He was just going to have to come up with something more creative.

One way or another, he was going to blow Logan Mac-Roy right to hell.

Teeth grinding, he lowered the rifle—just as the wrist-band the client had given him heated up again. He hissed in discomfort at the vicious burn.

What the fuck was that about, anyway? The client had said it would prevent him from being detected, but by what? By whom? MacRoy didn't seem to have a fucking clue he was being hunted.

And he wouldn't. Not even when he died.

Standing at what Logan had said was a safe distance, Giada scanned the woods as he rigged the bursting charge he'd use to blow up the mortar.

She had the distinct feeling they'd just dodged a bullet.

They'd been about to walk outside with the mortar when it hit her that the cell phone was wired to the explosive cone just as the mercury switch had been. She'd barely managed to zap the cell before Logan stepped outside.

What the heck am I dealing with here? This bomber was obviously no amateur, but he wasn't using magic either. Yet if he was nothing more than a mortal, a spell should have detected him. But every time she tried to do a scan, it was as if something blocked her.

I don't like this. I don't like this at all.

The mortar detonated with a thunderous boom and a soaring plume of smoke.

Giada, Logan, Josh, and his mother watched the show from a safe distance at the edge of the field. "Wow!" The little boy's blue eyes looked huge as he clapped both hands over his ears. "Wow!"

"Yeah," Giada echoed grimly. "Wow." If she hadn't been able to disarm that thing . . .

"All right, Josh, show's over." Karen Harper dropped a firm hand on her son's shoulder and turned him firmly around. "Time to go home and fix dinner."

"But Mooooommm . . ."

"Dinner sounds good." Logan gave Giada that easy smile of his as the two moved away, Josh still wheedling fruitlessly. "I know this great Mexican restaurant up the street."

What the heck—I deserve a celebration. "Sure." Giada gave those dark eyes a reckless smile. "Why not?"

TWO

Chico's was dimly lit, with sombreros and black velvet paintings of matadors hanging on the walls. It also served the best Mexican in three counties, which was why it was always packed.

The Latino waiter guided Giada and Logan to a dimly lit corner and took their drink orders as they contemplated the menu's selection of gastric WMDs.

Giada's margarita turned out to be electric blue and served in a salt-encrusted glass roughly the size of a goldfish bowl. Her eyes began to glaze before she'd finished half of it.

Logan resolved to drive her home. And wondered whether he'd end up pouring her into bed while he was at it. His cock twitched in silent approval of that idea. *Stop that,* he told it. *No seducing the coworker. Especially when she's drunk.*

Which didn't mean he couldn't seize the opportunity to pump her ruthlessly for information. Maybe he'd be able to figure out if she was a Maja. Okay, not exactly fair—but if she was lying to him, she didn't deserve fair.

"So your file says you've got a PhD in organic chemistry." Plucking a tortilla chip from the basket between them, Logan dunked it into the accompanying bowl of salsa, then

popped it in his mouth. He paused a moment to let his abused taste buds adjust to the salsa's nuclear bite. "Quite an accomplishment for a twenty-five-year-old." Since it took about six years to work your way through the master's and doctorate programs, most people were at least twenty-seven before they attained a doctorate.

"Actually, I was twenty-three when I got my Piled Higher and Deeper." Giada dunked a chip in the salsa, bit into it, then hissed and gulped margarita. "Early bloomer," she managed, when she quit gasping. "I started high school when I was eleven."

"That is early." He dipped, munched, and downed a cooling swallow of his Coke. "Was it rough, going to high school that young?"

"Sucked. Everybody else was at least six inches taller. And to make matters worse, I was a fat little kid." She crunched, sipped, and shuddered before taking another bite. He wasn't sure whether she was brave or masochistic. "And I'm a freaking genius, which didn't help." Blinking slowly, Giada added in a tone of realization, "Shouldn't have said that last part." She appeared to worry about it for a moment before shrugging. "Anyway, IQ is just a number. Doesn't mean a darn thing."

"Doesn't it?"

"Nope." She shook her head. " 'Cause being smart doesn't keep you from being stupid. They had me tutor this guy once. Captain of the football team, quarterback. You remind me of him some. Gorgeous. Shoulders to die for. Face like . . . well, something gorgeous."

Oh, she *was* drunk.

"I was so gone over him." She sighed in remembrance. "Fat little twelve-year-old, helping studly eighteen-year-old get through calculus. He was so nice to me. Didn't realize he was treating me like one of his brat little sisters. Even called me Squirt. Did I get a clue?"

Since she seemed to actually expect an answer, he said, "Uh, no?"

"*Heck* no. I finally screwed up my courage and confessed my luuuuv."

Logan winced in sympathy. "Didn't go well, did it?"

"He was very kind." She blinked hard. Logan had the horrifying suspicion the shine in those beautiful eyes was tears. "Very kind." Heaving a sigh, Giada eyed her drink. Less than a third of it was left. "I need to stop drinking this."

"Yeah," he said gently. "You really do."

She shoved the glass as far across the table as she could reach. Logan took it into protective custody.

"I was fourteen when I went to college," she continued. He suspected her eyes were not quite in focus. "I'd started growing boobs by then, shooting up and slimming down, but all that made me was jailbait."

"I gather you didn't get asked out a lot."

Giada snorted. "Not by anyone who wasn't creepy."

Out of sheer curiosity, he asked, "I trust I'm not creepy."

"Nope, but then, I'm not jailbait anymore."

He gave her a crooked grin. "No, you're definitely not jailbait."

He didn't think she was a Maja either. She was just too damned artless. He wasn't even sure she knew how beautiful she was. Somehow he got the impression that in the back of her mind, she was still that fat little girl who was too smart for her own good.

He wondered what quirk of his personality found that so appealing.

"Wait a minute," Logan told Giada as they pulled up in front of the six-story cream building that was the Daniel Morgan Inn. "If you try to hop out of the truck right now, you'll fall on your head."

He swung out of the bomb truck cab and jumped down, then strode around to open Giada's door. There was no way she could manage the metal steps down from the truck's high seat, not with all the tequila she had on board.

Giada blinked owlishly at him, then placed her hands on his shoulders and allowed him to swing her down.

She swayed against him on her long legs, and he braced

her there. Her breasts felt delightfully full and soft against his chest. The scent of her hair seemed to arrow straight to his groin. Logan swallowed, looking down into her wide gray eyes. Her lips parted, full and naked of lipstick. The temptation to kiss her rolled over him like a wave.

"You feel really good," she murmured.

He swallowed with an effort and managed, "And you are *really* drunk." Somehow he found the self-control to take a step back from that lovely, delightfully female body.

"How am I going to get to work?" A worried frown line formed between her delicate blond brows. "My car is back at the sheriff's office. Isn't it?"

He sighed. "I'll give you a ride in the morning. What floor are you on?"

"Third. 304." She fumbled the long strap of her purse onto her shoulder, then moved off across the parking lot for the front door of the hotel, swaying dangerously on her short heels. Logan caught up to her and took her arm, steadying her. Breathing deep of her seductive scent.

Do not seduce the coworker.

Logan walked Giada to her hotel door with careful courtesy, but did not ask to come in, pointedly, like a man holding tight to his self-control. After telling her he'd pick her up in the morning, he strode off down the hall as she watched with drunken admiration.

He really did have the most incredible butt. Might even be worth catching a fly or two.

"Ribbit." Giada closed the door and turned with a sigh to let her back fall against it. The room promptly did a slow revolution. Pointedly ignoring the effect, she made for the bed and fell facedown atop it.

A cat leaped silently up onto the bed. Technically speaking, the Daniel Morgan Inn was not a pet-friendly hotel, but nobody saw Smoke if he didn't care to be seen.

He strolled up to her body, black as India ink at midnight, except for smoke gray stripes across his forelegs and

rear haunches. She turned her head to stare woozily into the unearthly crystalline blue of his eyes.

"Hi there, Smoke," she murmured as he made his way onto her backside.

He paused to knead her ass with sheathed claws, then strolled up to her shoulder and settled down, a warm, furry weight.

"They almost got us today." Giada swallowed tequila-flavored bile at the thought of just how close she and Logan had come. "But it wasn't a sniper like the others. It was a bomb."

The cat growled deep in his throat, a rumbling sound she could feel in her shoulder blade.

"I managed to disarm it with my magic, but Logan got suspicious."

"Well," the cat observed in a basso masculine voice, far outsized for his seven-pound body, "the boy has never been stupid."

"No, he's definitely not stupid." Handsome, seductive, and suspicious, but not stupid. "I think I convinced him I'm just a mortal, but I don't like this. I don't like this at all. Lying to him—now, *that's* stupid. He needs to know what's going on. If I hadn't had a vision of what was about to happen, he'd have triggered that booby trap."

The cat eyed her in feline disapproval. "You know your orders."

"Yeah, well, the orders need to change. I'm going to go talk to them."

"Better brush your teeth first." Smoke jumped off her back and thumped to the floor. "You smell like tequila."

Giada cast a spell to sober herself up, then took a shower to complete the process. After stroking on a little eye shadow, then adding blush and lipstick to relieve her imminent-hangover pallor, she donned black jeans, boots, and a red tank top. For once, she let her blond hair down to spill in curls around her shoulders. A silver studded belt completed the Goth-chick look.

She'd gotten heartily sick of playing Dr. Shepherd, CSI Barbie.

Smoke leaped onto her shoulder and rode with regal calm, his long black tail tickling her back as it lashed back and forth.

It was full dark now, so casting spells took no effort at all. The gate appeared in the center of the room, a rippling shimmer of Mageverse darkness. Giada stepped through eagerly, sighing in relief as she felt the tides of magic lap around her body.

She might have been born mortal, might have spent most of her life unaware of the magical potential in her Latent body. But now that she was a witch, she craved the alien energies of the Mageverse—energies as natural as gravity or electromagnetism in the mortal universe. Energies everyone called magic for lack of a better term.

Giada badly wanted to understand those forces, wanted to formulate a theory to explain them, find answers to the questions nobody else had ever thought to ask.

What were the physics of magic?

As glittering currents lapped at her senses, she considered possible experiments before reluctantly putting the thoughts aside. Keeping Logan MacRoy alive was the priority. She could play later. But still, Giada couldn't help but look skyward and smile at the alien constellations overhead.

A new universe. All hers to explore.

Later, she reminded herself. Logan came first.

Sighing, she took a look around. She'd gated in near the Pendragon home. Even for Avalon, it was in a very upscale neighborhood, with Victorian mansions, Gothic Revivals, and French châteaus, each more elaborate and beautiful than the next.

By comparison to its massive neighbors, the Pendragon house looked—well—*tiny*, as if the family saw no need to impress anyone. Three stories tall, built of solid gray stone with a slate roof, it was surrounded by mounds of white rosebushes that seemed to glow in the moonlight. Ivy climbed its walls to form a leafy green veil, and a trio of massive

oaks presided over the front yard. There was no high brick wall to keep visitors out, nothing to prevent anyone from walking up the stone pathway to those arched double doors of thick, shining dark wood.

Giada's boot heels tapped on the three stone steps that led up to the modest porch. Despite her confident stride, her heart hammered in her chest. *They invited me. They said I could come anytime I wanted.*

Which didn't stop her mouth from going dry.

Before she could reach up to knock, the door opened. A slim blonde stood in the arched doorway, barefoot and smiling in jeans and a green polo shirt. Her eyes were wide and blue in her lovely face, her skin as dewy and ageless as a twenty-year-old's.

"Why, hello, Giada," said Guinevere Pendragon, once High Queen of Britain. "Come in, please. How's my son?"

"That's . . . a long story." Giada walked inside as the Maja stepped back to let her enter.

Gwen frowned. "That doesn't sound good."

"Hello, Gwen," the cat rumbled from Giada's shoulder. "You look beautiful, as always."

Guinevere smiled in delight and reached up to scratch between his pointed ears. "Smoke, you silver-tongued devil. How are you?"

The cat sighed. "Fine, considering your son keeps getting called out in the middle of the night for every fire in Greendale County."

"Well, he *is* an arson investigator."

"I know, but he's running my tail off." The cat lashed the body part in question.

"Bitch, bitch, bitch." The owner of the laughing male voice stepped around the open door, plucked the cat off Giada's shoulder, and inflicted a brisk rub between his pointed ears. Though no taller than average height, the man was so brawny and broad-shouldered, he gave the impression of being much bigger. Dark hair fell to his shoulders, and a thick mink brown beard framed his stubborn jaw. Otherwise, he looked enough like Logan to be his older brother.

In reality, he was his father. Arthur Pendragon had survived fifteen tumultuous centuries as mankind's vampire protector, his witchy wife by his side.

The fact that she knew King Arthur still had the power to get a squeal out of Giada's inner fangirl. "Hello, sir," she managed, and was proud her voice didn't squeak.

"How's the boy?" Arthur asked, handing Smoke over again, having apparently finished rubbing the cat's fur the wrong way. With a long-suffering sigh, Smoke scrambled back onto Giada's shoulder.

She cleared her throat. "Well . . ."

"They damned near blew him up," Smoke announced, sounding like a ruffled James Earl Jones. "Luckily, Giada disabled the bomb, or you'd be holding a funeral right about now."

Gwen's eyes widened in horror. "Bomb?"

So much for breaking the news gently. "I'm afraid so, ma'am." Giada gave her report, keeping it as brisk and matter-of-fact as possible, trying to avoid any emotion that would add melodrama to the account. Listening without comment, the couple escorted her to the living room and guided her to a seat.

"I remembered the cell phone just as we were about to walk outside," Giada finished, stroking Smoke absently. "I suspect I disabled it just in time." She shook her head. "That could have ended really badly."

"Multiple detonators." Arthur rubbed both hands over his bearded face. "The bomber has to be a professional."

Gwen frowned. "And you think he was somehow keeping you from detecting him with magic?"

"But if he's some kind of sorcerer, why use bombs?" Arthur rose from his seat and began to pace. "None of this makes sense."

"I think this conversation requires coffee," Gwen announced, standing up. "Be right back."

"She doesn't like to conjure when she's trying to think," Arthur explained as his wife disappeared around the corner, presumably into the kitchen.

Giada nodded and fell silent to let him pace in peace. Still stroking Smoke, who curled comfortably in her lap, she gazed around the room. It was cool and airy under a high, beamed ceiling, dominated by a fieldstone fireplace big enough to roast an ox. Massive furniture in buttery brown leather clustered around a low coffee table of cream granite on curling bronze legs. Tapestries and paintings adorned three walls, all depicting medieval scenes of jousting, hunting, or court life.

The fourth wall hosted a huge flat-screen television and an entertainment center. Beside it, a set of shelves held an impressive collection of DVDs, everything from a boxed set of *The Sopranos* to the complete works of Monty Python.

Elvis had his very own shelf.

She was still smiling at that when Gwen walked in, deliberate as a geisha, carrying a coffee service on a heavy, intricately scrolled silver tray. The former queen sat down next to her and poured two cups of coffee, steaming and fragrant, into delicate Waterford cups. She handed one to Giada, who accepted it nervously. The china was so thin it was practically translucent. God forbid she break it. Balancing the saucer carefully on her knee, she watched as Gwen poured a saucer of cream for Smoke. The cat hopped onto the coffee table and settled down to drink in dainty laps, purring like an outboard motor.

Guests served, Gwen poured her husband a crystal goblet of something deep crimson. Probably her own bottled blood. Giada made a mental note to make a donation herself, the sooner the better. Her blood pressure would soon start to spike if she didn't. Majae needed to donate blood as desperately as their vampire counterparts needed to drink it.

Well, she'd worry about that later. Logan was a far more immediate concern.

"You can see why I'm worried," Giada said as she stirred her coffee. "That mortar . . ." She shook her head. "The bomber couldn't have designed a more lethal trap for Logan. Disposing of that kind of device is routine for his squad. They do it on a monthly basis. If I hadn't been there . . ."

"Logan would be dead now." Arthur drained his glass and began to pace again, moving with a swordsman's muscular power and balanced grace, lethal and silent on his feet.

Giada blinked, suddenly recognizing that fluid stride. Logan walked the same way.

Smoke lifted his head from his saucer, licking cream from his whiskers. "And Giada might have died with him, powers or no powers. Even if she could have gotten a shield up in time, it might not have been enough to save her from a bomb going off in her face."

"We know, Smoke." Gwen's gaze was somber as she put her cup down with a restless clink. "We are very grateful for everything you're doing to protect our son. Particularly considering that we lost another Latent yesterday."

Giada sat up, frowning. "Another one? That brings the total to—"

"Twelve," Arthur growled. "Counting the hit-and-run night before last. Twelve of our people who could have become Magekind. Given your experiences with Logan, it's painfully obvious these are not accidents."

Gwen shook her blond head. "But the other attacks don't sound anything like this."

Smoke cocked his head. "Which suggests a gang of several criminals rather than just one. And a very well-funded gang at that. Any idiot can run down a target in a car or shoot them in a drive-by. A booby trap with two different detonators sounds like a professional, not a nutjob with a grudge. Who have you pissed off lately, Arthur?"

The Magus grimaced. "Who *haven't* I pissed off?"

"Could be a terrorist," Giada pointed out. "The Magekind has been running all those operations in the Mideast."

"I doubt it. None of those fanatics knows who I really am, much less who my son is." Arthur clenched his fists restlessly, as if aching for someone to punch. "Dammit, I wish I knew what the hell was going on here."

At first, the Magekind had believed the deaths were accidental, or possibly random crimes of violence. Car crashes, muggings, drive-bys, pedestrian hit-and-runs. Law

enforcement, too, had failed to realize there was even a connection, since the cops hadn't known the victims were all Latents. Which was no surprise, since the cops didn't even know Latents—or the Magekind—existed.

A month ago, Arthur and Gwen had grown concerned enough to ask Giada to keep an eye on their son. She was the obvious choice, since she'd only become a Maja four months before, and Logan didn't know her. Too, Giada, having been a chemist, could pass herself off as a mortal forensic specialist looking for additional training.

She hesitated a long moment before broaching the next point. It was going to take delicate handling. "Given the situation, are you sure keeping Logan in the dark is a good idea?"

Arthur snorted and walked over to pour himself another goblet of blood. "Giada, if Logan knew what you were, he'd throw you out on your pretty little ear."

"Sir, your son is not an idiot. Given all the other deaths, surely he'd realize he needs protection."

"Not likely. That kid has his father's hard head."

"Not to mention a healthy dose of the Pendragon ego," Gwen muttered into her teacup.

"But . . ." Giada began desperately.

Arthur snared her in a forbidding black stare. "But nothing. Once you told him the truth, he wouldn't want you around. You're too damned much temptation, for one thing. He's got it in his head that he doesn't want to become a vampire yet, and you could make him forget that."

"But you'd better not." A muscle flexed in Guinevere's delicate jaw. "I don't want my son thinking we trapped him. Morgana tried that, and he's never forgiven her. I'm not going to be put into that position."

"Which means you'd better keep your distance." Arthur folded his brawny arms and leaned a shoulder against the fieldstone fireplace mantel to glower. "Latents are pretty damned tempting to unbonded Magekind, and vice versa. If you get too close, you could find yourself in deep with him before you even know what hit you."

This was going to be a disaster—she knew it. But damned if Giada could tell Arthur Pendragon no. She sighed. "Yes, sir."

Ten minutes later, Giada was walking back up the cobblestone path with Smoke riding her shoulder. "I told you so," the cat rumbled in her ear.

Giada gritted her teeth in frustration. "Shut up."

Smoke sniffed. "Well, if that's the attitude you're going to take, I hear an azalea bush calling my name. God knows what trouble the boy's gotten into by now."

A cat-sized gate opened in midair, and he leaped through it with a flick of his midnight tail. Giada sighed and opened her own gate back to the hotel.

Weary to the bone, Giada undressed and slipped into bed. She flipped the comforter over herself, lay back, and folded her arms under her head, staring blindly up into the darkness, her mind grinding through the events of the day. When Guinevere had asked her to take this job, Giada had hoped it would turn out to be a giant waste of time—that no one was actually targeting Logan after all. Maybe all those deaths really had been some kind of horrible coincidence.

Today had revealed what a pointless hope that had been. Logan was definitely the target of a skilled professional assassin who meant business.

Yeeeeesh.

With a sigh, she rolled over onto her side, snuggled into the comforter, and closed her eyes. She'd better get some sleep if she meant to stay alert.

She was going to have to stay on her toes if she wanted to keep him alive. While, God help her, simultaneously keeping her distance.

Piece of cake.

Yeah. Right.

THREE

"Mmm," the male voice hummed in her ear, the sound as dark and rich as some particularly sinful chocolate.

Giada lifted her head, only to realize she couldn't see a damn thing. She lay on her belly, draped across something soft. A pile of pillows? Her hands rested across the small of her back. When she tried to pull her arms around in front of her, she found she couldn't move. Thin chains clinked, and something cool and metallic circled her wrists.

She was handcuffed. And, judging by the feel of silk against her face, blindfolded.

She should have been terrified. Yet all she felt was a kind of rich, erotic intrigue. As if some part of her knew exactly what was going on, and wasn't worried in the least.

"You smell delicious," the man purred. She could sense the warmth of his body hovering over hers, almost touching, but not . . . quite. A strong male presence braced himself over her in the darkness. *"And you look even better. All long and slim and beautiful."*

Fingertips glided across the cheeks of her bottom, just a hint of warm contact, delicately teasing. She drew in a

breath, impossibly aroused. Set her thighs the slightest bit apart in silent invitation.

A male finger drifted down the curve of her butt, dipped in between her thighs, found the fine curls there. "So soft," he breathed. "Like down."

That wickedly teasing finger slipped along the seam of her lips, not quite dipping between them. Yet the warmth and promise of his hand made her grow wet in swelling anticipation.

Giada found herself arching upward, lifting her backside, pleading for more.

Warm male lips touched her cheek. Opened. Teeth caught her flesh in a not-quite-bite, a wicked little promise of further pleasure. Giada groaned, her arousal spiraling.

She'd never felt so deliciously helpless in all her life. Bound, blindfolded, teased by a man she didn't know.

"Ohhhh, yeah," he breathed. "You're getting wet, aren't you? Ready for me."

"Yes," she whispered. "God, yes."

"You want me?"

"Yes."

"You want my cock?"

The rough eroticism of the word made her shudder. "Yessssss." A desperate hiss through clenched teeth. God, she wanted him so bad. Wanted his hands, his thick shaft, his strong, hot body grinding into hers. She craved him as she'd never craved a man in her life, craved him as a junky craves a fix.

"Good. Because I want you, too." He breathed the words into her ear, his lips brushing delicate flesh as they moved in wicked promise. "I want your mouth and your pretty breasts and your wet little pussy." His voice dropped into a growl. "And I want your blood."

"Oh, God!"

His hands went suddenly, deliciously rough as he dragged her thighs apart and mounted her, lifting her ass, angling her upward. He drove his cock into her wet, swollen flesh

in one hard stroke, even as his mouth found her leaping pulse.

She felt fangs pierce her skin, the first rush of blood as he began to drink in long, hungry swallows.

Just as his hand found the length of silk that blindfolded her. Snatched the thin scarf away.

Gasping, grinding up into his powerful thrusts, she met her own gaze in the mirror. And saw the man braced over her on muscled arms, eyes glowing vampire red as he fucked her in long, furious thrusts.

Logan MacRoy.

Giada jerked awake. A flick of will activated the bedside lamp, sent light spilling across her bed.

The bed that held no one but herself.

No Logan. No vampire lover with a taste for blindfolds and bondage.

What the heck was up with that?

Giada sat up and raked both hands through her hair. Her fingers caught in the tangled mass, and she tugged in sheer sexual frustration. She'd never had a dream that nakedly erotic.

Had it been a dream? A product of her body's attraction to Logan colliding head-on with Arthur's orders? Or had it been something more?

Something like, say, a vision of the future?

Maybe it was just a dream. She fell back against the pillows and stared at the hotel room ceiling, nibbling her lower lip. *Could have been. I'm attracted to him. It would be only natural to have a dream like that about a guy who turns me on. It didn't have to be a vision.*

Yet she'd never had an erotic dream that intense, that vivid. Of course, she hadn't had a whole lot of erotic *anything*. The vampire who'd made her a witch had been only the second lover Giada had ever had. Since then, she'd been so busy trying to learn to use her magic, there'd been no time to even think about sex.

Well, she was sure thinking about it now.

Not a good idea. Sex with a Latent could have serious implications.

Like Logan, all Latents were descendants of one of the original knights or ladies of the Round Table. As such, they carried Merlin's genetic spell in their DNA, a spell created when Camelot's chosen few had drunk from the wizard's enchanted Grail. If the spell was never activated, Latents eventually died of old age, just like any other mortal.

But if a member of the Magekind made love to a Latent, the spell would be activated, triggering a magical transformation. The men became vampires, while the women gained magical powers. Apparently Merlin's own alien race followed the same pattern—male vamps, female magic users.

It took at least three sessions of lovemaking to activate Merlin's Gift—sometimes more. Good thing, too, because the transformation could have unpredictable results. Giada had heard of Latents going insane from the transformation. As a result, it was strictly forbidden to Change someone without the permission of the Majae's Council, which determined who could safely acquire all that power. Logan himself had already been cleared years before.

Unfortunately, sometimes the council made mistakes. One of Giada's fellow Latents had contracted Mageverse Fever, forcing the Knights of the Round Table to hunt her down and execute her. She'd been trying to murder another Latent at the time.

Transforming people was definitely not something to screw around with. Especially not King Arthur's beloved son.

Better damned well not be a vision.

She lay over the pile of pillows, her backside lifted in seductive invitation, pale and deliciously curving in the moonlight. Her delicate wrists were handcuffed together at the small of her back, and a silk scarf blindfolded her.

Helpless. She was so deliciously helpless.

Logan's cock jerked in dark arousal at the sight of her lying there, long legs parted. Ready for him.

He touched her, fingertips tracing the luscious curve of her bottom. The scent of her arousal teased his senses, rich and ripe, blending with the delicate floral scent of her hair.

He could hear her heart beating, thumping strong and hard with her excitement. The sound made his fangs slide slowly from their housings in his jaw. Lust raked him with delicate needle claws.

"Ohhhh, yeah," he breathed. "You're getting wet, aren't you? Ready for me."

"Yes," she whispered. "God, yes."

"You want me?"

"Yes."

"You want my cock?"

"Yes! Oh, yes!"

Suddenly unable to wait any longer, he caught her slender hips, angled her upward. Entered her tight, wet body in one hard stroke that made her gasp and jerk her hips. Even as he began to thrust, she drove back at him, grinding eagerly. The sensation made his head spin.

He braced himself on his arms and lowered his head as he fucked her, breathing in her rich scent, loving the hot beat of her heart. His fangs twinged. Unable to wait any longer, he dipped his head, found her banging pulse with his lips.

Bit deep. She gasped in blended pain and pleasure.

Her blood flooded his mouth, more delicious than anything he'd ever tasted, hot and seductive and impossibly arousing. Unable to resist, he drank in long swallows, greedy for her, loving the snug grip of her sex around his aching cock, loving the way she whimpered in breathless delight.

The orgasm hit him in a ruthless, blinding flood, sweeping him up and away.

When it was over, he collapsed against her, panting. "Oh, God," he moaned, taking his fangs from her throat. "I never experienced anything like . . ."

Blood covered her mangled throat. Panicking, he jerked the blindfold off.

Giada's beautiful gray eyes stared at nothing, blank and dead.

Logan jolted awake with a strangled gasp of raw terror, his heart banging a kettledrum beat of panic. "Jesu!" He groped for the bedside lamp, switched it on.

And collapsed in raw relief.

A dream. Thank Merlin, it had only been a dream.

But then, he'd known that. He'd been having variations of the same nightmare since he was fourteen years old, with whatever girl he was attracted to at the time playing the starring role.

Though come to think of it, this nightmare had been more detailed than usual. More intense. Almost like a vision.

Except vampires didn't have visions. And anyway, he was just a Latent. Still.

Thank God.

In the inky shadows under an azalea bush, Smoke yawned. Gods and devils, he was bored. He could almost wish the boy would come pelting outside and roar off in his police car, lights and sirens flashing, headed to another of his damned arson investigations.

Instead, it seemed Smoke was doomed to another night of agonizing ennui trapped under the row of bushes outside Logan's sprawling brick split-level. Familiar territory, since it was the same house where Gwen and Arthur had raised the boy.

Smoke had been a regular guest back then, having taken interest in Logan during his visits to court with his parents. Lonely mortal boy, surrounded by immortals, with a brilliant, questing mind Smoke had delighted in educating.

The Mageverse was not, by and large, a good place to raise a mortal child. Exposure to all those magic-wielding

immortals tended to encourage bitterness, if not psycho-pathy. Witness poor Bors's son, Richard, who had tried to murder Arthur in an act of death magic last year.

So Gwen had taken an eighteen-year sabbatical from the Mageverse for the child's sake, with Arthur in and out as his duties permitted. The couple had bought the house here on the theory that the surrounding small town was a good place to raise children. Smoke gathered Logan had purchased it from them after graduating college. He . . .

Something rustled, interrupting Smoke's train of thought.

Someone cursed. Loudly.

"Shhh!" a drunken young voice hissed back. "We don't want to wake him up!"

Smoke lifted his head off his paws. *Oh, now this sounds interesting.*

He stuck his head out from under the bushes in time to see four teenaged boys sneaking toward the massive oak that reigned over Logan's front yard. All were dressed in black jeans and T-shirts or hoodies, apparently in some laughable idea of stealth. Each carried a roll of toilet paper.

Ahhhhh, yessssss. Entertainment.

Smoke slid from beneath the bush, casting a spell in a ripple of sparks and energy that rolled from his black nose to the tip of his twitching tail. Then he padded up behind the boys as they surrounded the oak.

Black as he was, the boys didn't see him until one of them wound up to cast his roll of toilet paper over the tree.

"And what," Smoke purred, "do you lads think you're doing?"

The boys wheeled. Four pairs of eyes widened, faces going bloodless in the light of the full moon. And to Smoke's delight, the pranksters screamed in chorus like terrorized little girls. All four dropped their rolls and fled like all the demons of hell were at their heels.

He watched them go, tail swishing lazily, and contem-plated pursuit with a certain wicked glee.

A door opened and the porch light flicked on, flooding the

front yard. "Smoke, is that you?" Logan demanded, sounding sleepy and irate. "Jesu, what the hell are you doing? I almost shot you."

"Saving your oak from being festooned with toilet paper." The cat turned.

It was just as well Giada wasn't here. Logan stood in all his shirtless glory, barefoot and wearing only a pair of jeans he hadn't bothered to zip, his nine-millimeter in one hand. He shook his dark head in disgust. "Probably my neighbors' kids, aka the Four Stooges. Those idiots try something at least once a month. I always run them off before they get started." He grimaced. "I think I've become a challenge."

"Somehow I doubt you'll have that problem again." Smoke grinned, revealing gleaming fangs the length of daggers. Fangs that went with the rest of his eight-hundred-pound body. "Aren't you going to offer me a saucer of milk?"

Logan snorted. "More like a turkey platter. Unless you want to switch forms before you terrorize the rest of my neighbors . . ."

"Oh, very well." Another wave of magic, and Smoke's tiger-sized body shrank down into house cat dimensions once more. He strolled up the brick steps and leaped easily into Logan's arms.

"What are you doing here, anyway? I haven't seen you in months." Logan gave him an absent ear scratch.

"I was bored. I thought I'd drop by." He cocked his head, eyes narrowing, as he enjoyed the sensation of those long fingers digging in. The boy had a talent for finding the perfect spot to scratch. He hummed in pleasure as Logan turned to carry him back into the house. "So, what have you been up to? Anything interesting going on?"

"Well, there's this new chemist I'm training at work . . ."

Smoke sniffed in feigned disdain. "I'm not interested in the activities of some balding nerd."

One corner of Logan's lips twitched up. "Believe me, she's not a nerd, and she's definitely not balding."

The cat gave him an innocent blink. " 'She'? Do tell, my boy. Do tell."

* * *

Terrence reclined on a stack of thin, dingy pillows on his sagging bed at a no-tell motel off I-85. He could have afforded better, but better meant maids. Maids who might be a little too nosy for his comfort. The Stay-N-Rest was a long-term occupancy motel that only afforded maid service between customers. Which meant he could leave his suitcase of bomb-making materials under the bed without having to worry some silly bitch would get curious.

So, pencil in one hand and a slice of pizza in the other, he felt free to sketch an idea for another bomb on the pad propped on his knees.

The encrypted cell phone vibrated on his belt. Terrence grimaced and dropped the slice of pepperoni pizza back in the Domino's box. He wasn't looking forward to this conversation.

"Status?" the client demanded. He thought she was female, but it was hard to tell, given the heavy filter that distorted her voice.

"No luck." He winced as he said it, feeling an unaccustomed sting of shame.

"*No luck?* They said you were the best. Did they lie?"

"No, they didn't lie," Terrence snapped back. "Somehow he disabled it. I have no idea how he realized . . ."

"Was someone with him?" the client interrupted, her distorted voice gone even sharper. "A woman?"

"Yeah, a blonde. But . . ."

"Did your wristband get hot?"

"Yes." He leaned back against the lumpy pillows. "Mind telling me what that means?"

"As a matter of fact, I do mind. I will contact you with further instructions. Keep your cell charged." The line went dead.

Terrence swore viciously, flipped the phone closed, and slid it back into its clip. What the hell was he dealing with here? Should he cut his losses and walk?

What if she'd decided to cut *her* losses and call the cops? Report the mad bomber holed up at the Stay-N-Rest?

Then she was one dead bitch, because the cops would never hold him. They never had. Then he'd find her, and he'd kill her. And he'd take his time. You didn't cross Terrence John Anderson and live.

On the other hand, she was paying him a hell of a lot of money to off the cop and make it look like an accident. Half a million. Exactly what MacRoy had done to piss her off that bad was a question he'd never asked. Mostly because it was none of his fucking business. All he cared about was the color of her money. Judging by the half she'd paid up front, it was his favorite shade of green.

So he'd sit tight and humor the bitch a little longer.

Picking up his pencil, he went back to work designing the bomb that would be the death of Logan MacRoy.

Logan sat in the black leather easy chair in the living room, absently rubbing Smoke's head and enjoying the soothing rumble of the cat's purr. After that god-awful nightmare, a conversation with his old friend was just what he needed to calm down.

He'd missed Smoke over the past few years. During his childhood, the cat had been the only confidant he'd had. He'd had to lie like a sociopath to every other boyhood buddy, at least when it came to talking about the family. Not that they'd have believed him if he had told the truth. *My father is King Arthur?* Yeah, right. As far as his mortal friends were concerned, his mother, "Gwen MacRoy," was a single parent with a great deal of money that allowed her to do whatever she damned well pleased.

So Smoke had been the only one he could talk to about the pressures of being the child of a legendary hero. Which was why Logan didn't hesitate to confide in him now. Felt like old times. "I'd wondered if she might be a Maja, but the more I thought about it, the less likely that seemed."

He ran his hand slowly down the length of the cat's back from ears to tail tip, absently enjoying the silky texture of Smoke's fur.

His friend blinked one eye, cat fashion. "Oh? Why?"

"She has a doctorate in organic chemistry, and when I got her going on the subject, she knows current theory better than I do. Had my head spinning. No way a Maja would be able to fake that. Hell, most of 'em don't even know how to use a computer."

"Neither do I."

"You don't have opposable thumbs."

Smoke sniffed. "At the moment."

Logan ignored that. "I have no idea why the hell one of the big pharma companies didn't snatch her up. According to her file, she taught chemistry at some little community college for a while, but apparently wanted to get back in the lab. She says she took the forensic chemist job with the Greendale department because she couldn't find anything else, but she'll be bored spitless in a week. That woman is a genius."

"I wasn't aware you found your job boring, boy." The tip of the cat's tail flicked.

He shrugged. "Testing drugs gets a bit dry after a while. Which is why I started working arson investigations and joined the bomb squad."

"You always were ADD."

Logan laughed, and the two fell into a comfortable silence. Stroking the cat slowly, he meditated on the sound of Smoke's rumbling purr in the darkened room. The last of his nightmare-induced tension drained away.

It had only been a dream, after all. He wasn't a vampire, and he had no intention of becoming one anytime soon. Giada was safe from him.

"What I don't understand," the cat said at last, "is why you fear becoming a Magus."

Logan stiffened, his peace instantly draining away. Sometimes it was like the damned cat read his mind.

Apparently oblivious to his sudden tension, Smoke con-

tinued. "When you were a boy, following in your father's footsteps was all you could talk about." He angled one ear. "Afraid of being lost in Daddy's shadow?"

"Dad doesn't cast a shadow. Dad is a fucking total eclipse. I came to terms with that when I was sixteen."

"And? Have you suddenly decided you can't live without chocolate after all?"

Logan smiled a little at that. When he was ten, he'd told Smoke the only thing he didn't like about the idea of becoming a vampire was giving up Tootsie Rolls in favor of chewing on girls. "Not quite. Girls have more appeal than I thought."

"So why don't you have fangs? Morgana predicted you'd be a fine Magus before you could walk, so I know you've been cleared."

He definitely didn't want to have this conversation. For one thing, he didn't want to trigger a rerun of that fucking nightmare. "That's a long story, and it's late. I need to hit the sack."

"Don't give me that," Smoke said roughly. "Something happened to you when you were fourteen. No one will tell me what, including your mother, and she's never hesitated to tell me anything. Neither did you, once upon a time. All I know is that you suddenly started keeping secrets."

"Don't worry about it, Smoke. It was a long time ago. I'm over it."

"Obviously not, or you'd be a Magus."

Dammit, when the cat got an idea in his head, he was like a dog with a bone. "I have a satisfying career I'm not ready to give up. That's all there is to it."

"I caught you *crying*, boy. You never cried. And you wouldn't tell me why."

There was a note of hurt in the cat's voice he'd never heard before. Guilt needled him, but he couldn't bring himself to dredge up the whole ugly story. "I'll tell you later, Smoke. Just . . . not tonight."

"Fine." The cat rose and leaped out of his lap, radiating offended dignity. The door opened, apparently at a wave of magic, and Smoke stalked out. It slammed behind him.

"Great." Logan scrubbed both hands through his hair, rose, and went back to bed.

Maybe if he was lucky, he'd even be able to sleep.

The alarm went off way too early. Giada groaned as she rolled out of bed and stumbled into the bathroom to let the shower pound her groggy brain awake.

As the warm, hot spray rained over her body, the details of the night's erotic dream replayed in her mind in uncomfortable detail.

Had it been a vision?

Somehow it didn't feel like a simple dream, maybe because it had been so kinky. She'd never had bondage fantasies before, so why would her unconscious mind generate one about Logan?

And how the hell was she supposed to face him this morning with the memory of that incendiary whatever-it-was playing in her head?

She got out of the shower, dried off, and went to work on her hair and makeup. She'd just finished dressing when her cell rang. She scooped it off the counter. "Hello."

"MacRoy's Taxi Service," announced a voice that sounded entirely too cheerful. "Hungover?"

"No, no thanks to you." Giada grabbed her purse off the bed, waving at Smoke as she headed for the door. He must have come in during her shower. The cat twitched an ear in reply as she closed the door behind her. "How could you let me drink all that tequila?" she continued to Logan. "I babbled like an idiot."

"I wouldn't say 'idiot.' You were a very cute drunk."

"Oh, thanks a lot." Just what she didn't need to hear. "Be down in a minute." She snapped the cell closed and headed for the elevator.

Distance, Giada. Keep your distance.

And for God's sake, don't think about that stupid dream.

FOUR

Logan had apparently swapped the bomb truck for his department-issued unmarked Impala in a very coplike dark blue. He leaned over to open the car door for her. As usual, he wore his black fatigue pants and a black knit shirt embroidered with a gold sheriff's star.

He gave her a rakish smile. "Good morning."

"Morning." She slid into the seat. "Thanks for the ride." It even sounded grudging to her ears.

"My, we're grumpy this morning." Logan lifted a thick, dark brow. "Sure you're not hungover?"

"Rough night. Didn't sleep well."

"Bad dreams?"

She felt her cheeks begin to heat and quickly turned her head to look out the window. "Something like that."

The Greendale Sheriff's Office was a former corporate headquarters that had been sold to the county when the corporation in question built more upscale digs. It was accordingly much nicer than the taxpayers of Greendale County would have otherwise been willing to spring for. Three

blocky stories of mud brown brick, the building was pleasantly ugly, but at least it had plenty of room for the assorted divisions of the sheriff's office. Including Logan's lab.

After stopping by Evidence to pick up the day's tests, Giada and Logan headed for the lab with a thick stack of manila envelopes containing what might—or might not—be crack cocaine, marijuana, or meth. Each sample would get two separate tests: a presumptive chemical test conducted by hand, then a mass spectrometer run in which liquefied samples would be vaporized and analyzed by computer. The two tests had to agree, or charges would be dropped.

Giada had been handling the testing process for a week now, but she already worked with speed and competence. Logan watched her weigh the first sample—a few pebble-sized crystals the narcs suspected of being methamphetamine. Then again, the crystals could just as easily be rock salt. The tests would clear up that issue.

Giada wrote the crystals' weight on a fresh bag, then cut a few fragments off one with a scalpel. Teeth gently nibbling her lower lip, she tapped the residue off the blade into one of the wells of a white ceramic tray. She picked up a bottle of Marquis solution, a mix of sulfuric acid and formaldehyde, drew an eyedropper of the liquid, and started to squeeze it into the well.

The dropper's rubber bulb promptly broke. Acid squirted up from the bulb, splashing right into Giada's face. "Arhhhh!" She recoiled, hands flying up to her burning skin.

Thirty-six seconds! Logan realized in horror. They had only thirty-six seconds to wash the acid off, or it would start eating its way into her face.

"Come on!" Grabbing her by the shoulders, he hustled her across the lab to the shower station. Slapping a hand against the eye-wash tap, he caught the back of her head and pushed her face into the six jets of water that blasted across the station's sink. The spray splattered around them, soaking his uniform pants. He ignored the sensation, interested only in saving Giada from a scarring chemical burn.

She started to straighten, sputtering, but he gently pushed

her head back down. "Not yet! Make sure we've got it all off."

Finally Logan decided it was safe to let her rise, wet and gasping. "You okay, babe?" Worried, he grabbed a paper towel and helped her mop her dripping face. "Did it get your eyes?"

"No, no, just splashed along my temple. Darn, that burns!" Giada shook her head hard, sending droplets flying. "Should have checked that dropper first. Ow!"

"Let me see." He turned her around and tilted her chin up.

"Guess the rubber of that bulb must have gotten so old, it just broke." She blinked up at him, water streaming down her cheeks.

"Probably. Sorry." There was a burn across her left temple, but luckily the acid had missed her eye. "Doesn't look too bad, but we'd better put something on it anyway."

Logan steered her into the supply closet where the first aid kit was kept. He tugged on a pair of rubber gloves and thumbed the top off a tube of Neosporin. She angled her head to the side for him, letting him spread the gel across the burn.

"Looks like you'll be fine." Logan eyed the string of pin-prick holes the acid had burned in the collar of her blouse. "That shirt's never going to be the same, though."

"What?" She glanced down and froze. "Oh." A tide of charming pink rolled over her cheeks.

Following her gaze, Logan caught his breath.

The thin cream fabric of her blouse was soaked through, plainly revealing the lace of her bra cupping her full, pale breasts. Her nipples were a delicate pink, tips drawn tight as budded roses. Logan swallowed hard, his mouth going dry.

Giada looked up at him, her eyes very wide, gray as storm clouds, water beading on the tips of her long lashes. Her lips parted, as pink and temptingly lush as her nipples.

Abruptly he was aware of her scent—a trace of jasmine and something clean and herbal. Her breath gusted against his mouth, smelling faintly of mint. Desire hit him, and he hardened in a sweet rush.

Logan took her mouth before he even knew what he was going to do. Her soft lips yielded under his, opening eagerly for the thrust of his tongue. She moaned, a tiny, arousing sound that made his cock jerk.

God, she was sweet. Mint and Giada, a combination that made his head swim in furious need.

His mouth moved over hers, sure and hot and possessive. She shuddered in helpless arousal as he hardened against her belly, the thickness of his erection shocking and exhilarating. He felt so damn big, so muscled and strong.

Just like last night's vampire dream. The dream that might have been a vision . . .

What the hell am I doing?

Giada jerked away from him with a convulsive jolt, feeling as if somebody had Tasered her. For a moment they stared at each other. His eyes were dark, hungry. Predatory as those of his dream self.

Was she destined to give him the forbidden Gift? Despite his parents' orders and his own stated desire to remain mortal?

This is a really, really bad idea.

She whirled and fled the closet, dashing across the lab for the door.

"Giada!"

She ignored him, racing around the corner toward the ladies' room. Staggering inside, she fell against the door, breathing hard in a combination of fear and frustrated desire.

What she saw in the long vanity mirror over the double sinks confirmed her worst suspicions. She looked like the star of a wet T-shirt contest.

"Damn!" Spotting a hand dryer, Giada twisted its nozzle around and stepped in close in an effort to dry her blouse.

Bad. This was bad. First erotic dreams, then he'd barely touched her and she'd gone up in flames. Was she that darned desperate?

Giada had never had this much trouble controlling herself with a man before. It seemed Arthur hadn't been kidding about the attraction between Latents and Magekind. Yet when she'd been a Latent, she hadn't felt this kind of insane lust for Renaldo, the vampire who'd Gifted her. They'd made love the required three times and gone their separate ways. She'd never given him another thought.

So why was Logan developing into an obsession?

Another glance at the mirror confirmed she was presentable again, though she needed to run a brush through her hair.

But what the heck was she supposed to do about that kiss?

What the hell had just happened?

One minute Giada had been going up in flames in the sweetest kisses he'd ever had. The next, she'd been running for the door. Had he completely misread the situation?

Logan replayed the kiss in his mind—not exactly a hardship. She'd gazed up at him, looking every bit as dazed as he felt, smoky desire in those gray eyes. Her lips had parted, and then he'd kissed her.

And she had, by God, kissed him back. That was not the kind of thing a guy misread. Especially not when she'd melted against him like hot butter in the sun. She'd even gotten his shirt damp with her wet blouse; he could feel the thick knit lying cool against his skin.

Giada had given him plenty of subtle signals before that, too. He'd caught her gaze lingering on his body more than once, though she'd looked away as soon as he caught her at it.

So why had she run? There'd been outright panic in her eyes when she'd pulled away. What was worse, she'd fled as if she was afraid he'd chase her.

Had he actually frightened her?

That thought did the trick of wilting his lingering erection in a hurry. The son of Arthur Pendragon did not terrorize women. Or take advantage of them.

Or rip out their throats.

The sick memory of the nightmare rose in his mind, making his stomach twist in horror. *Vampires don't have visions,* he reminded himself firmly. *It was only a nightmare.*

Besides, he wasn't a vampire. And even if he had been, he would never have hurt a woman. Real vampires, unlike fictional ones, were not at the mercy of their hunger for blood. Only blood-mad rogues attacked their lovers, and there was no reason to believe Logan was in any danger of going mad when he did receive the Gift. He wasn't some inexperienced kid without the willpower to control his own body and his own appetites.

The dream had been a nightmare. That was all.

As for Giada—he had no idea why she'd taken off like a scalded cat. She wasn't some inexperienced kid either.

Unless he'd misread the situation. Badly.

The lab door creaked as it swung open, and he heard Giada's heels click as she walked into the room. Logan stepped out of the closet and met her gaze steadily. "Do I owe you an apology?"

Giada hesitated, two flags of bright red blazing up on her sculpted cheekbones. He relaxed slightly. A woman didn't blush like that over an unwelcome advance.

Instead of answering, she avoided his gaze and walked over to the black marble counter where the abandoned meth test still stood. She swung open one of the glass-fronted cabinets and reached inside to take out another bottle of Marquis solution, then carefully squeezed out a droplet of acid into the sample well. "We can't do this."

"Do what?" Logan took a careful step closer.

Her head jerked up and she gave him a warning glare. "You know what."

"Kiss? Flirt?" He stopped and leaned a hip against the counter. "Have an affair?"

"An affair is not an option." She bit the words out and picked up a Sharpie, then pulled the evidence bag over to write the results of the first test across the front.

"Why? You're not in my chain of command, and you don't work for me, so there's no regulation against our getting involved. You're just here watching another chemist work. Unless there's somebody back home . . ."

Her gaze met his with an angry snap. "I wouldn't have kissed you if there had been."

"So why?"

"Because I don't want to. It complicates things." She used the scalpel to slice a fragment from the suspected meth crystal, then tapped it into a test tube. "I'm trying to learn my job, and I don't need the distraction."

"Fair enough." Taking a deep breath, he fought down both the stab of disappointment and the desire to argue. "I'll keep my distance."

Giada looked up at him with a trace of suspicion. "Just like that?"

"Yeah." He squared his shoulders. "I don't believe in trying to pressure a woman into doing something she doesn't want to do. Especially not when it comes to this particular topic."

Gray eyes narrowed, studied him. Then, slowly, she nodded. "Good. Because an affair wouldn't be a good idea."

Who are you trying to convince? Logan wondered. *Me—or yourself?*

Then he gritted his teeth. *Cut it out. If she doesn't want to get involved, that's the end of it.*

As for that part of him that perversely found her resistance intriguing—he'd ignore that, too, just as he did his lingering frustration. As Arthur had taught him from the time he was twelve years old: *"The lady always calls the shots, boy. Otherwise it's too damned easy for the one who's bigger and stronger to bully her into something she doesn't want to do. And that's dishonorable."*

Honor was everything. It might be old-fashioned to believe that, maybe even a little sexist, but he didn't really care.

A Pendragon was honorable above all.

* * *

Guinevere settled into a seat at her favorite table out on the elegant stone patio of the Majae's Club. Cherry blossoms scented the morning air, and a light breeze stirred the mounds of ferns that surrounded the wrought iron table. She sighed in contentment and sank back in her chair to look out across the city of Avalon. The trees were in full bloom, surrounding the magical mansions with great clouds of delicate pink and white blossoms.

Lifting her wineglass, Gwen sipped, savoring the light Zinfandel with its raspberry notes. *Delicious.* She picked up her fork and prepared to tuck into her Mediterranean chicken.

Morgana Le Fay, plate in hand, dropped into the chair across the table from her. "I see you and Arthur finally came to your senses about the boy." She took a delicate bite of her club sandwich, her white teeth framed by violently red lips. The lipstick precisely matched the eye-popping scarlet of her tailored suit.

Gwen narrowed her eyes over her fork and drawled, "Have a seat, Morgana."

Ignoring the sarcasm, Morgana took another bite, a contemplative expression on her coolly beautiful face. The breeze stirred a black curl against the high, creamy angle of her check. "The girl isn't who I'd have picked, but you obviously know Logan's tastes better than I."

Gwen set her jaw. "We did not send Giada to seduce Logan. Her job is strictly to protect him from whoever's killing those Latents."

Black brows drew low over brilliant blue eyes. Morgana straightened in her seat. "Whyever not? I told you, we need that boy. I have *foreseen* it." Arthur's half sister had always put great store in her visionary gifts.

Gwen leaned forward in her seat and used her best ferocious glare. "And I told *you*—Logan will decide when and if he becomes Magekind, not you. And not us. He will not

be tricked, he will not be seduced. He will make the choice of his own free will."

"And what if his dawdling costs Magekind lives, Guinevere?" Crimson lips peeled back from her teeth as she bit off every word like something bitter. "We have a responsibility to our people! And that includes making difficult decisions, like reminding a boy of his duty."

"Logan is not a boy. He's a thirty-one-year-old law enforcement officer who risks his life on a daily basis. He *does* his duty."

"And what if he gets himself killed before he gains an immortal's ability to heal his injuries? What will those high morals be to you then, eh?" Morgana leaned forward and tapped a long red nail on the table. "I'll tell you—ashes. Ashes in your mouth. Believe me, you won't like the taste."

Morgana rose to her feet and stalked off the patio, her red stiletto heels clicking an angry rhythm.

Gwen tossed down her fork. Suddenly she was no longer hungry.

The child's backpack sat in solitary splendor in the middle of the empty parking lot, not far from the bright red building that had once been a Circuit City. Tinkerbell's painted face smiled from the backpack's plastic surface, seeming to watch the four-foot-high machine rumbling steadily closer.

The robot gleamed in the hot afternoon light, caterpillar treads clanking on the pavement. It stopped eighteen inches from the backpack and started maneuvering back and forth, working to position the two steel tubes mounted on its front. Finally the twin barrels were aimed squarely at the zipper on the backpack's side. For a moment, there was no sound at all except the ping of metal heating in the sun.

Water exploded from one of the barrels in a furious, hissing blast. The zipper burst open under the pressure, and the backpack seemed to explode, scattering bits of equipment all around: an egg timer, the guts of a big lantern battery,

wires, a thin silver tube about the size of a number 2 pencil, and three red sticks of dynamite.

Again, the parking lot went silent.

After a moment, a man lumbered down the steps of the bomb truck parked three hundred feet away, moving carefully in the massive green suit he wore. Made of Kevlar and fire-resistant Nomex, the suit weighed almost a hundred pounds, including thick metal plates tucked into chest and groin pockets. The helmet alone weighed thirty pounds, between its bulletproof faceplate and radio unit.

Ignoring the scattered sticks of dynamite, the bomb tech bent over to pick up the small silver tube in careful bare fingers. After securing it in a thick, hard plastic cylinder, he gathered up the tube's dangling wires and twisted them together, then tucked them into the case. Finally, he put the cylinder into an armored box and locked its lid.

"Done," he announced into the radio.

The door of the bomb truck swung open and the rest of the squad emerged to collect the scattered parts of the device. With the blasting cap detached and rendered safe in the ammo box, the rest was okay to handle.

Giada, trailing behind Logan, frowned at the tech's bare hands. "Why doesn't the suit have gloves or boots?"

Logan shrugged. "You wouldn't have the dexterity you need to disarm a bomb if you were wearing gloves."

"But what if the bomb went off?"

"They'd call me 'Stumpy.'" The bomb tech pulled off his bulbous helmet and grinned, his face red and slick with rolling sweat.

Mark T. "Mount" Davis was a hulking six-two deputy with a boyish face and a dark blond buzz cut. The nickname came from his silver name tag, which listed him as "MT Davis." This, Giada gathered, was considered sophisticated humor by cop standards.

Davis turned toward Samantha Taylor, who had driven the robot using the remote controls in the truck. "Good shot with the water cannon, Sam. You hit that battery dead-on."

She grinned in pleasure at the compliment. Barely five-

four in combat boots, Taylor was a sturdy thirty-year-old
with a snub nose and a wicked smile. Between her build,
her bulletproof vest, and her weapons belt, she looked like
a redheaded fireplug.

Logan once told Giada that Taylor never hesitated to
wade into any fight, which made her beloved of her fellow
cops. He liked her because of her rock-steady calm—an
invaluable quality for a bomb tech.

Sam slanted Logan a grin. "All I've gotta say is that it's
lucky Logan doesn't build bombs for real."

He'd designed the training device used for today's exer-
cise. Both the blasting cap and the sticks of dynamite had
been dummies.

Logan grinned. "I only use my powers for good."

"That's not what Gladys Miller said."

"Bite me, Davis."

"You ain't my type. Though Miller'd probably do it if
you asked her nice."

"Miller's got a crush on our boy," Sam explained to
Giada.

"Gladys Miller?" Giada blinked. "The old woman in
Evidence with the personality of a rabid weasel?"

Sam laughed. "I see you're already a member of the
Miller fan club."

"I'm thinking of dumping a bucket of water on her to see
if she'll melt."

Logan grinned. "You're just holding a grudge because
she keeps trying to steal your ruby slippers."

"Speaking of movie references"—Giada lifted her chin
in the direction of the robot—"how did y'all get your hands
on the Terminator?"

Lieutenant Tom Billings spoke up as he strode along
beside them, straight-backed as the marine he'd been,
elegant in a pin-striped blue shirt and tailored gray slacks.
His dark, smooth head gleamed in the hot afternoon sunlight. "Bought it with a Homeland Security grant last year."
He slapped Logan on the shoulder. "Man's got a talent for
sweet-talking the feds."

At least I'm not the only one who finds him hard to resist, Giada thought.

She helped the squad gather up the remains of the phony bomb. After watching Taylor drive the robot back up the ramp into the truck, she joined Logan in the cab.

Back at the sheriff's office, Giada slid out of the truck as the other members of the squad pulled in.

Taylor got out of her car as the bomb squad's fifth member trotted up with a well-gnawed red rubber ball.

The big Lab sat back on her cinnamon-furred haunches and grinned a hopeful doggy grin. "Hey, there, Jenny." Sam bent and picked up the ball, then sent the toy sailing across the parking lot. Jenny barked happily, whirled, and raced after it.

"Jenny, where'd you go?" A skinny twelve-year-old boy raced around the corner, only to skid to a stop as Jenny trotted over. She dropped the ball and panted at him. The kid scooped up the toy and flung it across the parking lot. The dog barked, whirled, and galloped in pursuit, tongue lolling in joy.

"Andy, dammit!" A young girl ran around the same corner. Spotting Logan, she stopped and proceeded at a more dignified pace. She was a pretty teen, no older than sixteen or so, with big brown eyes and long, dark hair she must have worked over with a curling iron for at least an hour. "Hi, Logan." The narrow-eyed look she sent Giada was far from friendly.

"Hi, Heather." He gave the girl a smile before turning to Giada. "Giada, this is Heather Jones, the sheriff's granddaughter. The hooligan chasing Jenny over there is her brother, Andy. Heather, this is Dr. Giada Shepherd. She's a forensic chemist from Tayanita doing some training with me this month."

"Nice to meet you, Heather." Giada held out a hand.

The girl shook it with a distinct lack of enthusiasm. "Hi."

Looks like Logan's made another conquest, Giada thought dryly. *And I'd bet money he hasn't got a clue.*

Taking pity on the girl's obvious desire to talk to her

crush, Giada wandered over to Samantha Taylor, the dog handler. "Cute dog."

"Thanks." She accepted the drool-covered ball from Jenny and gave it another sailing toss.

Giada eyed the Lab's blue collar as she trotted away. It read, "Accelerant and Explosive." "What's with the collar?"

"Refers to the substances she's trained to detect. I use her for arson scenes and bomb searches."

"She's a K-9?" Now a little worried, Giada turned to watch Andy wrestle with the dog, giggling as Jenny licked his face.

As if reading her mind, Taylor shook her head. "She's not patrol-trained. I wouldn't let her play with the kids if she were." Patrol dogs sometimes bit people they didn't know well, especially if they thought their police handlers were in danger.

Giada relaxed. "Oh. Had her long?"

Taylor shrugged. "Just a couple of months. Somebody the sheriff knows donated her. I've worked with dogs before, so he asked me to take her." She lifted her voice into a shout. "Hey! Jenny, don't roll in that! I'll have to clean you up with a fire hose."

The deputy went off to collect her dog. Giada's gaze returned to Logan, who was listening patiently as Heather related some adventure from cheerleading practice.

Good thing he'd decided to play the gentleman after that searing kiss. Giada would have hated to spend the next month fending off his breathtaking efforts at seduction. *I'm darned lucky he backed off.*

So, demanded a small voice in the back of her mind, *why don't I feel lucky?*

She told it to shut up.

That night, Giada still felt no luckier.

Which was why she sat on her hotel room bed, soothing her wounded ego with half a pint of Chunky Monkey. When her conscience ranted, she promised it two extra

miles during her daily run in the morning. She tried not to indulge her inner fat little kid too often, but sometimes a girl had to do what a girl had to do.

Logan had given up on seduction a little too easily. He could have at least had the decency to look regretful.

I'm being perverse and immature. Aloud she muttered, "So I'm perverse and immature," and fed her inner FLK another spoonful of chocolate comfort.

Music chimed a tinkling note over her head, drawing her gaze upward just in time to see bright blue light spark. Something white fluttered through the air to plop to the bedspread in front of her knees.

Giada put the container of ice cream on the nightstand, stuck the spoon in her mouth, and examined the object. It was a fine cream envelope with her name written on the front in a beautiful swirling script. Tossing the spoon in the container, she picked it up and turned it over. Her eyes widened. A red wax seal held it closed, embossed with the image of a hawk clutching a dove in its talons. She recognized the symbol instantly.

Morgana Le Fay's seal. Oh, crap. What have I done now?

Heart in her throat, Giada carefully broke the wax. The paper inside was fine, heavy velum with a single line of beautiful script. "Dearest Giada—I would like to meet with you at my home at your earliest convenience.—Morgana Le Fay"

Translation: *now.* Morgana was the liege of the Majae's Council—the elected leader of the witches, just as Arthur led the vamps. You did not keep your liege waiting.

Giada scrambled off the bed, staring down at her oversized sleep shirt in dismay—*I need clothes!*—then realized she could just conjure something suitable. She zapped herself into one of her CSI Barbie suits, then created a gate and stepped through, her heart in her throat.

What does Morgana Le Fay want with me?

FIVE

For witches as for mortals, a huge, elaborate home was a status symbol. But in Avalon, a mansion didn't represent how wealthy you were, but how much magic you could command. The older and more powerful the Maja, the more Mageverse energy she could manipulate and maintain in the form of a house.

Which was why Giada lived in the Mageverse equivalent of a double-wide—a two-bedroom brick ranch that was all she could manage after four months as a witch.

Morgana lived in the Avalon equivalent of Versailles.

It was all Giada could do not to gape as the Maja admitted her into a château that seemed more museum than home. Black-and-white marble lay underfoot, polished to a mirror sheen, while the ceiling soared two stories overhead. Gilt-framed paintings by Renaissance masters hung on the wainscoted walls, as white marble statues posed in serene elegance on graceful pedestals. Everywhere Giada looked, gold and crystal and rich, gleaming wood dazzled the eye.

"Thank you for coming, my dear." Morgana's voice was so deep and purring, it brought to mind the witch from Disney's *Sleeping Beauty*.

"I'm honored to be invited." Giada dipped an awkward curtsey.

Morgana nodded in acknowledgment. She looked every bit as impressive as her home, dressed in a floor-length crimson gown straight out of the Middle Ages. Flowing bell sleeves swirled around her long white hands, and the bodice that cupped her cleavage was embroidered with gold and decorated with gems. The scarlet velvet made her skin look impossibly pale, particularly in contrast to the dramatic black curls that tumbled around her delicate shoulders. An emerald pendant hung around her neck on a thin gold chain, nestling between impressive breasts the color of cream.

Why is she working so hard to impress me? The thought flashed through Giada's mind and was instantly squelched. God forbid it show on her face.

Apparently it didn't, because Morgana turned and led the way across the foyer into an elegantly appointed sitting room. "Would you like some wine?"

"Ummm." Giada had been staring around at the sitting room, taking in the marble and gold fireplace with its flanking Greek goddesses. She bit her lip. What if she got drunk and said something stupid? Would refusing be rude? Probably. She managed a smile. "That would be lovely."

Morgana seated herself on a settee of a deep and verdant green, gesturing gracefully for her guest to join her. Giada obediently perched, smoothing her black skirt carefully over her legs.

The Maja picked up a crystal decanter from a side table. Moving with deliberate grace, she poured a dark ruby red wine into a pair of wine flutes so delicate, they looked as if they would shatter if you breathed on them hard. Giada accepted the proffered flute with more care than she'd used to lift the booby-trapped mortar.

The Maja sipped from her own glass, studying Giada around its fragile rim. "I understand Arthur and Guinevere have chosen you for the honor of protecting their son."

"Yes, my liege." *And you care, why?* She managed not to ask.

Morgana smiled, revealing teeth so white, she looked more vampire than witch. "Call me Morgana, child. I know how uncomfortable you Americans are with titles."

"Ah. Thank you." She sipped, expecting something a bit too dry and sour for her—her father had always said Giada had a barbarian's tastes when it came to wine. Instead, it was heady, deliciously sweet. "Oh, this is good!"

A dark brow lifted ever so slightly. "You sound surprised."

Giada froze. "No, ma'am."

Morgana laughed, a waterfall of pealing notes. "Relax, child. I don't bite." A long-nailed hand touched the emerald nestled in her cleavage. "At least, not young girls."

In the middle of another sip, Giada almost choked. *Does that mean she bites older girls, or just boys?*

The Maja's smile widened. "Occasionally."

Oh, my God. Is she reading my mind? And what the heck does she mean by that? She put the flute down on the glass coffee table with a clink. "Is there something I can do for you?"

"You're doing it, dear. My nephew's life is very valuable to me. To us all." Green eyes gleamed up at her. Morgana stroked the emerald again, slowly, almost teasingly. "My visions tell me he will become a very great Magus. The Magekind needs him. Desperately."

Giada's stomach promptly knotted into macramé. *I think I see where this is going. And I don't like the destination.* "I'm sure he will be—when he decides to accept the Gift."

Cat eyes considered her. "You could . . . *encourage* him to embrace his destiny."

"Arthur and Guinevere have ordered me not to tell Logan I'm a Maja."

Morgana's smile was as thin as a razor, and just as sharp. "So don't tell him."

Giada's eyes narrowed. "They also ordered me to stay out of his bed. Repeatedly. And I will not disobey them."

"Will you not?" There was a note of silky threat in her voice.

Giada swallowed and lifted her chin. "No."

Lush lips thinned, and Morgana's voice snapped like a whip. "I am your liege!"

Giada stared at her, anger beginning to heat her veins. *She wants me to seduce him into the Gift without warning him!* "And I gave. My. *Word*."

"You're from the twenty-first century. Your word is . . . flexible."

Now she saw red. "No. It's really not."

Morgana settled back against the settee's arm and eyed her, gaze now cool with calculation. "No. I see it isn't." Her dark head tilted as she studied Giada with unnerving intensity. "You're not the most powerful Maja, are you?"

"No." Giada met her gaze without flinching, anger making her reckless. "And yes, you *could* fry me like a mosquito in a bug zapper."

"Oh, child! So melodramatic!" Once again, Morgana threw back her head in pealing laughter. It was beginning to seem a little over the top. "I have no interest in hurting you! I want to help you. After all, you're all that stands between my beloved nephew and a very ugly mortal death."

Riiiiight. Giada just looked at her, brows lifted.

"And I do want him to survive long enough to become a Magus." She reached behind her neck, thrusting out her impressive cleavage as she took off her emerald necklace. The gemstone swung with a hypnotic glitter as she extended it to Giada. "This will amplify your connection to the Mageverse, allowing you to draw power more easily."

Giada eyed the gem warily. "That's very generous, but I couldn't . . ."

"Do you wish to save Logan's life or not?"

She blew out a breath and extended her hand. "Well, when you put it like that . . ."

Morgana poured the emerald and its golden chain into her palm, sending a hot tingle racing up her arm.

Concealing a shiver, Giada looped the necklace over her head. "Thank you." She meant it.

Giada had lived most of her life as the most gifted person in the room. Finding herself a less-than-powerful witch grated on her. Particularly now, when everything depended on her magical skill.

Morgana gave her a curt nod and rose from the settee like a cat uncoiling. "Keep it with you. You'll need it."

Knowing a dismissal when she heard one, Giada rose and bowed. "Thank you, my liege."

The witch nodded and escorted her to the door. Giada fled, feeling she'd made a narrow escape.

Morgana watched the young Maja stride across her garden. A gate appeared before her like a glowing doorway of light, and she vanished through it in a ripple of magical energy.

Slumping, the Maja swung her front door closed. There would be repercussions for this night's work. The girl wouldn't discover the deception—she didn't have the power.

Guinevere, however, did.

Arthur's wife would know the minute she touched the necklace that it was spelled to do more than enhance the child's power. She and Arthur would be furious. So would Logan and Giada, for that matter.

But it wouldn't be the first time Morgana had angered her half brother, and it wouldn't be the last. She wasn't looking forward to facing his rage—or Logan's either, for that matter. But she'd long since accepted the fact that someone had to do the jobs others were too honorable to do.

Morgana didn't enjoy such jobs, and she certainly wasn't proud of doing them, but she'd always done what was best for her people no matter the cost.

And she always would.

"Is he dead?"

The woman tightened her grip on the cell phone. "No."

Her father swore, hissing curses in a deadly voice. "Use-

less female. I should have known you would not have the stomach for this."

"My stomach is not the problem." She took a deep breath and wrestled her irritation into submission. Father had never recognized her strength, her determination. All his hopes had rested on her older brother's shoulders, despite Trey's obvious flaws.

But she'd sworn that by the time she was done, he'd see her worth, strength, and intelligence. She'd prove she was more than the mere female he considered her. "They've got a witch watching him. She disabled the first bomb."

"They suspect?" Alarm rang in his voice. "I told you they must learn nothing!"

"And they haven't." With an effort, she kept her tone cool and level. "They simply suspect someone is targeting their Latents. And they'll never learn anything different, because I'm going to take care of her. Once she's gone, Arthur's spawn will be dead within the day."

"Good. I want that bastard Celt to suffer as I have."

"He will."

"But carefully. I do not want our shame common knowledge. Too many enemies would turn it against me."

Her eyes narrowed. "Don't worry, Father. They'll never trace any of this back to you. I have taken great care to make sure the assassin knows nothing. And you know I will never betray you."

"See that you don't."

His tone sent ice creeping up her spine. She could almost feel the weight of his fist. She licked dry lips. "How is Mother?"

"No better. She is sedated most of the time." He sighed. "She fears how our people will react if this becomes known. And her grief . . ." Silence stretched, vibrating and taut. "She has never been strong, even for a female."

Her fingers tightened on the cell phone. "Our people will know only what you want them to know. And Arthur will pay in blood."

* * *

In the dream, Giada was tied up again.

Red silk scarves bound her spread-eagled to the four-poster bed. Moonlight flooded through the window, painting Logan's muscled body in silver light as he reclined next to her. His eyes blazed red, and fangs glinted in his lazy smile as he twirled a long white plume between his fingers.

The feather danced over one nipple as Logan teased her with delicate little strokes. She chuckled at the ticklish sensation, squirming. He watched her twist in her bonds, blatant male possessiveness in his gaze. "Mmmmm," he purred, his voice so deep, the sound alone was enough to make her hot. "Don't you look good enough to eat."

Giada grinned up at him. "You're a bad man, Logan MacRoy."

"Oh, darlin', you have no idea." He grinned back, wicked. "But you will."

He drew the ostrich feather along the full underside of her breasts, then floated it across her ribs to make her jerk and giggle.

Giada looked up at him, loving the way he studied her as if trying to decide what luscious, wicked thing he was going to do next. Her mock helplessness in her silken bonds only added to the sweet heat. She knew how completely safe she was with him.

He lifted his eyes to hers, lids dipping lazily as he stroked the feather over her stomach, teasing first her belly button, then the spread of her thighs. He bent his head and breathed softly, puffing into the soft nest of hair there until she smiled in anticipation.

"You smell wet," he murmured, his smile hot.

Giada laughed. "I am wet. You have that effect on me."

"Yeah?" He rolled between her legs. "Let's see just how wet I can make you."

Logan bent his head and parted her lips with his fingers,

*then settled down to lick. The first pass of his tongue made
her squirm. Pleasure swirled through her, lazy and hot. He
nibbled, teased, stretched one arm up her torso to flutter
the feather over the curve of her breast. She rolled her hips
in helpless pleasure at the delicate sensation.*

*Heat expanded through her in gorgeous waves, growing
hotter and more intense with every swirl of his tongue. She
surrendered to the passion, let it crash through her.*

*Until he rose between her thighs and settled on top of
her, weight braced on one arm, his gaze predatory. Taking
his cock in hand, he aimed it for her slick opening. And
thrust in one hard, demanding stroke that buried him to
the balls.*

*They caught their breath together. He felt so thick, so
overwhelming and delicious. He reared back, plunged deep
again. And again. And again, rolling his powerful ass in
those breath-stealing lunges.*

*Giada cried out in pleasure. Orgasm stormed through
her, tearing a ragged yowl from her throat. Logan growled
back as he lowered his head to seek the thumping vein in
her neck. And bit, sinking his fangs deep in one quick,
painless stroke.*

*Wrapped hard in his arms, impaled, surrendering, Giada
let herself fly.*

Only to wake, shivering, in the dark, her body thrumming with the dying echoes of her climax.

As she wondered yet again whether it had been vision
or dream.

Across town, Logan jolted awake, sweating, sick at the taste
of dream blood and the sight of Giada's bloodless corpse.
And tried desperately to persuade himself it had been only
a nightmare and nothing more.

The next morning dawned clear and bright, under a sky of
a particularly piercing shade of Carolina blue. The drive to

the sheriff's office required more patience than Giada usually had, as she negotiated the bustling Greendale traffic through the city's sprawling downtown. The stream of cars poured past clothing and antique stores crowded shoulder to shoulder with restaurants and bars. A couple of corporate headquarters presided over the low skyline with brick faces trimmed in cream and banks of windows like huge green mirrors.

In Greendale, anything over three stories looked like a skyscraper.

Finally reaching her destination, Giada drove her Toyota Camry into the sheriff's office parking lot and pulled into her assigned space.

As she got out, juggling a newspaper and a cup of cooling drive-through coffee, Logan looked up from locking his own car door. "Hey." His smile flashed as he walked over to her, and her too-susceptible heart began to beat far too fast with the memory of last night's dream. She barely noticed the rumble of a car pulling up behind her.

"Ready for another exciting day in the world of—" Logan broke off, his eyes widening in horror. "Gun!" He leaped even as he roared the warning, slamming into Giada with desperate, bone-jarring force, powerful arms wrapping around her. Coffee and paper went flying as they crashed down in a heap. A pistol fired with an oddly flat firecracker pop. Giada's head hit the pavement, touching off a cascade of stars behind her eyes.

She stared at the light show in dazed incomprehension as a car engine roared, accelerating away.

Someone just shot at us. For a stunned, breathless moment, Giada lay on the cold pavement, under Logan's warm, panting weight, waiting for the next bullet. It didn't come.

"Giada! Are you all right?" He peeled himself off her, dark eyes searching her face as he drew his gun. "Giada!"

She struggled to suck in a breath—but her stunned, frozen lungs refused to obey. *Got the breath knocked out of me.* She cast a quick spell, shocking her diaphragm into motion. "I'm okay," she wheezed.

"Great. Just relax." He rose into a crouch to snatch a look over her car hood, then holstered his gun again and pulled his cell phone off his belt. "Bitch's gone. Fuck, holy fuck."

"Jesus Christ!" a voice bellowed in the distance. "Mac-Roy, you okay?"

"Yeah, yeah, I just took a graze." He started running his hands over Giada's body in a fast, professional search for broken bones. "Call Dispatch and put out a BOLO for a black four-door Honda Civic with tinted windows," he said over his shoulder. "Late model, maybe a 2009. Driver was a white female from what I saw, red or brown hair, definitely armed. And call for an ambulance. I think Giada's hurt."

"Plates?"

"I was too busy eating pavement to get the tag number."

I'm supposed to protect him, and he saved my life. The thought slid through Giada's dazed mind, followed quickly by *Somebody just tried to shoot me.*

She might be immortal, but her ability to heal just about any wound would do her no good if somebody put a bullet in her brain. She'd be dead before she could hit the ground, much less cast a spell.

"Giada?" He touched her face to collect her dazed attention. "Can you tell if you're hurt anywhere? I hit you pretty hard."

"You saved my life." The words emerged as a croak. She winced and put a hand up to probe the back of her skull. Her fingertips discovered a very tender lump and something sticky. The bump pulsed a protest. "Ouch. My head."

"Just lie still. You don't need to go anywhere right now."

"What the hell happened?" a harried male voice demanded.

Logan looked up. "Somebody tried to shoot Giada. Shell casing should be right over there." He straightened to point. Giada's eyes focused on a snaking trail of blood down his left forearm. "God knows where the bullet is. Probably under the car somewhere."

She sat up so fast her head swam. Ignoring the sensation, she reached for him. "You're bleeding!"

"I'm fine." He gently urged her back down. "Be still, Giada. You don't know how badly you're hurt."

She frowned, studying the blood trickling down his arm. "Is that a bullet wound?"

He shrugged. "Just a graze."

"A graze?" She stared up at him, wanting badly to heal the wound, but knowing she didn't dare.

By now, cops and civilian employees had gathered around them, all talking at once. The deputies began to search the parking lot for the bullet and its casing. Light flashed, blinding her as something whined—an evidence tech with a camera.

A beefy gray-haired man crouched beside Logan to gaze down at her in concern. His face was long and craggy, with a hawk nose and a thick Wyatt Earp mustache. He wore dark brown slacks, a cream shirt that bulged over a slight potbelly, and a gold and brown checked tie. It took Giada a moment to recognize Sheriff Bill Jones as his sharp hazel gaze searched hers. "Do you know why somebody would try to kill you?"

Giada blinked up at him and lied over the wail of an approaching ambulance. "I don't have a clue, sir." *Except somebody's trying to murder Logan MacRoy. And somehow they've figured out that I'm here to protect him.*

Things had just gotten really complicated.

The next several hours were a blur of probing fingers and equally probing questions, along with assorted medical tests, none of which Giada enjoyed in the least.

Despite their best efforts, the ER staff of Greendale County Medical Center found nothing beyond a collection of scrapes and bruises caused by slamming into the pavement under Logan's shielding body.

Giada had indeed suffered a concussion, but she'd healed that herself in the ambulance. Morgana's emerald pendant was every bit as effective as the witch had promised, allowing her to draw energies from the Mageverse with no effort at all, daylight or no daylight.

She could have gotten rid of her road rash just as easily, but Logan had already seen the cuts, and she knew his suspicions would be aroused if they healed too fast. So Giada clenched her teeth and left the scrapes alone, ignoring their gritty sting.

Logan, too, had gone to the ER at the sheriff's insistence, ending up in the room beside her own. The minute their caretakers were distracted, he slipped around the curtain separating them. A thick white pad covered the bullet graze on his forearm as he studied her with brooding eyes. "You're sure you don't know who the shooter could have been?"

"Like I told the last dozen cops who asked, I haven't the faintest clue." Giada slid a hand over her head and grimaced. Her chignon had collapsed into a haystack of tangles, some of which were sticky with blood. Her favorite black suit would never be the same; a bloody hole had been ripped in her slacks over her left knee, and her white silk blouse was filthy and torn.

CSI Barbie was not looking her best.

"And before you ask," Giada continued, ticking off the items on her fingers, "no, I wasn't dating anyone back home, particularly not anyone with stalker ex-girlfriends who might want to blow me away out of jealousy. No, I don't know any crazy rival chemists or fired coworkers. No nutso roommates either. I have no idea why anyone would want to kill me." *Except that they want me out of the way so they can kill you.* "Maybe it was just some random fruitcake I cut off on the interstate. Who the heck knows?"

Logan gave her a tired smile. "I gather the detectives have been giving you the third degree."

"And the fourth and fifth degree, too. I think they're working on a doctorate." She slid off the gurney and winced as her knee protested. "I just want to go back to my hotel room and sleep for about twelve hours."

"About that . . ."

"Oh, jeez, what now?"

"I think you should come home with me." Logan held up a hand as if to block her protests. "Not so I can hit on

you again. You've got my word on that. If you are being targeted, I'd just feel better if you had someone with you."

Giada stared at him, bewildered. "You want me to stay with you?"

"If you're not comfortable with that idea, I can ask Sam Taylor—you know, the woman on the bomb squad? Jenny's handler? I'm sure she'd let you stay with her for a few days."

"No, I trust you. Especially considering you saved my life today." This could work, she realized. It would give her an excuse to stay close to him even when he wasn't on duty. "I really don't think anybody's after me, Logan, but I guess it wouldn't hurt to take precautions."

One thing was for sure, though. She was going to have to stay on her toes at all times. That gun could just as easily have been aimed at Logan as at her.

And she couldn't protect him if she was dead.

SIX

Logan insisted on giving Giada a ride to the hotel to pick up her things. She asked him to wait in the lobby while she took a shower and packed. He told her to take her time and went off to acquire a baggage cart.

Giada trotted up to her room as fast as her skinned knees would allow. "Smoke!" She pulled the door closed behind her. "Wake up, we've got a problem."

The cat opened one crystalline blue eye. "Oh, gods and devils, what now?"

Quickly, she brought him up to speed while she threw her things into suitcases. "I'll be checking out, so you'll have to gate to the Mageverse for the day."

The cat sat up, his tail curled over his toes, an expression of narrow-eyed thought on his furry face. "Actually, I can see how this would work very well. Hmmm."

"Whatever. Gate off now, before Logan comes up here and wonders why I've got a magic cat in my bed."

Smoke stretched his jaws in a silent feline laugh. "Oh, that does sound suggestive." Conjuring a gate, he disappeared.

* * *

Giada turned on the shower and waited for it to reach a comfortable temperature, staring blindly at the rushing water. An image flashed through her mind: *Logan charging toward her, fear and determination mingled on his handsome face. His body slamming into hers, taking her down . . .*

The trail of blood snaking down his muscled forearm . . .

He'd damn near taken a bullet for her. And she'd damn near died.

She stepped under the shower stream, gasping at the sting of water on cuts. *This is the second brush with death I've had in the last week.*

She hadn't let herself think about how close the bomb had come to killing them both, warding off the thought by telling herself she'd handled it. Saved them.

But she hadn't handled it today. She hadn't even seen it coming.

Leaning her forehead against the cool tile, Giada stared down at one scraped foot as it bled sluggishly into the swirling water. *I screwed up. I can't let them take me off guard like that again. I won't get lucky twice.*

And to think, the worst problems she'd had four months ago had been trying to find a job, an apartment, and a boyfriend, in no particular order.

Then came Christmas, and a witch named Pam.

Pam, who'd said she was the birth mother of Giada's father. Pam, who'd cast a spell that forced Giada's scientist's mind to believe in magic.

The Magekind, her grandmother explained, was recruiting. Would she like to become an immortal witch and help save the world from humanity's destructive impulses? Since the world obviously needed saving, and the immortality thing had sounded pretty good, Giada had said yes.

Turned out immortality only meant you didn't age. Somebody could still kill you.

You'd just leave a good-looking corpse.

I can't afford to screw up again, Giada thought, and started shampooing her hair. *So I won't.*

Logan's house was not what Giada had expected. Somehow she'd assumed he'd live in the mortal bachelor version of her own Avalon brick ranch: cramped and furnished in mismatched Goodwill castoffs.

Instead the home was a roomy split-level that appeared to date from the seventies, surrounded by blooming azalea bushes, a massive oak presiding over the newly mown front yard. A birdhouse hung from one branch, weathered dark gray, looking as if it had once been a Cub Scout project.

Inside, the split-level had the comfortable look of a family home, with a few exotic touches. There were tapestries she recognized as Guinevere's work, depicting unicorns and dragons, ladies and knights picked out in thin, bright yarn. Handwoven rugs provided rich contrast with the pale, mellow wood of the flooring. There seemed to be at least one bookshelf in every room, all of them crammed with well-thumbed volumes—not just the chemistry and forensics texts she'd have expected, but a collection of paperbacks ranging from science fiction to cozy mysteries.

"You've got a beautiful home," Giada said as she followed him up the wide carpeted stairs.

"Thank you." Logan wasn't even breathing hard as he juggled three of her suitcases. He'd refused to let her carry anything heavier than her makeup case. "I grew up here, actually. Bought it from my mother a few years ago when she . . . retired." He glanced around the hallway, his gaze lingering fondly on a tapestry of an armored knight. "I always loved this house."

The guest room he led her to was just as pleasant as the rest of the house. A dark blue comforter draped a sturdy pine queen-sized bed piled with pillows. The matching mirrored dresser and chest of drawers shared space with an empty computer desk and a brown leather swivel chair. The

carpet was also blue, though a shade paler than the spread, its pile thick and inviting.

Giada's gaze fell on a set of trophies lined up on the dresser. Basketball, baseball, football, one or two awards in swimming and track. She walked over to study them in dawning realization. "This was your room when you were a kid."

"Yep." He put her suitcases down on the bed.

"You *were* a jock, weren't you?" Which made sense. Latents tended to be stronger and more athletic than most people.

"'Fraid so." He glanced at the trophies, and she saw a flush spread across his angular cheekbones. "I keep meaning to stick those in the attic. Kind of ridiculous for a grown man to hang on to all that . . . stuff."

"Hey, I still have all my science fair awards." Giada shook her head, laughing softly. "I was such a little nerd. Guess I still am."

"Hardly." His smile was so warm and approving, her heart gave a happy little bump. "Why don't you unpack? I'll start dinner. How do you feel about lasagna?"

"My mouth just started watering. You cook?"

"Oh, yeah. My mom considered it a survival skill."

Giada snorted and walked over to unzip one of her suitcases. "Mine always said that's why God made Domino's." Her voice dropped to a mutter. "No wonder I was a little butterball."

He chuckled, brushing her shoulder with warm fingers. They left a definite tingle on her skin. "Come down as soon as you're ready."

She couldn't resist the impulse to ogle his ass as he walked out.

While Giada unpacked, Logan detoured into his own room and grabbed a pewter statue off the dresser, then quickly retreated downstairs with it.

In the kitchen, safely out of his guest's earshot, he put

the statue on the counter and eyed it. The muscular figure of the cat crouched, its eyes two shimmering moonstones.

He hadn't tried this in years. He hoped it still worked.

Clearing his throat, Logan said, "Smoke?"

Moonstone eyes flared with pure blue light. "Hmmm? Logan, boy, is that you? You haven't called me with that thing since you were eighteen."

"Yeah, well, I've got a problem. And I think I need magical help."

A cat-sized gate appeared in midair, and Smoke landed on the marble countertop with a soft thump. "What's the problem, boy?"

Quickly—he wasn't sure how much time he'd have before Giada came downstairs—Logan filled his friend in on the day's events while he started work on dinner.

Smoke's blue eyes widened in alarm. "Your friend was almost shot?"

Logan nodded grimly over the cutting board as he sliced up a bell pepper. "Would have taken a bullet right in the back of the head if I hadn't knocked her clear. As it was, she ended up with a bad case of road rash, but I didn't have time to be gentle."

"And you want me to protect her?"

"That's the idea. If you could stay close . . ."

"Boy, they're not going to let you bring a cat into the police department."

"Sheriff's office. The police are city. We're county."

One ear flicked in lazy dismissal. "Whatever."

"Anyway, if you could just hang around outside the building. Keep watch. If that bitch shows up again, track her. Please. I need to know why the hell she's after Giada." Hearing the stairs creak under padding bare feet, he added hastily, "But don't talk around Giada, okay? I don't want to have to explain the whole magic cat thing."

Smoke shot him a look of narrow-eyed disgust. "Have I ever talked in front of one of your mortal friends, boy?"

"Good point. Sorry."

Giada slipped into the kitchen before either could say

anything else. She wore jeans and a loose cotton shirt, a black leather belt cinching her waist, making it look even tinier than usual. Logan had never seen her in anything but business wear, and he blinked at the way the worn and faded denim hugged those elegant curves. *Damn,* he thought, *Giada can make anything look sexy.*

Then his gaze locked on the scrape across her high cheekbone. His heart gave a hot squeeze in his chest. *She came too damn close to getting killed today. Way too damn close. And I've got to make sure it doesn't happen again.*

Giada paused in the doorway, eyeing Smoke. "You've got a cat."

"Actually, I think the cat's got me." Logan returned to stirring the ground beef he was browning. "How're you feeling?"

"Head hurts a little bit, and I'll be really sore tomorrow, but at least I'm still breathing." Her smile was sudden and breathtaking. "And I've got you to thank for that. I had no idea the shooter was even there. If you hadn't pushed me down, I'd be dead."

To Logan's annoyance, he felt his face grow warm. To distract her from that ridiculous blush, he affected a John Wayne drawl. "Awww, little lady, 'tweren't nothing."

She stepped over to him, rose on her bare toes, and kissed him gently on one hot cheek. "Thank you." Her lips felt deliciously soft.

And incredibly sweet.

Following a very tasty supper—Logan was indeed a good cook—Giada cleared the table over his protests. After the day she'd had, loading the dishwasher finished off the last of her energy reserves. She dragged her battered body up the stairs and fell into bed. In minutes, she was deeply asleep.

As Smoke wandered outside to lurk under the bushes and watch for assassins, Logan retreated to his own room. He was too much a gentleman to glance in at his sleeping guest.

If he had, he might have noticed the point of bright green light burning beneath the cotton fabric of her T-shirt. The necklace Morgana had given her blazed against her bare skin, magic pulsing in its heart.

Logan loomed over her in the darkness, moonlight silvering his muscled shoulders. Giada's heart pounded as she looked down the length of her body into his hungry eyes. Eyes that glowed vampire red as he bent his head. His tongue flicked out, stroked the aching point of her nipple. Each lick made her head swim with sweet, searing pleasure. Warm fingers shaped her breast, squeezed, stroked, drew teasing circles on her flesh. She writhed, gasping.

Gods, he felt so good. So perfect.

She ached between her legs, a creamy pulse of need. She'd never felt like this, never needed a man with such ferocious, driving hunger.

She had to have him. Had to. *She thought she would go insane without the long, slick heat of him driving just where she needed it.*

"Logan . . ." Giada moaned . . .

And woke.

For a long, disoriented moment, she could only stare blankly at the ceiling. "Logan?"

But he was gone. There was no hard, heavy body pressing against hers, no hot mouth tormenting her breasts, no teasing hands. There was nothing but a wet, empty ache.

Another dream. Even more intense than the others.

So intense, in fact, that she suddenly realized one hand was thrust down beneath the waistband of her panties. The flesh between her legs was swollen tight, so wet it felt as though she'd been covered with melted butter.

Just another damned dream. Frustration clawed at Giada with stinging stiletto claws. God, she wanted Logan so bad.

Her legs scissored restlessly on the sweaty sheets. Her breasts ached, nipples drawn into desperate peaks.

He's right across the hall, the voice of temptation

breathed in a sighing devil's whisper. *All I have to do is walk ten feet.*

But she couldn't. Making love with him would be utterly irresponsible, a betrayal of the trust Arthur and Guinevere had bestowed on her. Logan did not want to become a vampire.

But just once wouldn't hurt, her aching body wheedled. *It takes at least three times to bring on the Gift. Maybe more. I could make love to him once . . .*

But if he made love to another Maja twice more, it *would* change him. *I have no right to make such a choice for him.*

Giada gritted her teeth and jerked her hand out of her panties to fist the sheets. *I am not going to do this. I'm not.*

Sleep. What she needed was to go back to sleep.

But every breath she took rasped hard nipples against the fabric of her T-shirt. The shirt was old, butter-soft from washing, but it might as well have been burlap from the way it raked her sensitive skin.

Logan's eyes shone at her through the darkness, glowing red with vampire magic. He smiled at her, his fangs white, sharp.

Only to vanish into the shadows like seductive mist.

She wanted to scream.

Three times she'd dreamed of him with this overwhelming erotic intensity. Or were they glimpses of the future? If so, did that mean she was destined to Change him?

And if it was destiny, what was the point of fighting it?

But I swore I wouldn't. She ground her teeth so hard, her skull filled with a sound like sandpaper rasping over cement. *I promised Guinevere and Arthur. Besides, he's my friend. He saved my life today. I can't repay him by betraying his trust. It's bad enough I have to lie to him.*

The muscles of her thighs jerked in spasms, and her belly clenched with craving. *Cut it out, Giada.* Squeezing her eyes tightly closed, she dug her nails into the mattress like a cat dangling from a tree branch.

Over a pack of rabid dogs.

I'm not going to do this. I'm not. Not. Notnotnotnot . . .

Eyes clenched shut, she didn't see the necklace give another demanding pulse.

When Giada opened her eyes again, she was standing in the hallway outside his door. She didn't even recall getting out of bed. Horrified, she turned to dash back into her own room.

"Giada?" Logan blinked at her from around the edge of the door. "Is something wrong?"

She was in his arms before she knew what she was doing.

Giada plowed into Logan so hard, she knocked him back on his heels. His gasp of astonishment was muffled by her mouth covering his with kisses that were more like famished bites.

Automatically, he enfolded her frantic body in his arms. She felt deliciously warm and soft and firm in all the right places, and his libido registered its enthusiastic approval with an instant hard-on.

She was moaning something between kisses, throaty little groans. Lost in a delightful sensory storm, it took him a moment to decipher the soft stream of whimpers: "This is wrong. I've got to stop. You'll hate me. But oh, God, you feel sooooo good . . ."

It took willpower he hadn't even known he had, but he managed to grab her upper arms and peel her off, gaining a couple of inches of space between them. Her eyes looked vague, dazed—and troubled. "Not that I'm not enjoying this, but what's going on? I thought you said you didn't want to sleep with me."

"I didn't, I shouldn't—but I *need* you." Gray eyes glittered up at him from her flushed face, and her lips were parted, ripe and tempting, strawberry rose. "I've been dreaming about you. Dreaming for days." Her nails dug into his back. "Please. I've never felt like this. I can't stand it. Please . . . Don't hate me!"

An alarm peeled somewhere in the back of his mind—was it a coincidence that he'd dreamed about her, too? But the sound was muffled by the thunderous rush of blood in his ears. He had to taste that mouth again.

Her lips opened under his, moist and eager. Tongues met, swirling together in a slick and maddening dance. Her hips rocked against his erection with a delicious pleading that made him feel as if the top of his head was about to blow off. Dressed only in a pair of cotton boxers, Logan felt the contact with a molten intensity that burned through his veins in shuddering waves.

No woman had ever turned him on this much, this fast. Not even Clea, the Maja Morgana had sent to seduce him. Clea, whom he'd had the sense to refuse.

That thought sent another slicing through the hot erotic haze. *Was* Giada a Maja? This wasn't the first time he'd wondered, but the idea had never seemed so likely. There was something abnormal about the savage mutual heat blazing between them now. Something that smacked of magic.

And I really should care.

Whatever it was that burned between them was more than magic. It wasn't just Giada's luscious little body that drew him. It was her intelligence, her strength, even her former fat-little-kid vulnerability. She got to him the way no woman ever had, with a strength that had nothing to do with how long they'd known each other.

It was as if she fit the empty parts of him like a key sliding into a lock, making him just as desperate to have her as she obviously was to have him. If he gave her a chance to come to her senses, this opportunity to forge something deeper might never come again.

So he kissed her back with all the skill and hunger in his soul, slipping one hand up to cup her breast, the other down to the damp fabric between her thighs. She made a sobbing moan of surrender—and closed her hand around his cock.

Growling in need, Logan lifted her into his arms and carried her into his bedroom to lay her down on the tumbled

sheets. Straightening, he looked down at her, his heart beating hard, his cock jutting with the strength of his need.

Giada's eyes were luminous silver in the moonlight flooding through the bedroom window. Her skin seemed to glow, pale and perfect. His mouth went dry as he bent to grab the hem of her top and pull it over her head, leaving her breasts beautiful and bare.

Round, sweet handfuls, they were tipped by blushing rose nipples. An emerald lay between the soft mounds on a delicate gold chain, adding an exotic flourish to her nudity. Her waist dipped to a swell of hips framed in tiny lace panties. Her legs looked impossibly long, lean with strong runner's muscles.

He stripped off his boxers in one swift, impatient move.

Giada caught her breath. God, he was beautiful as he rose to his full height, naked and brawny in the cool, pale light flooding through the window. His shoulders looked impossibly broad compared to his narrow waist and the powerful legs that were all chiseled muscle and bone. His cock jutted from a nest of fine, dark curls, curving slightly upward, its head fat as a plum, shaft so thick and hard she caught her breath.

She reached for her panties and stripped them off, then sent them sailing across the room. He grinned in an oddly boyish flash of teeth, and covered her in warm, velvet strength. She purred.

He kissed her. Lazy, sweet, and deep, stroking tongue and lip, brushing back and forth, teasing, nibbling teeth finding her chin, the tender lobe of her ear. Blowing to make her smile at the tickle.

The maddening hunger retreated even as he caressed her, becoming a bit more gentle, a bit more tender with every touch. Less like a possession than natural need. She gasped in relief, able to think again. *I should stop this.*

But his fingers feathered over her breasts, spinning

sensations she'd never felt before. Impossibly intriguing. Incredibly hot. She caught her breath and let her eyes slip closed.

Sex had never been all that satisfying for her. Her first college lover had been a virgin himself. When he'd penetrated her, she'd been too dry, and it hurt. She'd cried, and he'd stormed out in a huff.

Renaldo, the vampire who'd given her Merlin's Gift, had been far more skilled. He'd made sure she was aroused, and all three times had been satisfying—though the Gift itself had felt a lot like taking a direct lightning strike to the back of the skull. Yet he'd *never* made her feel like this.

Luscious curls of pleasure trailed in the wake of Logan's fingers, delicate as the brush of a butterfly's wings. His lips felt so soft, some magical blend of silk and satin, heated and tender.

He touches me like I mean something to him.

Renaldo had made love like a French chef preparing a meal—with skill and pride in his craft—but she hadn't meant anything to him. He hadn't *known* her. Hadn't wanted to.

Logan cradled her with every touch and kiss, silently assuring her how important she was to him. Each glittering sensation struck her starving soul like rain on parched earth.

That was what she couldn't resist. She might have found the strength to tear herself away had he offered her nothing more than desire. She could not say no to this exquisite tenderness.

"You're so beautiful," Logan breathed. There was absorbed wonder in his eyes as he looked at her, tracing the curves of her body with delicate fingertips.

Giada shivered. Caught her breath as he lowered his head. The tip of his tongue found the point of her nipple, sending hot jolts of sensation flicking along her nerves, piercingly sweet. She moaned and slid a hand into the raw silk of his hair.

He licked her, slow circles and figure eights drawn in wet

heat on aching skin. The desire that had calmed began to surge again, sweeter now, a warm purring thrum building in her bones.

Slowly, deliberately, Logan worked his way across her breasts, paying lavish attention to first one nipple, then the other, until he had her head rolling on the pillow in a delirium of pleasure.

Giada was floating in honeyed arousal by the time he started stringing tiny, stinging little bites down the rise of her rib cage. He paused to tongue her navel until she squirmed in ticklish protest. Then he just kept going, kissing his way down to her pelvic bone.

She caught her breath in helpless anticipation as he stirred the fine, soft hair over her mound with a fingertip. Spread her lower lips, oh-so-delicately, like a man parting the petals of a rose.

Lick.

Sensation zinged its way up her spine. Sparks flared behind her lids. "Logan!" She twisted, digging her nails into the thick muscle of his shoulders.

He made a low rumbling sound like the purr of a tiger. And covered her with his mouth, tongue swirling a hypnotic dance over wet and swollen flesh. Her hips jerked and rolled in helpless delight.

He licked, he suckled and teased. Drew back for a moment and slid a finger deep into tight, creaming depths. Made a deep, satisfied sound. "You *do* want me."

"God, yes!" She squeezed her eyes shut and dug one bare heel into the small of his back. "You're driving me insane!"

"Good. You've been driving *me* insane for days." A second finger joined the first, pumping, twisting. She rolled her hips, pleading.

"Now . . ." she panted.

"Hmmm." Logan tilted his head, eyeing her folds as they caressed his fingers with wet, swollen heat. "Not quite."

"Logan!"

He laughed and took her with his mouth again, licking her clit in tormenting little strokes that made her quiver.

She began to beg, rolling her hips against his face, so maddeningly close to her climax, but not . . . quite . . . *there*. "Logan, dammit!" she gasped, her voice strangled.

He laughed, a wicked rumble, and sat up. She was about to protest when he grabbed her thighs, spread her wide—

And drove to the balls in one hard lunge.

Her eyes flared wide, meeting his narrowed gaze as he froze, there, impaling her. "God!" His voice sounded strangled. "You feel . . ." A muscle flexed in his cheek, and his eyes closed as he began to pull out, slowly, slowly, a raking, delicious glide.

Only to fill her again the next moment, his pelvis pressing deliciously against her clit.

Thick, so damn thick, so damn long, all the way . . .

So damned wrong. She really wished she cared.

SEVEN

Giada clenched around him, a cream-slicked silken vise, so impossibly tight he wondered if she was a virgin.

But no virgin would feel like a heated peach, all juice and yielding flesh. Her exquisite runner's legs were wrapped around his waist, heels riding his ass, urging him on. Her slender arms gripped his shoulders with surprising strength until every sweet satin inch of her was pressed to every hairy male inch of him. She met his thrusts with rolling, eager hips as she moaned, gasped, cried out in reaction each time he drove deep.

Logan felt the orgasm gathering in his balls like a hot fist going tight. And tighter, and tighter, until he thought the pressure would . . .

"Logan!" She screamed his name in a high-pitched cry of delight. Her tiny inner muscles clamped down on his sawing cock with astonishing strength, pulsing as she climaxed.

He bellowed and came in a roaring explosion of a climax that tore through him like a convulsion, so hard that for a moment he wondered if it was the Gift. Throwing back his

head, Logan watched light explode behind his lids in searing shades of gold and green. Dimly, he felt Giada's slim body twisting in his arms.

Their eyes tightly closed, neither of them saw the emerald around her neck spit a final satisfied green spark.

Gasping, they collapsed together in a sweat-damp heap, unable to move for a long moment, hearts pumping in desperate lunges, lungs heaving.

With a groan, Logan finally rolled off her and drew her over across his chest. Giada lay there, boneless as a wet sponge, listening to his thundering heartbeat slow. Her own heart still pounded, and her muscles quivered like a hard-run horse's. Her entire body felt stunned with a kind of bewildered delight.

She'd never even known sex could be like that. No wonder everyone made such a big deal about it. She couldn't wait to do it again.

The memory of Arthur Pendragon's cold black gaze flashed through her consciousness. *"Do not sleep with my son."*

Giada winced. *I am so screwed.*

She'd broken a promise to King Arthur. He was going to kill her. *Logan* was going to kill her.

What had she done?

She had to tell Logan the truth.

Yes, Arthur had told her not to, but then, Arthur had told her not to sleep with his son, too, and look what had happened.

She was a weasel. She had all the willpower of a roll of wet toilet paper. He was going to hate her.

Gathering her courage, Giada lifted her head, bracing herself for his reaction. "Logan . . ."

"Oh, man," he moaned. The smile that played around his beautiful mouth was both sated and oddly sweet, tinged in an astonished wonder. "That was . . . amazing."

Diverted, Giada stared at him. "Really?" The word was such an obvious plea for reassurance that she winced. *Idiot. He probably says that to every girl he screws stupid.*

Logan brushed a tangled blond curl off her cheekbone and gave her a tender smile. "Yeah. Really."

Good grief, he means it. That look in his eyes . . . Something told her Arthur's son wasn't the type for facile sexual lies. She swallowed and licked her dry lips. "I have something to tell you."

He stroked the curl he still held between thumb and forefinger. His gaze was warm, indulgent. Almost . . . loving? "Yeah?"

Imagining the rage that would soon fill those dark eyes, the disillusion and betrayal, Giada cringed.

"I've never felt like this." The words burst from her, utter truth—but not the truth she needed to tell. Which was when she realized she couldn't stand to see those beautiful eyes chill into hate and anger.

Oh, God.

I won't touch him again, she told herself firmly. *It takes three times. Maybe more. I'll just stay away from him from now on. If we don't make love again, everything will be fine.*

He lifted his head from the pillow and took her mouth, the kiss tender, so deliciously seductive, her sated body quivered in response.

I am so screwed.

Giada felt delicious as she lay across his body, sweat-damp and breathing hard, warm and female and lovely. Her hair tumbled across his skin, cool curls tickling every time either of them breathed. Her breath puffed across his left nipple, which drew into a bead in response.

I think I'm in trouble.

The thought zipped in out of nowhere, and Logan frowned. *Shut up,* he told that little warning mutter. He did not want this lovely mood ruined.

But the mental mutter only got louder. *I am definitely in trouble.*

Logan was nobody's idea of a virgin. He'd been fourteen when he'd had his first lover, a pretty sixteen-year-old Latent with a yen to seduce the son of King Arthur.

There'd been a lot of Latents like that.

Since becoming an adult, he'd learned his way around a woman's body well enough that he no longer expected to be surprised. Giada had surprised him anyway.

Logan had no idea what had made this time so different. He suspected it was Giada herself. Giada, with her oddly innocent reactions to his touch, her beautifully responsive body.

Giada, who was mortal. Who could never become immortal because she wasn't a Latent.

The thought brought its own kind of grief.

Though Logan was in no hurry to become a vampire—and in fact meant to put it off as long as possible—he'd always known he had a duty to join the Magekind. Never mind that the thought made his stomach knot and sweat break out on his palms.

Avalon needed him, especially now. Over the past two years, the Magekind had fought a series of wars with some seriously nasty magical enemies. Arthur had lost far too many warriors in those battles—so many, in fact, he'd been forced to recruit a group of likely Latents en masse back in December. It had been an unprecedented move, because the Magekind usually recruited one Latent at a time. To bring in so many at once showed just how desperate they really were.

Arthur had asked Logan to take up Merlin's Gift with the new group, but he'd refused. He still wasn't sure he was ready.

Sooner or later, though, he'd have to accept the Gift. That meant leaving behind his mortal career, his fellow cops and coworkers. He would probably never see those friends again. They would grow old and die, while he continued on, immortal, un-aging, fighting at his father's side. He'd have no room for mortals in his life anymore.

Not even a mortal like Giada.

Brooding now, Logan stared at the ceiling, his hand absently stroking the cool gold silk of her hair.

If he hadn't been his father's son, what would he have done?

The answer was obvious. After tonight, he would have pursued Giada with all the skill at his command. Wined her, dined her.

And proposed.

Giada Shepherd was everything he'd ever wanted. Brilliant, lovely, and courageous. The woman of his dreams.

Oh, he could still court her—but only if he was willing to turn his back on his duty to his father. And he couldn't.

It was one thing to put the Gift off. He had, after all, a perfectly legitimate reason to wait. He wanted to be sure of his strength before he attempted the transformation. The price of failure would be entirely too high, not only for himself, but for his parents. So he'd wait until he was sure.

But he could not wait forever.

And that meant he and Giada had no future. Like it or not, he was going to have to keep his distance.

The spy prowled the bomb squad's equipment room, cell phone in hand. Pausing in front of the whiteboard hanging on the wall, she studied the duty schedule the squad members had filled in.

"According to my contact," she murmured, "Logan MacRoy will be on call with the arson squad Friday night."

"And you want me to make sure he's got something to investigate." Terrence John Anderson sounded, as usual, faintly bored.

She bared her teeth at the whiteboard. "*And* that it's the last investigation he ever conducts."

"I can arrange that."

Restlessly, the spy turned to pace again, striding back and forth across the room. "I think you'd be wise to make

sure there's at least one backup . . . device. That woman he has with him may be able to deactivate one of them."

"The tall blonde."

"Yes." She ground her teeth at the rise of impotent rage. Her failed attempt to shoot the little bitch grated on her. "The blonde. I think she's the reason your first attempt on Logan failed."

"I wouldn't think so. According to my research, she's just a chemist. I don't see how somebody like that would be able to disable one of my devices."

How *dare* he question her? With the skill of long practice, the spy kept the rage from her voice. "Trust me, she did."

"Okay, okay, don't get your panties in a wad. I'll make sure she goes down with him."

"Thank you." Her eyes narrowed. "Feel free to make the incident as spectacular as possible."

He paused a moment, surprise in his silence. "I thought you wanted this low-key."

"I've changed my mind." It would take something big to get her father's attention—and win his respect. "I have someone I want to impress."

Terrence laughed softly. "Oh, believe me—I can deliver impressive."

"See that you do." She clicked the cell phone closed and tucked it away. Blowing out a breath, she gazed around at the rolls of det cord and boxes of bursting charges. There were enough explosives in this room to turn the entire department into a crater.

It would be so easy to get Terrence in here and turn him loose. If she timed the bombing for shift change, he could take out three-quarters of the deputies and all of the department's administration, up to and including the sheriff.

It was definitely something to think about.

She let herself imagine it: the roiling smoke, the screams of the dying, the blood and missing limbs, men turned to hamburger in the blink of an eye.

God, she was so tempted.

But no. It was much better to try a surgical strike first. Otherwise, it might not be clear to Arthur that their true objective among all those dead cops had been his precious son.

And she wanted him to know.

Terrence put his cell back on its belt clip, a smile of anticipation on his face. Finally! He'd been going out of his mind with boredom stuck in this hotel room, waiting for the client to let him know when she wanted him to make another attempt.

Generally, he did not allow those who hired him to dictate how he did his job. But this one was paying him a great deal extra to indulge her.

Now she'd given him permission to carry out the kind of deadly artistry that was his forte.

Better yet, this one would be a challenge. He'd never tried to combine an arson with not just one but a series of bombs. Bombs designed specifically to take out first responders.

Dead cops. Dead firemen. A sense of power rolled over him, exhilarating and arousing. Terrence hardened behind his zipper in a rush of heat and swelling lust.

His mind raced as he started considering the possibilities. First, though, he'd need to find a house he could burn to provide the setup he needed.

He contemplated whether to arrange civilian fire victims. It was a tempting idea, but perhaps a little too ambitious. If he tried to plant devices while the victims were at home, the chances of getting caught were just too great. Armed homeowners, someone calling 911—

Definitely too dangerous.

So he'd look for a place whose occupants were on vacation. Somewhere there were no neighbors, or the other residents were gone during the day. It would take time to find a place like that, and still more time to design and plant his devices.

He'd have to work like a dog to get everything ready, but he should be able to finish his preparations by Friday.

A cold smile playing around his lips, Terrence picked up his notebook and digital camera and headed for the door.

Smoke dozed, eyes half-closed, under his favorite azalea. He'd walked his usual warding spell around the yard, so it was safe enough. The ward would wake him if anyone tried to cross its boundary.

He rather hoped someone would. He was looking forward to sinking his fangs into the bastard who was tormenting Giada and Logan.

"Smoke!"

He jerked fully awake at the low hiss. "Giada?"

Skimming out from under the bush, he found her looking miserable as she stood on the house's brick front steps. She wore jeans and a wrinkled inside-out T-shirt that looked as if she'd donned it in the dark, and her face gleamed with silver tear tracks in the moonlight. Alarmed, he demanded, "What's the matter?"

"Let's move away from the house." She sniffed and headed for the woods at the edge of the backyard. "Logan's asleep, and I don't want to wake him."

Worried, Smoke trotted after her. When he judged they'd put enough distance between themselves and the house he asked the obvious question. "What's the boy done now?"

"It's not him." Her lips trembled. "It's me. I had sex with him! I tried not to, but I just couldn't stop."

The story emerged in a whispered rush, nasal with tears. Smoke looked up at her, his tail tip twitching in suspicion. There was something wrong with this story. Smelled like a spell to him.

"I'm coming up." He gathered himself and jumped. She caught him automatically and drew him into a cuddle. He suspected the hug was more for her comfort than his.

As she continued her tearful self-flagellation over her lack of control, Smoke gave her a thorough but unobtrusive sniff.

The child definitely smelled of magic other than her own. The alien scent led right to the emerald pendant around her slender throat. One more good sniff, and he recognized the dark blend of musk, cinnamon, and magic. *Morgana's been a busy girl—again.* "Where did you get that necklace?"

Giada glanced down at the stone and sniffed again. "Morgana gave it to me. It's supposed to enhance my powers during the day. Works, too."

That's not all it's doing. He flicked the end of his tail, thinking. It would make Giada feel better if he told her she was the victim of a spell, but then she'd promptly dump the necklace. He wasn't sure that was such a good idea. Morgana was arrogant and often too ruthless by half, but on this particular occasion, she was also right.

It was past time Logan became a Magus.

Even the boy knew it. The only unknown was why he was stalling. His fears obviously had something to do with whatever had happened when he was fourteen. The cat huffed, irritated with Logan's uncharacteristic secrecy.

"What am I going to do, Smoke?" Giada moaned. "I can't let this happen again. But how can I prevent it, when I don't even understand why I lost control this time? The need—I've never felt anything like it."

The cat winced at the prick of unaccustomed guilt. "Don't be so hard on yourself, child. Logan wants you, and he can be very seductive."

"Yeah, well, he wouldn't want anything to do with me if he knew I was Magekind." She frowned, head down, studying the leafy ground in front of her sneaker-clad feet. "I wonder if I should tell him."

"God, no. Arthur ordered you not to, remember?"

"He also told me to stay out of Logan's bed. Maybe I should tell *him* what happened and ask him what to do."

"He'd hit the ceiling." And Gwen would take one look at the necklace and spot Morgana's fine hand at work.

"And then he'd rip a strip off my hide." Giada sighed. "But I deserve it. Might as well open a gate and get it over with . . ."

Alarmed, Smoke realized he had to nip this in the bud—fast. "I think not. Now that you've experienced the effect, I'm sure you can fight it." *Not likely.* "Go back to your own bed and try to get some sleep. It takes at least three exposures to trigger the Gift, remember? Logan will be fine."

"Are you sure?" She frowned, concern drawing a line between her blond brows. "I really think I should report in."

You certainly should. But since that didn't suit Smoke's plans at all, he lied without twitching an ear. "There's no point in getting Gwen and Arthur stirred up over this. You won't let it happen again."

"But Smoke, you don't know what it's like!"

He had a pretty good idea. Giada didn't stand a chance. "I have faith in you, child."

Actually, he did. Of all the females he'd met in Avalon, Giada was the most perfect for Logan. And since the boy was no fool, it wouldn't take him long to realize it.

Of course, after Logan became a vampire, there would be a royal row—literally—when the truth came out. Smoke would have to take his share of the blame, but it wouldn't be the first time he'd had to disappear until tempers cooled. They'd eventually see he was right and get over it.

It took some coaxing, but he finally got Giada to go back inside. He slipped back under his bush with a sigh of relief.

It was close to dawn when he heard his name whispered again. "Smoke!"

Logan. He was surprised it had taken the boy so long. Poking his head out from under his bush, he glowered up at his friend. "What?"

Logan crouched and studied him with a frown. "Is Giada a Maja?"

Oh, gods and devils, Smoke had been afraid that question was coming. "No." It was distasteful lying to the boy, but it wasn't as if he had a choice.

"Damn."

Smoke flicked an interested ear at the mutter. "I thought you didn't want to become a Magus."

"I don't." Logan sank onto his butt in the grass and folded his long legs tailor-fashion. "But I'd rather Giada wasn't mortal."

Suddenly Smoke felt much better about taking so many liberties with the truth. "Like the girl, do you?"

"She's perfect." He grimaced. "Except for the whole getting old and dying thing. And I can't stay mortal for much longer. Dad needs me."

"He's needed you for years, boy."

"But not if it means taking my fucking head."

Smoke flicked his ears forward and stared. "What skull worm do you have now?"

Logan lifted one shoulder in a half shrug. "Same one I've had for years."

"And isn't it time you tell me about it?"

He didn't answer for so long, Smoke began to wonder if he ever would. Finally the words emerged in a frustrated growl. "What if Morgana's wrong about me being able to handle the Gift? She's been wrong before."

Smoke studied him, eyes narrow. "Who was she wrong about when you were fourteen?"

"Jimmy Cordino." Logan looked off across the yard, staring blindly toward the dawn. "He was one of Kay's descendants. You know how Dad was about Kay." Kay, Arthur's foster brother, had been a courageous, capable warrior, one of the original Knights of the Round Table. He had been killed in an air strike during World War II. Arthur had been heartbroken.

"Everybody said Jimmy even looked like Kay, who was his great-grandfather. That summer, Dad took Jim under his wing—teaching him sword-craft, how to ride, shoot— everything he thought a Magus should know." Logan's smile was very faint. "I hated Jimmy's fuckin' guts, and it was mutual. I was jealous of how much attention he was getting from Arthur, and he was jealous of me being

my father's son. Then he got the Gift, and it all went to
hell."

The Pendragon Home, Avalon, October 15, 1991

Logan jerked awake to blink at the ceiling in dazed confusion, wondering what had pulled him out of sleep.

Ah. There it was.

The creak of the stairs under someone's weight. Probably Mom or Dad, home at last. They both kept vampire
hours, something he had yet to adjust to this early in the
summer.

Yawning, Logan rolled out of bed and padded, barefoot,
into the hall. "Hey, how did it . . ."

Jimmy Cordino stood there, pale blue eyes wild, pupils
shrunk to black pinpoints in the hall light. Blood smeared
his face and splattered his white shirt and faded jeans. Even
his blond hair was matted in red, sticky clumps.

"What the hell happened to you?" Logan demanded.
"You look like shit."

"I killed her." Jimmy didn't even sound like himself. His
voice was too high, more like a kid's than the twenty-one-
year-old he was.

Which was when Logan's sleep-stunned mind began to
catch up to the situation. A chill spread over him. "Killed
who?" He took a step back—and froze as a sudden horrifying thought shot through his alarm. "My mom? Is my mom
okay?"

"Not her!" Jimmy sneered, his lifted lip revealing inch-
long fangs. "The Maja. The Maja Arthur set me up with.
The one they told me to fuck." He laughed, his voice spiraling into a chilling giggle. "Well, I definitely fucked her."

Sweet Jesu, he's gone blood-mad. Logan licked his lips.
"You'd better get out of here. Dad's on his way home." *I
hope.* Despite years of combat training from the time he
could walk, Logan knew damned well he was no match for
a blood-mad vampire.

There was that chilling laugh again. "You better pray he is, you spoiled little fuck."

Okay, that was *definitely* his cue. Logan whirled for his room, planning to lock the door behind him. If he could only delay Jimmy even a few minutes, Dad would . . .

The vampire was on him before he even took half a step, clamping a forearm across his throat. Logan gagged at the vicious pressure.

"Logan!" Arthur roared from downstairs, his voice shaking with a combination of rage and fear Logan had never heard in it before.

"Up here, 'Dad.' " Jimmy's breath reeked with the smell of blood as it gusted against Logan's face. "Come talk to your itty bitty boy. And *me*."

"You even nick that boy with a fang, and you're dead." Arthur's voice sounded so flat and cold, even Logan felt the chill. Booted feet rang on the marble floor in long running strides.

"I'm dead anyway." Jimmy's bitter laugh had a sobbing edge.

The vampires appeared at the foot of the stairs. Logan's knees went weak with relief. Arthur and his best knights— Lancelot, Galahad, Tristan, and Gawain, moving like silent wolves at his back. They all wore identical expressions, faces frozen, eyes narrow and icy with a terrible rage.

"Let the boy go, Jimmy," Arthur said, starting up the stairs in a slow stalk. He carried Excalibur naked in his hand, the sword glowing with boiling energy as it reacted to his fury.

Jimmy shrank back as the arm around Logan's neck began to shake. "Don't kill me!" The naked plea was shocking after all those cocky threats.

"You killed *her*." Arthur's black eyes burned. "Left her with her throat ripped out in the bed where you'd made love."

"I didn't mean to! I lost control. I was just so"—his voice cracked—"hungry."

"I know." A faint hint of compassion warmed Arthur's

eyes. "Don't compound your mistake, Jimmy. Let the boy go."

Jimmy's arm only tightened, hauling Logan off his feet, to choke helplessly as the young vampire retreated down the hall. "You'll kill me."

"We can't let you murder again, Jimmy." Arthur's voice softened. "And I don't think you want to. Do you?"

"But I didn't mean to!" It was a wail, a boy's pitiful cry of anguish and fear. He braced a shoulder against Logan's bedroom door as if his knees had gone weak. "I won't do it again! I swear it! Just give me a chance!"

"You can't control it, Jimmy. I'm sorry we did this to you." *I'm sorry we made you a monster.* He didn't say the words, but still, they rang in the silence.

"Fuck you, old man!" Jimmy screamed, a howl of defiance. His free hand fisted in Logan's short hair, jerked his head to one side. Out of the corner of his eye, Logan saw the flash of descending fangs . . .

A feminine hand thrust through the surface of the closed bedroom door as if it were water. A spell blasted from slender fingers, right into Jimmy's blood-maddened face. Blinded, the vampire staggered.

As blind as his captor, Logan felt the woman grab the collar of his pajamas. She jerked, dragging him out of Jimmy's hold and right through the door her magic had rendered insubstantial.

Logan's stunned gaze fell on his mother's white face. Guinevere's arms closed around him in a ferociously tight hug as he heard the liquid *thunk* of Excalibur biting through bone and flesh.

EIGHT

"My father blamed himself for Jimmy's blood-madness." Logan stroked a hand over Smoke's back as if hypnotized by the sensation of glossy black fur. "He always said they shouldn't have tried to turn him so soon. Maybe if they'd given him more time to mature, he could have controlled the hunger."

Smoke lashed his tail in agitation. "Logan, you're thirty-one, not twenty-one. *And* you've got a will harder than a Sidhe sword. You won't go rogue."

"That's what Dad says." He shook his head. "But you didn't see the look in his eyes the night he had to behead Jimmy. And I keep thinking —what if it was me? He's still not over killing Mordred during the rebellion, and that was fifteen hundred years ago."

Smoke twisted around and reared on his hind legs, the better to look directly into Logan's eyes. "He won't have to kill you, Logan. You're stronger than Mordred, and you're sure as hell stronger than Jimmy Cordino."

"I hope you're right." A muscle flexed in his chiseled jaw. "Because I don't think Arthur could survive killing another son."

* * *

Giada thrust her face under the shower spray and let the cool water pound the last of the sleep out of her sluggish brain. She dreaded the day.

She was going to have to explain to Logan why it was impossible that they continue their—what? Romance? Affair? It felt like more than that, and yet it couldn't *be* more than that. And once she told him the truth, as she eventually must—he had a right to know he'd had his first exposure to Magekind sex—he'd want nothing to do with her again.

The thought sliced a dagger of pain into her heart.

Suck it up, Giada. Concentrate on the job.

She headed downstairs twenty minutes later in a severe black suit, her hair bound into a French braid so tight, her face ached under her minimal makeup. Her sensible flats clicked on the hardwood floor as she walked into the kitchen, following the scent of frying bacon.

As she walked in, Logan looked around and gave her a polite smile. "Good morning. Sleep well?"

Giada examined his expression for a possible double meaning. Instead, there was only the mannered stretch of lips over teeth, as if he were addressing a stranger. She frowned. "Fine."

"Good. Breakfast'll be right up. There's a jug of orange juice on the table."

"Is there anything I can do?"

"Nope, got it all under control."

"Oh." Feeling awkward, Giada sank into her usual seat and watched him work. She had the distinct feeling she was being ignored. *Okay, what the hell is this?*

She'd expected to have to explain why last night's unforgettable experience couldn't be repeated. But evidently Logan hadn't found it all that unforgettable. In fact, he was making her feel like a drunken one-night stand he was too polite to show the door.

Had she been *that* bad?

* * *

Giada sliced off a fragment of the thumbnail-sized object the narcs thought was a crack rock. She dropped it in one of the wells of the ceramic tray, conscious of Logan's cool, professional gaze as he watched over her shoulder.

You'd never know he'd made passionate love to her the night before.

How did guys do that—act as though nothing got above the waist? It was as if they had an emotional force field at the navel. "Captain, she canna take much more!"

Okay, when she started channeling *Star Trek* reruns, it was time to get a grip.

"Logan!" a boyish voice piped from the hallway.

"Incoming," Logan murmured, looking toward the lab's double doors. "Sheriff's grandkids are loose again."

He walked over to let them in. Giada refused to let her eyes drift to his butt as he walked away. *Keep your mind on the drugs, Giada.*

For the next few minutes, she managed to do just that as Logan and Andy retreated to his office to examine the dummy grenade the construction crew had dug up at Camp Cleveland that morning.

"You guys been fighting?"

Giada glanced up and found Heather Jones watching her. She opened her mouth to deny it, then noticed the sympathy in the girl's eyes. "Is it that obvious?"

"Well, umm . . ." Heather's gaze shifted as she struggled to decide whether a polite lie was called for.

Giada smiled slightly. "Under the circumstances, I figured you'd cheer."

It was Heather's turn to wince. "It's that obvious?"

"Only a little."

The girl sighed. "Guess it doesn't really matter. I'm sixteen, and he's so . . . not." She contemplated the age difference before shaking her head. "Even if he was interested, it would be kinda overwhelming, you know?"

"Not to mention a little creepy." She dropped the pink test solution on top of the sample and watched it turn blue. "Yep, that's crack."

"Love sucks."

Giada blinked and looked up at the girl, whose expression was a wry blend of pain and humor.

Heather shrugged. "Just sayin'."

"It does have its moments. You speaking from recent experience?"

"Guy at school. He's a jerk."

Giada nodded wisely. "You'll have that."

From Logan's office, there came a chimpanzee shriek, followed by a thump. Logan and Andy laughed.

Giada looked over her shoulder toward the office. "What the heck was that?"

"Logan's got this toy. It's a little stuffed monkey with rubber bands for arms, and you shoot it like a slingshot. When it hits the wall, it . . ."

Thump! "Cheeeecheecheee!"

Logan and Andy hooted.

Giada and Heather exchanged a look. "Boys," the girl said with elaborate disgust.

"Yeah, that about sums it up."

Logan watched Giada prepare a run on the mass spectrometer, loading tiny tubes of solution into the circular tray. Slotting the loaded tray into the computerized device, she hit a button to send the injection arm swinging around. It stabbed a needle into a tube's rubber cap, sucked up the solution, and started heating it into a vapor for analysis.

The mass spec probably had to work twice as hard in the icy atmosphere Giada was throwing off. She'd been giving him the cold shoulder ever since he'd decided he had to shut their romance down two days ago.

He wondered yet again whether she was hurt or just

pissed. She wouldn't talk to him even when he tried to broach the subject, so he had no idea.

It's for the best. It certainly makes it a hell of a lot easier to stay away from her.

Yeah, right.

Logan was still watching her cool, elegant profile when his cell chirped. He plucked it out of its belt clip. "MacRoy."

"Saddle up, CSI," drawled Hillsborough fire chief Jordan Gray. "I got a fire for you. Looks suspicious as hell."

Logan unsnapped one of the pouches on his fatigue pants and pulled out his notebook and pen. "Where?"

Gray rattled off the address, then hung up. Logan promptly called Mark Davis, who helped him work arson scenes. "Hey, Mount? MacRoy. Hillsborough Fire Department just called. They've got a fire they want us to check out."

"Gotcha. Mind giving me a ride? My cop car's in the shop."

"Sure. Meet me at mine." He headed for the lab door.

"Wait up." Giada strode after him. "I'm going with you."

Logan gave her a tense nod, though inwardly he groaned. He'd been hoping for a break from the Frost Queen, but evidently she had no intention of letting him off that easily.

It's your own damn fault, his conscience told him. *You know better than to get involved with a mortal.*

He told it to shut the hell up.

Mark "Mount" Davis picked up on the tension between Logan and Giada two minutes after getting in the car with them. He promptly tried to fill it like the good Southern boy he was, telling them about the latest adventures of his three-year-old. "That young'un's a pistol. My mama loves to run out her lower dentures at the grandkids. Tara said, 'Don't be so uncouth, Grandma.' Uncouth! Ha! Now, where the hell did she get a word like that?"

"Bright little girl," Giada observed.

"Girly girl, too. Loves walking around on her tippy-toes and wearin' frou-frou dresses. Probably gets it from that Ballet

Barbie DVD she watches all the time." His besotted grin made him look even more boyish. "We're gonna get her in ballet class. Lori, her mama, studied dance for several years when she was little. Tara takes after Lori a lot, which is a real good thing. Wouldn't want her to take after me, that's for damn sure."

He fell silent, probably contemplating some brilliant imaginary future for his child. Logan turned the Impala cautiously down a narrow gravel road that snaked between the trees, barely wide enough for a fire truck. Several hairpin curves later, they spotted the red and white whirling lights of emergency vehicles parked on the side of the road.

To the right of the trucks, a black plume of smoke writhed sullenly into the air from one of those small brick ranch-style houses so common in the South. Holes gaped in the roof where the firefighters had vented the blaze with their axes. Several thick yellow hoses snaked across the house's front yard, past a pink Big Wheel and a swing set.

Kids. Giada felt her stomach clench in dread. "We got any fatalities?"

"Don't know," Logan said shortly, pulling in behind a massive red fire engine with the words "Hillsborough Volunteer Fire Department" painted in gold across the rear.

Giada got out and went to help the two men unload their equipment from the trunk—half-face cartridge respirators, leather workman's gloves, a camera, shovels, hard hats, and a bottle of Dawn dishwashing liquid. Logan handed her the pair of fire boots she'd been issued, and she quickly changed into them, all the while praying the civilians had gotten safely out of the house.

At last, booted and equipped, she tromped across the yard at Logan's heels as he went in search of the fire chief. The sound of glass breaking made her jump, and she looked up to watch a firefighter heave an armchair through the broken window.

"They're overhauling the house," Davis grunted.

Giada frowned. "They're what?"

"Overhauling." He gave her a smile. "Means throwing out anything that might catch fire in a flare-up later."

"They call it overhauling. We call it evidence eradication." Logan watched with disfavor as a set of drapes sailed after the chair. "It's hell investigating a fire scene. Half the evidence goes up in flames, and the other half gets doused with water and tossed out on the front yard."

"Hey, CSI!" a hearty voice called. "You gonna catch me a firebug?"

"That's the plan," Logan said as a heavyset man in turnout gear strode across the yard toward them. Balding and ruddy-faced, Jordan Gray had an impressive belly and bloodshot hazel eyes. Logan introduced Giada, who presented her hand for a firm shake.

After giving Davis a slap on the shoulder, Gray sobered, his soot-smeared face going grim. "If this ain't arson, I'll eat my boots. Bastard wasn't subtle about it, neither. Looks like multiple points of origin in the kitchen."

"Anybody at home?"

"No, thank the good Lord. Neighbors said the family just left for Disney World." He sighed. "Only good news in this whole mess. I called the daddy's cell, told them they just lost damn near everything they got. They're on their way back."

"Who called it in?"

"Passerby saw the smoke. Called on his cell."

"Passerby, my ass." Logan snorted. "There is nothing on this road but this house. Ten bucks says Dispatch talked to the arsonist."

"I wouldn't take that bet. I thought the same thing when I got out here."

Logan looked over the house with grim eyes. "Homeowner pissed anybody off lately?"

"Not that he knows of." Gray scratched his sooty forehead. "Crossed my mind to wonder if he or the wife's got something goin' with somebody on the side."

"A jealous somebody? Could be." Logan put his fire helmet on and gestured for the others to do the same. "Noticed there's a natural gas hookup on the side of the house. You turn it off?"

The chief snorted. "Do I look like a fuckin' idiot to you?

I got no desire to get my fat ass blown into orbit. First thing we did when we rolled up was turn off the power and turn off the gas."

"Good to hear. Can we get started?"

"Yeah, it's out, mostly. Wet as hell in there, though." Gray shook his head. "Sure hope you find something the detectives can use to catch this fucker. I don't need no fire-bug in my town."

"You and me both." Logan nodded at Giada and Davis, and all three started toward the house.

Comfortably settled on a camouflaged deer stand midway up a leafy oak, Terrence watched through his binocs as MacRoy led the blonde and one of his fellow arson techs into the house.

A smile on his face, Terrence pulled out a cell phone and dialed.

This'll rock your world, MacRoy.

On the opposite side of the house, deep in the stand of thick trees that surrounded it, an oval of air sparked and wavered, as if with swirling heat.

Smoke hopped through the cat-sized gate and sniffed the air. He'd spent the last week trailing around after Giada and Logan, determined that if anyone took another shot at them, he'd be there to do something about it.

He started toward the fire scene, soundless and dark as a shadow moving over the leaves. *Hope the bad guy is still hanging around. I'm going to give that bastard a very ugly surprise.*

With the help of one of the firefighters, Logan, Giada, and Mount Davis washed their boots down in a bucket with the Dawn detergent.

"The idea is to avoid tracking petroleum products onto

the scene," Logan explained when Giada questioned him about it.

She frowned. "But there've been a dozen firefighters wandering in and out of that house. God knows what they've tracked in."

"They're them. We're us. And we have to contend with defense attorneys looking for any excuse to tell a jury we're sloppy."

"You know why lawyers wear ties?" Davis asked the Hillsborough firefighter, a thin man whose face was seared red by radiant heat.

"Nope."

Deadpan, Davis explained, "Keeps the foreskin from rolling up over their heads."

Logan nodded. "Be hard to bullshit a jury otherwise."

A wicked light sparked in Davis's eyes. "They'd be all, 'Ummmph! Ummmph!' "

"We can only fantasize."

As the firefighter guffawed, Giada eyed the three. "You guys are bent."

Logan grinned and started up the brick steps. "It's taken you this long to notice?"

The door had been kicked open and hung half-off its hinges. The air was heavy with the greasy, acrid scent of smoke and the reek of half-burned upholstery. Coughing, Giada stared around cautiously as she followed the men inside. The place was dark, the only light coming through the broken windows. The walls were black with soot, and the floor was piled with tattered pink insulation and chunks of board covered in something white and slimy. The carpet squelched underfoot, so soaked she wondered how it would ever dry.

"What the heck is all this stuff?" She played her flashlight over a pile as she stepped across it.

"They call it 'fall down.' " Logan caught her elbow to help her across the pile. "Chunks of the ceiling. Firefighters cut a hole in the roof to douse the fire from above. All that

water hits the wallboard, and it just crumbles into chunks of wet gypsum."

Looking up, Giada realized she could see the house's rafters. Daylight streamed through a ragged hole in the roof. "They don't fool around, do they?"

"Nope. We'll start in the kitchen. Watch your step. Floor might not be solid."

Carrying their gear, the three tromped across the piles of fall down, past a couch burned down to its metal springs and wooden frame. The area around it was seared black.

"Not liking that couch," Davis said to Logan. "Looks like a point of origin to me."

Giada studied it, wondering what had led him to that conclusion. "Why?"

"Fire does not burn downward," Logan explained. "The only way you get a low burn—like that couch—is if the blaze started there or something burning falls on it. It's an interior wall, so no burning curtains. Ceiling could have caught, but there'd be more searing on the fall down, and that looks like it was caused by water damage."

She fell silent, digesting that, as they climbed over the debris and headed into the kitchen.

The damage there was extensive—cabinets burned to carbonized shells of wood, table and chairs blackened. A coat of greasy soot covered every surviving surface, and fall down littered the floor with slimy piles of insulation and wallboard.

Logan surveyed the devastation and grunted. "Yeah, he got busy in here. Let's take a look at the rest."

They headed back through the living room and into a short, blackened hallway. Giada noticed lighter swirls through the soot, then a handprint planted in the middle of the wall. She nodded at the marks. "Firefighters?"

"Yeah." Mount gave her an approving smile. "During a fire, the whole house is pitch-black with smoke. Only way you know where you are is to find a wall and follow it."

She frowned. "Doesn't the fire provide some light?"

Logan shook his head. "Not once the smoke gets thick enough. Inside a burning house is a damned scary place to be, even with a breathing pack and turnout gear."

Which is saying something, Giada thought. *Especially coming from a man whose idea of a good time involves acid and high explosives.*

They walked through an open door. In contrast to the chaos in the rest of the house, the room beyond was almost completely undamaged. A frilly pink canopied bed occupied one side of the room, under a pile of stuffed animals. A child-sized pink flowered couch dominated the other end, next to shelves crammed with picture books. Dolls peeked from a plastic toy box, all big eyes and tangled polyester hair.

Giada wandered over to examine the couch. A Tickle Me Elmo sat there in lone splendor, looking oddly mournful. She winced, imagining what would have happened if the little owner of all these toys had been home.

"Why is there no damage—" She stopped, putting the evidence together. "The door was closed."

"Exactly." Logan nodded at a black palm print on the cream-painted wall. "Firefighter opened the door and came in hunting a window to vent the smoke through. It was still pitch-black in here, which was why he followed the wall."

"So since there was no fire at this end, the firefighters didn't bother venting the roof."

"Right. No holes, no water, no fall down."

They found the bedroom across the hall just as undamaged, though the reek of smoke was everywhere. The homeowners would have a heck of a time ridding their surviving belongings of the stink.

Giada's gaze fell on a framed photograph sitting on a gleaming cherry bureau. Compelled, she moved over to study it. The family of three was achingly young, dressed in their Sunday best for the portrait. The father had a long, rawboned face and short-cropped blond hair. One big-knuckled hand rested on the shoulder of his wife, who smiled at the camera, her little daughter in her arms. Like her husband,

she was blond, but her features had a delicate prettiness that was echoed in her daughter. The little girl grinned in pure joy from the safety of her mother's arms.

Giada winced. Just a day ago, they'd walked through this house, had breakfast in the kitchen, watched cartoons in the living room. She could almost see the little girl dancing at the thought of meeting Mickey Mouse.

Instead they were coming home to blackened chaos. All because of some arsonist who'd wanted to see their house go up in flames.

Assuming it wasn't more sinister than that.

Giada frowned, suddenly uneasy. Could this be connected to the attempts on Logan? An arson fire, designed to draw him out, set him up. Kill him.

Her stomach twisted into a knot. Whether or not he was a player with a taste for seducing coworkers, he didn't deserve to die at the hands of some assassin with a grudge against the Magekind.

Damned if that would happen on her watch.

They returned to the kitchen to start clearing away the fall down so they could see whether there was any sign of pour patterns on the floor—trails of accelerant leading to a doorway, ignited by a tossed match. Giada shoveled through her assigned pile of debris, listening absently as the men talked points of origin. Even as she worked, she scanned with her magic, searching for psychic impressions left by the arsonist.

And sensed absolutely nothing.

Giada frowned, puzzled. She should have found something, some mental shadow, even during the day. Especially with Morgana's necklace amplifying her powers. But there was nothing.

Which strongly hinted that either the arsonist wasn't the assassin she was hunting—or he *was* the same guy, and had powers of his own, enough to block her scan.

But how? The Magekind had just fought a war to drive

all the evil magic users from the planet. The magical barrier that kept out the Dark Ones had been re-erected so the aliens could never return.

Could be a Sidhe criminal, though. King Llyr had killed his vicious brother, but that didn't mean there wasn't some new magical player.

Probably not a Dire Wolf, though. Merlin's werewolf creations didn't have the ability to work spells beyond shapeshifting. Besides, they were good guys, created to keep the Magekind from going rogue.

Could be a dragon. A lot of them don't much like humans . . .

A breeze blew through the kitchen door, bringing a whiff of petrochemicals. She frowned. "Do you smell gas?"

Logan looked around at her, a line forming between his thick brows as he sniffed. "Yeah, I do."

"Thought the chief said he'd had the gas turned off." Davis wiped a bead of sweat from his temple with a gloved hand, leaving a streak of soot.

"I think I'll check it again." Logan rested his shovel against the blackened wall and headed out the kitchen door that had been half-splintered by a fireman's axe. He returned a few minutes later, looking unhappy. "Chief's right. Valve was shut off."

Maybe, but Giada still smelled an unmistakable gas reek, even through the lingering odor of smoke. She looked down at her shovel to hide her concentration as she scanned with her magic once more.

The blast lifted the roof right off the house, blowing out the last of the glass and lighting up the twilight with a hellish glow.

Shit! Giada's stomach wrenched in horror. *Another booby trap. The bastard must have sabotaged the gas shut-off.* Which meant he was probably getting ready to trigger some kind of incendiary device that would blow all three of them right to hell.

NINE

Giada grabbed for the natural gas line with her magic. Just as she'd suspected, the assassin had disabled the needle inside the valve, preventing it from closing off the flow of gas. Yet the valve control would still turn, so Logan and the firefighters would have no way of knowing it had been sabotaged.

Conjuring a vise of magical force, Giada clamped the line closed. A second spell sent a cold wind blowing under the house, carrying away the gas that had been building under the house's foundation.

A scan found the incendiary taped to one of the house's concrete supports. It was a simple enough device, designed to produce a single spark. Just enough to detonate the gas.

If she'd been a couple of minutes later finding it . . .

Giada leaned against her shovel, sick and nauseated from the close call.

"Hey, you okay?" Logan asked, crouching beside her, concern in his dark eyes. "You look pale."

She straightened guiltily. "Fine." The word emerged as a mumble. "I'm fine."

Unconvinced, he eyed her. "Give us a minute, Mount."

"Sure," the big cop said. "I need to go take some pictures of the rest of the house anyway." Catching Giada's puzzled expression, he explained, "Gotta document the crime scene." He bent over to dig the digital camera from an equipment bag, then ambled out.

A warm hand came to rest on Giada's shoulder. She looked up to find Logan gazing down into her face.

"You're good at that," she told him, exhaustion making her a little too blunt.

"Good at what?"

"Looking like you care." As anger narrowed his dark eyes, she silently cursed herself.

She hadn't intended to say that out loud.

"And . . . bang." Terrence pushed the send button on his cell and waited for the blast.

Nothing happened.

"Fuck!" He sat up straight on the deer stand, peering through his binoculars. The house remained stubbornly undamaged. How the fuck had the blonde managed to bugger his device?

"Well, not this time, bitch." Viciously, he thumbed another set of numbers on his cell and hit send, triggering the backup device he'd planted.

BOOM!

With a grin of satisfaction, he watched the detonation lift the roof off the house.

The shock wave rolled from the rear of the house, picking Giada and Logan up and slamming them into the cabinets like the batting hand of an angry giant. The carbonated wood crumbled into ash under the impact, and they hit the floor, stunned and helpless.

Which was when Giada felt Mark Davis die.

Agony blinded her as a hail of ball bearings ripped

through the big cop's body. Her abused eardrums couldn't even detect her own screams.

A muscled arm closed around her waist and jerked her effortlessly off the ground. Giada almost fried her would-be attacker with a spell before she realized it was Logan.

His lips moved, something that looked like "Come on!"

She let him hustle her through the kitchen door and down the brick steps. "Mount!" Giada still couldn't hear herself yell, though that didn't stop her from trying. "The bastard killed Mount!"

She'd failed. She'd failed them all. She'd seen the blast, found the first device the bomber planted, and made the lethal mistake of thinking that was all there was. And Mark Davis had paid for her error with his life.

She thought of the little girl he'd bragged about, the bright three-year-old who walked on her tippy-toes and called her grandma "uncouth." The little girl who now had no father because *Giada had failed.*

Logan pushed her into the arms of the firefighters who staggered out to meet them. Even as they surrounded her, he turned back toward the house. His soot-streaked face looked as stunned and blank as the firefighters'. Blood covered his chin from a split lip and swollen nose.

The Hillsborough chief grabbed Logan's shoulder as the men gathered around him, mouths moving, arms gesturing. The argument was short, fierce, and utterly silent, as if somebody had hit the mute button on Giada's personal soundtrack. The expression on Logan's bloody face was savage as he finally jerked free of the chief and headed for the house over the firefighters' evident protests.

The house stood smoking, its formerly undamaged end now blown to hell, roof half-collapsed. Giada and Logan had survived only because they'd been in the kitchen, at the opposite end of the building.

Davis had been standing in the hallway with his camera when the improvised claymore mine had gone off. The bomb she'd seen too late.

The assassin had planted the device in the little girl's room, inside one of the cushions of that little pink flowered couch.

Which was why Giada was going to kill him.

With all the firefighters distracted by Logan, she turned and walked toward the woods. The woods from which an assassin would be watching as he gloated over a good man's death.

Oh, yeah. The bomber was going to die. Screw trials. Screw mercy.

Giada was going to fry him like an egg.

Smoke raced through the woods, his small furry body a streak of black. He'd been trying to track the arsonist by scent when he'd heard the house blow. For a moment, his heart simply stopped in his chest as if gripped by a giant's fist. Then he'd forced himself to calm down and reach for Giada and the boy, and he'd found them both, dazed but alive.

But there was something wrong with the girl. He couldn't touch her mind. It was as if she'd shut down.

He found her striding through the woods, her face blank and bloody and soot-streaked, clothes dirty and torn. "Giada!"

She didn't respond to his voice, just kept moving in that mechanical stride, like a windup toy with a broken spring.

"Giada, child, what's wrong?" Panic touched him. He knew Logan was uninjured, so what . . .

Death. He felt the ugly psychic reek of it. One of Logan's men had died.

Smoke cursed softly in a language that had been dead long before the birth of the Christ. Logan being Logan, and Giada having the same overdeveloped sense of responsibility, they'd blame themselves. "Giada . . ."

She ignored him utterly. He scanned her and realized why. The blast had damaged her hearing just as her friend's death had wounded her soul.

None of his cat forms would do for this. He had not walked on two feet since old King Dearg Galatyn had ruled the Sidhe, but one did what was necessary. Sighing, he gathered his power and let it roll.

Giada jolted backward, startled, when the man appeared by her side. For a moment she thought it must be the one she hunted, until she recognized the crystalline slit pupils and the inky fall of hair striped with silver. "Smoke?"

His lips moved, shaped words she couldn't quite make out. His face was both stunningly beautiful and utterly masculine, ears forming elegant Sidhe points, nose an aquiline sweep, sulky mouth drawn into a frown of worry. He looked like sin and sex, and he made her uncomfortable as hell.

Then he took her face between broad, long-boned hands, and she froze. Magic poured into her, warm as a father's kiss, and she found herself relaxing into it.

With a loud crackling pop, her hearing returned. "I'm sorry, child." Smoke's voice sounded the same as always, deep and rumbling, though now it seemed to suit his big body.

Her eyes stung. "He's dead, Smoke. Mount's dead."

"I know, my dear. I know." Those were not empty words. Sadness darkened his pale eyes like a shadow over the moon.

She wanted to crumple into his arms and sob out her pain and failure, but that would be a betrayal. She had a killer to find. It was the last thing she could do for Davis, and she was not going to fail him this time.

"How?" Giada choked out. "How did I miss this? I should have seen it. I should have known."

Smoke shook his head. "The killer has to be blocking our magical scans somehow. There's no other explanation."

"Unless I'm just not powerful enough."

He gave her an impatient look. "I know you want to wallow in your guilt, my dear, but I can assure you, I am *definitely* powerful enough to detect him."

"So how is he blocking us?"

Smoke shrugged broad warrior shoulders. "When we catch him, we'll ask him."

"Mount! Dammit, Mark, answer!" Logan shouted. He couldn't have heard a reply even if his partner had made one—he was still stone deaf—but he knew the firefighters would. They'd waded into the debris with him, gone grimly to work with shovels and gloved hands to throw hunks of roof and wallboard and two-by-fours aside as they searched for the missing cop. From the corner of one eye, he saw whirling blue lights appear as patrol cars approached, eerily silent in his deafened world. No surprise—an officer was down. Every cop in thirty miles would show up to help search.

Then Logan found the first hunk of red-splattered wallboard.

And knew.

He heaved it aside with an utter disregard of its value as evidence, unaware of the prayers he was chanting. Heaved another chunk aside, forgetting to disguise the Latent strength that was so much greater than a human's.

When he found Mark Davis crumpled between two chunks of red-soaked wallboard, Logan crashed to his knees in the wreckage and almost impaled himself on a broken two-by-four. For a long moment, he simply knelt there, staring.

His friend was unrecognizable.

Men gathered around, stood staring in frozen horror. He was dimly aware of someone staggering, falling over a pile of board, then vomiting in helpless spasms. He was too busy trying to control his own rebelling stomach to care.

A thick arm slid around his waist and helped him to his feet. As he stood, his gaze fell on yet another red-splattered chunk of wallboard. This one was dimpled with an odd pattern of metal circles. A river of ice slid over him.

Logan grabbed the chunk of board and stared at it in horror. "Jesu!" He wheeled toward the dazed crowd of

firefighters and cops, raised his voice in a bellow he couldn't even hear. "Pull back! Get the fuck out of here!"

The man beside him jerked him around with a hand to his shoulder. It was only then that he recognized Sheriff Bill Jones. The man looked blasted, older than his years, grief aging his pale eyes. His lips shaped a single word: "Davis . . ."

Logan lifted the chunk of wallboard and pointed at the metal dimples. "Those are ball bearings, Sheriff. Mark was killed by an antipersonnel device specifically intended to kill first responders. And there may be more than one. We've got to clear this scene *now*."

They moved through the woods wrapped in an invisibility shield Smoke had generated with an ease Giada could only envy. He was back in cat form now, though he was a very big cat indeed. She wouldn't want to be the assassin when Smoke got those dinner plate–sized paws on him. His claws were the length of steak knives, and just as sharp.

"He may be able to block magic," the cat murmured as he ghosted along. "But I doubt he's thought to block scent. And I have a very good nose."

He knew what he was doing, too, working a spiral pattern in the woods surrounding the scene. It was a damned good thing they were invisible, given the furious activity around the house. Gazing back the way she'd come, Giada saw that the cops had strung crime scene tape and corralled the crowd that always shows up for a fire. Judging by the grim expressions on the deputies' faces, somebody had finally realized Mark had been killed by a bomb.

She probably should have told them that before she left, but it hadn't even occurred to her.

Giada frowned. She was keeping too many freaking secrets. It was one thing when she'd thought Logan was the only one in danger and she could use her magic to contain the situation. But it seemed the other cops were now targets, too.

If she'd told Logan the truth, would Davis still be alive?

Oh, yeah, she'd blown it in a big way. And there was no way to repair the situation. Imagining Logan's reaction when she came clean, she winced.

"I've got the bastard's scent." Smoke didn't even lift his head from the ground as he headed off into the woods. "This way."

Giada's lips twisted into an expression halfway between a snarl and a grin. The one thing she could do was avenge Mark's death. And by Merlin's Cup, she was going to do just that.

The spy slipped into the woods, intent on finding Terrence Anderson before Logan's little blond witch did. That Giada Shepherd was out looking for him was apparent from the fact that she was nowhere to be seen.

Damn good thing the spy'd had the foresight to give Terrence one of the sorcerer's bracelets. Otherwise the witch would have been all over him days ago.

As it was, this was a perfect opportunity to rid herself of the blonde.

She was looking forward to it.

Logan walked over to one of the paramedics. His hearing had finally returned, though it had brought a pounding headache with it. He was starting to wonder if he had a concussion. He asked the guy for an Excedrin and a cup of water, then moved on to his real objective. "What was wrong with Giada? Was she badly hurt?" Jesu, he hoped not.

The paramedic's long, pleasantly homely face went blank. "Giada?"

"Yeah, the blond woman who came out of the house with me. Didn't one of you guys take her to the ER?"

The guy shook his head. "We're the only unit here, man. We haven't taken anybody anywhere."

Logan tensed. *Then where the hell is Giada?* When he

hadn't seen her after he'd found Mark, he'd assumed she'd gone to the emergency room.

"Shit." Turning away, he scanned for a bright blond head among the milling men.

Giada was nowhere to be seen.

He glanced uneasily toward the woods. Could she have been taken?

Rein in the imagination, MacRoy. Nobody's going to kidnap a woman in front of fifty cops and firefighters.

But she might have walked off on her own. Particularly if she was still disoriented from the blast. Following that uncomfortable hunch, he headed for the woods.

The assassin sat on a camp stool he'd put on a deer stand mounted in a tree, staring intently through a pair of binoculars at the police working the murder scene. A broad grin of murderous delight stretched his mouth.

Smoke looked up at Giada—though not far up; in his current form, his head came to her hip. "Shall I do the honors?"

"Hell, no. He's mine." Giada summoned her power through Morgana's emerald, letting it lift her skyward like a leaf sailing on the wind. Fury pounding a drumbeat in her head, she snarled silently as she rose toward the tree stand. The bomber was so intent on his binoculars that he didn't notice when she drew even with him.

"Hello, you murdering pig," Giada purred. "That was a good man you killed."

The assassin jerked around so fast, he almost fell off his perch. Giada relished his expression of uncomprehending astonishment as he gaped at her floating body. "What the fuck?" His voice cracked on the last word. "How'd you . . ."

"I'm a witch." She felt her lips draw into a smile that wasn't the least bit pleasant. "And I'm going to show you magic that will make you scream for the rest of your very short life if you don't tell me who the hell hired you. Now."

His mouth worked silently before he managed, "This ain't possible."

"Obviously it is, or it wouldn't be happening." Magic poured from her hands, ripping him off his stand and dragging him into the air. A second ball of force clamped around his throat. He choked, kicking. Giada watched his face darken with snarling satisfaction.

"Don't kill him, child," Smoke called from below. "At least, not yet."

She let up the pressure on his windpipe and added just enough support to keep from breaking his neck. Judging from the way his face was going dark, he probably had his doubts. "Now, let's try this again. Who. Hired. You?"

His mouth worked, but no sound emerged. She let up on the pressure another fraction, and he squeaked, "I don't know!"

"Now you're just being insulting. Guy like you? You know. Or you've certainly got a damned good idea. Otherwise . . ." She tightened her grip on his throat. "Not feeling the need to keep you alive."

His eyes wheeled like those of a panicked horse, face purpling as he gagged out, "She's got money. Never . . . never tried to haggle. Gave me what I wanted."

Giada loosened her hold another fraction. "She? And how much money?"

"Three million."

"You were underpaid. What did she want for her three million?"

"MacRoy dead. With a lot of collateral damage. Wants to send a message to somebody."

"Who?"

"I can't . . ."

She cranked down on the force again. *"Who?"*

"His father! MacRoy's father!"

"You know, I'm still not hearing her name." Something crunched. He choked. "I really want her name."

* * *

This would not do at all.

The spy studied the situation, and did not particularly care for the view.

Giada Shepherd hovered on a cloud of magic that foamed around her like a fountain of glowing force. Coils of the same energy wrapped the assassin's neck and torso in strangling bands.

Who'd have thought the little twit was capable of that kind of magic?

To make matters worse, at the base of the tree crouched an enormous feline . . . *thing.* It was black, but far too massively built to be a panther. She thought it looked more like a tiger, what with the pewter fur striping its brawny black haunches and massive forelegs. Its head was longer and more elegant than a tiger's, with long ears rising to tufted points. It radiated such power, the witch looked like a firefly by comparison.

Fear iced the spy's spine. She could not afford to leave Anderson in the witch's hands—it would not take the little blond bitch long to wring out every detail the bomber knew. Which might be nothing . . . but then again, perhaps he knew entirely too much. God only knew what information he'd unearthed.

So. The cat first. The cat was most dangerous. Luckily, the spy had approached from downwind, so the big beast had not scented her—yet.

As if sensing that thought, the creature's head swung in her direction. Instantly, the spy exploded toward it in a furious rush of muscle and power. If she didn't strike fast and hard and *now*, there would be no second chance.

The cat roared, rising onto its powerful haunches to meet her with extended claws. Magic poured from its open jaws, boiling like an electrical storm. The blast slammed into the spy's face with such force, it would have killed anyone not of her kind.

Before the cat could register that its blast had done nothing, she locked both hands in its ruff. Clawed paws ripped her forearms, but she ignored the pain, whipped into a spin,

and heaved. The beast yowled as all eight hundred pounds of it sailed through the air to slam into a tree trunk halfway across the clearing. The furry body bounced, landing in a dazed heap. Crackling like a volley of rifle fire, the tree toppled, landing right on top of the huge cat.

Giada shouted something that sounded like "Smoke!" The spy looked up. The witch hovered fifteen feet in the air, staring in shock toward the downed cat.

With a snarl, the spy rammed her shoulder into the tree the assassin was perched in. The trunk snapped in two like a matchstick. As it fell, it hit the Maja dead-on, cutting her startled scream short. She plummeted.

Terrence yelled as he, too, dropped like a rock.

Magic rained down around the spy in silent silver sparks as the Maja hit the ground in a crumpled jumble of arms and legs. The spy ignored the pyrotechnics and grabbed Terrence by his Kevlar vest the instant before he slammed to earth.

The bomber took one look at his rescuer and shrieked like a child.

"Shut up!" The spy slapped a clawed hand over his mouth. It covered his entire face. One eye rolled white and wild up at her, and he went still. She wrinkled her nose at the pungent smell of urine. "Pah! Coward."

Tucking her hireling under one arm, the spy padded over to examine the fallen witch. Blood smeared Giada's still face, and her eyes were closed.

It would be so easy to kill her.

One quick slash of the claws, and the witch would no longer be a problem. The spy licked her fangs, considering.

Father wouldn't like it. If the Magekind examined the body—and they would—they would quickly determine *what* had killed her, though they still wouldn't know who.

An investigator would be sent to determine the identity of the killer. Father would not appreciate having to shield her from such an investigation.

Perhaps she could make it appear a simple human murder instead. Yes, that could work.

She looked down at the bomber still tucked under her forearm. "Where's your gun?"

Terrence didn't answer. Probably speechless with terror. Disgusted, the spy looked around until she spotted the rifle lying on the leaves. She started toward it . . .

And froze. Leaves rustled and crackled in the distance, the sound of cops running clumsily through the woods. A familiar male voice called, "Giada! Giada, where are you?"

Logan.

The spy peeled her fangs back from her teeth. Shoot them both? Tempting thought.

"This way!" he shouted. More bodies came crashing through the woods. Oh, hell, it sounded like he'd brought half the cops in the county. It would take them time to find this spot, but if she shot the girl, the shotgun blast would bring them running. All those guns and Tasers—it was entirely too likely they'd take her down. And with Logan still alive, that wasn't a risk she could afford to take. Killing him had to take priority.

She had to get out of here now, or this entire situation would explode in her face.

Cursing under her breath, the spy wheeled and fled, carrying the unresisting form of the bomber under one arm like a bag of soggy, urine-scented potatoes.

T E N

Smoke took a gasping breath as his eyes flew open. Pain seared through him, so sharp and strong he had to fight a whimper. All he could see was a blur of green.

He blinked, managed to focus his eyes, realized after a moment that his vision was obstructed by leaves.

Gods and devils, that—*thing* had dropped a tree on him. And judging by the pain, at least one of its broken branches had been driven through his haunches like a spear.

Taken like a week-old cub. Disgusting.

While the thing—it had looked like a cross between a wolf and a grizzly bear—had shrugged off his magical blast as if he'd been tossing marshmallows. Had it been a Dire Wolf? He'd never seen one of the creatures, but the beast had certainly fit the description he'd heard.

Smoke lifted his head. Pain wheeled through his body in countless red-hot points of agony, a constellation of suffering. He could feel blood flowing from dozens of wounds, matting his black fur. Had he been the mortal animal he appeared, he'd be dead. As it was, he didn't exactly feel healthy.

With a low growl, he sent out a magical probe. The crea-

ture that had attacked him was more than a mile away, moving fast in the opposite direction.

Well, that's something, anyway.

The same scan told him that Logan and a mob of cops were headed in his direction. As if things weren't bad enough, Giada lay in a broken heap, her life force dim and fading. She'd be dead in minutes if he didn't move fast.

He breathed out magic, and the tree dissolved in a shower of sparks—just as that wolf/bear thing should have done. Freed of impaling branches, Smoke sought the form he hadn't held since . . . Actually, he couldn't remember.

He'd been Sidhe, of course—less than an hour ago, in fact. But it had been a long, long time since he'd held *this* form. Power rolled over him in a storm of energy and raw will, healing his injuries, banishing pain and blood as his body shifted, shrank, expanded.

Feeling one hell of a lot better, he rolled to two feet. But as he straightened, he became aware of something else. It was one thing to be Sidhe. It was something else again to be a demigod.

He had forgotten the raw power of his true form, the way the magic crackled and foamed in his blood. Forgotten its hypnotic song.

Why had he walked away from this?

You know why. And you don't want to go there again. Pain, blood, the pleas he hadn't had the power to answer.

The failure.

Well, he wouldn't fail this time. He could do this. He strode over to the fallen girl, who lay with one leg pinned under yet another tree. Crushed.

Gods and devils, she was bleeding out.

Smoke reached down, hooked a hand under the tree trunk, and lifted, heaving it easily out of the way. It hit the leafy ground with a crash. Dropping to one knee, he sent power feathering over the girl, trying to sense her injuries.

Bad. Even worse than he'd thought. Her heartbeat stuttered . . .

And stopped.

Smoke's own heart lunged into his throat as he spread a big hand over Giada's still chest. His skin glowed against hers, casting a cool blue light that brightened to blinding as his magic went to work.

It took a moment even with his power, but her heart finally began to beat again. But the sound was not the strong, steady thump it should be. He had to work fast if Giada was to survive.

Smoke gathered in yet more power from the Mageverse, sent it flooding into her, seeking out the fractured bones, the punctured liver, the pooling blood. One by one, his magic found her injuries and coaxed them whole again. Her fluttering heartbeat steadied, strengthened. She sucked in a rough breath and coughed, a helpless hacking sound.

He frowned, suddenly sensing something he'd never realized before. Giada had real power—far more than she had ever evinced.

Something was blocking her access to it.

Some secret disbelief, some cool fear was keeping her from reaching her full potential. He thought it might be her scientist's mind, which had never been fully convinced she could break the laws of physics. Even the spell Giada's grandmother had cast to make her believe in magic had not eliminated those doubts. But you needed belief to use that kind of power, so she'd been left half-crippled.

Smoke knew he could break that mental barrier, give her full access to the magic that was her birthright. But should he do it?

"Giada? Giada, dammit, answer me!" Logan was far too close now, crashing through the woods as if Smoke had never taught him better, followed by a small army of cops.

Feh. There was no more time to dither. A flick of power, and it was done.

Giada's eyes flew open, her expression startled. He didn't have time to explain. It was more important to clean up her bloodied, dirty clothing and dissolve the last fallen tree into mulch.

"Smoke?" she rasped.

"Later, child." Shifting to his favorite feline form, he slipped off into the underbrush even as the police flooded the clearing.

Nobody even looked twice at the house cat ghosting away from the scene.

To his vast relief, Logan found Giada lying on her back in the leaves, staring up at the trees overhead. Her expression was dazed; she must have been hurt more than she'd thought.

"Hey." He sank down beside her. "You okay?"

"Umm." She blinked at him slowly. "Yeah."

Logan did not care for the way she said that. He wasn't entirely sure she even knew who he was.

"Jesus Christ!" It was the sheriff, leading the pack of searchers at Logan's heels, his expression irate and worried. "Is she all right?"

"I'm fine." She tried to sit up, groaned, and promptly lay back down again.

"You stay here," Logan told her, then looked up at Jones. "Where are the paramedics?"

"On their way with a stretcher."

"I said I'm *fine*." Obviously intent on proving it, she reeled to her feet.

Logan rose to join her, looking her over in concern. She had no visible injuries, but she was swaying like a pine tree in a high wind. Reaching out, he steadied her with a hand on her elbow.

"You don't look fine." Sheriff Jones frowned as the other cops gathered around them in an interested mob. "You need to get checked out. You could have been hurt in that blast more than you think. And what the hell were you doing, running off into the woods like that?"

"Looking for the killer." She swayed.

Blue eyes narrowed. "Dammit, you're a civilian. Hunting bad guys is *our* job." The big man's jaw worked in frustration, and he made a throwaway gesture with one hand.

"Wasting my breath. You don't even know what planet you're on." He glowered around in irritation. "Where the hell are the paramedics?"

"Right here, Sheriff," a man called, carrying a backboard into the clearing.

Giada managed a glare, swaying. "I don't need a doctor."

"I say you do," Jones told her firmly. He glanced at Logan, hovering by her elbow. "And while you're at it, check out the lieutenant," he told the paramedic. "He doesn't look so good either."

"Yes, sir." The man put down the backboard as his partner dropped the medical kit beside them. "Have a seat, y'all."

Logan didn't even consider offering an argument. He felt like crap— bloody, exhausted, and nursing a headache that felt as if a Dire Wolf was whaling away on his skull with a hammer.

"Come on." He pulled Giada gently to the ground. "Let the nice paramedics do their job."

Terrence John Anderson hung across the monster's furry shoulder and worked hard not to heave. Vomiting down the creature's back wouldn't be the best career move he'd ever made.

In fact, it would be right up there with taking this fucking job to begin with. The witch was right—he'd been underpaid. Three million was nowhere near enough to deal with this shit. Witches. Monsters. Men who wouldn't fucking *die*.

And he'd pissed himself. The scalding humiliation of that made him want to kill something. Again.

Right when he was getting ready to heave last night's moo goo gai pan into its fur, the monster came to a skidding halt in the leaves.

A moment later, Terrence hit the ground with a teeth-rattling thud. Despite his rebelling stomach and throbbing ass, he didn't waste time scrambling to his feet.

The creature towered over him, seven feet of muscle, fur, claws, and really, *really* big teeth.

Jesus Christ, he thought, staring up at it in disbelief, *it's a freaking werewolf.*

Its head was unmistakably lupine, with a long, fanged muzzle and pointed ears. Thick fur the color of cinnamon covered its head and shoulders in a fluffy mane that fell to surprisingly round, full breasts. The fur was shorter elsewhere, a fine red-brown pelt, though it thickened over the creature's groin. Its—her—body had a lean elegance that reminded him of a leopard's. And her claws were the length of Ka-Bar knives.

A ball of ice formed in his stomach. She could rip him apart and eat him before he knew what hit him. He took a step away and said the first thing that came into his head. "I've got money."

"You should." Her eyes gleamed down at him, bright as the LEDs on a bomb timer. "I paid you enough up front."

Okay, that was a good sign. Capable of rationality. Maybe he could—*This thing had hired him?* "You're my contact?" She didn't sound like the woman on the phone. He wouldn't have mistaken that deep, growling voice for anything human.

"Yes." She leaned down until her muzzle was a foot from his face and peeled her lips off long, gleaming white teeth. "Which is why I strongly suggest *you don't give me up to any fucking witch.*"

"Wouldn't dream of it." The words emerged as an embarrassing squeak.

She snorted, stirring the hair on his head. "You were about to sing like you were auditioning for *American Idol.*"

Terrence licked his lips and dared, "Nobody said anything about witches."

She tilted her massive head. "Would you have believed me, asshole?"

There was no percentage in answering that one. "So what do you want me to do now?"

The werewolf turned away and began to pace, moving with odd grace on legs more like a dog's than a biped's. "MacRoy is still alive, but you tossed a fine wasps' nest among those cops today. That was good."

Maybe she would let him live. "Thank you."

She shot him a narrow-eyed stare that made him step back a pace. "I'd be happier if MacRoy was dead."

He gave her a sickly smile. "I'd be glad to try again. I like a happy customer." That was closer to groveling than he liked to come.

Another gusting snort. "I'll bet." The silence stretched as she paced. The werewolf moved with amazing silence, considering she had to weigh four hundred pounds. "I want something bigger next time. Something really dramatic. Civilians." She gave her massive head a short and decisive nod. "Lots of dead civilians, something that will send a message nobody can ignore." Pivoting, she lifted those knifelike claws in an unmistakable threat. "But this time MacRoy dies. Or you do."

Terrence stretched his mouth into a semblance of a wide smile. He was all too aware of his wet pants. "Got it."

Yeah, he got it. Him or MacRoy—and the werewolf would kill him in a way he really wouldn't like. So it would damn well have to be MacRoy.

It was late afternoon when Logan stepped out on the deck outside his house, his broad shoulders slumped, one big hand wrapped around a beer bottle as he leaned a hip on the railing.

Giada pulled the French door open and stepped outside. She still felt vaguely as if she were floating, power fizzing just under the skin. Whatever Smoke had done to heal her had quite a kick.

Even the call to the Mageverse had been effortless, daylight or no daylight. Guinevere hadn't been happy to learn a Dire Wolf was involved. Still, it did explain how the killer

had been able to block their magic. She'd said they'd contact the Direkind as soon as Arthur woke from the Daysleep. Their new allies should be able to help them track the killer down easily enough.

Then she'd thanked Giada for saving Logan's life. Her gratitude had stung, considering what had happened to Mark.

Giada eyed the beer bottle in Logan's hand as she crossed the deck to join him. "Should you be drinking that?" The ER doctor had said Logan had a mild concussion.

"No." He took a deliberate swallow.

"Ah." She badly wanted to heal him. Though the sun was still up, power buzzed through her like the snap and crackle of electricity. Her own power, not the emerald's.

Unfortunately, Logan would definitely notice any attempt to heal him, no matter how subtle she was about it.

Maybe when he was asleep . . .

Giada frowned. On second thought, that sounded a bit questionable.

It seemed she'd been doing questionable things a lot lately. The results had not been good, especially for Mark Davis and his family.

Guilt stabbed her, a knife-twist of pain right in her heart.

As if reading her mind, Logan spoke. "The sheriff's telling Mark's wife right now." He took another deliberate swig of his beer. "Her whole fucking life is imploding. And then she's got to tell her daughter Daddy ain't coming home. Ever."

Giada winced. "I'm sorry." The words were automatic—and utterly useless.

"So'm I. He was my man, and I let him get killed."

"How could you have prevented it?" She crossed the deck, drawn as helplessly to his pain as iron fillings to a magnet. "You had no reason to believe somebody was targeting first responders." *Because I didn't tell you you're the target of an assassin.* Another vicious stab of guilty pain accompanied the thought.

"I was his superior officer." A muscle worked in his tight jaw. "It's my job to foresee possibilities and look out for my men."

Giada studied Logan's stony profile, seeing his father clearly in the line of his nose, the sweeping angle of his brows, the jut of his chin. Which was probably why what he'd just said sounded as if it had come out of Arthur's mouth. It probably had.

"What, you were supposed to use your X-ray vision to detect that bomb, then fly Davis to safety?" Giada asked tartly. "Hate to break it to you, but that's a badge on your chest, not a big red S."

He slanted her a look and snorted. "Your inner nerd is showing."

It was on the tip of her tongue to snap, *And your Arthur is showing*. But that, of course, would open a can of worms the size of boa constrictors.

She could only grind her teeth in frustration.

The thing was, Giada had a point. Logan was only human—but he didn't have to be.

If he'd been a vampire . . .

You would have been in the Daysleep, dumbass, because it was still daylight.

But given a similar situation at night, could he have used his vamp abilities to detect the bomb?

Maybe, maybe not. It was impossible to tell. And pointless to wonder. Mark was dead, and nothing would change that. As Dad liked to say, *"Woulda, coulda, shoulda. Didn't."*

And in this business, you didn't get a second chance. If you fucked up, people died. Logan had fucked up, and Mark's wife and daughter would spend the rest of their lives with an aching emptiness instead of the man they loved.

There were things Logan could do to make their lives a bit easier, things he *would* do. Mark's insurance would kick

in, and the deputies would band together to do whatever they could for the fallen cop's family, just as they always did.

But Logan had access to considerable financial resources as the son of Arthur Pendragon, resources he rarely tapped. He would make sure Mark's bright little girl went to college, that she and her mother wanted for nothing. But none of it would make up for Mark's loss.

Neither would finding the bastard who had done this and making him pay. Logan was going to do it anyway, just for the sheer joy of taking the murdering bastard down. Even if it meant fucking the first Maja he could find and becoming a vampire.

Even if it meant never seeing Giada Shepherd again.

That thought hit him with a sword stroke of pain, an ache that rivaled his guilt. He turned to look at her hungrily, studying her face in the light of the setting sun. Rose and gold painted the line of her nose, the soft tilt of her lips, the rounded curve of her chin. Her hair was down for once, distilled sunlight lying in tousled curls around her shoulders. Her black T-shirt had bright green lettering that read, "Don't make me get my flying monkeys." The shirt was a little too tight, emphasizing the round, lovely swell of her breasts. Jeans clung to her runner's thighs, faded almost white over the knees and fly.

And she was mortal.

Mortals and Magekind could never marry. He had never questioned that rule. The truth of it was too self-evident. It was one thing to grow old with someone, but to grow old while your partner remained young caused inevitable bitterness and jealousy. It was better to let a mortal find happiness with another mortal.

But Logan had also never fallen in love with a mortal before.

As that thought sliced into his consciousness, he froze, stunned by its sheer power.

In love? With Giada Shepherd?

Holy hell.

He certainly wanted her. Logan remembered the hot, slick grip of her sex, those long, warm legs wrapped around his waist, the taste of her hard nipples, her intoxicating response to his every hard thrust.

But there was more to the attraction than her eager body or her elegant blond beauty. There was that keen intelligence, that sly sense of humor, the courage that had her returning to the job even after a would-be killer took a shot at her.

She was the kind of woman he could imagine spending the rest of his life with. Too bad it wasn't possible.

Too bad it was time for the Gift. He'd put it off by telling himself he wasn't ready to attempt the transition, but in truth, he'd had the needed emotional maturity for a while now. He was not a kid anymore.

Maybe on some level he'd been waiting for his Gwen—the Maja who'd capture his heart and draw him into a spiritual Truebond so profound, they became one being.

Instead, he'd met a mortal who made him want what he couldn't have.

"There is such pain in your eyes." Giada lifted a hand and laid it against his cheek. Her fingers felt cool and smooth. "I'm so sorry about Davis."

He started to tell her his pain was not caused by Davis—or not only by Davis. But before he could speak, she rose on her toes and covered his parted lips with her own.

The kiss was exquisitely gentle, an offer of comfort, as delicate as a rose petal. Yet it detonated in his consciousness in a rolling burst of feral need.

His mind catalogued each dizzying sensation: her breasts, so lusciously, delightfully soft, the tips pressing hard against his chest. The warmth of her long legs against his. Her fingers threading through his hair. Her tongue, stroking wet and slick through his lips to touch his own.

Raw sex. Pure tenderness.

With a low groan of hunger, Logan caught Giada's hips and pulled her against him, wanting to touch every inch of her with every inch of him.

God, she felt incredible. Strong, slim, delightfully female, seduction incarnate.

He was going to have to give her up. There was no choice. But not now.

Not tonight. He could have tonight.

Logan kissed Giada with a white-hot intensity that made her breath catch. Strong hands tugged her against his hips, branding her belly with the hard length of his cock. Arousal curled through her, a response to all that heat, that delicious male strength.

He slid a hand up under the hem of her shirt to take warm possession of her breast. A thumb teased her nipple to full hardness, sent sweet arousal flooding through her. He bit her lower lip, gentle but demanding, and she opened to him with a soft, helpless groan.

Lust boiled up in her, sizzling like water over white-hot stones. Fierce, aching—yet somehow alien. Coming from outside her.

What the hell?

Something burned in the back of her mind like a bright green fuse snaking through her body, setting her afire.

A spell?

Giada frowned and sought out that green thread with her own power. It was the work of an instant to trace it back to its source: the stone around her neck.

In a flash, so much became clear. The mindless lust she'd felt that first time that had erased her self-control, driving her to make love to Logan despite all the reasons it was a really bad idea.

Morgana, you bitch.

A flick of will, and the spell winked out, no match for her new strength.

But Logan's mouth still moved on hers, coaxing and delicious. One hand cupped her breast under her shirt, thumb flicking her nipple, teasing it hot and hard.

Morgana's spell might be gone, but the desire remained.

Her very own desire, blazing up from her body, her blood. No spell needed but the one Logan cast.

God, he felt good. Too good.

In a flashing moment of clarity, Giada realized she couldn't sleep with him. It would be his second time, and she had no right to keep him in the dark.

It was time to tell him the truth. To hell with Arthur and Guinevere and their orders. A cop was dead because they'd told her to keep her mouth shut. True, they couldn't have predicted the way this had gone south, but Davis had still paid with his life.

Like it or not, she had to come clean.

Her stomach promptly tied itself into a sick knot. Logan was going to be furious. He'd never touch her again. Never kiss her with so much heat and longing.

She opened her mouth for the hungry thrust of his tongue, wanting only to drink him in a little longer. She just wanted to extend this fragile moment so she'd have something to remember in the bitterness that would follow.

His strong hands came up to cup her face, cherishing her. Such a sweet illusion. Tears stung her eyes.

I've got to do this now, or I never will.

She pulled away with a painful effort, as though ripping the scab off a deep and bleeding wound. Opened her mouth . . .

Not yet.

The vision hit her in a stunning wave of images, each flashing so quickly, there was barely time to register them. *Logan, fangs gleaming in his mouth. The sheriff's grandchildren, Andy and Heather, wearing identical expressions of terror. Heather looking pleadingly up at Logan. Something was strapped around her chest.*

Something that had a timer.

Logan leaping at the red-furred Dire Wolf who held Andy a terrified captive in her arms. Giada herself, hurling blasts of flaming magic at yet another werewolf, this one even bigger, who shook off her attacks with contempt.

I can't tell him yet.

It was wrong, she knew it in her guts. But she also couldn't ignore her vision. If she told him the truth now, those kids were dead. Even if it meant suffering his rage, she had to make love to him.

What if she explained what she'd seen? No, he'd be too pissed off to believe her. Morgana had tried to play him too often.

Oh, God. He's going to hate me for this.

"Giada?" Logan frowned down at her, his gaze concerned as he brushed a thumb over the single tear rolling down her cheek. "What's wrong?"

"Nothing." Her smile trembled on her lips. Winding her arms around his neck, she rose on her toes and kissed him, deep and slow, letting her body lean into his. She kissed him as if it would be the last time she ever touched him.

Because it probably would be, at least with this kind of sweet passion. She might convince him he had a duty to become a vampire, but she knew their third time would be angry at best. The very thought made her chest ache.

So let me have this last sweetness.

Logan could taste tears in her kiss, yet her mouth was so exquisitely hungry, almost desperate. As if somehow she knew there was no future for them. He badly wanted to soothe her, but he didn't have it in him to lie. So instead he kissed her back with all the starved intensity in his soul.

When he could finally bring himself to pull away, he was breathing hard. So was she, despite the tears that beaded her lashes like gemstones.

"Come inside." Logan caught one cool, delicate hand to draw her after him, then pulled off the ridiculous shirt she was wearing before they were even inside, dropping it heedlessly on the deck. Her bra followed the moment the door was closed behind them.

He stepped back a fraction, the better to enjoy the exquisite sight of her. Her breasts curved in sweet invitation, creamy and full and tipped with tightly erect pink nipples.

Dropping to his knees before her, Logan took one of those hard tips in his mouth. She tasted as delicious as she looked, musk and woman and need. Her moan of pleasure shot to his head like heated bourbon. His cock, already erect, jutted into his fly so hard it hurt.

The delicate pleasure of Logan's tender suction made Giada shudder in helpless delight. She threaded her fingers through his hair and let her head fall back.

Teeth raked gently over the erect bud of her nipple, sending another exotic spiral of delight up her spine. Heat gathered in her belly, muscles drawing tight with need.

Logan began to explore, one big hand palming her other breast, thumb and forefinger plucking, rolling, stroking. His free hand traced her body, finding the dip of her waist, the rise of her hip. He paused over the ticklish plane of her belly, making her giggle, before continuing on to stroke the long muscles of one thigh.

She closed her eyes, floating in the spell he wove with his hands and mouth. Yet each sweet sensation carried an echo of pain, because he'd never touch her like this again. And she deserved no better. Davis had died today, and she hadn't saved him.

No. Don't think about that. She'd pay the price for her failure, but for now, she needed this silken hour. The memory of it would get her through the rest.

Her eyes snapped open as a sudden bolt of desperation shafted through her. She dragged herself away from that impossibly tempting mouth. "I've got to touch you. Now. Please . . ."

Hot eyes softened to tenderness at whatever he saw in her face. "All right."

Logan stood and led the way to the rug that lay in front of the fieldstone fireplace. The thick, soft yarn depicted a knight in gleaming armor kissing a lady in an intricately embroidered green gown, the colors delicate and lovely. Recognizing Guinevere's work, Giada winced. She banished

that flash of guilt as he turned to face her. Grabbing the hem of his shirt, she dragged it over his head.

As always, the sight of Logan's sculpted masculinity took her breath. She stopped to drink in the sight of him dressed only in jeans, his cock hard and hungry behind his fly. Laying a hand against his muscular chest, she savored the firm warmth, the soft, dark hair that dusted his skin. Unable to resist, she bent and kissed one small male nipple. Her tongue flicked out for a delicate lick, and her eyes slid closed in delight.

She would never forget the way he tasted. Not if she lived to be older than Merlin himself.

Suddenly greedy, Giada reached for the snap of his jeans. The hiss of the zipper sounded impossibly loud against the backdrop of their quickened breathing.

Looking down at the arrow of boxers and tight flesh she'd revealed, Giada caught her breath. The ripe head of his cock thrust over the blue cotton waistband, dark with need. She sank to her knees.

He caught his breath. "Giada, for God's sake—I'm not made of steel."

"Could have fooled me." She aimed a quick grin up at him, then grabbed jeans and boxers simultaneously and began dragging them down over his powerful thighs. He bent to help her skin them off, kicking them away with a careless flick of one big bare foot.

Giada looked up from her knees. He jutted over her head, balls round and furred, the shaft long, thickly veined, dark with arousal. She rose a little until her mouth was even with his erection. He stiffened with an indrawn breath, anticipation in his eyes.

She promptly decided to keep them both in suspense a little longer.

Her hand went right past his cock to trace the jutting angle of one hip. Leaning forward, she kissed him there, aware that her tumbling blond hair teased along his cock as she moved.

He groaned. "You've got a sadistic streak, woman."

Giada gave him wide eyes and a slow, deliberate blink. "Who, me?" Then she ran her tongue over the thin, sensitive flesh across his pelvis. Paused for a nibble right at the crest of the bone, then began to string kisses all around his abdomen, letting the fall of her hair brush and tease his jerking shaft.

A big hand closed in her hair. Giada literally felt him resist the urge to pull her head where he so obviously wanted it. Laughing softly, she turned and pressed a kiss to the side of his cock. It jerked upward in reaction, hot against her lips. She gave him a quick little lap of her tongue. "Mmmm," she purred. "Château D'Logan, a particularly bold vintage."

"Wench."

Giggling, she stroked a hand up one strong leg, savoring the textures of warm skin, muscle, bone, the soft dusting of hair. Her fingers discovered the firm pouch of his balls, surrounded in dark curls, drawn tight to the underside of his cock. She cupped him, and that long shaft jerked again.

"Giada . . ." Logan's voice sounded ragged.

She smiled ever so slightly . . . and engulfed him without warning, swooping as much of his cock into her mouth as she could manage. His breathing caught.

He tasted of salt and male musk and need. The single bead of arousal on the tip of his cock was just slightly bitter. She suckled hard and felt him shudder, his knees almost buckling.

Giada smiled in satisfaction around her mouthful of thick shaft. *I may not forget this*, she thought, *but you won't either. Even if you never speak to me again.*

Logan wasn't sure how much more he could take. Giada's mouth felt exquisitely hot and wet as she suckled him in slow, strong pulls. She was the most erotic sight he'd ever seen as she knelt on that colorful rug, one hand wrapped around his cock, her hair teasing his thighs as it swung with her movements, her lips circling him. He could feel the

climax burning up his spine like a fuse, throwing hot white sparks of pleasure as it ran.

This was going to be over way too fast if he didn't do something. Now.

It took far more willpower than he'd thought he even had to pull out of her silken mouth. "Enough." His voice sounded ragged to his own ears. "I want to play, too."

"You weren't enjoying that?" She pouted at him, but the glint in her gray eyes told him she knew better.

Logan lay down on the floor on his back and drew her to kneel astride his face. "I'm not even going to dignify that with an answer." He licked her in a single long, satisfying stroke.

"What was the question again?" To his immense satisfaction, the last syllable of that word spiraled upward into a squeak.

"Dunno. But I think the answer is sixty-nine." Her giggle became a yip as he parted her delicate pink lips with his fingers and started giving her the attention she deserved. She was deliciously wet already, all cream-slick flesh, tight and rosy. The scent was so incredibly arousing, he shuddered at the storm front of need that roared through him. He hadn't even realized he could get this turned on.

Savoring that need, loving the taste and scent and textures of her, Logan swirled his tongue over and around each silky fold. He reached his free hand down her body to find one breast, began to pinch and twist the tight little nipple.

As if in echo, slender fingers closed around his cock, and she took him in again, one long and ruthless swoop into delight. He suspected his eyes rolled back in his head.

The first hot spasm shot up his spine, making his thighs jerk and his back arch, tearing a strangled cry from his lips. A hot tide of energy rolled over him next, swirling and wild, ripping a startled yell from his lips.

She stopped, lifted her head. "Logan?"

"Stop. I'm about to come." He'd thought for a moment he'd already lost it, but his balls were still tight, still aching with frustrated hunger.

And he wanted *in* her.

Logan's thrumming control snapped like a bowstring, and he caught her around the waist. Tumbling her onto her back on the soft rug, he rose over her, took her delicious legs in his hands, and spread her wide.

He drove his cock deep in one ruthless thrust. Giada's lovely gray eyes flew wide in surprise, and she gasped.

With an effort of supreme will, he managed to stop. "Did I hurt you?"

"No, no, *God* no!" Her long legs curled around his waist, dragging him close with surprising strength. "Don't stop!"

So he braced himself on his arms and began to ride in long, searing strokes that made them both shudder.

How does it keep getting better? Giada wondered wildly as his body rocked hers with each breath-stealing lunge. He filled her completely, thick and amazing, the muscles of his braced arms working as he moved. Sweat gleamed on his shoulders, and his powerful chest heaved. His gaze was focused on her face, his dark eyes wide with wild delight. A muscle in his jaw flexed as though he were grinding his teeth, fighting for control.

Lifting her head as he lowered his, she found his mouth. He didn't stop thrusting as they kissed desperately, tongues swirling, tasting each other, hungry for every sensation.

Ravenous.

She could feel her orgasm building hotter, drawing tighter, with every driving stroke.

Closer. Closer . . .

I don't want it to be over so . . . The explosion of pleasure detonated in her belly and rocketed up her spine.

And magic flooded from her hands, her eyes, her mouth, in a river of sparks that spiraled around him and dove into his flesh.

Oh, no! Not this soon! It was only a preliminary burst—it would have been far more intense otherwise—but it was enough to blow the secret.

With a gasp, Giada struggled to contain the flashing energy, but it was too late. She heard his shout of surprise.

He convulsed with a roar, coming, his last furious thrust wringing another climactic pulse of magic and pleasure out of Giada's dazed body.

Even as she cried out in helpless delight, her heart sank. Dammit, her second time hadn't been anything like this. Probably because a human's body had to make a more dramatic change to become a vampire, with everything from bone and muscle to digestive system changing into its new, more powerful form. Her own body had stayed basically the same; only her brain had changed to allow the manipulation of magical forces.

Not that it mattered. He knew now. And he was going to be furious.

ELEVEN

The combination of magic and a violent orgasm wrung Logan's body like a rag. When he finally collapsed on the floor beside Giada, he felt dazed, as stunned as if she'd hit him with a board. He lay there for a long moment, staring blankly at the ceiling.

"I'm sorry." She sounded hoarse.

"Morgana?" This was going to hurt. Once he could feel again, it was going to hurt like a bitch. "Did Morgana send you?"

"No. Well, yeah, kind of. There was this necklace . . . But no, she didn't send me. It was your parents."

He discovered he could in fact move when his head jerked to stare at her. The fury that roared through him blasted away his numb shock. "My *parents* put you up to this?"

"No! No, not to seduce you! They ordered me not to sleep with you, but Morgana . . . and then I couldn't . . ." She broke off and shook her head. "I'm making a mess out of this. Look, Logan, there's an assassin after you. Somebody's killed twelve Latents so far. Arthur and Guinevere were afraid you'd be next. And they were right. He's tried to get you at least twice I know of."

Suddenly a lot of things were painfully clear. "But you saved me. That's why that woman tried to shoot you in the department parking lot—to get you out of the way."

"I think so, yeah." She sat up, looking miserable—and infuriatingly delicious in her nudity.

He looked around for his clothes, found his T-shirt, and dragged it over his head. "That's why Davis died—because this bastard was after me and missed?"

She raked both hands through her tousled blond hair as he located his jeans and boxers. "Yeah. There was more than one bomb, but I didn't realize that. The gas we smelled at the scene—he'd rigged the line to explode, but I deactivated it. I didn't realize he'd set a second device." Giada met his gaze, anguish in her eyes. "I fucked up."

"That's not all you fucked," he growled with deliberate vulgarity as he pulled on his clothes. "If Arthur ordered you not to sleep with me, why in the hell did you do it anyway? *Twice?*"

She bit her lip as tears welled. "The first time, Morgana had given me a necklace that compelled me to . . . And this time"—her voice dropped—"I had a vision."

"A vision." He snorted. "Where have I heard that one before?"

For the first time, a flare of anger pierced her visible misery. "I'm not lying, Logan. I saw the sheriff's grandkids. Heather was wearing some kind of suicide vest with a timer, and she was terrified. And a Dire Wolf had Andy. You attacked it. You were a vampire."

"So why in the hell didn't you just tell me any of this? 'Hey, Logan, an assassin is after you, so Daddy sent me to play bodyguard.' "

Storm-cloud gray eyes narrowed. "Because Daddy said you were too stiff-necked to let me hang around if I was up front about this." Her anger was every bit as hot as his now. "Arthur said they needed a Maja who was also a chemist, so the bodyguard would have an excuse to stay close."

"So you *are* a chemist." He curled his lip. "At least there's one thing you didn't lie about."

"You know, I've saved your life twice now, you jackass. So get off my back." She bounced to her feet, gorgeous and naked in her rage. He couldn't quite subdue his erotic appreciation as she stalked over to her discarded jeans and jerked them on.

"Twice? I count once. And since I damned near took a bullet for you, Witchypoo, I figure that makes us even."

She wheeled to face him. "Not even close. Remember the mortar in that old man's farmhouse? It would have blown you to hamburger if I hadn't disabled it first."

He was far too pissed to concede the point. "Fine. I'm grateful. That still doesn't give you the right to make me a vampire without a little fucking warning."

"I did what I had to do." Giada jerked her zipper up. "I'm sorry I lied to you, but if you weren't such a stiff-necked idiot, I could have told you the truth!" Opening the French door, she reached out, snatched her T-shirt, and jerked it on over her head.

Then, without a backward look, she stalked out onto the deck.

"You know," Smoke drawled, "she's right. You are an idiot."

Logan whirled to see the cat standing in front of a shimmering dimensional gate. "Where the hell have you been?"

"Hunting your would-be killer."

"Did you find him?"

"He seems to have some kind of magical shielding." The gate vanished as Smoke sauntered over to the coffee table and leaped onto it with no effort whatsoever. "That's the reason Giada has had so much trouble tracking him down."

"Giada said she thought it was a Dire Wolf. Magic just bounces off those bastards."

The cat hesitated. "I think it's more than that, Logan. The bomber is human, so we should have been able to detect him easily. Something blocked us. That implies . . ."

"Magical shielding." A chill of dread ground across his heart like a glacier. Logan followed the cat and dropped

onto the couch. "God, tell me it's not those damned Dark Ones again."

The Dark Ones, alien magic users who fed on life force, had tried to invade last year. The resulting conflict, christened the Dragon War, had damned near destroyed the Magekind. And if Avalon had fallen, humanity itself would have been next.

"I doubt it." Smoke's ears flattened as his black tail lashed. "I'm told the barrier around the Twin Earths has been strengthened, so such an invasion shouldn't be possible again."

"So how can this bomber raise a magical shield?" Logan leaned forward to brace his elbows on his knees, the better to meet the cat's blue-eyed stare. "The Direkind don't use magic. Are we sure that's what it was?"

"I saw this creature. It certainly fit the description I've heard, though I've never seen a Dire Wolf before. I didn't fight in the Dragon War."

Logan frowned, interested. "Why not?"

Smoke sat back on his haunches and curled his tail around his toes. "I was . . . otherwise occupied. And before that, of course, we did not even know they existed."

Logan knew his friend well enough to realize there was a lot more to the story than that, but he also knew better than to press. Smoke didn't answer questions he didn't care to answer, period.

Abandoning the subject with a mental shrug, Logan went on to a topic that bothered him far more. "Why did you lie to me, Smoke? I asked you if Giada was a Maja, and you said no."

The cat sat back and curled his tail neatly around his paws. "I have walked among the Magekind a very long time, boy. Giada is the best potential mate for you I've ever met. You two fit like a key in a lock."

Logan stared at Smoke in astonishment. "Let me get this straight. You were *matchmaking* when you lied to me?"

The cat's tail unwound from his haunches and started

to lash. "You felt it, too, boy. I could see it on your face every time you looked at her. You're in love with that girl."

"I don't even know her! The woman I fell for doesn't exist. She's lied to me from the moment I met her. I never even thought she was capable of that kind of deception."

"She wasn't the only one lying, boy. You never told her what you are either."

"Because I thought she was mortal! You don't tell our secrets to mortals. I was doing my duty."

"So was she." Another angry tail flick. "Arthur ordered her to lie, because he knew if she showed up and told you the truth, you wouldn't let her anywhere near you."

"Bull. I'm not stupid enough to turn down protection when I'm being targeted by a magical killer."

"You'd have seen her as too much temptation, and you know it. I've watched you with Majae for years, Logan. Any woman who tempted you too much was one you got the hell away from."

Logan opened his mouth for an angry retort, only to realize Smoke was right.

"Did you think we wouldn't notice, Logan? Everybody saw it. Why do you think Morgana sent Clea? She figured you'd only see her as a mortal fuck buddy, like the rest of your lovers."

That stung enough to tell Logan it had an element of truth. "I have a right to decide when and where—and with whom—I become a Magus. It's my life, Smoke. Especially since if I go blood-mad, somebody's going to have to kill me."

"You're not going to go blood-mad." The cat's ears flattened against his skull in frustration. "You're not some weak-willed little brat—that's the whole problem. You could teach stubborn to a dragon. The Hunger isn't going to have a prayer against you."

His real fear burst out of his mouth. "What if I hurt her?" Logan shot to his feet and began to pace. "Jimmy Cordino killed the Maja Arthur sent to Change him."

"Ah, so that's it." Smoke's voice softened. "Jimmy didn't love the girl who turned him."

Logan stopped his agitated pacing to glare at the cat. "For the last time, I'm not in love with Giada Shepherd. She didn't say a word in the past three weeks that wasn't a lie."

"Smoke."

Logan's head snapped around. Giada stood in the open doorway to the deck.

Giada's face was dead pale except for two bright flags of color on her cheeks. "I've got to go to Avalon to report to Arthur," she told the cat, without even glancing in Logan's direction. "I made a preliminary report to Guinevere, but he's going to want the details."

"I'll go with you." Smoke started across the coffee table as if about to hop down.

"No. Someone needs to stay with Logan in case they try for him again." Despite her cool tone, pain gleamed in her eyes. He could see it, though she refused to meet his gaze directly.

Dammit, how much had she heard of his argument with Smoke? Just enough to wound her, apparently. "Giada . . ."

She gestured, opening a dimensional gate. Before he could think of another word to say, she was gone.

Giada had miscalculated. Again.

Her heart sank as she performed a magical scan of the Pendragon home, detecting Arthur's sleeping mind inside. *Of course he's asleep,* she realized in disgust. *The sun is still up.* Being a vampire, Arthur would be in the Daysleep, recharging his magical batteries. Gwen was apparently out, probably consulting with other Majae about the new Dire Wolf problem.

Dammit. Giada wanted to get this over with. Take the punishment for her many sins, then retreat to her own Mageverse home to lick her wounds in peace.

She had no doubt there would be punishment. Arthur

did not suffer disobedience, and as for Guinevere—well, Giada would be lucky if the Maja didn't turn her into a frog for real.

Actually, spending the rest of her life on a lily pad didn't sound all that bad. At least in frog form she wouldn't keep reliving Logan's scornful words to Smoke: *"For the last time, I'm not in love with Giada Shepherd. She didn't say a word in the past three weeks that wasn't a lie."*

To make matters worse, he was right.

Brooding, Giada turned and looked across Avalon toward the setting sun. She probably had another half hour before Arthur woke. No point in going home when she'd just have to turn around and come right back. Might as well cool her heels in Guinevere's garden while she waited.

When Gwen and Arthur had first approached her about serving as Logan's magical bodyguard, they'd given her a tour of the flower garden that lay behind the house. Now Giada wandered into the backyard for a second look, hoping for a little distraction from the blend of nerves and raw pain currently knotting her stomach.

Rosebushes and various exotic Mageverse flowers rioted in bright blooms, perfuming the air with a delicious blend of scents. A spring danced in the garden's heart, water leaping from clustered stones to roll down into a little pool.

Fish swam lazily in the clear water, scales brilliant with color, fins and tails floating behind them like trailing scarves. A pretty wrought iron bench stood beside the spring, offering a lovely view of both pool and garden. Giada dropped onto it, numbly watching the leap and sparkle of the water in the light of the setting sun.

It felt as if someone had sandblasted the skin off her body. She'd never realized emotional pain could be so intense.

"I'm not in love with Giada Shepherd. She didn't say a word in the past three weeks that wasn't a lie."

Yet as much as those words hurt, they were nothing compared to the explosion of agony Mark Davis had felt when the assassin blew up the house. The pain she'd sensed would

probably haunt her as long as she lived. She knew the guilt would.

He'd died because she'd screwed up.

No, not screwed up. She'd *fucked* up. Davis was dead, and his wife and child were even now dealing with the loss. To add insult to injury, the bastard who'd killed him was still roaming free.

Yet another thing Giada had fucked up.

She'd been so intent on forcing the assassin to tell her who'd hired him, she hadn't even noticed the approach of his furry accomplice. Not until the creature had slammed Smoke into a tree and batted Giada out of the air like a slow baseball pitch. If it hadn't been for Smoke, she'd be as dead as Davis.

She was only dimly aware of the tears that started to roll down her cheeks.

Giada had no idea how long she floated in a swirl of misery before an alarmed female voice jerked her back to awareness. "Giada?"

She started and swiped her hands guiltily over both wet cheeks as Guinevere hurried across the garden toward her. To Giada's surprise, the garden was now twilight dark, the sun almost completely behind the horizon. How long had she sat in a stupor, anyway?

"What's wrong, child?" The Maja's eyes were too wide as she sat down on the bench and took Giada's hands in a warm, strong grip. "I felt your pain from three blocks away. Something else has happened. Is it Logan?"

"No, he's fine." *One sex partner from becoming a vampire, but fine.* "I was just thinking about Mark Davis."

Sadness flooded her lovely eyes. "Logan always spoke so fondly of him. And if I know my son, he's taking it hard—and probably blaming himself." She sighed.

"Is Arthur awake yet? I need to give you both the . . . details." *Of how I so totally screwed up. Oh, God, I dread this.*

Gwen frowned, her eyes searching Giada's face before her gaze softened. "He should be up in a few minutes. Why don't you come inside the house and have a cup of tea while he gets dressed?"

Giada doubted she could keep anything in her stomach, considering that it was currently a solid mass of knots. Still, it would give them both something to do with their hands. "Thank you, that sounds lovely."

When Arthur strode into the living room, Giada's teacup rattled on the saucer she'd balanced on one knee. The big warrior frowned at her, narrow-eyed. "What the hell's going on? Gwen said one of Logan's teammates is dead."

Giada realized his wife must have spoken to him through the Truebond psychic link they shared.

Gwen gestured him to a chair. "Have a seat and let the child talk, Arthur."

Unable to sit any longer, Giada put her cup on the coffee table and rose to her feet even as Arthur dropped into one of the armchairs.

Putting both hands behind her back and bracing her feet apart in an approximation of a parade rest, Giada began to tell the whole painful story. She left nothing out, from her stupidity in accepting the necklace from Morgana to Mark's murder to the battle she and Smoke had fought with the Dire Wolf.

She finished with the vision that had convinced her to make love to Logan for the second time, even though it meant violating the orders she'd been given.

When she finally stopped talking and dared look at Arthur, his sculpted cheekbones were scarlet with rage. Her heart sank as she braced herself.

Here it comes.

"Let me get this straight." He spoke in a terrifying whisper of rage that chilled Giada's blood to ice. "Despite your orders to stay the hell away from my son, you made love to him anyway. *Twice.* You failed to detect the explosive

device that killed one of his men, and which damn near killed both of you, too. *And* when you captured the killer, *you let him get away.*"

Giada lifted her chin and fought to keep her eyes from dropping from his hot black gaze. Her braced knees shook. "Yes, sir."

"And to make matters worse, my son now believes we set him up with a Maja seductress, despite my personal vow *on my honor* not to interfere with his decision."

Her head rocked back as his voice grew louder. "No, sir. I told him you ordered me to stay away from him. I took full responsibility for my actions."

Black eyes narrowed. "Wasn't that kind of you."

"Arthur," Guinevere snapped. "That's enough."

"It's not even close to enough, Gwen," Arthur snarled. "We trusted this girl with our son, and she botched it. We're lucky he survived her . . . protection."

"I'm aware of my mistakes, sir." Giada's voice shook, and she swallowed, fighting to steady it. "I deeply regret them, particularly Davis's death. I realize there's nothing I can do . . ."

"Actually, there is," Arthur snapped coldly. "Consider yourself confined to your Avalon residence. Spend your time thinking about the importance of following orders, so that in the unlikely event we ever entrust you with another mission, you won't fuck it up the way you did this one." He curled his lip. "And stay the hell away from my son. Don't visit him, don't talk to him, don't even look at him. And *especially* don't screw him." His eyes narrowed as he rose slowly to his feet. "And don't even think of disobeying *that* order."

She swallowed. Her head felt so light that for a humiliating moment, she wondered if she might faint. "Yes, sir. I won't, sir."

"Won't *what?*"

"I won't visit Logan, I won't talk to him, I won't even look at him. And I won't . . . make love to him. Again." Her voice shook.

Arthur lifted his lip, exposing his rage-lengthened fangs. "Get out of my sight."

Giada turned and fled for the front door, opening it with a burst of magic. She slammed one shoulder into the door-frame on the way out. Barely feeling the pain, she broke into a run the moment the door closed behind her.

"Arthur," Guinevere said in a deliberate voice, "Have I ever told you just how big an asshole you can be?"

He looked around at her, incredulous. "You can't be defending that little idiot to me."

Her blue eyes narrowed. "She loves our son, Arthur. And if he doesn't love her back, I'll be greatly surprised."

He snorted. "Logan's not that big a fool."

They'd had a lot of fights over fifteen hundred years of marriage. The one that followed that statement ranked with the worst.

It was full night as Logan sat in one of the lawn chairs on the deck, his third beer on his knee as he pretended to ignore Smoke. Which wasn't easy, since the cat crouched under a redwood end table glaring daggers at him. Black as his friend was, all Logan could see were ice blue eyes glowing in the dark like a pair of laser sights.

Nobody did contempt better than Smoke. He might as well have had a neon sign flashing over his head that read, "You're an asshole."

Logan took another long swallow of his beer and ignored him some more. Which would have been considerably easier if he hadn't suspected the cat was right.

He kept remembering the look on Giada's face as she'd told Smoke she was leaving. So much desperate dignity layered over so much pain.

Sucker, his harder self growled. *She lied to you. She deserved a chewing out.*

He only wished he could believe that. Unfortunately,

there was a tight little knot in his chest that insisted otherwise, even after half a six-pack of Bud.

Water under the bridge, he told himself. The real question was what did he do now?

Which was something of a stupid question, because the answer was so obvious.

He had to become a vampire.

The Gift would give Logan all the power he needed to avenge Mark's death. Especially considering that there was apparently a Dire Wolf involved in this mess. Presumably a rogue; Logan couldn't believe sane Direkind would involve themselves in killing Latents. Like the Magekind, the werewolves had been created by Merlin himself to safeguard the human race.

But one of those Dire Wolves was evidently more interested in killing than keeping anybody safe. And Logan was damn well going to take the murderer down—along with the assassin she'd hired.

But first he had to complete his transformation.

Which meant he'd have to find a Maja to sleep with him the final time. He'd always figured he'd seek out La Belle Coeur, the Maja court seducer often dispatched to help male Latents reach Merlin's Gift.

La Belle was not only exquisitely beautiful, she was said to be a thousand years old, with mind-blowing sexual skills. Logan had grown up listening to vampires rhapsodize about being transformed by La Belle Coeur's delicious ministrations.

What's more, La Belle was as kind and intelligent as she was beautiful. Logan had suffered from a rather painful crush on her as a teenager, a fact she'd been well aware of. Yet she'd always treated him with grave respect, even when he'd been an awkward fourteen-year-old. Now he could finally seek her out and experience the reality behind all his boyhood fantasies.

So why the hell do I find that idea about as exciting as washing socks?

He frowned. Somehow he had the feeling that making

love to La Belle would be a poor second to taking Giada to bed. Giada, with her long and lovely body, who'd responded to him with such innocent hunger. If she'd had more than a couple of lovers in her entire life, Logan would be greatly surprised. Yet he'd found the greatest pleasure he'd ever known in her inexperienced arms.

And he wanted that pleasure again.

Why not? The thought shot into his mind as if it had been waiting in ambush. She'd enjoyed their lovemaking every bit as much as he had.

True, he'd been graceless when he'd denied feeling anything for her. At the very least, he'd need to make a very sincere apology.

Maybe even bring her some roses.

All he had to do was start tying up the immediate details of his mortal life, and he'd be free to seek her out again.

Cheered, he finished off his beer and went inside to get some sleep.

As he passed, Smoke muttered, "Dumbass."

TWELVE

The spy reported to her father in his library. There, surrounded by Victorian elegance, facing her brother's portrait, she began her report. Her stomach clenched with nerves as she faced her sire's cold blue eyes. At any moment, she expected to feel his fist.

He had never had patience for anything he perceived as failure, and she knew he was going to be furious when he learned she'd been seen in Dire Wolf form. Especially since he'd warned her repeatedly to avoid detection.

When Arthur complained—and he would—the Southern Clans would send an enforcer with an order of execution to search for the unidentified killer. If he caught her, ugly questions would arise that could endanger her father, the Circle of Chosen—perhaps even Warlock himself.

Yet she'd had no choice. Permitting Giada to interrogate Terrence would have had the same result—only without any possibility of damage control.

There was, after all, always the chance she and her father could kill the Southern Clans' enforcer before he discovered the truth.

She only hoped her father would agree with her judgment.

Otherwise she might not walk out of this room alive. Completing her report, she braced herself for his reaction. And waited.

"You say this cat you fought had power." Her father leaned forward over the solid oak surface of his massive desk. His eyes burned hot with excitement. "What did it look like? Describe it."

The spy blinked. Pleased excitement was the one reaction she hadn't anticipated. "Yes, sir. Its magic felt . . . ancient. Powerful. Far greater than the Maja's. Greater than anything I've ever sensed." Even greater than Warlock's, though she didn't dare say so.

Her father gestured, impatient. "Yes, yes, I understood you the first time. But what did the cat *look* like?"

She frowned, wondering why he was so interested. "Big. Larger than a tiger, I think, but with the same kind of build. Very muscular. Probably close to eight hundred pounds. He was black, with silver-gray stripes on his haunches and legs. When he reared onto his hind legs, he was taller than I am in Dire Wolf form." Given that she was more than seven feet tall then, that was saying something. "His paws were huge, with long, knifelike claws. If I hadn't taken him off guard by hitting him from upwind, I don't think I would have survived."

Her father grunted. "No, probably not." She saw without surprise that he didn't seem disturbed by the idea of her death. He straightened his shoulders. "I must tell Warlock about this. In the meantime, stay close to Logan. Notify me at once if the creature appears again."

"What about the assassin?"

He gave her a wave of dismissal. "Tell him to hold off. I suspect Logan may be our best chance at obtaining this cat for Warlock. And if I'm correct, acquiring it could be the key to our success." The spy stared at him, working to keep the shock off her face. For months now, he'd talked of killing Logan as a crucial part of his revenge on Arthur. Yet one mention of this cat, and he seemed willing to put his obsession aside.

What the hell was going on?

He glowered at her. "What are you waiting for? Go. Go now!"

"Yes, sir." Knowing he'd tolerate no further delay, the spy whirled and strode out.

"Come in, Logan." Sheriff Jones gestured him to one of the seats before the massive cherry desk. "How are you feeling? And how's Shepherd?"

"She's fine. So am I." Physically, anyway. He managed not to frown as he put the sealed envelope he held onto the desk's shining surface, then dropped into one of the guest chairs.

"What the hell is this?" Jones glowered at the envelope as if it were a dead rat.

"My resignation."

"Hell." The sheriff slumped back into his red leather executive chair and rubbed both hands over his tired, angular face. "I had a feeling you were gonna do that. Get it off my desk—I'm not accepting it."

Logan lifted a brow. "I'm sorry, Sheriff, but you don't have a choice."

"Look, I know you're upset about Davis, but it wasn't your fault. You had no reason to think that fuckin' arsonist had planted a bomb to kill first responders. That kind of crap don't happen in this county."

Logan set his jaw. "He was my responsibility, Sheriff. And he died on my watch."

"And I'm responsible for *both* of you, MacRoy." The sheriff stared at him, gaze brooding, for a long moment. As if finally coming to a decision, he sighed. "Look, resigning right now is a really bad idea. Take some time off if you need to, but don't quit. I had to bring the ATF in on this, and it would look damn suspicious to them. They're gonna wonder if you want to get out of town because you planted that device." Alcohol, Tobacco and Firearms were often called in on bombings, particularly if a serial killer was suspected.

"They'd think I'm crazy enough to stay in the house, *knowing* the bomb was about to go off?"

Jones shrugged. "You know feds. They tend to suspect locals of being either crooks, crazy, or incompetent. Maybe all three."

Logan grunted, frowning. The sheriff had a point. Yet once he became a vampire, working during the day would be out of the question. Well, he'd just have to try to finesse the situation as best he could. "Okay, I'll just take some time off."

Besides, a badge might come in handy during his pursuit of the assassin.

"What about Shepherd? Isn't she supposed to be learning the job from you?"

"I've got a feeling she needs some time, too."

Not that he intended to give her any.

Logan followed Smoke through the dimensional gate that led to Giada's Avalon neighborhood.

"This way," the cat said shortly, tail lashing, as he trotted along the cobblestone street.

Oh, yeah. Smoke was pissed.

It had taken Logan an hour of argument verging on a shouting match to convince his friend to help him. Finally the cat had growled, "Okay, I'll take you. But don't be surprised if she turns you into a frog."

Which was why Logan had bought a dozen pale lavender roses that emitted a scent as exotic and lovely as they were.

Giada's neighborhood bore an astonishing resemblance to one of the lower-middle-class developments back home in Greendale County. The houses were all single-story brick ranches, utilitarian and small, with one or two bedrooms at most. Some were the most their Majae owners had the experience or power to construct. Most had been created by more experienced Majae as residences for young vampires or witches who couldn't yet build their own.

Giada's house followed that pattern, with the addition of

cream trim and bright flower beds in a riot of colors. She might not have had a lot of power when she built the house, but she'd done her best.

Logan's stomach gave a nervous flutter as he climbed the brick steps to the front door, positioned the bouquet of roses to his satisfaction, and took a deep breath.

From somewhere inside, he heard something that sounded like the theme song to *Buffy the Vampire Slayer*.

At least she was home.

He pressed the doorbell and listened to its musical notes peal through the house. And waited.

No answer.

Frowning, Logan looked down at Smoke. "Is she home?"

"She's home," the cat said shortly. "She's ignoring you. Not that I blame her."

Huffing out a breath, Logan leaned on the doorbell again. "Giada! Please come to the door. I'd like to apologize."

Music sounded so suddenly he jerked away. Pink, singing "U + Ur Hand" at a thunderous volume directly in his right ear. A spell.

So he yelled louder. "Giada!"

Pink informed him that he was going home alone.

Huffing in frustration, Logan looked down at the cat. "Would you mind asking her to talk to me?"

Smoke's blue eyes narrowed as his tail whipped back and forth. "Waste of time. You stepped in it this time, boy."

"Just tell her I came to apologize." He gritted his teeth. "Please."

"Won't do any good."

"Okay, tell her I came to grovel. She only did what she'd been ordered to do. I get that."

A nerve-wracking moment went by as the cat glowered up at him. "All right—for all the good it'll do you." With that, Smoke strolled through the solid surface of the door as if it had an invisible pet entrance.

Logan watched him go—and frowned at the ugly feeling the cat was right.

* * *

Smoke found Giada lying sprawled on a long sectional couch watching an enormous television. On its huge screen, a young blond girl drove a stake into the chest of a fanged person with a misshapen face. The monster promptly exploded into dust.

Giada scooped chocolate ice cream out of the large bowl she held in her lap. Licking chocolate off her spoon, she asked, "Do you think I'd make a good lesbian?"

"No. You like men too much."

"Not anymore." She took an even bigger bite. "Men suck."

The blonde leaped up and kicked another vampire in the face. He flew backward.

Smoke wandered over to sniff the bowl. The alcohol content made his eyes water. "What the hell are you eating?"

"Häagen-Dazs Rocky Road and Godiva Chocolate Liqueur."

Smoke shuddered. "You're going to spend the next three days making sacrifices to the porcelain god."

"Nope. Because I can do magic." Giada snapped her fingers, and tiny fireworks exploded over her hand like a miniature Fourth of July celebration.

Smoke sat down on the coffee table and curled his tail around his toes. "Logan wants to apologize. He wants you to give him Merlin's Gift."

"Too bad." She returned her attention to her magical television, her expression brooding. "Anyway, Arthur ordered me to stay away from him. I can't talk to him, I can't even look at him. And I'm sure as hell not supposed to sleep with him. Tell him to go find himself another witch."

"He wants you."

Her head jerked around to stare at him. "I. Don't. Care." She gestured. Before Smoke could block the spell, he was sitting on the front porch next to Logan.

Thoroughly disgusted, Smoke looked up at his friend. "Told you so."

"Why the hell not?" Logan demanded.

"To start with, Arthur gave her a direct order not to so much as look at you, much less have sex."

"My love life is none of Dad's business!"

The cat snorted. "Try telling him that."

Logan bared his teeth. "Oh, I will."

"My relationship with Giada is none of your business," Logan growled at his father. "Rescind your order."

"Forget it. *She disobeyed me.*" Arthur spoke through his teeth, big fists clenched. He and Logan stood nose to nose and toe-to-toe as they glared at each other in the middle of the Pendragon living room. "House arrest is the least she deserves."

"Morgana's necklace . . ."

"Was not the reason she slept with you the second time. *That* she did deliberately, just as she deliberately did not report to me after the first time you made love."

"Actually," Smoke said distantly, "I convinced her not to."

"You?" Arthur wheeled on the cat, who lay cradled in Guinevere's arms as the two watched the brawl like spectators at a tennis match. "Why the hell did you do that?"

"Because she's perfect for him—which you'd know if you weren't so bullheaded." Smoke flicked one pointed black ear in feline disdain.

White teeth flashed in a snarl. "You do not get between me and my warriors, godling."

Smoke's pupils contracted to slits. "You do not command me, Arthur Pendragon."

Gwen tightened her grip on him, as if to keep him from leaping down and transforming into something that could do a great deal more damage than a seven-pound house cat. To her husband, she said, "I told you Logan was in love with her."

Logan stiffened. "I didn't say I was in love."

She shot him a glower. "You didn't have to."

"I *cannot* have my warriors ignoring my orders." Arthur's voice sank into the deadly whisper that communicated rage far more clearly than any bellow. "When I lead my people into battle, a moment's disobedience could kill us all."

"We're not in battle, Arthur." Gwen glared at him even as she maintained a firm grip on the cat.

"Davis could tell you differently," Arthur snapped. "If, that is, that idiot Maja hadn't gotten him killed."

"She's not an idiot," Logan ground out between clenched teeth. "She's quite literally a genius, and I wouldn't be here now if she hadn't saved my ass—twice. She may lack experience, but that doesn't make her incompetent."

"She still disobeyed a direct order. When I was High King, I had warriors flogged for less."

"Knights," Gwen corrected coolly. "Not ladies. You've never laid a hand on one of my ladies. Not even me, and I deserved it."

Arthur huffed. He eyed Logan a long moment. Whatever he saw in his son's face made his own expression warm fractionally. When he spoke again, his tone was a bit more conciliatory. "So. Despite her mistakes, you seem to have a high opinion of this girl."

"She's brilliant, she's got courage. She doesn't back down. And . . ." *I want her.*

Arthur's dark gaze softened. "But do you love her?"

Logan opened his mouth for an automatic denial. Then he closed it again and sighed. He'd never been able to lie to his father. "I don't know. I know I was falling for the woman I thought she was, but I'm not sure now how much of that was real. All I'm really sure of is that I want the chance to find out. Besides, it's time I become a vampire. I need a Magus's powers to avenge my friend, not to mention all the Latents those bastards have killed."

"You don't need the girl for that," Arthur pointed out. "Any Maja will do as well. La Belle Coeur—you had a crush on her, as I recall."

"Yeah, when I was fourteen. I haven't been fourteen in a long time." He met his father's gaze steadily. "I want Giada,

Dad. Rescind the order. Find another way to punish her if you have to, but don't keep us apart."

"Dammit. Very well, then." Arthur's eyes narrowed. "But make no mistake—she *will* be punished." His voice dropped to a mutter. "As soon as I can come up with something appropriate."

"Thank you." Knotted muscles relaxing, Logan allowed himself a smile.

"Orders notwithstanding, there's no guarantee she'll agree to give you the Gift."

"I can take care of the rest, Dad."

"It's not going to be that easy, boy," Smoke observed. "She's pretty pissed."

"And I'm pretty stubborn." He gave them all a grin and headed for the door.

As it closed behind him, Smoke looked up at Guinevere. "He has a great deal to learn."

"It's that hard Pendragon head." Guinevere bent and let the cat leap to the floor. "I'd better get her new orders sent before the shouting starts." She disappeared through the hallway door, leaving Smoke and her husband alone.

"Does Giada love him back?" Arthur asked in a low voice.

"Oh, yes." Smoke looked up at him. "But he hurt her more than he realizes. She's very young and very vulnerable."

"And very beautiful." Arthur stared blindly at the door his wife had vanished through. "A woman like that can find a man's vulnerabilities and pry him apart." A very faint smile touched his mouth. "Or make him more than he ever was before."

The great black wolf bounded through the thick mountain woods, sending a squirrel fleeing from his path with a panicked squeak. Ordinarily, he would have entertained himself with a chase, but there were more serious matters on his mind at the moment.

It was dark in the mountain woods this night, with only a thin sliver of moon providing any light at all. But the wolf's eyes were so sensitive, he found his way to the sheer gray-granite cliff with ease.

As he stopped before it, a section of the cliff face began to shimmer, melting away like a mist. A great black cave entrance appeared. The wolf trotted into it. The minute he vanished into the darkness, the opening disappeared as the cliff face solidified again.

Inside, the wolf paused as a soft, dim light began to radiate from the tunnel walls, for even one such as he couldn't see in total darkness. The beast shut his eyes and bent his head, concentrating. He began to glow, his outline flaring bright, shifting. When the light vanished, a man stood in the beast's place.

George Devon Jr. straightened his broad shoulders and ran a manicured hand over his dark hair, making sure no strand was out of place. He'd worn what he considered casual clothes—a pair of dark tailored slacks and a navy silk shirt that made the most of his athletic build. His feet were shod in expensive loafers, a match for the black belt that circled his narrow waist. A thick gold ring glinted on one hand, adorned with a black gem in the shape of a styl-ized wolf head. An iridescent shimmer danced over the ring's stone with every move he made.

He padded down the long tunnel, feeling his stomach flutter with nerves. That annoyed him. Men trembled in his presence, awed by his wealth and power. *He* did not tremble.

But Warlock was no ordinary man—or even Dire Wolf.

Still, Devon was damned if he'd cower before the immortal, so he forced confidence into his stride, arrogance into the tilt of his dark head. The pose felt natural to him, habitual.

Rounding a corner, he stepped into a cavern so brightly lit, his dark-adjusted eyes were momentarily blinded. He stopped, knowing that's exactly what Warlock intended.

His guests' temporary blindness gave the immortal an advantage if he chose to kill them.

"Lord Devon." Warlock rumbled his name with the faintest edge of warning growl. "What brings you here this night?"

He resisted the urge to lick his dry lips. "My daughter has made a discovery I thought might be of interest to you."

"Your *daughter*?" There was the faintest note of incredulous contempt in Warlock's voice, as if no woman could have discovered anything worthwhile. Which was true enough. Still, unlikely as it seemed, the girl *had* found something.

Devon's sight began to clear, and he blinked hard as the cavern came into focus, its gray stone walls glittering with flecks of quartz.

Warlock loomed over him in Dire Wolf form—eight feet tall, his fur a short white pelt over most of his body, except for the thick mane that fluffed like a lion's around his lupine head and fluffed around his heavy sex. His eyes gleamed, bright orange flecked with gold—warm colors given a chill by their feral, inhuman expression. The immortal rarely deigned to assume human form. "So tell me what this *daughter* of yours has found."

Devon drew himself to his full height under Warlock's ancient gaze. "The Maja who has been guarding Arthur's son was accompanied by some kind of cat. Much bigger than a tiger, and black, with silver stripes on the haunches. She said it was surrounded by ancient magic more intense than anything she'd ever felt."

Warlock's head jerked up, his orange eyes widening with astonishment. "She saw the godling?" It was barely a whisper. An enormous hand fell on Devon's shoulder and squeezed in demand. Devon hid a wince as long claws dug into his flesh. "Tell me. Tell me everything . . ."

Giada stared at the parchment scroll with its flowing handwritten script, not sure whether to be relieved or furious.

"In light of your service in saving the life of our son, be advised that your house arrest has been rescinded, and you now have permission to have whatsoever contact you choose with Logan MacRoy.

"In lieu of said house arrest, you are hereby ordered to present yourself to Magus Lord Arthur Pendragon for training in sword-craft. Maja Lady Guinevere Pendragon will likewise instruct you in magical combat. Such training will commence after you have successfully completed your current mission of identifying and aiding in the apprehension of those who have sought to kill Logan MacRoy."

It was signed by both Arthur and Guinevere.

"Damn." She let the scroll roll closed and tossed it on the coffee table, throwing a brooding look at the front door. Logan would be showing up any minute now.

At least Arthur hadn't *ordered* her to sleep with him, so she could always say no.

If, that is, she could muster sufficient willpower.

She flung herself back on the couch—and grimaced as the room revolved around her. Her stomach rolled, threatening to expel everything she'd eaten in the last two days.

Smoke had been right about the Rocky Road/chocolate liqueur combo.

Shuddering, Giada cast a healing spell on herself. Magic poured from her hands to swirl around her body in a cascade of light. The nausea promptly faded as the spins slowed and stopped. She closed her tear-swollen eyes in relief.

Maybe when Logan showed up, she'd just pretend to be asleep. Come to think of it, she could even arrange a magical coma, just for a week or two. Let him find some other witch to pester with his delicious kisses and strong, warm hands and massive . . .

Shut up, Giada.

Despite her best efforts, remembered images and sensations stormed through her mind: Logan, gloriously naked, bracing his big body over hers as he prepared to thrust deep.

His mouth moving over her skin, seducing her so tenderly, spinning glorious sensations over her body. His hands, his teeth, his roar of pleasure . . .

Then he turned on you like a rabid wolf, she reminded herself. *Are you going to stick your head between his jaws and let him take another bite*?

She'd have to be an idiot.

Yet even as her common sense warned her to keep away, there was a part of her that longed for him. A very big part of her. Way too big.

I'm in love with him. She threw an arm over her face as her eyes began to sting. *Dammit, I am* not *going to start crying again. I've got to quit acting like such a wimp. I'm a Maja, a warrior of Avalon.*

The doorbell rang. "Giada?" Logan called through the door.

She lifted her voice and hoped she sounded angry instead of agonized. "Go. Away!"

"Look, would you please let me in? I want to apologize."

"Send a card."

"Giada . . ."

"Logan, I don't want to hear . . ." An image flashed through her mind—*Logan, lips drawn back from fangs as he roared in rage. A huge black Dire Wolf loomed over him, massive as a grizzly as it struck out at him with enormous claws.*

More images came, faster and faster, sucking her down into a chilling nightmare blur. *Devices with timers counting down. Gaping jaws with bloody teeth. Heather and Andy, faces tear-streaked and white with terror. Slashing claws, eyes that glowed with magic and mad rage. A white wolf, a red wolf, and a black wolf.*

Logan again, fangs bared. Agony, hot and burning, as phantom jaws ripped into her flesh . . .

She screamed.

THIRTEEN

Logan stared at the closed door, feeling his stomach sink deeper with every minute she refused to come to it.

Then she screamed.

It was a cry of pure, distilled terror. Spiraling into a name: "Logan!"

"Giada!"

Another scream, even more piercing than the first, accompanied by the thump of a body hitting the floor.

Logan reared back, swung a booted foot up, and sent it smashing into the door. It burst open in a rain of splinters, and he plunged inside, gaze sweeping the room, looking for enemies, wishing he had his gun.

The living room was empty except for Giada, writhing on the floor, her screams slicing his heart like razors.

He was on his knees beside her with no memory of crossing the room. When he snatched her into his arms, one flailing hand slapped against the side of his head with a Maja's strength. He winced and caught her wrist. "Giada! Giada, baby, what's wrong? What's happening?"

Her eyes rolled, wild and wide, not seeing him at all. He

knew that expression from his boyhood, on those occasions his mother had a particularly bad vision.

But Gwen had never convulsed like this. He started to go for the cell phone on his belt, only to realize it wouldn't work in the Mageverse. Besides, the Greendale County Rescue Squad couldn't exactly open a dimensional gate.

What was worse, neither could he. He couldn't even use magic to call for help.

Heart pounding a furious drumbeat of terror, Logan dragged her close. "Giada! Giada, it's all right, you're safe! Come on, baby, come back, come back . . ."

He was just about to snatch her off the floor and carry her in search of the nearest Maja when she went completely limp. Terror iced his veins, until he realized she was still breathing.

After an endless moment, she blinked and focused on him, her gray eyes dazed. "Logan?" Her voice broke, raspy from screaming.

His relief was so great, he thought for a moment he was going to pass out. "Hey. Hey, baby, you're back!" He smoothed her tangled blond hair back from her face.

"Where did you . . ." She stopped to clear her throat, swallow. "How did you get inside?"

"You started screaming." He gave her a strained smile. "I kicked in the door. What happened?"

"Vision." She closed her eyes, only to pop them open again, fear on her face, as if she'd seen something horrible in that instant.

Logan stroked her face, trying to soothe her. "What did you see?"

"Dire Wolves. Three huge Dire Wolves. One of them was snow-white. Another one was black." She licked her lips. "And one had red fur like the one that attacked Smoke and me when we caught the bomber."

"So there were three of them?"

She nodded, rubbing a hand over her face, her expression weary. "And I saw the sheriff's grandkids again. They were terrified. We've got to warn him."

"And tell him what? There are werewolves after Heather and Andy? Yeah, that'll go over well."

She glowered at him. "Well, we can't just let them have those kids, Logan."

"Of course not, but we can get Smoke to keep an eye on them. Heather loves cats—she'll be happy to let him hang around. And if it comes down to a fight between Smoke and a Dire Wolf, my money's on Smoke. He can assume any damn form he wants to, and he could give Merlin a run in the magic department."

Giada considered the idea, then nodded. "Yeah. But we're going to have to get him over there now. I don't want to leave those children alone one minute more than we have to. I'd better call him."

Five minutes later, Smoke was sitting on Giada's coffee table, listening with tail-lashing attention as she described her vision. "Bastards," he snarled. "Involving children in this mess. Of course I'll guard them."

Logan frowned. "We've got to warn the clans they've got rogues again."

Smoke snorted. "If I know Arthur, it's already done."

"Wonder why they're having so much trouble policing themselves? The last one had been killing human women for years before Lancelot and a Mageverse team killed him."

Giada nodded. "Kat and Ridge. I know her—she's Lancelot's daughter. Became a Maja at the same time I did. I heard something about a werewolf serial killer murdering her sister when Kat was only ten or so."

"That's the one." Logan grimaced. "The clans estimated he murdered twenty women. Just ripped them apart. The cops thought they'd been mauled to death by dogs."

"And on that note—" Smoke stood up, his tail lashing, "I'd better gate before one of those furry bastards gets to those kids. Good luck, children." A cat-sized oval rippled into existence in midair, and he leaped through it in a single lithe bound.

"Judging by what I saw, we're going to need all the luck we can get," Giada muttered.

"Speaking of that vision . . ." He watched as she scrubbed both hands wearily over her face. "What else did you see?"

"You. You were a vampire. And you were really pissed off." She looked away from him. "I guess this means we're supposed to fuck now." There was a note of bitterness in her voice.

Logan blinked at her tone. "Not like this." The words were automatic. So was his feeling of revulsion.

"You've got to Change, Logan. And apparently, I'm the Maja who's supposed to Change you." The resentment in her gaze sliced into his soul.

"It can wait." *Merlin's Cup,* Logan thought, *Smoke was right. I really screwed this up. And if I don't find a way to fix things, it's over between us before it even gets started.* His mind raced desperately as he looked for a way to cool the situation off. "Let's go for a walk."

"A walk?" Her gaze was incredulous. "Logan, we're on the clock. God knows what those rogues are going to do next. Not to mention that damned bomber."

"Look, Smoke's watching the kids. The wolves won't be able to touch a hair on their little heads with him on the job. Besides, we know it's not going to happen until after I've Changed. That means we've got some time."

"I'd rather get it over with."

"You make it sound like a trip to the dentist."

She shrugged.

Shit, he really had *screwed things up royally. So go for the one argument she can't refute.*

"I doubt I could get it up now if my life depended on it. Let's just . . . take a walk. You know Mermaid Beach?" When he'd been a boy, Gwen had often gated them there to swim in the ocean, walk on the white sand, and watch the Merkind who gathered to sing and play in the shallows.

Giada lifted her shoulders in that dismissive shrug again. "Whatever." With a flick of her fingertips, she opened a gate. His mind working furiously, Logan followed her through.

* * *

Giada had to admit, the beach was beautiful at night. Long white curls of breakers glowed in the moonlight as they flung themselves onto the milky sand. The wind from the sea carried the smell of salt and distant voices singing, high and haunting.

"Merkind," Logan said, his voice quiet, almost reverent. Bracing his hands on his hips, he stared out over the horizon, his expression dreamy. "They love to rest on the rocks at night and sing praises to the moon."

Giada slanted a glance at him through her lashes. *Well, he does know how to stage a seduction.*

Logan glanced at her just as the thought crossed her mind. Evidently he read it on her face, because his broad shoulders hunched.

He tucked both big hands in the back pockets of his jeans. "You scared the hell out of me when you screamed. I thought the bad guys had gated into your house or something."

"How the hell would they get through Avalon's shields?" The city's wards were constructed to allow no one but Magekind through unannounced.

Logan shrugged. "Happened before. Geirolf's worshippers gated in once, and the Dark Ones . . ."

"Which is why Merlin strengthened the wards during his last visit."

"I didn't say it made sense. Sometimes fear doesn't."

They stood side by side in silence for a long moment, listening to the Merkind sing. "Guess it's no wonder you're twitchy," Giada said at last, "what with that rogue after you."

He turned to frown at her. "Giada, I was afraid for *you.*"

"I can take care of myself."

"I've been a real dick, haven't I?"

Startled, Giada turned to look at him. She considered giving him a proper Southern belle's denial, then decided on honesty instead. "Yeah, pretty much."

Logan winced. "Yeah. When I found out you were Maja, I stopped treating you the way you deserve."

"I lied to you." *Just shut up,* she thought at him. *Stay a jerk. Don't drag me back into love again. I don't think I can take it.*

"You just did what you were supposed to do. I don't blame you for that," Logan told her, moonlight glinting in his dark, serious gaze.

That's big of you. She managed not to say it out loud. *I'm supposed to make love to him, not slice him into verbal sushi.*

"Thing is, I've got a really lousy history with Mageverse women, both Latents and Majae." Correctly interpreting her gaze, Logan added, "I'm not making excuses, just explaining."

"I heard. Clea and Morgana."

"That's just the latest chapter. I lost my virginity at the age of fourteen to a sixteen-year-old Latent. God, she was gorgeous." Gazing out to sea, he smiled in remembrance, though the curve of his mouth looked a little bitter. "I thought she was in love with me. Wrong. She just wanted to bang Arthur Pendragon's son. Figured I could use my pull to make sure she got Merlin's Gift."

"I hope Arthur didn't fall for it."

"Hell, no. When I told him I was in love, he chewed me out and gave me a lecture on being a sucker."

"Maybe not the best message to give your teenage son."

"Not an ordinary teenager, no. But the fact is, he was right. Latent girls made plays for me on a regular basis after that."

"And you had to beat 'em off with a stick. Poor you." She winced mentally the minute the words were out of her mouth.

He gave her a long look. "Yeah, okay, I had that coming."

"Sorry. That was bitchiness above and beyond the call of duty."

Logan smiled faintly. "Anyway, when I turned nineteen, Morgana decided it was time I got the Gift. Suddenly every gorgeous single Maja in Avalon found me irresistible. I finally stopped coming to the city at all. A guy can only

take so much. Then Clea showed up last year, trying to pass herself off as mortal. And I almost fell for it." He shrugged. "Like Dad said, I'm a sucker."

She cocked her head and studied him, curious. "Just why did you work so hard to fend off all those beautiful women? Why *are* you still a Latent?"

Logan was silent a long moment. "I wasn't sure I was up to controlling the transition."

As Giada listened in growing horror, he described his boyhood run-in with Jimmy Cordino. "What really got me was the idea that if I went blood-mad, Dad would have to kill me, too. He'd consider it his duty. And he's already had to kill one son."

"The one that led the rebellion. Mordred."

"Right. It was fifteen hundred years ago, and he's still not over it." Logan's gaze turned distant. "I didn't want to be responsible for destroying Arthur Pendragon." One shoulder went up in a half shrug. "Though could be I'm giving myself too much credit. Dad's pretty damned tough."

Remembering the look in Arthur's eyes when he talked about his son, Giada strongly suspected Logan was right that Arthur wouldn't survive killing him. Still . . . "You know, the Majae's Council isn't wrong very often. Odds are if Morgana's said you'll make a good Magus, you're not going to have any trouble with the transition. Besides, you're not a kid anymore."

"Exactly. Which is why I've decided it's time. But more than that, I *want* to be with you, Giada." He met her gaze with dark, steady eyes. "I don't know what we have here. I don't know if I'm in love with you, and I don't know how you feel about me. But I know I want to find out."

Giada found she couldn't hold the stare any longer, so she looked blindly out to sea. "You hurt me, Logan. You hurt me badly."

"I know." He said the words very softly. "And I can't tell you how sorry I am for that."

"I don't trust you." She turned back in time to see pain flash across his face.

"I don't blame you."

"Then why risk it? Why not just fuck one more time and forget the whole thing?"

"I don't just want a fuck, Giada." A muscle worked in his jaw. "If that's all I wanted, I'd go ask La Belle Coeur. I want *you*. I want to touch you, to hold you, to taste your mouth again. And I want us to find out what we have, because if we don't, I think we'll regret it for a very, very long time." He caught her hand in his. "Take a chance with me, Giada. Take a chance *on* me."

Those eyes of his. So dark, so hungry. Hungry not just for her woman's body, but for her soul. A smart woman wouldn't let him have it.

As her heart sank, Giada realized she wasn't a smart woman.

She was in his arms.

It happened so fast, with no intention on her part, as if her body had gotten tired of her brain's dithering and taken what it wanted.

That first contact sent a bolt of heat through them that was more than simple human desire. It was need. It was magic. His Latent's body recognizing her, Merlin's Gift awakening, sending a pure pulsing chime through bone and muscle and flesh.

They shuddered in each other's arms, gasping at the magical reverberation that shook them like matched tuning forks. The last of her reservations disappeared like dew in the morning sun.

"Damn," he breathed. "First time that's happened."

Giada started to reply, but his mouth came down over hers in a hot kiss. Magic spilled from tongue to tongue and back again. She shuddered as it flooded her every cell like a jolt of electricity.

Logan cradled her face between his broad, warm hands, still kissing her, tasting her. He bit gently at her lips, and when she groaned, he swirled his tongue deeper. When its tip touched her own, she felt another electric pop. It should have hurt. Instead a luscious sizzle spread through her, and

she shivered, whimpering as delicate claws of need pricked her flesh.

He rumbled something hoarse and masculine, catching the hem of her shirt. An instant later, the T plopped to the sand, leaving her breasts cupped in the lace and silk of her bra.

Logan gazed at them, heat flooding his eyes. "God, you're exquisite."

Dropping to his knees, he paused a long moment, staring at her, reverent as a supplicant. When he finally reached up and cupped her, she let her head fall back at the strong warmth of his hands. His thumbs brushed back and forth over the peaks of her nipples, teasing them into hard buds.

Logan looked up to meet her eyes. Moonlight reflections danced in the darkness of his stare, and he swallowed. Then, slowly, he leaned forward and pressed a gentle kiss right between her breasts. His lips lingered there, as if tasting the beat of her heart.

His mouth moved, stringing slow kisses up the rise of one breast, following the line of pale lace, finally closing over the jutting tip. With a purr of satisfaction, he suckled her through the silk, drawing strongly. Each pull of his mouth sent another hot spark leaping along her nerves, until her entire body smoldered. Giada reached up and threaded her fingers through his mink-soft hair, cradling his head.

At last Logan reached behind her for the clasp of her bra. A flick of his fingers, and it fell away, joining her T-shirt on the ground. He drew back, admiring the nipple he'd so skillfully brought to a throbbing pitch of need.

Then he swooped in on the other one and began to lick and play. Teeth rasped as his tongue flicked, and his mouth closed tight in another dizzying suckle, as he thumbed the other nipple, driving her hunger higher.

And higher yet.

His free hand found the snap of her jeans, worked it open. The zipper's hiss sounded over the sigh of the wind.

Giada spread her arms wide and sent magic dancing over the sand around them. When the sparks faded, they knelt on a satin comforter piled with pillows.

Logan released her nipple long enough to grin up at her. "Nice."

She grinned back. "There are some places sand just doesn't belong."

He laughed and grabbed the waistband of her jeans, then began tugging them down her legs. "Good point."

It didn't take him long to get her naked. Her running shoes and socks joined her discarded clothes, and he caught her around the waist to tumble her back on the comforter.

"Aren't you forgetting something?" She gave him her best wicked smile.

He slanted her a playful leer in return. "Nope. Looks like I've got everything I need right here."

"But you're still dressed." Giada raised herself up on her elbows. "Unless you want me to take care of it." Her right hand took on a threatening glow as she let her wicked smile go a little evil.

"Uh, no." He laughed. "Knowing you, you wouldn't give 'em back."

"I doubt the Majae would complain at the sight of you wandering naked through Avalon." The glow around her hand got a little brighter.

"Maybe, but my fellow Magi would still be ragging me about it centuries from now." He jerked the shirt over his head and threw it aside.

She laughed, feeling so damned good, she felt guilty. Somewhere Mark Davis's wife was crying for him. *That is not a good line of thought right now.*

Then Logan reached for his zipper, and she forgot what she had to feel guilty about.

He took his time with his jeans, easing them down over his hips so slowly, she was seriously tempted to just zap them off.

His cock emerged, contained only by black boxers that weren't entirely up to the job. The hard male jut made her mouth go dry.

Giada rolled up onto her knees and caught his boxers in both hands. The head of his cock peeked over the waistband,

a bead of arousal riding its rosy curve like a tear. She leaned in and licked it away.

His gasp was gratifying as he jerked upright.

She smiled and dragged his boxers down his brawny thighs, tugging his jeans the rest of the way off as she went. To her frustration, she discovered she couldn't get them off over his shoes. "Dammit!"

"Such language!" Laughing, he plopped his butt down on the comforter and pulled off his shoes himself as Giada watched with possessive greed. Much to her satisfaction, he was soon as naked as she was.

He threw his jeans and shoes aside and lay back, folded his arms behind his head, and grinned. He made a luscious picture, all tanned muscle against the bright scarlet of the comforter, a pile of sky blue pillows behind his dark head. "Now what?"

"Now," she growled, "I've got you just where I want you." And she pounced.

Swinging a leg astride him, she settled down and bent to taste his tight male nipples, letting her hands roam, exploring the muscled topography of his broad chest, his abdomen, the round bunch of biceps and triceps. Dark hair dusted his tanned skin, soft and fine, and she stirred her fingers through it, intrigued.

She was acutely aware of his cock, brushing her belly as she moved. Thick, hot, promising, a tempting distraction.

His hips rolled, silently begging her to touch the big shaft, cuddle his furry balls, and taste him there.

Smiling to herself, Giada ignored the wordless entreaty.

For once, she felt powerful, as sexy as a goddess. Probably because that's the way he looked at her, his dark eyes dazzled, his face tight with his effort at controlling his own need. She decided to tease him a little more.

Sliding down the length of his body, Giada bent to taste the rosy head again.

God, he was hard. And thick, and hot, his balls drawn tight to the underside of his cock. Silently pleading.

She closed her mouth over him . . .

The magic jolted through her in a hard, hot pulse, dragging a muffled yelp from her mouth as Logan, too, cried out.

Lust shot through her, abrupt and demanding, jerking her out of her mood of lazy sensuality. She had to ride him. Had to fuck him.

Now.

Giada whipped upright and grabbed Logan's cock, aiming it upward. Driven by furious need, she impaled herself in one hot swoop. They both gasped.

He felt huge, delicious. Her every cell sent up a silent, demanding yowl, driving her upward, only to grind down again, impaling herself on his thick heat.

"God, Giada!" Logan stared up at her, his eyes wide, almost dazed.

"More!" She needed more. Harder. Now! *Now now now nownownownownow* . . . Desperate, she started pumping up and down on his erection even as he ground up at her.

But it wasn't enough. *She needed more.*

Giada arched backward, grabbed her ankles, forced herself down, then dragged herself up, tormenting both her own tight, creamy flesh and Logan's thick cock with sizzling pulses of delight.

It felt like something huge was gathering deep in her womb, some exotic blend of magic and sex, furious and wild as a thunderstorm, all crackling tension straining to escape. She needed to free it, had to, but she couldn't quite . . .

As if he sensed her desperation, Logan's big hands grabbed her hips and pulled her down, only to push her back up as they rolled and ground and strove together, trying to force that last little bit that would . . .

"Yes!" It was a scream of relief as much as climax, blending with Logan's roar of pleasure.

Giada's scream spiraled into a shriek as the magic exploded in her belly, jerking her back like a bow as the first desperate pulses poured out of her body. And into his.

The magic went on and on, jolt after blazing jolt, rippling

through her body in long contractions, forcing itself into him until he convulsed, his big body writhing under hers.

Giada looked down. Magic danced around him in a whirlwind of energy, hot and golden, growing brighter and brighter with each pulse from her core.

Until all she could make out was furiously boiling energy in the rough shape of Logan MacRoy.

Merlin's Cup, they didn't tell me it would be like this!

Even as the half-fearful thought flashed through her mind, another magical detonation shook her, one even more furious than those that had come before.

The force of the spell shot through her so hard, it picked her up and threw her like a rag doll. She landed in a heap, dazed and blinded.

When she lifted her head, she saw Logan shining like a star fallen to Earth.

Which was when he began to scream.

FOURTEEN

Every muscle of Logan's body cramped and jolted as wave after wave of magic poured through him. Giada's power had triggered Merlin's Gift, and now it was tearing through his body, remaking every cell.

Pain flared along his nerves, as searing as the white-hot pleasure of orgasm. His vision became a curtain of blinding gold.

A subjective eternity went by before the pain began to fade, the pulses of magic slowing as his body completed its transformation. The golden energy began to drain away, leaving him lying limp on the comforter, legs and arms still twitching helplessly from the final spasms.

Blinking, dazed, Logan saw stars burning overhead, brighter than he'd ever seen them. That damn mermaid seemed to be singing directly in his ear in high and piercing notes. He turned his head to look for her, but there was nothing there except the ocean, flinging itself in curling whitecaps that beat against the sand.

The night seemed much brighter, more like twilight than full dark. And the ocean roared like a storm, all thunder and wind.

"Giada?" he rasped. Clearing his raw throat, he tried again. "Giada?"

"Ummm. Yeah?" She sounded as hoarse as he did. Probably because she was shouting. Had she gone a little deaf?

Turning his head, he spotted her at last, lying half-off the comforter as if something had picked her up and thrown her. She sprawled there, naked and sweating, looking just as dazed as he felt. "You okay?" he managed.

"Think so." She licked her lips and stirred weakly. "You?"

He considered the question for a long moment. "Don't know. That was . . . nastier than I expected."

"I don't remember my transformation being this violent." Odd, she didn't look as if she was shouting, but her voice rang as if amplified. "It . . . hurt, but not like this."

A fragment of remembered conversation crossed his mind. "Lance told me once that getting a Magus's Gift is rougher than the Maja version. Probably because it changes our bodies more than yours."

They fell silent, panting together. Even their breathing seemed loud. And the mermaid's music had acquired a percussion section, a thunderous *thump thump thump* that gradually slowed, settled into a slower rhythm.

Except the sound wasn't a drumbeat, Logan realized as he recognized it at last.

Heartbeats. Hers and his. *He could hear their hearts beating*, even over the sighing thunder of the ocean.

His hearing had become far more sensitive. All his senses had sharpened, which was why the night seemed so bright.

Wondering, Logan spread his fingers across the comforter. He could feel each fiber beneath his fingers. And the air smelled of salt and wind and . . . something delicious. Sex and magic and blood.

And woman.

Giada.

His limp cock stirred on his belly. Something else moved in his mouth. Frowning, Logan ran his tongue along his

teeth. Fangs. He had fangs. They'd emerged at the scent of Giada on the wind.

Yeah, he thought. *I'm a vampire.*

He caught his breath as a sudden compulsion engulfed him—the need to touch Giada, to drink in her scent and taste her skin. He rolled over onto his hands and knees, felt the distinct tremble in his thighs, and decided he wasn't up to standing.

So he crawled.

Still looking a little dazed, she watched him come. The closer he got, the stronger her seductive scent grew. When he reached her at last, he cuddled in against her side and buried his nose in her hair to drink in that intoxicating smell.

His cock, stone-hard again, nudged her hip. He shuddered. Her skin felt impossibly fine-grained against his body, like sun-warmed silk.

Almost as intrigued as he was aroused, Logan touched her, stroking his fingertips over her delicate nipples, across the jut of her hip and the soft flesh between her thighs. The beat of her heart picked up speed, taking on urgency with every thump. The perfume of her body intensified, his cock jerking in reaction.

And his fangs ached, as demanding as his erection. Hungry for her.

Giada caught her breath as Logan stroked her, his gaze wondering, as if he'd never touched a woman before. Amazement softened his dark eyes and the line of his mouth. His nostrils flared, as if to drink in the smell of her skin, her hair. He lowered his head and licked one nipple, then sighed in pleasure at the taste.

"You remind me of a cat in catnip," Giada told him, and giggled as he found a particularly sensitive spot with his fingers.

"I feel like one, too." He nuzzled her breast, then cupped it. "The way you smell. The way you taste. I've never

experienced anything like it." He took her nipple into his mouth and began to suck. His eyelids drifted shut, his expression one of pure delight.

After the physical storm of his transition, she'd have thought herself too drained for arousal. Yet each touch, each flick of his tongue, each caress sent another hot little flame licking along her nerves. Giada squirmed at the growing heat. "Logan . . ." She reached for him.

His hands snapped around her wrists, pinning them to the comforter as he reared over her. A low, feral growl sounded, more like Smoke's than anything human. His gaze burned into hers as he settled between her legs. With a moan of helpless arousal, she hooked her ankles over his butt, opening herself for him.

He drove into her, the thrust jolting her. Giada caught her breath. He filled her so mercilessly full. His cock felt hot within her, and his big body surrounded her in heat and strength.

Logan began to stroke, long, deep, hard. Still holding her wrists pinned, he settled against her, so close she could feel his breath on her throat. His lips opened, and she felt the prick of fangs. *He's going to bite me*, she thought, surprised when the idea brought only a thrill of arousal. She threw back her head, inviting him to do whatever he wanted. "Yes," she whispered. "Do it. Do it now."

And he was gone.

Startled, Giada lifted her head, feeling suddenly cold without his heat. The sea wind raised goose bumps across her naked body. "Logan?"

It took her a moment to spot him. He stood at the edge of the water, wavelets foaming around his ankles. His shoulders looked tight as bridge cables, and his hands were fisted at his sides.

She sat up and flipped one corner of the comforter over her body, seeking its warmth as she frowned at him. "What's the matter?"

"I almost *bit* you." He sounded shaken.

"Uh, yeah. You're a vampire. It comes with the territory."

He turned, and she frowned at the torment on his face. "What if I hurt you?"

"You won't. Besides, I'm a Maja." She grinned, trying to lighten the moment. "If you do something I don't like, I can turn you into a frog."

"You don't understand." Despite his obvious worry, his cock bobbed, still fully erect. When he spoke, she saw the tips of his fangs. "I don't just want you. Giada, I *hunger* for you."

"Good. I hunger for you right back."

Logan whirled to face the ocean as if he didn't trust himself to look at her any longer. "For God's sake, put on some clothes. My control isn't that good." His voice dropped. "And you're too damned beautiful."

Giada blinked, impossibly flattered. There was no doubt he meant every word. She opened her mouth to say something flip, then frowned and shut it again. His hands were shaking, and it looked as if every muscle in his body was drawn tight in his battle for control.

By all rights, she should be afraid. After all, he was a big, powerful man even for a human. As a vampire, he had superhuman strength he hadn't yet learned to control. Between that and the fact that the hunger of new vampires was powerful enough to drive some of them mad . . .

She really should be afraid.

But she wasn't. Now all she had to do was convince him to trust himself as much as she did. Which was more than a little ironic, since she'd told him not an hour ago that she didn't trust him.

Seems she'd lied to both of them.

"Logan." Giada moved up behind him and touched his strong, naked back. He trembled under her hand.

"Giada, *please*." He gritted the words through set teeth. "Gate out. Gate out now. I don't want to hurt you, dammit."

"You won't."

He shot a tormented look over his shoulder at her. "I could." His eyes caught the moonlight, flashing red.

"Yeah, you could. But you won't." Giada looked up at him, hoping her serene certainty showed on her face. "I *know* you, Logan. You're a strong man, a good man, and you won't lose control."

He stared at her. "You sound so damned sure."

"Because I am. Your body may have changed, but Merlin's Gift didn't touch your soul. You're still the same man you've always been. Just like your father."

As she spoke, his gaze dropped to her throat and lingered there, hunger flashing nakedly across his face. He dragged his eyes away. "I'm not my father. I've never been that strong."

"Oh, bullshit."

He blinked, startled at the uncharacteristic curse, and looked at her just as she'd intended.

"You just transformed, Logan. You're hungry because your body needs blood."

"I'll go to the Lords' Club." A muscle flexed in his jaw, and he turned to stare at the horizon again. "They've got bottled blood there."

"Bottled blood won't work for your first time. You don't just need blood, you need the magic you'll get from me. You *know* that." She took a step closer until one bare breast brushed his arm. "Just as you know Majae need to donate blood as much as vampires need to drink it. I haven't donated in weeks."

He frowned, dragged out of his absorption with his own transformed body. "Giada, that's dangerous. You've got to at least bottle it every couple of weeks, or you could end up having a stroke."

"Exactly." Deliberately, she laid a hand on his shoulder. His skin felt almost hot enough to burn, blazing with a fever of need. "That's why I want to give it to you. Now."

Logan had never felt such hunger. His hands shook with the driving need to take her, to press his fangs into her throat and feel her blood fill his mouth. To gulp hot red life from her veins.

He thought of the junkies he'd met in his law enforcement

career—people willing to whore or steal or kill for whatever drug held them in thrall. He'd always felt nothing but
contempt for those people.

Now he understood. And he realized the only difference
between them and him was he'd never known that kind of
razor-blade need.

Now he did.

He thought about all the debased things he'd seen junkies do—the lies, the casual betrayals of family and friends
and lovers. A junkie's drug was a jealous god that permitted
no love of anyone or anything else.

Which was why he had to get the hell away from Giada
and her soft, tempting throat. He turned and started to walk
away, ignoring his body's frustrated howl of need.

"Damn you, Logan MacRoy." He'd never heard her
sound so furious, not even when she'd thrown him out of
her house.

He kept going.

The spell hit him in an explosion of sparks. The next
thing he knew, he lay spread-eagled in the middle of the
comforter. He tried to roll to his feet again, only to find
himself pinned.

He lifted his head to see bands of golden light binding
his wrists and ankles. "What the fuck is this?"

Giada walked over to stand over him, her fists propped
on her hips, irritation on her lovely face. "What does it look
like, you big idiot?"

To his horror, she straddled his hips and coolly settled
herself on top of him. Sweeping her hair aside with one
hand, she positioned herself so that her throat touched his
mouth. Every square inch of the rest of her lay spread over
him—soft naked breasts pressing against his chest, her wet
sex against his erect cock, her long legs clasping his hips.

His body roared. Fangs, cock, demon hunger all clamor-
ing to *take her now*.

"Get *off* me!" He bore down hard, clinging to his self-
control like a drowning man grasping a life preserver. *He
was not going to kill her, dammit.*

Her only reply was a tempting little wriggle. The feel of her nipples brushing his chest, her mound rubbing his shaft—Sweet Jesu, it was pure, distilled torture. And the scent of her skin rolled over him with every breath he took, so exotic, so sweet, all sex and magic, begging him to sink his aching fangs deep.

No. I will not. Logan began to fight his magical bonds, trying to rip free, but they held him fast when solid steel would have ripped like paper.

Maybe he could reason with her. "Giada, I dreamed about this. Twice. Both times, you were tied up and . . ."

She lifted her head and looked at him, surprise on her face. "Was I lying on my stomach with my wrists bound behind me? And the second time you had an ostrich feather, and then you . . ."

He stared at her in horror. "And then I ripped out your throat."

Her head rocked back. "No, you didn't. God, what a revolting idea."

"Giada, I had the same dream, the same vision. And I killed you both times."

"Then it obviously couldn't have been a vision, could it? Not even a Maja can die twice. Besides, vampires don't *have* visions. Majae have visions, and the only thing I saw was both of us having one hell of an orgasm."

He stared up at her. "Giada, I can't take the risk."

"It isn't a risk, Logan. You're not going to kill me." She leaned down and kissed him, softly, with breathtaking tenderness.

He didn't dare move. Images from the dream roared through his head in blood and horror.

"Logan," Giada breathed against his mouth. "Sweetheart, it's all right. Somehow we linked as we dreamed, but your mind turned it into a nightmare. You won't hurt me."

"But what if I do?" Another minute ticked by, savage in its torment. He clamped his teeth shut. Giada squirmed against him, sweet and merciless and delightfully naked.

Another minute. Another. He lost track of time, shaking in his bonds like a man in the grip of malaria.

Another minute. "Giada," he gasped. "Giada, please!"

She made no response other than that luscious, vicious little wiggle.

Eternity ticked by like sand in an hourglass falling in slow motion.

"I can't help but notice," she said at last, sounding a little hoarse, "that I'm still alive. Shouldn't you have ripped out my throat by now?"

He said a few words he'd never used to a woman in his entire life. Dad, who had never touched him in anger, would have beaten his ass with a sword sheath. He didn't care.

"Wow, that was inventive." Giada sounded amused, damn her. "You do realize I dropped the spell ten minutes ago. The only thing holding you still is you."

Giada sat up. To his shock, her face was wet with tears. She stood, turned on her heel, and started to walk away. "Do whatever the hell you want. I'm done."

Logan was on his feet before he realized it, so fast he stumbled. He caught himself and strode after her. Grabbing her by one delicate shoulder, he spun her around and hauled her into his arms. "Why did you do that?" he demanded into her hair. "I could have hurt you!"

"No, actually you couldn't." Her voice sounded stuffy with tears. "That was kind of the point, jackass. You don't have it in you to hurt a woman. Vampire or not, you're the strongest man I know." She laughed, sounding a little watery. "Maybe not the *smartest* man I know, but definitely the strongest."

She was right. Including the part about him being a bit dim.

The realization rolled over him, abrupt and startling. He wasn't going to hurt Giada when he fed. If he'd lacked that kind of strength, he'd have lost it the minute she put her throat against his teeth.

Logan wasn't Jimmy Cordino. He'd met others like

Jimmy as a cop; he should have recognized the kid's type long ago. Jimmy had been a twenty-one-year-old idiot with a psychopathic streak the Majae really should have sensed before they authorized his receipt of the Gift. *And I'm none of those things. Not kid, not psychopath, and not out of control.*

It was time to prove it. He caught Giada's delicate chin and tilted her head up. Lowered his own. And bit, making it as fast and clean as he knew how.

She breathed a purr as his own senses exploded with the taste, the scent, the raw eroticism of possessing Giada. Blood filled his mouth, and he swallowed, shuddering at the searing intensity, the pumping, amazing pleasure. The beat of her heart was loud in his ears, a pounding throb. He realized he could monitor how much he took from the strength of the sound.

So he forced himself to slow down, spin it out, listening carefully, trying to keep his attention on the beat rather than his own rioting senses. It was hard—Merlin's Cup, it was as hard as his cock—but after the lesson in self-control she'd just given him, he knew he was up to the job.

Feeling more confident, he cupped one exquisite breast. And began to drink in earnest.

Giada's eyes widened in stunned delight as his lips moved on her throat, gently reverent.

It wasn't the first time she'd fed a vampire. There'd been the Magus who'd given her the Gift—right now she couldn't even remember his name—but that had been nothing like this exquisite worship.

Logan's lips moved so softly on her skin as his fingers caressed her breast, teasing pleasure from her nipple with gentle little squeezes. His other hand slipped down her belly, found her lower lips, slid between. She arched, sucking in a breath as he started tracing lazy circles over her clit. The arousal that had chilled to guilty ash as she tormented him now flared hot enough to make her quiver.

His cock pressed hard against her belly. She wrapped one hand around its demanding width, began to stroke as she let her head fall back in surrender.

God, she loved the way he filled her hand, so feverishly hot, so hard, his skin like satin over a warm steel rod. A flick of magic slicked her hand with oil as she stroked him lazily. His fingers wove their own spells—runes of arousal and pleasure drawn over nipple and clit, pausing to dip between her nether lips to find her slick, tight core.

With a helpless moan, Giada sank against him, listening to his rough breathing over the sigh of the ocean and the distant song of mermaids worshipping the moon. His fingers thrust and teased, his mouth drew, and the orgasm gathered in the pit of her belly like a burning storm. Her stroking hand moved faster in time to his busy mouth. The pleasure built, hotter, more furious with every touch and stroke, until she wanted to writhe under its delicious lash.

Then it burst free, jerking her into a bow against his hands. She screamed, her hand tightening over his cock. He stiffened, and his shaft began to pulse in long liquid jets against her belly as he growled in dark pleasure.

Her knees gave, almost dumping her to the sand, but he gathered her against him and cradled her, releasing her throat at last. They leaned against each other, both breathing hard, as he began to lick the twin wounds in her throat.

At last he stirred, lifting his head to stare once again toward the horizon. "Sun'll be coming up soon."

"The sun . . . ? Oh, God, I've got to get you home." She straightened away from him reluctantly. "You'll need to go into the Daysleep." A flick of her fingers opened a gate, and they stepped through together, leaning on each other like a pair of drunks.

The car pulled up in front of the sheriff's office. Bill Jones grinned broadly and stepped forward to open the rear door. His grandson leaped out of the backseat and fell into an enthusiastic bear hug. Heather scooted out after her brother

and gave her grandfather a hug. The kids gave their mother a good-bye wave and disappeared into the building with the sheriff.

Smoke stepped out of a gate into the shadows cast by the building's manicured hedges. He paused just long enough to cast an invisibility shield around himself, then walked through the glass door as if it was no more substantial than mist.

This seemed like a perfect opportunity to check out what was going on at the sheriff's office. That rogue Dire Wolf seemed to know entirely too much about the department, including such details as Logan's work schedule. Smoke badly wanted to find out how she came by her information.

Just inside the glass doors, he stopped dead, the fur along his back bristling in alarm.

Magic. The smell of alien magic hung in the lobby, subtle but unmistakable. Not Magekind magic. Something else.

What in the name of all the gods and demons was this? And why hadn't Giada sensed it?

Smoke realized the answer almost as soon as he thought of the question. Up until he'd eliminated the block on her magic, her powers had been weak during the day. And once they'd been strengthened, she'd returned to the Mageverse.

Which had left the Dire Wolf spy free to roam the department at will.

If Smoke could just discover who the mole was, they'd be that much closer to stopping the killer permanently.

So he put his nose to the industrial brown carpet and started working his way through the lobby, through a closed door, and down a corridor, magical senses alert.

The hallway was a soup of smells—no surprise, considering that more than three hundred officers worked for the department, plus assorted civilians. When you added witnesses, suspects, and victims to the list, teasing out who was who would be damned difficult.

What's more, the mole had apparently been all over the building for months, laying down a variety of trails of

different ages. The scent was strange—a blend of dog and human. Which wasn't all that surprising for a Dire Wolf. As he'd thought from his glimpse during the fight, the scent was also unmistakably female.

Yet the odor wasn't exactly the same as that of his attacker. Perhaps because the creature had assumed a different form?

Then again, it would just about have to. Even humans would have noticed a seven-foot fanged monster among them.

MAGIC.

Smoke froze in his tracks as his own power leaped within him. He hunkered down and inhaled deeply, drinking in the scent. This new trail was very, very fresh, having probably been laid within the last hour.

He slipped along after it, resisting the impulse to move too quickly. It wouldn't do to run right into the creature. He didn't care to precipitate a fight that could end in humans being injured—and far too many questions being raised.

He had not gotten to be as old as he was by being reckless.

The scent trail led down one corridor, then another. Smoke followed it patiently, dodging oblivious cop feet, until it led to a closed door. The trail did not emerge again.

Which meant the mole was still inside.

Smoke crouched outside the closed door, listening hard, tail twitching as voices argued on the other side.

"Sam, you can't seriously think MacRoy would knowingly have anything to do with getting Davis killed." The male voice sounded incredulous. "Logan's a damn good cop."

"Then why in the hell would he try to tender his resignation? You heard the sheriff. He had to talk MacRoy out of handing in his badge right then." The woman's voice rang clearly, hot with anger.

"Knowing Logan, he just feels guilty because he couldn't swoop down like Superman and fly Davis to safety." The man snorted. "His sense of responsibility has always been a little overdeveloped."

Smoke laughed silently. That was putting it mildly.

"I hope you're right," the woman growled. "But the fact is, we both know how damned good MacRoy is with explosives."

"So you're suggesting, what? He planted that bomb himself so he could disarm it? And instead, Davis tripped it?"

"He wouldn't be the first cop who got somebody killed while trying to play hero."

"Taylor, if you really believe Logan MacRoy's capable of something like that, you're not thinking clearly. I think you need to go take a couple of days off and get your head back on straight."

Silence ticked by in icy seconds. Finally: "Is that an order, Lieutenant Billings?"

"Do I have to make it one?"

She swore viciously. Smoke jolted as he heard feet stalking toward the door. He whipped around and shot off down the hall.

It wouldn't do to let the mole realize they were on to her.

The door banged open, and the mole froze as the scent of Mageverse magic hit her senses in a wave. She'd been concentrating so hard on the argument with the lieutenant, she hadn't realized someone was eavesdropping.

Judging by the wild feline cast to the scent, it was the tiger creature Warlock was so interested in. She concentrated hard to penetrate the illusion the beast had cast, saw a blur of black. Except the small form disappearing around the corner didn't belong to a tiger of any kind.

It was a house cat.

The Demigod was a shapeshifter of stunning power, if he could manage a transformation into something so small, yet still retain human-level intelligence.

Automatically, she started to lunge in pursuit, only to have a fierce jerk on her leash bring her up short.

"Cut it out, Jenny," Deputy Samantha Taylor snapped,

angry impatience ringing in her voice. "The lieutenant says we've got to go home for the day."

For a moment, Amanda Devon considered sinking her fangs into her "handler's" ass, then thought better of it. She needed to talk to her father. There had to be some way they could use this new knowledge to lure the Demigod into a trap.

And avenge her brother's death by killing Logan MacRoy.

FIFTEEN

Giada lay in the darkened bedroom listening to the steady sigh of Logan's breathing. He'd gone to sleep as if clubbed the moment the sun came up. Yet though she'd been up all night, she couldn't seem to wind down enough to drift off herself. Her mind kept skipping over the events of the night like a stone across a lake.

Her threatening and confusing visions, the dizzying pleasure of making love to Logan, the fierce explosion of his Gift. Yet forcing him to yield to his own hunger had been the most difficult and painful event of the night. Come to think of it, it was the most difficult and painful thing she'd ever done, period.

Logan had vibrated against her in a tormented battle against his own vampire drives for fear of hurting her, even as she'd deliberately pressed her throat to his mouth.

Giada had realized there was a chance he'd lose control as completely as he feared, but she'd never thought it was much of a risk. Logan would never hurt a woman, regardless of the provocation.

She did, however, realize just how painful the struggle had been for him. His brush with death at the hands of

Jimmy Cordino had scarred him more deeply than anybody had realized, including his parents. Yet Magi had to drink the magical blood of Majae—or die. He had no choice, particularly since he couldn't gain his full powers without drinking directly from a Maja.

But did she have the right to force him to confront his fear? Especially by grinding his face into her throat?

It was a good thing he'd finally seen the light. She'd been on the verge of gating off so she could collapse in tears. Listening to him beg her to release him had made her feel like a rapist.

And maybe that feeling wasn't all that far off the mark.

Yet after all that, he'd still brought her to a delicious orgasm that, in retrospect, only increased her guilt.

There was no doubt about it. Whatever his flaws, Logan was an instinctively gallant lover who seemed driven to make sure his partner had an even better time than he did.

Which was yet another reason Giada had fallen for him.

If she'd had any doubt about her feelings, last night had blown them right out of the water. Not only was he gorgeous and intelligent, but his basic decency had been bred right into the bone, despite the game-playing of various Majae that had also instilled a certain cynicism.

Not that Giada herself had any room to talk, considering last night's ugly little game. If they'd ever had a chance at anything more, she'd probably killed it right there. How could he feel anything for a woman who'd bound and tormented him, regardless of the reason?

The only man she'd ever really felt anything for, and she'd blown it royally.

Perfect, Shepherd. Way to go.

Logan's eyes sprang open. He stretched, a delicious sense of strength and well-being rolling through his body. Propping himself on his elbows, he drew in a breath—and his eyes widened.

SEX.

The air was full of it, warm and dark and female. His cock instantly hardened against his belly into a fierce and demanding length as his fangs slid to full extension.

Giada lay curled against him, deeply asleep. He rolled over and lowered his head, unable to resist the temptation to bury his face against the silken tumble of her hair.

He frowned. There was a trace of salt in her scent. Not the warm musk of arousal, but something else. Sadness. Grief.

She'd been crying.

Alarm rolled through him, banishing his lust. Had he hurt her the night before? He had been very careful when he'd bit her, but he'd also been very turned on. And vampire strength was much greater than human. What if he'd hurt her without meaning to?

He rolled over and found the bedside lamp, flipped it on. Winced as the flood of light made his eyes water as though he were staring straight into the sun at high noon. He jerked his eyes away from the lamp and waited for his sight to adjust.

"Logan?" She yawned hugely.

He sat up and began to examine her anxiously. Propping herself on her elbows, she blinked at him. To his relief, he saw no signs of bruises. Which didn't mean much; there was no sign of his bite, either. Majae could heal their own injuries just as Magi could. "Did I hurt you last night?"

She frowned up at him. "No, of course not."

"Are you sure?" He searched her gaze carefully.

"Yeah, why?"

"You were crying." He brushed a thumb across her cheek, found he could detect a faint salty grit against her skin. God, his sense of touch was incredibly acute now. "I can smell your tears."

"Yeah, but it wasn't because of anything you did. More what I did."

He frowned. "What do you mean?"

Giada lifted one shoulder and looked away. "I was pretty nasty to you last night—binding you with my magic until you bit me."

He examined her face. "Yeah, that was a little high-handed, but you were right. I needed to drink from you, which meant I had to stop being a wimp."

Giada snorted. "Of all the words I'd use to describe you, 'wimp' doesn't make the list." She met his gaze with a steady, straightforward stare. "I'm sorry I was such a bitch, Logan."

"Yeah, well, the word 'bitch' doesn't exactly leap to mind when I think of you, either, Giada."

He thought she relaxed a little. "Umm. Good." After a pause she said, "I'm sorry anyway."

Logan shrugged. "I suspect I had it coming. I haven't exactly been the model of chivalry the past couple of days. I think you used the word 'jackass' a time or two. Which was probably generous. 'Asshole' might have been more apt."

Giada laughed. "Well, maybe a little." To his relief, her gaze lightened, and a teasing smile flitted across her mouth. In his relief, he caught her in his arms and hugged her.

"Ow!"

"Shit!" He let her go and rolled off the bed to examine her anxiously. "Did I hurt you?"

She rubbed her ribs, wincing. "A little, but it's just a bruise. I think your full strength must be coming in."

Logan raked his hands through his hair in frowning thought. "That makes sense. From what I've heard, you usually have to drink from a Maja and go through at least one Daysleep before you really complete the transformation." He was going to have to be damned careful, or he'd hurt someone without intending to.

Which meant he'd better keep his distance from Giada. Which was, dammit, the last thing he wanted to do. He had to get a handle on his new strength quickly.

Especially since, if Giada's vision was correct, he'd soon have to go up against that Direkind killer and her pet

bomber. Logan frowned. "I need to go see Dad and get in some combat practice."

"Good idea." Giada grimaced. "Come to think of it, Arthur and Guinevere have ordered me to present myself for more training, too." When he frowned at her, puzzled, she explained, "In lieu of house arrest for disobeying orders."

He winced in sympathy. "You may end up wishing they'd left you on house arrest."

She lifted a brow. "Oh?"

Logan nodded, remembering some of his more memorable teenaged infractions. "Dad's combat sessions tend to leave bruises, especially when he's pissed."

"Oh, *that* sounds like fun."

"He probably won't be that rough on you, though, since you're female. Dad's pretty old-fashioned when it comes to women."

"Yeah, but he also seems to take the concept of obeying orders very seriously." Giada raked her hair out of her eyes and grimaced. "He's going to kick my ass."

Logan gave her a sympathetic smile as he walked over to open the bedroom door. "Maybe, but he'll kick mine, too. Much harder."

He twisted the knob. With a screech of tortured metal, it gave like putty under his hand as the metal tongue tore through the doorframe.

They stared at the damaged door for a moment of mutual stunned silence.

"Maybe I'd better take care of opening doors for a while," Giada said at last.

"Yeah. That would probably be a good idea."

Arthur jerked the door open before they even had time to knock. Nonplussed, Logan met his searching gaze.

A grin of pure relief spreading across his face, Arthur snatched him into his arms with such power, Logan's feet left the ground.

"He did it, Gwen!" his father yelled, thumping his back before dropping him back on his feet. "The kid finally did it!"

"Hey," Logan protested. "I thought you said you knew I could manage the transition without any problem."

"Hell, we were never worried about the transition. Come in, come in." Arthur stepped back, waving them both inside. "We were afraid you'd have a fucking car accident or get shot or blown up or some damn thing before you got around to it." He gave Giada a huge, sunny grin. "Thank you, girl."

She stared at him in total confusion. "Wait a minute—didn't you order me to stay away from him?"

"That," Gwen said as she hurried down the hall to hug her son fiercely, "was because we were trying to hide how desperate we were for him to accept the Gift. We didn't want either of you to think we'd sent you to trap him." Stepping out of his arms, she muttered, "Though Merlin knows I was tempted."

Logan met Giada's confused gaze and shrugged.

"When you have children, you'll understand," Guinevere told him, tucking his arm into hers and leading them toward the sitting room.

"Actually, I'm here to ask you for combat training," Logan told his father. "I just trashed Giada's bedroom door."

"Occupational hazard of getting the the Gift," Arthur told him with a snort. "We'll head to the training center and start working on your reflexes. Luckily, I've been training you for years, so you've already got a better foundation than most new recruits."

Logan shook his head. "Still won't be easy. My strength is so much greater, I'm afraid to touch anybody for fear of breaking bones."

"Don't worry about it," Arthur said. "You break anything of mine, I'll turn into a wolf and heal."

"And promptly bite me on the ass."

"Well, yeah." His father's grin faded. "I'm afraid I've got some bad news, though. Smoke just contacted Gwen.

He found out who our Dire Wolf is. We're going to move on capturing her tomorrow night. Then we'll deliver her to the Direkind for justice."

Logan gave Arthur a wary look. "How is that *bad* news? We find the psycho, we stop the killings."

"It's Samantha Taylor."

He was so stunned, it took Logan a moment to respond. "Oh, hell no. Smoke's wrong. I've known Sam for two years, long before any of this started."

Arthur shrugged. "She could have had this planned for a long time."

"Why didn't I sense it?" Giada said, her gray eyes wide with distress. "The magic around that thing we fought— you could have cut it with a knife. If Sam is the Dire Wolf, I should have known it the first time I met her."

"Maybe she was blocking your senses," Gwen suggested. "We know there was something keeping you and Smoke from tracking the bomber. It's logical that this Sam has the same ability."

Giada frowned. "And where the hell did that come from? Direkind are like Magi—they can't use magic beyond their ability to shift."

"Maybe there's something they haven't told us." Gwen's expression went thoughtful. "Though I suppose it's logical that they'd have some means of blocking magical senses. After all, Merlin wanted them to remain hidden from us in case we ever turned against humanity."

"When are you moving on this, Dad?" Logan asked. "I want a part in the takedown, but there's no way in hell I should go into combat until I've got better control of my abilities."

"Tomorrow night." Correctly interpreting Logan's expression, Arthur held up a hand. "I want to take my best knights on this, but I've got all three Round Table teams working connected operations in Spain, Pakistan, and Afghanistan. Those ops are balanced on a sword point, so I can't do anything tonight. Still, I should be able to shake at

least Galahad and Lance loose long enough to snatch that bitch wolf after sunset tomorrow."

Logan frowned. "But what if she puts together another bombing in the meantime?"

"I've got a couple of Majae staking out her house. If they have to, they can call in more witches and take the little bitch down." He sighed. "I don't particularly want to do that—I hate sending Majae against a Dire Wolf, since the furry bastards are spell-resistant—but sometimes you've got to make the best of a bad tactical situation."

Logan frowned. He didn't like the delay a damned bit, but he saw his father's point. Besides, he wanted a chance to look Taylor in the eye and find out why the hell she'd done this.

The training center was a sprawling facility designed to test the skill and endurance of Magi and Majae alike. There were target ranges, mazes with magical attackers, dueling circles, and assorted enchanted traps intended to test reflexes, strength, and agility.

Logan and Arthur headed to the strength training area, dark heads together as they talked. Giada trailed after them with Guinevere. The older Maja conjured a padded seat and gestured for Giada to join her.

"I thought you'd want to start the magical training you and Arthur specified as my punishment."

Gwen waved a hand. "There'll be plenty of time for that later. We don't want to miss this."

Which was a damned good point, Giada decided, as Arthur led his son over to a hulking SUV.

"Oh, yeah." Gwen settled back. "The lift-the-SUV trick. You can tell a vamp what he can do all day long, but he'll never really believe it until you make him test his limits."

"But Logan grew up among vamp . . . uh, Magi."

Gwen shook her head. "Doesn't matter. It's too great a jump. You can know something like this intellectually, but

until somebody makes you push your strength to the wall, you don't really believe it."

Logan eyed the SUV, took a deep breath, squared his shoulders, and walked over to it. Quickly, he bent over, grabbed the big vehicle's bumper, and pulled upward.

And ripped the bumper right off.

Arthur's bellow of laughter carried across the grounds. Logan stared at the twisted piece of metal in his hands, his expression nonplussed.

Giada sat up, alarmed. "Hey, his hands are bleeding."

"Magi may be much stronger than humans, but they are not made of steel," Gwen told her. The expression on her lovely face was serene. "Arthur will show him how to change and heal in a moment. In the meantime, he needs to learn the proper technique."

Arthur walked over to the truck, crouched, positioned his hands under the vehicle's body, and lifted. He then walked up under it, shifting his hold as he went, until he balanced the SUV over his head as easily as a man lifting a sheet of plywood.

"Damn." Giada blinked in astonishment. "I didn't realize they were that strong."

"He's showing off," Gwen told her. "Logan's not quite strong enough to do that yet. A Magus's strength increases over time, as he feeds and absorbs Mageverse energies."

Giada frowned, thinking it through. "Does that mean a Magus weakens if he's trapped on Mortal Earth?"

Gwen nodded. "Yes, though we can usually find him fairly quickly if something like that happens."

When his father put the truck down, Logan stepped forward, positioned his hands where Arthur had, and lifted it with a grunt of effort. The front end of the car rose as he heaved upward. Giada watched the powerful muscles of his back ripple with effort, the cords straining on the side of his neck. She drew in a breath—and yelped as his arms suddenly gave under the weight. The SUV started to fall . . .

And stopped with a groan of tortured metal, hovering in midair as he dove clear.

"Thanks, Mom!" Logan called.

"Wasn't me." Guinevere jerked a thumb in Giada's direction.

Which was when Giada realized she was on her feet, magic pouring from her hands as she held the big vehicle suspended. She'd acted on pure frantic instinct. Startled, she lost her magical grip. The truck hit the ground with a thunderous crash.

Gwen sighed. "We lose more SUVs that way." Eyeing Giada, she added, "Smoke was right—you are stronger than we thought."

They fell silent, watching Logan attempt various feats of strength under his father's tutelage. "Have you ever heard of a Maja and a Latent sharing dreams?" Giada asked Gwen suddenly.

The Maja gave her a sharp look. "Did you and Logan . . . ?"

"Yes. At least twice we had the same dream. Well, more or less the same. He dreamed he killed me in both of them . . ."

Gwen swore so foully in gutter Latin that Giada blinked in surprise. "Jimmy Cordino." Her tone made the name sound like an obscenity. "I suspected that little bastard was why Logan was so reluctant to accept the Gift."

"You were right."

She grunted. After a thoughtful moment, she added, "It is interesting that the two of you linked in your sleep. Even if you'd already made love first, it's . . ."

"But we hadn't. Not then." Giada's cheeks heated in horror at what had just come out of her own mouth. *For God's sake, she's his mother.*

"Oh, really?" Blue eyes widened in surprised interest. "That *is* unusual. You two could probably form a really strong Truebond." She considered that a moment, then added hastily, "That is, if you wanted to."

"Umm. Well. That's good to know." What the heck did you say to a statement like that coming from a man's mother? Deciding discretion was the better part of valor,

Giada proceeded to concentrate very hard on Logan and Arthur.

"Don't do that, boy." Arthur gave him a cuff across the back of the head. "If you're that hungry, go bite that girl of yours."

Logan realized he was absently sucking one of the cuts on his fingers left by his attempts to lift the SUV. His own blood did not taste nearly as good as Giada's—but it wasn't all that bad either.

He snatched his finger out of his mouth, mildly revolted at himself.

Arthur shook his head. "You need to heal those cuts. Time to get in touch with your inner wolf."

"Okay." He took a deep breath and blew it out. "What am I supposed to do?"

"Imagine the form you want to take. Got it?"

He frowned, remembering the dark-furred wolf he'd seen his father become. "I think so."

"Now, reach for your magic. And let it take you." Dark sparks swirled in Arthur's eyes, flooded the whites of his eyes, washed over his skin in a blinding flood that swirled, changing shape. For a moment, Logan thought he smelled dark forests and moonlit nights.

Then the magic was gone, and a huge black wolf stood where his father had been. The big beast looked up at him expectantly.

Logan obediently closed his eyes and pictured a wolf . . .

And nothing happened. He frowned, puzzled. Where was the wolf? It had always looked so easy when the knights called up their beasts.

Wolf?

Nothing answered. His body did not flow into the change he'd seen the others make with such ease.

"Nothing's happening."

"Shhh," his mother said as two sets of light footsteps approached. "Keep your eyes closed. You're fighting it. Help him, child."

A delicate hand touched his cheek. It seemed he heard Giada's voice whispering in his mind, though she made no sound. *Reach out into the dark, out into the wild woods where the moon paints each leaf of every tree in silver, where the magic breathes cool shining breaths and soft feet pad over rustling leaves. Do you feel it?*

"Yes," he breathed. And he did.

There it was, the moving darkness, ancient and huge and powerful. The magic hit him like a tsunami, flashing through skin and bone and muscle, twisting and tearing. There was a moment of intense pain . . .

When the world came back, it returned in a furious sensory assault—smell, sight, touch, all so intense that they seemed to batter his brain. It took him a long, disoriented moment to realize he stood on four feet. He tried to walk and damn near fell on his . . .

Muzzle?

Wolf teeth snapped inches from his ear. He bounded straight up like a startled cat.

That was the key, he realized. *Don't think. Let the body follow instinct.*

His father pounced on him with a happy growl, almost but not quite sinking long white fangs into his furry flesh. Logan rolled to all four feet and began to run, moving faster than he ever had in his life, Arthur in playful pursuit.

Hours later, Logan staggered over to take the silver goblet his mother held out to him. It was full of such blessedly cold water that for a moment he wasn't sure whether he'd rather drink it or dump it over his head.

He ended up downing it and asking for a second cup. That was the one he poured over himself, sighing in relief as his sweating flesh instantly cooled.

"Stop drooling, child," his mother said.

He looked around, surprised—he hadn't been aware he'd *been* drooling—only to find Giada blushing.

Oh. He hid his grin behind the cup.

"I think the boy needs a dozen eggs, Gwen," Arthur announced. "Giada hasn't seen him juggle."

Logan dragged his gaze away from his lover's bounding pulse. "Juggle?"

He'd just spent hours transforming to wolf form and back again, then lifting one god-awful weight after another. His every muscle ached, and his legs shook like those of a horse who'd been run too hard. Now his father wanted him to demonstrate a skill he'd mastered when he was twelve?

Out of the corner of one eye, he saw something white sail toward his head. Automatically, he reached up to snag the egg out of the air, just as he'd done when he was a teenager.

And promptly found himself holding a handful of yolk.

"Gently, boy, gently." Arthur gave him a toothy grin. "You wouldn't want to leave bruises on Giada's white skin, would you?"

Good point. He set his teeth and reached out to catch another egg.

Crunch.

Dammit.

SIXTEEN

By the time they returned to Giada's tiny ranch, it was barely an hour until dawn. Logan couldn't remember the last time he'd been so exhausted. Arthur had run him hard, and he'd pushed himself even harder. He had to be ready for the raid on Sam Taylor's house.

"I still can't believe Sam's a killer," Logan told Giada as she gestured, opening the front door with a spell. "She's always seemed like such a good cop."

"I know what you mean." She took his arm to guide his steps, in the process flooding his senses with her delicious scent. His fangs twinged, and the Hunger growled through his blood. "I liked her, too. But if Smoke says she smells like Dire Wolf, she's a Dire Wolf."

"Yeah." He resisted the urge to lean into her, knowing he probably smelled like a wet dog himself.

"What *is* Smoke, anyway?" She led him down the short hallway toward her bedroom. He could hear the rush of the shower already running—she'd apparently magicked it on when they'd come in.

"Who the hell knows? He and Dad have been friends for most of a thousand years or so. He's a lot like a real cat—he

comes and goes on his own schedule. He's been known to disappear for years, only to show back up as if he'd never been gone. Never mentions what he's been up to, either. Very mysterious."

The bathroom was surprisingly large, considering the size of the house. It had both a sunken tub and a glassed-in shower, both in gleaming rose marble that matched the rose-specked white ceramic tile on the floor.

"I'm a big fan of bathing," Giada told him, a touch defensively.

Logan grinned down at her. "What a coincidence. So am I." He reached for the hem of his sweaty T-shirt, grimacing as his sore muscles complained.

Without commenting, Giada brushed his hands out of the way, grabbed the shirt, and pulled it off over his head when he lifted his arms. He toed off his running shoes and stripped out of his pants, acutely aware of her warming gaze. He just wasn't sure he had the energy to do anything about it.

When he stepped under the shower spray, he sighed in pleasure as the hot water began to pound his aching muscles. Knots began to un-kink, and he leaned one hand wearily against the cool tile. Closing his eyes, he relaxed as the spray began a rhythmic pulsing that was no doubt magically induced.

He really needed to scrub the sticky blend of sweat and egg yolk out of his hair and off his skin. Unfortunately, he felt as if he'd been run over by an Arthur-shaped truck, and he doubted he had the strength.

Just as that thought crossed his mind, a pair of hard nipples brushed his back.

Suddenly he felt a whole hell of a lot more lively.

Logan turned around to find Giada deliciously naked and standing in the shower as she worked a foaming cake of soap in her hands. Her smile was wicked. His cock stirred and rose in pure appreciation at the heat in her eyes.

Yep. He was definitely less tired than he'd thought.

* * *

There's nothing like a wet, naked man with a truly impressive hard-on to make a girl feel welcome. Giada grinned, watching Logan's dark eyes crinkle at the corners as he smiled down at her in hot appreciation.

She felt pretty damned appreciative herself. His broad, powerful chest was gemmed with beads of water, glistening runnels snaking down rippled abs toward his jutting cock. His dark hair was slicked tight to his head, and droplets shone on his high cheekbones and dripped from the cleft in his chin.

Her fingers itched to touch him. She reached out with the cake of soap and began to trace it over his chest. She almost purred in satisfaction as he let his head fall back with a groan of deep male pleasure.

Unable to resist, Giada stepped in closer, let her soapy hands roam, and watched in absorbed fascination as trails of bubbles rolled down strong ridges and hollows. Slowly, gently, she ran the tips of her nails over his skin, following fascinating masculine contours. So strong, so warm under her hands. Almost feverish. He shuddered in pleasure.

Her hand trailed lower, hesitated just above the broad jut of his cock. He went still under her fingers, as if holding his breath. Hiding a secret smile, she trailed one finger back up, circled his navel, and slanted a look up at him through lowered lashes.

He was watching her with a hungry intensity that reminded her of a tiger at a waterhole. Her nipples budded under the heat of that feral gaze.

Her hand flashed down to cup his balls. Logan jolted with a low male growl. "Playing dangerous games, there, sweetheart."

"That's okay." She gave him a deliberately cocky grin. "I loves me some danger."

He grinned back in a slow, deliberate revelation of very sharp fangs. "Good." The hint of menace in the word sent a delighted little thrill down her spine.

She tilted her head back and rolled his balls between her fingers, gently, tenderly, then let just the tips of her nails scrape carefully along the underside of the fuzzy sac. His cock jerked upward in response like a rearing horse. She brought her other hand into play, rubbing the cake of soap slowly up and down the thick rod, watching foam slide and drip along its veined contours. "You have a beautiful cock. It's so long. Almost as thick as my wrist." She released his tight testicles and started running her hand along the soapy shaft. Back and forth, concentrating on the slick, delicious textures, watching droplets of water bounce against his taut flesh.

One big tanned hand covered her smaller one, slid the soap out of her fingers. Giada looked up, still stroking his heavy erection, as he began to work lather between his own palms.

Soapy fingers found one breast and pinched its hard nipple, sending hot little thrums of pleasure along her nerves. The hard, slick edge of the bar slid over the other breast, then dipped under its heavy curve, then up again to rasp against its tip. Back and forth, back and forth, each pass teasing her, ripples of delight pulsing through her veins like waves of honey, hot and thick and impossibly sweet.

He drew in a sharp breath. She realized suddenly that her hand had tightened around his soapy cock. "That feels good," he whispered.

She gave him a slow and crooked smile, shivering a little as he ran the bar of soap down the curve of her belly. "So does that."

The bar paused in silent request right over her mound. Knowing what he wanted, she set her feet a little farther apart. Letting him slide the soap between her lower lips, right across the hard little nubbin of her clit. She shuddered, impossibly aroused. "That feels even better."

"Good," he breathed, watching her through hooded eyes. "Very good." He extended his middle finger, sliding it between her lips, almost entering.

But not quite.

The sensation of that soapy fingertip sliding across her sensitive folds was maddening. Giada let her head drop back against the cool tile of the shower stall. Her moan sounded impossibly erotic to her own ears.

The soap hit the bottom of the tub with a *thunk*, slid unnoticed toward the drain as he dropped to his knees. She looked down at the top of his gleaming wet hair as he spread her lower lips with two fingers and leaned in. He paused a moment, watching with absorbed interest as the stream of water washed away the soap from her fine blond fuzz.

His mouth covered her so suddenly, she jolted up onto her toes. Her hands fell automatically to the back of his head, cradling it as his tongue slipped between her lower lips. The raw power of the sensation made her shudder in hot delight. He lapped her clit like Smoke working on a saucer of cream—slowly, with relish, his dark lashes fanning his cheeks. One finger slid up into her opening in a slow, seductive pump. Giada quivered helplessly.

He circled his tongue around her nubbin, drew a lazy figure eight, and pumped that finger. In. Out. In. Out. His free hand reached up, found one breast, and cupped. His thumb brushed her nipple, back and forth, in the exact same rhythm as that busy tongue. Flick, stroke, pump.

Giada let her head fall back, hot jolts of electric pleasure rolling up her spine, fine muscles pulsing in her abdomen. She was so damned close to coming. So close. But not . . . quite . . . there.

"Logan . . ." The word was more whimper than anything else.

A second finger joined the one inside her, a dazzling double stroke that made her pant. His other hand pinched her nipple hard enough to send a sharp jolt of delight through her belly. He twisted those tormenting fingers.

But they weren't enough. What she wanted was cock. Thick, hard, driving inside her.

Her hands curled into fists in his hair. "Logan, for God's sake—*fuck me!*"

He was on his feet before she felt him move, strong

hands closing around her ass to pull her off her feet with no effort at all. With an eager little gasp, Giada wrapped both arms around his neck and hooked her knees over his narrow hips.

He impaled her in a slick and ruthless rush. They both gasped at the sensation of his big shaft driving deep into her wet sex. "God, Logan!" she managed, as he rolled his torso, pumping in farther, harder, deeper.

"Sweet Merlin's Cup, you're tight!" he gritted through set fangs, shifting his grip to support her back.

She dug her nails into his back and hooked her ankles together, then began to roll her hips. The spasm of delight that whipsawed through her had her gritting her teeth and hunching harder, seeking more, reaching deeper.

He groaned, the sound deep and tortured in her ear, as he began to thrust with slow, exquisite care. "Let me know . . . if I go too deep," he gasped.

"Fine! I'm fine! More!" Close. So damn close, so damn fast. She just needed a little bit . . .

The climax hung just beyond her grasp, hot and white behind her eyes. Giada curled her nails in and ground down on his cock, using all the power in her thighs and calves to try to wrench out that last little bit of friction she so desperately needed.

Big hands helped, sliding under her thighs, lifting her as if she weighed nothing.

"More, Logan!"

He leaned forward, braced her back against the cool tile, tightened his grip on her ass, and began to hunch in a furious hammering drive that made her throw back her head in a yowl of feline delight.

Her climax burst free like a star going nova, spilling bright sparks through her belly in hot rhythmic pulses. Her yowl spiraled into a shriek.

Logan growled in reply, leaned forward, and put his mouth against her hammering pulse. The quick pain of his bite added a wicked additional jolt to her orgasm, kicking its fading quivers back into another ferocious convulsion.

She twisted against him, screaming, only distantly aware of his answering groan and the hot pulse of his jerking cock deep inside her belly.

When it was over, they clung together, breathless as shipwreck survivors, stunned and quivering.

Dammit, she thought. *It just keeps getting better. I am so screwed.*

And so in love.

There was a witch outside the house.

Amanda Devon growled softly as she reared, paws planted on the windowsill as she stared at the woods behind Sam Taylor's house. She could feel the bitch out there, radiating magic to her Dire Wolf senses.

"Shush, Jenny," Sam snapped, before returning to her phone call. "Lori, I just wanted to tell you how sorry I am. If there's anything I can do, you just ask. Mark was a damn good man, a damn good cop. We're all just sick . . ." She paused. Amanda could hear Lori Davis crying stormily for her dead husband. "Oh, honey . . . Honey, you're going to make yourself sick. You've gotta be strong for Tara . . . You want me to come over?" She sighed. "Okay, if you're sure . . . Don't worry, I will definitely be at the receiving tomorrow. Me and every cop in Greendale County. Everybody loved Mark . . . Okay, honey. Now, I mean it about callin'. Anytime. You need me to keep Tara, whatever. Anything. Promise me? . . . All right. Bye, sweetie." She clicked the phone off and sighed, raking her hands through her long red hair. "I swear to God, if I find out Logan had anything to do with this, I'm gonna put a bullet in his brain."

Amanda ignored her, still concentrating on the witch.

This was bad. Very bad. It meant they'd figured out what "Jenny" was. But why hadn't they moved against her yet?

Must be waiting for nightfall, when they could mobilize the vampires. They'd be aware that she was resistant to magic, which meant there was damned little witches could do to her.

A hand latched onto her collar and tugged hard. "Get down off that windowsill, dog. You're scratching the hell out of the wood."

Amanda turned a glare on the human, who took a step back from her snarl. "What the heck is wrong with you, Jenny?"

I'm not in the mood to play doggy, human. And I need to get the hell out of here before the sun sets.

She had to shift forms and escape. But she couldn't do it in front of Taylor.

Taylor, whom Logan considered a friend. What if Taylor, like Davis, died a hideous and bloody death? Wouldn't that inflict a little additional pain on her enemy?

Besides, she was really sick of playing big, goofy dog . . .

Samantha took a step back, going pale. "Jenny?"

God, she was bored.

Sherri Carson yawned hugely as she leaned back in the camp chair she'd conjured. She'd been on edge when she'd first replaced Smoke on guard duty, but she'd quickly realized her greatest problem was not going to be an attack from a rogue werewolf.

It was going to be staying awake.

Sherri was determined not to blow this. She'd been a Maja for only four months, and had spent most of that time training for magical combat. On this, her first mission, she was determined to make sure Sam Taylor didn't disappear before Arthur's knights showed up to take her into . . .

A shriek rang out, shrill with terror. Sherri jolted to her feet, staring at Taylor's house in shock. A wave of psychic agony slammed into her magical senses, and she began to run for the house, knowing even as she ran she should call for backup. But it would take too much time and magical focus to punch a spell message through to the Mageverse. And right now, Sherri knew she just didn't have the luxury.

A woman was dying, and Sherri was the only chance she had at survival.

The glass door was closed and locked, but it dissolved like morning mist when Sherri's spell blast struck it. She plunged through the opening, her heart in her throat.

PAIN. Choking, strangling, fighting to breathe . . . Couldn't breathe, couldn't . . . Blood, her blood, everywhere . . . Vicious eyes glaring down into hers, triumphant and savage.

Sherri's stomach drew into a solid knot of terror and forced its way into her throat. Swallowing, she stopped, listened hard.

A gasping, bubbling sound. Like someone struggling desperately to breathe. *Dammit, should have called for backup, you idiot. Move. If you don't move now, she's dead. A healing spell could save her life.*

Gritting her teeth, she strode down a short hallway toward that pitiful sound.

A sound that was growing steadily fainter.

Dammit, Sherri! Quit being such a freaking puss.

She broke into a run again, headed for the source of the dying breaths, knowing each second she delayed put the woman another instant closer to being beyond help.

Samantha Taylor lay sprawled on her back in the bedroom, her throat a red ruin, her mouth working helplessly, her eyes going glassy even as Sherri knelt beside her.

Oh, hell! Sherri grabbed for the Mageverse with all the power within her, calling the magic as she reached down to try to heal the woman's shredded throat.

A rumbling snarl sounded. She jerked her head up.

The creature loomed over her, a towering, red-furred monster whose eyes burned gold and narrow over bared knife-sharp teeth.

Sherri acted on pure instinct, transforming the power she'd called into a searing ball of flame that she blasted right into the Dire Wolf's face. It roared, startled, shaking its red-maned head.

The flames winked out.

Oh, shi—

A furry red hand slashed downward before she could even finish the thought.

* * *

Arthur stared down at the empty camp chair, his hands curling into armored fists. "Where the fuck is she?"

Giada and Logan exchanged a look. Then the whole group—Giada, Logan, Arthur, Gwen, Lancelot, and Galahad, plus their Majae wives, Grace and Caroline respectively—turned toward Samantha Taylor's house. They were almost eerily silent in their enchanted plate armor, swords at their hips or sheathed across their backs.

Logan drew his own blade and started for the home with long, enraged strides. Giada plunged after his armored back. "Dammit, Logan, let me scan!"

"Scan, then!" he snarled.

She sent power pouring over the house in the moonlight.

And sensed the house still shivering with the echoes of violent death and scaring agony.

"Oh, hell!" Giada started to race past him. Logan reached out, grabbed her wrist, and jerked her around.

"Dammit, do you *want* to run into an ambush?"

"They're dead, Logan!" she snapped. "Sam and Sherri are lying in there, dead!"

His head rocked back, eyes narrowing in a wince of pain, before he recovered to growl, "Then getting yourself killed won't do them any good, will it?"

"Is the werewolf there?" Arthur demanded, his black eyes cool as he drew Excalibur.

"She's gone," Gwen said. "She killed them both and vanished."

After a quick search of the house, the group gathered around the bodies of the two dead women.

The young Maja lay over Samantha Taylor's body, her head at an unnatural angle. "Oh, child." Guinevere reached out and closed Sherri's staring brown eyes. "Why didn't you call for help?"

"She sensed Sam dying," Giada said. "She was so desperate to save Taylor, she walked right into the Dire Wolf's ambush."

"At least she got off a spell blast." Arthur gestured toward a blackened area high on the wall. The center of the area was white, forming the outline of a non-human head.

"That's a Dire Wolf, all right." Gwen raised the visor of her helmet to study the burn more closely. It was almost seven feet off the ground. "Female, by the size. A male would be even bigger."

Giada threw her a wild look. "Bigger?"

"And immune to magic." Grace studied the outline. "Sherri hit it hard. Anything but a Dire Wolf would have burned like a torch."

Arthur crouched to breathe in deeply, using his acute vampire sense of smell. "The creature was in dog form when she attacked Sam. Then she transformed to Dire Wolf to attack the Maja." He rubbed his knuckles thoughtfully over his bearded jaw.

"Jenny," Logan snarled. "She was the fucking K-9 all along."

Gwen fisted her hands on her hips. "Why didn't Smoke realize the Dire Wolf was the dog, not Sam?"

Lancelot shrugged his broad shoulders. "The mortal handled the animal so often, its scent was all over her. And hers was on it."

"Smoke wasn't the only one the Dire Wolf fooled." Giada looked down at the bodies, feeling battered by her own profound failure. "I didn't sense it either. Why the heck did Merlin give these werewolves so much power?"

"When he visited during the Dragon War, he told me he'd feared the Magekind would misuse their abilities and begin abusing mankind." Arthur rose to his feet again, his expression weary. "Apparently it had happened before with some of the other guardians Merlin's people created on other planets."

"But if they watch us, who watches them?" Giada asked.

"They're supposed to police themselves, apparently."

"Yeah, well, they're doing a piss-poor job," Logan growled. His armored glove creaked as he curled one hand into a fist. "So are we going to call them in on this or what?"

"I already contacted the man they named as their ambassador. Devon said they would look into it." Arthur frowned, brushing his thumb over his lower lip.

"Devon?" Lance looked up sharply. "The same Devon who was the father of that fucking Dire Wolf serial killer?"

"That's the one." Arthur shook his head. "I talked to the head of their council about the man, but he cut me off at the knees. Informed me George Devon is one of their aristocracy, the Chosen. He swears Devon's from an ancient family, completely beyond reproach."

"Wait—Dire Wolf serial killer?" Caroline looked at Lancelot. "The one who killed Kat's sister? He had an odd name—Trey or Tip or something."

"That's the one." Lancelot nodded. "His real name was George Devon III, which is where the Trey came from."

Giada remembered the story all too well. Trey had been torturing and killing blond mortal women for years. One of his victims was the half sister of Lance's daughter, Kat. When Kat became a Maja, she tracked Trey down, just in time to prevent another murder. It took Kat, Lancelot, and Kat's lover, Ridge, to save the girl and kill the Dire Wolf.

Arthur's eyes narrowed in calculation. "As I recall, Trey's father, George Devon Jr., was not particularly pleased when we informed him his son was dead."

Logan met his gaze and knew they were thinking the same thing. " 'Not pleased' enough to seek revenge?"

"He made all the appropriate noises of horror and contrition, but I could smell his rage." Arthur rubbed a hand over his bearded chin. "I thought at the time he was furious at his murdering son, but what if it was me he was angry at? It would explain a lot, wouldn't it?"

"As in, 'You killed my son, so I'll kill yours'?" Lance asked.

A pause slid by, hot with growing anger. When Arthur

finally spoke, fangs showed in his snarl. "I think I need to have a word of prayer with that manicured little fucker."

"Before you whip out Excalibur," Gwen pointed out, "remember this is a *female* Dire Wolf we're dealing with."

"So I'll give him a minute to explain before I cut off his fucking head."

"Arthur . . ."

"Look, we can fight over who does what to whom later," Logan interrupted. "I need to call 911 to report Sam's death."

His father stared at him. "Logan, this is a magical murder. We cannot afford to have your detectives investigate this."

"They're not going to realize magic was involved, Dad. The autopsy will say she was killed by a dog bite. They're going to assume Jenny went nuts and attacked her—which is basically what happened."

"What about Sherri?" Arthur jerked a thumb at the burn mark on the wall. "Not to mention the outline of the seven-foot-tall monster on the wall?"

"We can remove that." Gwen eyed the mark thoughtfully. "Along with all signs of Sherri and her blood."

Grace nodded. "And the glass door she blew open."

"Probably need to create some way the dog could have escaped," Giada said thoughtfully.

"That's simple enough," Logan said. "We could just say the door was standing open when we drove up."

Arthur frowned. "According to Smoke, Taylor told your lieutenant she thought you killed Davis. They're going to wonder what you're doing here."

He shrugged. "I'll just tell 'em I dropped by to talk. It's still early enough for a visit. It'll be pretty damned obvious I didn't kill her." Logan looked down at Sam's body, his expression brooding. "No human did that."

"Technically speaking, you don't have to get involved with this at all," Arthur pointed out.

Logan glowered at him. "She's one of my squad mates. I'm damned if I'm going to leave her here to rot."

"Of course not. But we could make an anonymous call to 911. When the officer arrived to check out the call, he would discover her."

"That would only raise more questions. She's obviously been dead awhile, which means it's too late for a passerby to call because she heard screams. Which would make detectives wonder if the killer made the call. Since the killer is supposed to have four legs and a tail—not a good plan."

"Logan, I could call the cops," Giada pointed out. "You could go with Arthur to hunt the killer."

He hesitated a moment, then shook his head. "What if the Dire Wolf came back after we left?"

"Why would she do that?"

"Why did she kill Sam? She's nuts."

"Logan's right—he should stay with you. I don't want to end up with another dead Maja." Arthur looked at his knights. "In the meantime, let's pay a visit to Trey's dear old dad and find out what he knows about this mess."

"I'll stay with Logan," Giada said. "We'll go get his car, drive up as though we just got here."

"I will take Sherri home and prepare her for her death ceremony." Grace looked down at the Maja's twisted body, sadness in her eyes. "Such a bloody, stupid waste."

Arthur's lip curled. "And someone is damned well going to pay."

Gwen turned to Logan and extended her hand. Magic sparked in her palm, solidifying into a cell phone. "If you get separated from Giada, use this."

He lifted a brow as he took it. "I gather it's not really a CrackBerry?"

"Nope. Magic. It'll connect you right to me, and Arthur and I will come running."

Logan clipped it onto his belt. "I just hope we won't need it."

"Believe me, kid—so do I."

* * *

"You got trouble," Charlie Myers said in his smoker's rasp. "I told Arthur your husband had nothing to do with this mess, but I don't think he believed me. Suspicious bastard— begging your pardon, ma'am."

"That's quite all right." Joan Devon gripped the phone in a white-knuckled grip, ignoring the pain of her wounds. A savage joy rose in her as she listened to the Southern Clans chieftain.

This was just the opening she needed.

"I told him no Chosen would have anything to do with killin' Latents," Myers continued, "especially not a Devon."

"Well, given that my son murdered all those human women, one can see how Arthur might have found your assurances a bit hollow."

"Ah." Myers sounded taken aback. "Yeah, but Trey was . . . well, begging your pardon, ma'am, but Trey was crazy."

And so is my husband. Why do you think Trey went mad? Joan did not say so out loud, however. That was not a fact to share with the likes of Charlie Myers. She did have her pride, after all. "Thank you for your concern, Mr. Myers. I will deal with the situation."

"You'll let your husband know?"

"Of course," she lied. "Good-bye, Mr. Myers."

"Ah. Okay. Umm, good-bye, Mrs. Devon. You take care, now."

Joan clicked the portable phone off and gently cradled it. She looked around the bedroom with its overturned furniture, ripped bedspread, and trail of bloodsplatter. Did she have time to pick up?

Probably not. The damage was too extensive to repair in the time she had. And anyway, they would want tea.

Her gaze caught on the portrait of her family hanging over the massive four poster. Trey and Amanda, smiling happily to either side of her, George standing behind them all, tall and strong and smiling.

He could hide so much behind that well-bred smile.

Hatred rose in her, black and choking. She'd tolerated too much for too long. Too much death. Too much madness.

And Warlock. She'd tolerated Warlock for far, far too long. Well, she was done with that.

He was behind it all, she knew. That damned sorcerer had set all this in motion, stolen her children, her pride, her husband, put them all on the path to destruction.

But she would have her revenge. She would pay for it, of course—pay in heart's blood. Not that it mattered. In all the ways that counted, she'd lost Amanda long ago. Like George, her daughter had always seen her as weak.

She wasn't weak. She was a woman of the Chosen, and she had more strength than the men of her class ever gave her credit for.

Sometimes being underestimated was quite useful.

Briskly, Joan rose from the bed and limped toward the hall. She needed to prepare the tea.

Sheriff Bill Jones crouched by Samantha Taylor's bloody body. Giada couldn't help but notice he knelt in the same spot Arthur had occupied an hour before.

"It looks like her own fuckin' K-9 killed her." He shook his head, his expression weary and sick. "I let my grandchildren play with that dog." He looked up at Giada and Logan. "So you found her like this?"

Logan nodded. "The kitchen door was standing open."

Jones's eyes narrowed. "So y'all just walked right on in?"

"We spotted the blood trail on the floor. Thought we'd better investigate."

"We called 911 as soon as we found her." Giada's gaze dropped to the trail of bloody dog tracks that led out of the room and down the hall to the kitchen door. She'd conjured it herself, just as she'd removed the blast marks from the hallway and all traces of Sherri's blood from the carpet. She'd also repaired the glass door and removed the camp chair from the woods.

The fact that she'd tampered with evidence in the process gave her a queasy feeling in the pit of her stomach.

Unfortunately, the only alternative had been to leave Sam to rot in her own bedroom, and Giada was no more willing to do that than Logan was.

Jones straightened. "So what were y'all doing here to begin with?"

Logan met his gaze steadily. "I wanted to talk to her."

"About her belief you had something to do with killing Davis? I'd imagine that pissed you off."

"I had no intention of starting trouble, Sheriff."

"I'd fuckin' well hope not, since if you did, it didn't end too well for Sam."

"So you think, what? I showed up and sicced her own dog on her?"

"Don't be a smart ass, MacRoy."

Anger sizzled through Giada. "Logan would never hurt any woman. Especially not a fellow cop. And the idea that he'd have anything to do with killing Mark is just ridiculous."

Jones eyed her, his gaze cool. Though Giada could feel her cheeks getting hot, she refused to drop her eyes.

"You done?" he drawled at last.

She gave him a slight, cool nod. The tips of his mustache twitched into something suspiciously close to a smile. "Good, 'cause I agree with you." He turned a cool, steady gaze on Logan. "I've known you seven years now, MacRoy, and I'd sooner suspect my own son-in-law of killing Mark Davis than you. You're a good cop, a smart cop." The sheriff shook his head. "But I've gotta tell you, coming over here was fuckin' stupid. Sam had a temper, and she woulda jumped your ass in a heartbeat. As it is, you're damned lucky those wounds are obviously dog bites, or you would be in deep shit."

Logan sighed. "Yeah. But I wish to God I'd had to deal with Sam's redheaded temper instead of finding her like this."

"You and me both, boy." His expression brooding, he watched as the evidence tech shot pictures of the dead woman. "Damn, I'm tired of standin' over my people's

bodies. Just makes me sick in my gut." He looked around at Logan and Giada again. "You two coming to Mark's receiving tomorrow night?"

Logan nodded. "I want to pay my respects to the family, and I doubt I'll be able to make the funeral."

Jones frowned, obviously wondering what would be more important to Logan than his teammate's funeral. There was no way to explain that since the service would be held during the day, Logan would be unconscious, out cold in the Daysleep.

"What time is the receiving?" Giada asked, obviously hoping to divert the sheriff's attention.

The receiving of friends was an old Southern tradition, generally held at the funeral home the evening before the funeral so those who couldn't attend the service could pay their respects.

"They're expecting a pretty big crowd, so it'll run from six thirty to ten P.M.," Jones said. "I figure half the departments in the Southeast will send representatives, plus a sizable percentage of the public."

It was fairly unusual for a Southern cop to fall in the line of duty. The last time a Greendale County deputy had died on the job had been in 1973.

An ambulance crew approached, leading a stretcher. Logan, Jones, and Giada stepped aside to let them put Samantha in a body bag. "Our visitors might as well stay in town," the sheriff said, watching grimly. "Gonna have to hold another one for Jones in a couple of days. Hope we've killed that damn dog by then."

Logan exchanged a look with Giada. Jones wasn't the only one with plans for Sam's killer.

Which was when his magic cell phone rang. He moved off down the hall as he flipped it open, Giada at his heels. His father's voice spoke. "We're moving on George Devon."

"We'll be right there." Logan closed the phone and turned to Giada. "Let's go."

SEVENTEEN

The werewolf lived in a mansion.

Arthur and his team of knights and Majae gated into a huge, dour room lined with bookshelves and leather tomes. The air smelled of dust, ancient paper, and the lingering odor of cherry pipe tobacco. Under that lay a strange, exotic scent that reminded Arthur of a combination of ozone, fur, and deep woods. He knew that smell from the Dragon War.

Dire Wolf.

Eyes narrow, he scanned the room. An oxblood leather chair sat behind a massive desk of dark, heavily carved wood that occupied one end of the long room. The opposite end was dominated by a fireplace of black marble flecked in red quartz that reminded him a little too much of blood.

A life-sized painting hung over the fireplace: a young blond man dressed in cream jodhpurs and a red jacket. His chin tilted at an arrogant angle, hauteur in his cold blue eyes. A pair of fox hounds lolled at his booted toes.

"Trey?" Gwen muttered.

"Trey," Arthur confirmed.

Galahad snorted. "Looks more like something out of the nineteenth century than the twenty-first."

"Which was probably his whole problem right there." Arthur lifted his chin in silent signal and started for the door, Excalibur naked in his gloved hand. His team followed him, silent as ghosts, moving out into the hallway to begin a fast, efficient search.

They'd found no trace of George Devon Jr. beyond the scent of Dire Wolf, when light steps and the faint ring of metal sounded on the stairs.

Arthur turned in the corridor, Excalibur in his hands, conscious of his wife beside him, ready to throw a spell.

"Hello, Arthur Pendragon. And Lady Guinevere, of course," the woman called in a voice flavored with a Charlestonian drawl that sounded both cultured and wealthy. "Welcome to my home."

Arthur tensed, exchanging a quick glance with Gwen. Despite the elaborate courtesy in her voice, the woman smelled of blood.

They watched, tense, as she reached the top of the stairs, a silver tea service in her hands. She was a slim, delicately built woman, dressed in a robe of heavy cream silk that made her skin appear almost ghostly. Thick hair curled around her shoulders, a rich, dark chestnut shot with silver. Fine lines fanned around her large, hazel eyes and bracketed her full mouth. She was probably in her mid-fifties.

Blood streaked one long, trailing sleeve of her robe.

"You're bleeding," Gwen said.

The woman glanced down, lifting one thin forearm. A set of deep claw marks raked in a spiral along its length, the blood dark and dried on her pale skin. "It's nothing. It will heal when I transform."

"Who hurt you?" Arthur asked, anger glinting in his dark eyes.

A faint, dry smile curled her lips. "My husband is a traditionalist. I questioned his judgment in reference to our daughter."

Arthur tensed. "Is he home?"

"No." The faint smile flashed again. "But your knights

are welcome to search the house for him if you wish." She started toward the library with the heavy tray, then paused to look at them. "Will you join me?"

"Of course," Gwen said, exchanging a telling glance with Arthur. They barely needed their Truebond to communicate anymore.

He sheathed his sword and dipped his head in a half bow. "Lead the way, madam."

Cautiously, they followed her. As they passed one of the bedrooms, Lance stuck his head into the corridor. Arthur nodded, silently indicating that his warriors should continue the search.

The Dire Wolf woman put the tray down on a small black marble table before the fireplace and gestured at the three oxblood leather chairs that surrounded it. "Please sit."

"I don't believe we've been introduced," Gwen said as they obeyed.

"Oh, dear." The woman looked momentarily flustered. "I'm sorry, I'm Joan Devon. Tea?"

"Yes, please." Arthur studied her, frowning. The woman seemed entirely too calm about having her home searched by a team of armed vampires and witches.

And it had been a woman who'd killed Samantha Jones.

"I hope you'll excuse our descending on you like this, but we have suffered some serious losses lately," Arthur said. "Latents have been murdered, and my son has been targeted."

"Yes, I know. Sugar? Cream?"

They said they'd take both. As the woman prepared three cups, Gwen met her husband's gaze and spoke through their Truebond psychic link. *She hasn't poisoned the tea, anyway.*

That's good to know. Is it just me, or does she seem a little . . . odd?

More than a little.

"The death of our son hit my husband very hard." Joan presented Gwen with a cup, then gave one to Arthur as well.

"The Chosen put great store by their sons." Her mouth flattened. "Much more than their daughters. Tradition again."

Arthur's eyes narrowed. "Do the Chosen have a tradition of revenge, madam?"

She did not blink. "Yes, Lord Arthur. I'm afraid we do."

The silence that followed that statement seemed to crackle with their growing anger.

"Mrs. Devon, has your husband been killing Latents?" Arthur asked, his voice deceptively calm.

"Technically, I don't believe my husband directly murdered anyone." Joan sipped her tea, her expression serene. "But he did coordinate the killings."

"What about the bomber that tried to kill my son?" Gwen demanded.

She considered the question. "I believe my daughter hired that particular assassin." She could have been commenting on a shopping trip, for all the emotion she showed.

Gwen and Arthur exchanged a look. "And yet you're willing to just *admit* that?"

She looked up at the painting over the fireplace. "Like my husband, I am a traditionalist. I fear I have kept my silence for too many years on too many subjects. And it has occurred to me recently that perhaps I have mistaken cowardice for duty."

Compassion dawned in Gwen's blue eyes as she studied the woman's profile. "I'd imagine that would be a painful realization to make."

Joan snorted. "My dear, you have no idea."

"A woman willing to make such a statement is no coward, Mrs. Devon," Arthur said quietly.

"I let my son kill far too many innocent women. That was definitely the act of a coward, for I feared the rage of my son and my husband, just as I feared the rejection of my fellow Chosen."

"Judging by your wounds, you had good reason to fear," Gwen said quietly.

"Perhaps." She put her cup down on its saucer with a soft, definitive click, as if coming to a sudden decision.

"You need to know that there is one Dire Wolf who can do more with magic than simply shift forms."

Gwen and Arthur exchanged a quick look. After a pause, he said, "That is indeed news, Mrs. Devon."

"Unlike the rest of the Direkind, he is not mortal. It's said Merlin himself gave him his powers in the Dark Times. And he is very, very powerful. He leads an elite group of Chosen males who consider him semi-divine. My husband is one of them."

"What's his name?"

"They call him Warlock." She met Arthur's eyes. Such rage flashed in her gaze, he felt a chill. "Warlock put my son on the path that destroyed him. The path that destroyed my family. And I would see him dead for it."

The werewolf's name was Gordon Bryson IV, and he had teeth like stilettos. Logan could count every one of them in the lip-rippling snarl he aimed at Arthur. "I will tell you nothing, Pendragon."

Which wasn't exactly a revelation. Neither had the other two Dire Wolves Joan Devon had named as members of Warlock's inner circle. They'd resisted so savagely, the knights had ended up killing them.

They'd tracked this third Dire Wolf to his own very expensive condo. Everything in the place seemed to be black, made of chrome, or covered in white leather, with the exception of the werewolf himself. He looked like a grizzly bear, and had the temperament to match.

"You and your furry friends have been killing my people, Gordon." Arthur lifted Excalibur at a menacing angle, sending light dancing down its four-foot length. "Talking is the one thing that will keep you alive. Where is Warlock?"

The wolf threw back his golden head and laughed in a series of chilling barks. "Where you will never find him, Celt. Kill me if you can."

Arthur's lips peeled back from his own teeth. "Oh, we can."

Gordon lunged at Arthur, massive clawed hands reaching toward his throat. Logan stepped in, slicing at the monster's massive forearm with his own blade, forcing the Dire Wolf to twist aside. Lancelot struck, raking his blade across the monster's furred belly. Roaring in pain, Gordon swung at his head, but Grace blocked the Dire Wolf's claws with a thrust of her oval shield.

Magic was no good in this fight. They were down to medieval weapons against claws and fangs. Logan had earlier asked Giada to conjure him a Glock, only to discover Dire Wolves shrugged off bullets like rainwater. A surface-to-air missile might have done the job, but you couldn't use a SAM in a condo without killing a lot of innocents.

Normally, the racket they were making would have drawn the county's cops like bees to peaches, but one of the witches had cast a noise-dampening spell over the entire building. The combatants could hear one another, but the neighbors would sleep on, undisturbed.

It ended with shocking speed. Gwen danced forward, swinging her sword like a baseball bat as she screamed a taunt. Gordon dodged, realized she'd been left wide-open by the momentum of her own weapon, and lunged under her guard.

The Dire Wolf didn't know her well enough to realize he was being suckered.

Excalibur descended like a lightning bolt. The Dire Wolf's head bounced, hitting the shining marble tile yards from his tumbling body. His blood painted the white walls in a scarlet arc.

Arthur eyed the corpse with disgust. "Well, that was an utter waste of time. Didn't get a word out of the son of a bitch."

Galahad turned to study the horizon through the glass French doors. "Sun'll be up in an hour or so. I don't think we have time to keep beating the bushes for Warlock."

"I can mobilize my women," Morgana said. She'd gated in to join the hunt, judging it to be of higher priority than

the Afghan operation she'd been running. "We can continue the hunt in the day."

"Make sure you take only the Majae who are competent with sword and shield," Arthur told her.

She sniffed. "Since when do I need you to tell me how to wage a campaign?"

Arthur only grunted in response. "In the meantime, the rest of us need to get some Daysleep." He turned to Giada, Gwen, Caroline, and Grace. "That includes you lot. It's been a tough night, and tomorrow is likely to be just as bad. I want you fresh for when we find that bastard Warlock." His expression went grim. "Because we'll sure as hell need you then."

Logan watched as Giada worked her way through a conjured pizza with delicate greed. She had offered to share, but one whiff of cheese made him feel a little queasy.

Which was actually a good thing, since his system could no longer handle any food but blood. Realizing that, she'd laughed at herself for making the offer. "I've got to get used to you being a vampire," she said, taking another bite.

What he really wanted to bite was her. She looked long and lovely as she reclined against the beige fabric back of her sectional couch. Her blond hair was still damp from the shower they'd shared, and her long legs were bare beneath the frayed hems of her cutoff jeans. She wore a black T-shirt printed with a devilish smiley face and the words, "Lead me not into temptation—I can find it myself."

She was definitely not wearing a bra.

"I've been thinking." He hesitated a moment, trying to decide how to approach the topic. *Might as well just go for it.* "Did you see the way they fought?"

Giada looked at him over a slice of pepperoni. "What, the werewolves?"

"No. The Truebonded couples. Like Grace and Lance, Caroline and Galahad. And my folks. They were so . . . coordinated."

"Well, yeah." She nodded, took a sip from a can of Coke Zero. "It was pretty impressive. Perfect teamwork. Like the way Gwen lured George in so Arthur could take him out. All without saying a word."

"That's the Truebond."

"I know."

He took a deep breath. "I've been thinking we should do it. Truebond."

She froze, a piece of pizza halfway to her mouth, her storm gray eyes going wide. "Us? But we're not even married."

"You don't have to be married to Truebond."

"But you might as well be! Truebonds can't be severed, Logan. When you link two souls, divorce is not an option."

Was the idea so distasteful to her? "It's better than dying. The Direkind were created by Merlin himself. We need every advantage we can get."

Something flickered in her eyes. Pain? "So you're suggesting a marriage of convenience?"

"I've watched my parents use their Truebond all my life. It makes them far more formidable than they would have been separately." He tried out a smile. "And I can say that from personal experience as a former teenage boy."

"But if one of them dies, the shock would kill the other."

"They've been Truebonded for fifteen hundred years, and nobody's managed to kill them yet. And believe me, plenty of people have tried."

"Got me there." She smiled very slightly, though there was no humor in her eyes. "But I've got to ask—why me? There are a heck of a lot of single Majae who'd jump at the chance to Truebond with you."

But they're not you. He wanted to say those words, but they seemed naked, as if they said more than he was ready to admit. So instead he said, "I know those Majae. I think you and I together could be more effective than I'd be with any of them. We're a better fit."

Her gaze cooled so sharply, he thought, *Oh, hell.*

When she spoke, it was with no inflection at all. "Well, that's logical."

And logic, he realized suddenly, was not the right way to talk someone into a union of souls. "Just think about it." He took a deep breath. "Think about this."

Logan leaned over, tilted her chin up, and kissed her, slowly, carefully. Her lips were cool and still under his at first—so still he felt a chill. He didn't push, just brushed his lips over hers, gently, a request instead of a demand.

At last her lips softened from their cool line, parting under his. Her stiff body relaxed, and her tongue brushed his mouth. He opened for her gratefully, letting her taste him.

Tasting her, so sweet and hot, he shivered in the sudden rise of need.

There may have been cool logic in the reasons he'd given her to Truebond with him, but there was nothing but heat in his kiss. Her body—her illogical, hungry body—leaped in reaction.

Logan deepened the kiss, big hands slipping around her shoulders to pull her closer. Despite all the reasons she shouldn't, she sank against him, enjoying the hard muscled strength, the way his fingers stroked so tenderly over her arms. Desire slid through her like molten chocolate, slow and sweet and warm.

She moaned into his mouth, the sound a helpless admission of just how much she wanted him.

And I can have him. The thought flashed through her mind. *If we Truebond, he's mine. United that way, he'll learn to love me.*

But what if he doesn't? Logan pulled the T-shirt off over her head, his eyes darkening at the sight of her bare breasts. It would be a little slice of hell to be in love with Logan MacRoy, while knowing beyond doubt he didn't love her in return.

But what if she refused to Truebond with him and he died in the fight with the Dire Wolves?

No, *that* would be hell. Spending the rest of a very long life wondering if she could have used the Truebond to save him.

While being without him. Forever.

But what if she couldn't make him fall in love with her? What if he came to resent her?

But if he died because she didn't do this . . .

As her mind skittered in indecision like a panicked squirrel, she grew irritated with herself. Logically he was right—they needed every advantage they could get. If there was a cost later, she'd pay it.

She closed her hand over his, stopping the stroke of his fingers over her nipples. "I'll do it. I'll Truebond with you."

There was a flash of relief in his eyes. Relief that became a frown as he gazed into her face. Apparently he didn't like what he saw there. "Are you sure? If we do this, we can't go back."

She didn't let her gaze drop. "I'm sure."

"Do you know what to do?"

Giada shrugged. "I just gave you the Gift, so we're half-way there as it is. I just need to deepen the bond."

"Then if you're sure . . ."

"Are *you* sure?" She had to ask.

He smiled, but there was tension in the line of his mouth. "I've never been more sure of anything in my life."

Yeah, right. Giada took a deep breath and reached out to lay a hand on the side of his face. Closing her eyes, she reached for her magic. Here in the Mageverse, it responded in a hot gush of energy, eager to be shaped to her will. She let it flow through her, out to her hand, to her fingertips and palm, to pour into his flesh, his mind. She felt him stiffen against her, catching his breath at the bright burn. She opened her eyes.

There are sparks flashing in her gaze. God, she is so beautiful.

Giada jolted, realizing the alien thought was his. In her surprise, she almost lost the connection, but she grabbed for

it again, adding more magic to the thin thread like a woman spinning yarn. Strengthening it, binding them tighter . . .

Hunger.

Giada caught her breath as the need rose in her, sudden and sharp. The need to feel her slick nether lips sliding the length of his cock in gorgeous waves of pleasure. The need for her blood flooding his mouth, flavored with hot copper and burning with magic.

It was Logan's need. Logan's hunger. So sharp and hot it touched off her own desire to feel him driving deep, to feel the sharp bite of his fangs and the spreading pleasure of his mouth drawing hard.

Hunger fed hunger, each enhancing the other, building in a furious feedback to maddening heights.

Hands clawed at buttons and zippers, fabric tore in impatient fingers. Until they were both naked. This time there was no sweet, leisurely foreplay, no sensual teasing. They didn't need it. They just needed that hot and total connection.

She swung astride him, wrapping her legs around his hips. His arms cradled her close as their mouths sealed in a ferocious kiss as necessary as oxygen. His fingers found her breasts, pinched a hard nipple into stinging pleasure as he bore her backward into the sectional's cushions. Positioning himself at the opening of her slick lower lips, Logan entered in one driving, breathless thrust.

They both cried out, the sounds of their voices blending, his deep rumble underlying her higher cry. Overwhelmed by mutual need, they ground against each other, his lean hips rocking against her softer belly, her heels digging fiercely into his ass, arms wrapped tight against each other as they strove hard for the orgasm they could feel building.

They kissed as they fucked, tongues slipping in and out in time to hard, jarring thrusts that drove the pleasure higher, higher, higher. Until Giada had to rip away to breathe, throwing her head back, knowing he'd take the gesture as the offering it was.

He covered her banging pulse with his lips, still thrusting

in short little digs, so damned close they could both taste it, in a mutually crazed sliding into madness.

His fangs bit deep, and she gasped at the sharp sting. Cried out as he began to drink, the taste of her own blood on her tongue like liquid magic, a searing echo of what he experienced with each hot swallow.

And still he pumped that meaty cock into her cunt, fierce long thrusts, greedy for that dizzy soar and swoop into orgasm. She dug her nails into his back, feeling the hot sting on her own shoulders even as he felt his/her cock in his/her sex, the magic rendering irrelevant the question of what anatomy belonged to whom. It was all hers, all his, blood and dick and pussy and fangs, a crazy melding, building to . . .

Explosion.

The climax was like nothing they'd ever felt, a rocket ride into heat and light, blinding, overwhelming. She screamed for them both, his mouth busy on her throat as her voice spiraled into a high and breathless shriek.

Until they tumbled down again, still linked cock and cunt, fangs and throat, mind and mind, hearts pounding in a single hard beat.

Together.

EIGHTEEN

Giada lay with Logan's broad, warm body curled around her, listening to the strong, slowing beat of his heart. Both brawny arms looped around her, cuddling her close. And it felt . . .

Good. Really, really good.

He drifted off to sleep, his active, questing mind falling into misty drowsiness as the sun approached the horizon. Giada knew when it rose because he went out like a birthday candle blown by an eager child.

This Truebond was . . . amazing. Really, there was no other word for it. To be united with a man like Logan, no longer completely alone as every human being ultimately is within his own skull. Able to hear his every thought, feel his sensations, share his dreams and his hopes.

As he could feel hers.

What would he think of her when he woke up at sunset, and they began to explore this new connection?

It wouldn't take him long to realize she was hopelessly in love with him. She wouldn't be able to hide it, as she'd hidden her feelings in the erotic storm they'd just enjoyed. He was a smart man; he'd know.

And then what?

Giada frowned into the darkness, imagining what he'd think when he perceived the depth of her crazy love—when he didn't feel the same way. As she was sure he didn't.

Oh, he desired her—that much was plain from the erotic hunger she could sense through the Truebond. But love? Love the way she felt it for him?

No way.

She had good reason to love him, after all. He was Logan MacRoy, son of King Arthur, chemist, cop, and vampire. A man who disarmed bombs because somebody had to do it.

And she was . . . well, Giada Shepherd. She had a doctorate in organic chemistry, and yes, she was a Maja so she could do some really cool magic. And true, mirrors didn't exactly break when she walked by. But let's face it—Logan was far above her on the Hotness Scale.

Giada winced. Boy, it sounded juvenile when she put it like that. But juvenile or not, there was an element of truth to it.

She didn't want him to know how much she loved him. Not yet. Not until he'd learned to love her.

At least a little.

Smoke purred like an outboard motor as Heather Jones absently stroked his fur, her nose in a Stephanie Meyer novel. Groaning and hooting by turns, her brother sat on the floor, furiously manipulating his Xbox 360's controllers with agile thumbs. On the den's enormous flat screen, his elf alter ego attacked an army of orcs with a flaming sword, whooping battle cries as he fought.

Despite his lazy pose on Heather's stomach, Smoke was just as busy as the boy. Earlier, he'd walked a warding spell around the Jones family's sprawling Dutch Colonial Revival, three stories of creamy yellow siding, dark brown shutters, and brown gambrel roof. The spell probably couldn't keep the Dire Wolves out—they seemed to ignore all magic but

their own—but it would warn Smoke if they tried to mount an attack.

Since the children's parents had gone to Mark Davis's receiving of friends, it was up to him to keep the kids safe. And he was determined to do just that.

Luckily, Heather was a sucker for big blue eyes and soft fur. All he'd had to do was show up outside the house this morning and meow. She'd seen him, decided from his lack of a collar and tags that he was homeless, and begged her mother to let her adopt him. Mrs. Jones was now running a "cat found" ad in the paper—which, of course, would get no response.

Smoke planned to be gone before she decided to take him to the vet and have him fixed. That just wouldn't do *at all*.

Shuttering his eyes, he concentrated on looking lazy. It wasn't difficult; everything about the house was comfortable, with pale green walls accented in cream, lots of colorful throw pillows and rag rugs, and a jungle's worth of houseplants. The den furniture was wicker, with thick, bright green cushions.

Just as he was fighting off dropping into a doze, Andy's elf zigged when he should have zagged, got sliced by an orcan axe, and gave such a realistic death shriek that Smoke jerked in alarm. "Dammit!" Andy yelled.

"Language," Heather said, without looking up from her book.

"Bite me!" her brother growled back.

She snorted. "Not in a million years."

Smoke was just settling down again when a sensation of menace slid over him, raising every hair on his back into a bristle of alarm.

Power. Evil. Magic so powerful and malevolent, he hadn't felt the like since the Dark Ones murdered his Sidhe tribe to feed their vile appetites.

Godling, a voice growled in his mind, deep and chilling, *I come for you.*

What in the name of all the gods and demons was *that*? Ice slid over his heart as he bolted to his feet.

"Hey, watch the claws," Heather said, frowning over her book at him. Smoke realized he'd unconsciously dug into her jeans-clad thigh. He jumped down, landing with a thump on the beige carpeted floor as his heartbeat broke into a thundering gallop of pure panic.

That thing will kill these children. Smoke would be a target, too, of course, but whatever-it-was would definitely go after the children.

Creatures like this always did.

Bodies lay strewn across the village—women, children, old men, hacked, burned, half-eaten among the piles of ash and stone that had once been huts. He'd stumbled across the smoking, stinking mud, staring in horror at what was left of his tribe. Too late, he realized the Dark Ones who'd ambushed him in the forest had been a diversion. The real target had been those he loved.

His people. The descendants who'd trusted him.

Self-hate rolled over him like a wave of lava, searing him with the burning weight of his guilt. They'd given him their love, sung songs in his worship, chosen their most beautiful maids to lie with him in hopes of a demigod's sons.

And he had failed them when they'd needed him most.

They'd died in agony, victims of creatures who'd devoured their suffering with greedy enjoyment.

Smoke shook himself hard in an effort to banish the psychic scar of his darkest memory. His fur floated in the air with the violence of the movement, but it didn't help.

Once again something else was coming to kill innocents under his protection. These two pretty children would end up lying in their own blood, eyes empty and staring while he suffered the memory of their deaths all the rest of his immortal, pointless life.

No. Gods and devils, not this time. This time he would not fail. He would die if that's what it took, but these children would live.

Smoke drove his mind into the core of the Mageverse

where his purest power lay coiled and waiting. Power he'd walled away all those centuries ago.

Now he tore that wall down with a single fierce thrust of will. The magic came shrieking back, a cyclone whirl of energy that shredded his cat guise like rice paper in a gale.

It *burned*. The pain blazed mercilessly along every neuron and cell, until his brain seemed to ignite like a bonfire in his skull.

Andy and Heather screamed, high, startled shrieks that barely rose over the thunderclap sonic boom of his transformation. In that moment, he went from seven-pound house cat to his true guise—a tall, broadly built Sidhe warrior, clad in enchanted plate armor, a battle-axe in one hand. The only sign of the cat he'd been was the V-shaped silver stripes running through his long black hair.

For half a beat, the children just blinked at him. "What . . . Where did you . . . ?" Heather stammered, rolling off the couch and backing away.

Smart child.

"You have pointed ears!" Andy blurted.

"There's no time for that." He cast a spell, quick and ruthless, ensuring he'd get neither argument nor questions from his charges until they were safely elsewhere. "Come."

Drawing again on his power, he prepared to cast a gate to Avalon. Once there, they'd . . .

It was like punching his fist into a wall of solid steel. The energy of his gate slammed into a force barrier that bounced it back on him. He barely managed to dissolve the spell in time to keep from being incinerated by his own creation.

You go nowhere, godling. The voice hissed in his mind like a nest of snakes, its writhing mental touch making him recoil.

Smoke snarled a curse in a language that hadn't been spoken in millennia. Grabbing Heather's upper arm in one hand, he gave Andy a light push down the hall. "We've got to get out of here. Quickly. Get to the garage."

Firmly under his spell, neither child questioned him

as he hustled them along. The skin between his shoulder blades tightened and itched in warning dread with every step they took.

The sense of menace became a sickening presence. Claws scraped on the wooden floor.

Smoke jerked around.

The creature that had gated in behind them was nearly nine feet tall, with fur as thick and white as a polar bear's. His eyes glowed orange, and his muzzle was wolfish, a match for the erect ears and bushy tail. A fluffy mane flared around his head to run down his chest all the way to his sex. Gold glinted against pale fur: a medallion engraved with intricate runes that matched the wide rings on each clawed finger.

Magic boiled around the creature like a hurricane front, a seething, glowing cloud, flavored with malevolence.

This had to be Warlock, the sorcerer werewolf Guinevere had warned him about in her psychic message.

The Dire Wolf smiled, thin black lips framing very white teeth. "There you are."

Heather screamed, the sound piercing with an instinctive terror even Smoke's calming spell couldn't suppress.

"Get the car and get out," Smoke told the children, giving them a shove down the hall. "Run."

As they sprinted away, he faced the werewolf, lifted his war axe, and prepared to buy the children time to escape.

"I have dreamed of finding something like you," Warlock said, moving closer with an odd, stalking grace, studying him with pleased interest. "I can pull a great deal of power from my clans, of course, but you—the power I'll get from you would increase that by an order of . . ."

Smoke didn't let him finish, lunging to swing the axe in a hard diagonal arc. The blade struck some kind of magical shield and bounced away, the pain of the abortive strike jarring his arm to the elbow.

He didn't pause, rotating the axe's three-foot-long shaft in both hands as if it were a quarterstaff. Mentally, Smoke

cursed. The walls of the hall were too damned close together to swing the axe properly.

Luckily, he had thousands of years of combat experience, and he knew how to compensate for the problem. Sending a spell shimmering down the handle, he swung the axe with all his strength. The enchanted weapon passed through Sheetrock and studs like a ghost, going solid as it shot at the Dire Wolf's grinning muzzle. The sorcerer's magical shield flared gold . . . and the axe slid through it, too, solidifying the instant before it . . .

Warlock jerked his head back as the blade flashed past, missing his nose by a cat's whisker. Smoke spun to add to the axe's momentum, roaring a battle cry as he aimed for the beast's chest. Again the Dire Wolf danced away at the last possible instant.

And in the kitchen down the hall, the children screamed. And something laughed, a rumbling evil chuckle.

Smoke whirled to throw himself into a plunging run down the hall.

He had to get to the children.

"Where are you going?" Warlock called, outraged. "You're fighting *me*. The humans are not your concern!" The floor shook as the creature pounded after him, footsteps like thunder rolling under the children's shrieks.

NINETEEN

Heather screamed again over the bang of a screen door. Smoke shot through the kitchen entry, jumped across an overturned chair, raced to the other side of the room, and hit the screen door so hard it flew off its hinges. The splintered door banged into the garage wall and tumbled into his path again. He fended it off with a forearm and ran past the Joneses' white Saturn into the moonlit front yard.

The bastards had backed a dark blue van into the curving paved driveway, parking at an angle so the bulk of the vehicle hid their actions from curious neighbors.

Heather hung limp and unconscious over the brawny shoulder of a female werewolf, while a male with black fur handed Andy up to a mortal human crouched in the van's open rear door. Yelling, the boy struggled hard, legs kicking, fists swinging. The man cursed and backhanded him, a single vicious slap. Andy clutched his head and started crying, gulping sobs of pain and fear.

Smoke snarled, conjured a knife as he ran, and threw it with a hard, skillful flick of his wrist. It thunked into the human kidnapper's shoulder, and the man fell back, yelping in pain and clawing at the weapon.

The female Dire Wolf whirled toward Smoke, her eyes going wide in her red-furred face. She grabbed Heather's jaw in a clawed hand that engulfed the teen's entire head. "Back off, or I'll break this little bitch's neck."

He conjured another blade, preparing to launch it with an extra kick of magic to give it greater speed. The Direkind might be resistant to magical blast attacks, but steel was steel. And one could still use a spell to add kinetic energy to any weapon.

But in the instant before he launched the knife, he sensed a blast boiling toward him. Smoke ducked, but the powerful bolt caught his shoulder, spinning him off his feet and into the air. Even as he tumbled, he curled his body, trying to roll with the bolt—only to slam into a bubble of energy that sucked him in with a pop. The bubble instantly clamped down on him like a vise. Pain tore a gritted curse from his compressing lungs.

Growling in fury, Smoke tried to blast free from his prison, but the globe only drank his magic down and tightened still more. His ribs creaked from the vicious pressure until he couldn't draw breath to scream.

"Ah, better. Much better," the white Dire Wolf said in his deep, oily voice. "Let me attend to the hostages, and then we can get down to business."

Andy Jones stared in numb fear at the elf man, who writhed five feet off the ground, his darkening face contorted in pain. Without even glancing at him, the giant white werewolf strolled over to the van, big head tilted in casual interest. He looked like something out of one of Andy's video games, walking on legs curved like a dog's, a big white monster with orange eyes and a whole lot of teeth.

Andy froze, not even daring to breathe. They'd cuffed his hands behind his back, and he felt sick and helpless.

"Take your hostages and go," the white werewolf told his captors. "I will be busy with the godling for quite some time."

"As you wish." The black monster ducked his head in a kind of bow.

The white one turned and walked back to the elf, moving quickly on his big paws, like he couldn't wait to do whatever horrible thing he had planned.

The wolfgirl handed Heather up to the black werewolf. He flopped her over one furry knee to handcuff her wrists behind her back.

"I'm bleeding!" the regular guy whined, clutching the knife buried in his shoulder. "I need to go to the emergency room!"

"Shut up," the black werewolf snapped without looking around. He added to the wolfgirl, "Change back and drive."

"To the target?"

"Not yet. We need time to prepare. Just find someplace to park out of sight."

She nodded and closed the van door. A minute later, the engine started and the van lurched, backing up. It got really dark and quiet, except for the guy making kind of sobbing sounds of pain as he breathed.

The monster's breath gusted against Andy's arm, smelling like blood and raw meat. Andy did not want to imagine why. He'd probably start screaming again, and he had the feeling he needed to be really quiet.

The van stopped and accelerated forward. Andy braced his shoulder against the metal wall behind him and huddled on the carpeted floor next to his unconscious sister. His bruised face ached, and the handcuffs hurt. He wanted his mother.

Had the white werewolf killed the elf?

The regular guy spoke from the bench seat against the opposite wall. "If you think I'm gonna be able to rig the devices with my shoulder like this, you're nuts."

"You'll find you can do whatever I tell you to do," the werewolf said. "Because you won't like the consequences if you don't."

Devices? What kind of devices?

He didn't dare ask.

* * *

Smoke's ribs ached as he struggled to suck in a breath against the crushing weight of the Dire Wolf's magic.

"They say you were a god once." Blazing orange eyes regarded him through the energy globe. "You certainly have a lot of power." Black lips stretched into a grin. "At least, for the moment. I'm going to take it all away."

Sheer rage helped him draw a breath. "Fuck . . . you."

Warlock laughed. "Have a little dignity. That is no way for a god to talk."

Smoke could only snarl in reply. *I must get out of this thing. Gods knows what those furry bastards are doing to the children.*

As desperation clawed at him, he scanned the trap that held him, seeking some flaw he could use to break the thing open and escape. Unfortunately, the globe was as smooth and featureless as a titanium egg. And every bit as strong.

So maybe he could *create* a weakness. Smoke picked a spot on the field between his feet and stared at it, concentrating fiercely as he focused his magic into a white-hot beam, bright and fierce as a laser. Then he shot that beam of a spell straight down into the globe's bottom.

Which promptly sucked it up like a sponge.

Smoke curled his lip and kept trying, drawing more power, then still more, bearing down to force the spell into the tightest point he could manage.

"Oh, yes," Warlock purred. "Give me more, godling."

Smoke jerked his head up to meet the creature's orange eyes. Eyes that glowed brighter as the spell burned hotter.

Gods and demons, the globe is feeding him my power. Cursing silently, Smoke shut down his spell.

"Don't stop," the Dire Wolf said. "I still hunger."

Smoke called him a few choice words, rolling syllables of rage in a language that hadn't been spoken in millennia.

"I have no idea what you just said, but somehow I suspect it wasn't very nice." His grin mocking, the monster walked up to the globe as Smoke glared at him. "Never mind. I'll be

able to translate it myself once I have finished draining you."
The werewolf slid his ringed fingers into the globe as the
medallion around his neck began to glow. So did the rings.

Ice rolled across Smoke's skin, growing steadily colder
as the medallion glowed brighter. He could feel the boiling magic within him growing weaker as the globe drained
it away.

"Oh," Warlock purred, orange eyes shuttering in orgas-
mic pleasure, "that *is* nice."

The line of mourners snaked through the somber red-
carpeted halls of the Gayle Funeral Home. As the sheriff had predicted, hundreds of people had turned out for
Mark Davis's receiving, most of them cops from Greendale
County and its surrounding jurisdictions.

They were a quiet group, as might be expected, all too
conscious that going down in the line of duty could happen
to any of them without any warning at all. The fact that yet
another cop had fallen the day before—evidently a grue-
some victim of her own K-9 partner—only added to the
grim mood.

Logan, standing beside Giada in line, was conscious
of being surrounded by uniforms and badges with black
mourning bands stretched across them. A couple of days
ago, he would have felt like a member of the family in the
dress uniform he'd donned as a gesture of respect.

Now he felt like an interloper. He wasn't one of them
anymore.

He was a Magus, a vampire. One of Arthur Pendragon's
warriors. There was pride in that thought, but there was also
a certain quiet ache at leaving the law enforcement brother-
hood behind.

Yet painful or not, it was his duty. After they'd paid their
respects to Mark's widow, he and Giada would meet the
others to continue the search for Warlock and his rogues.
Logan had no doubt they'd find them, if not tonight, then
tomorrow.

There wasn't much Arthur Pendragon and his warriors couldn't handle. A werewolf sorcerer was just more of the same.

If only he was so certain of his skills when it came to more personal relationships. Logan slanted a look at Giada, standing slim and elegant at his side. The tailored black slacks and jacket she wore over that white silk blouse would have made most women look severe. Yet somehow the stern clothing only emphasized Giada's delicate femininity.

She really was one of the most beautiful women he'd ever met. Yet though he could feel her in his mind, a humming female presence, he sensed she was holding him at a distance. And he didn't know why.

Logan frowned, studying her cool profile under the tight gold twist of her hair. His mother had told him it could be difficult getting used to being Truebonded. Having someone else inside your head was not the usual human state of being.

The process would probably be even more challenging if you'd Truebonded as a survival strategy rather than a matter of love.

Had he made a mistake, asking Giada for a mental link so early?

Logan shook the question off. They'd done it, and now they were going to have to learn to manage their new psychic link, much as he was learning to manage his vampire abilities. They'd figure out a way to make it work, just as his parents had.

And God knew Arthur and Gwen had gotten through a bumpy patch far worse than this. His mother had basically forced the Truebond on his father by seducing Lancelot. Enraged by the one-night stand, Arthur had demanded a Truebond so she'd be unable to cheat on him again.

He hadn't been pleased to discover that was exactly what Gwen had intended all along. Thanks to the Truebond, Arthur had forgiven her for manipulating him—it was hard to stay furious at someone when they were part of you. Even so, he'd only recently forgiven Lance.

Logan found it hard to believe his mother had done

something like that to begin with; it seemed utterly out of character. But then again, it had been fifteen hundred years ago; she'd been only twenty.

Anyway, if Arthur and Gwen could get through something that serious, this . . . distance should be nothing more than an emotional speed bump.

Surely.

Heartened, he reached out to Giada, trying to brush her thoughts with his. Once again, she fended him off. He felt a stab of pain, sharp as a dagger's point in his chest.

Andy clutched his sister's hand, his head aching in a savage, rhythmic throbbing. The werewolf had hit him when he'd taken another swing at Regular Guy. He'd known he couldn't win, but he couldn't just give in. Not to what the bastards had in mind.

By the time he woke up, they were no longer handcuffed, and the guy—the *fucker*—was done with his preparations.

Head down, Andy stared at his sister's arm as they held hands. Her wrist was circled by a huge bruise that looked like the prints of the werewolf's fingers. She must have fought them, too.

Andy discovered he was proud of her.

"It's going to be okay," she whispered to him. Her voice sounded funny. Kind of raw, as if she'd been screaming. "Grandpa will save us."

"I know," Andy lied.

How would it feel to die? Would it hurt, or would it be so fast he wouldn't feel anything? He hoped it was fast.

Would he go to heaven?

Maybe he shouldn't have called Regular Guy a fucker. Except RG *was* a fucker. Anybody who would do something like this to two kids he didn't even know was definitely a fucker.

"I've lost a lot of blood," RG said. He was whining again. Dumbass. The werewolf was going to black his other eye. Served him right. "I did what you said. All you have to do

is arm the devices, and you've got a remote for that. Can I go now?"

The werewolf looked around. He'd gone to the front of the van to talk to the wolfgirl, who sat in the driver's seat. She'd turned into a regular human. Probably because the cops would have pulled them over if she'd still looked like a monster.

Driving while werewolf? Andy snickered.

"You have done well, human." But there was something in the werewolf's voice, something that made the hair stand up on the back of Andy's neck. "We've decided to reward you."

Oh, crap. Something bad was about to . . .

One minute the werewolf was leaning over the front seat of the van. The next, he was all the way in the back, on top of RG.

Who started screaming like a little girl.

Blood splattered across Andy's face, and it was all he could do not to scream himself. RG flailed at the monster, and more blood flew. Then the werewolf straightened and stalked away, leaving the guy lying on the floor in a bloody heap.

"You bit me!" Huddled on the bench seat, RG stared at the wolf accusingly. "Why did you bite me?"

"Because you're a fucker?" Andy muttered.

Heather snickered, then gave him a scandalized look.

"Oh, like you weren't thinking it," he whispered.

"I bit you," the werewolf said, ignoring them as he dropped into the seat behind the driver, "so you'll become one of us."

"If he doesn't die," Wolfgirl said. She was sitting turned sideways in the driver's seat. To RG, she added, "You have a twenty-percent chance of burning up in the transition."

"Odds are you'll survive, though." The werewolf licked the blood off his teeth. "And then you'll have more power than you've ever dreamed of."

RG's eyes took on a glitter Andy didn't particularly like. "So the next full moon . . ."

"Full moon, my bushy red tail." Wolfgirl snorted. "You'll change sometime in the next hour. The moon's got nothing to do with it. That's just a myth."

RG's eyes widened. "In the next *hour*?"

Andy and his sister exchanged a sick look. RG a werewolf? Every time Andy thought this couldn't get worse . . .

It did.

Pain clawed at Smoke, raking psychic furrows in his mind, ripping into memory, shredding his magic.

Eating his soul.

He'd battered the globe, first with spells, then with his fists and feet, trying to break through, to get the hell out before there was nothing left of him.

Nothing worked.

"Arhhhhh!" Warlock jerked his ringed fingers free of the globe and jumped back, shaking his hands as if he'd been burned. "Merlin's balls, you have as much power as the legends say."

Smoke managed to lift his head and snarl.

His thoughts crept like molasses through the universe of pain he inhabited. Pain in his skull, in his bones, in muscle and flesh, so great he shook with it in constant, rolling tremors.

The wolf regarded him through the globe, frowning. "This is taking too long. I'm going to miss the fun at the funeral home if I don't speed it up." Thin black lips rolled off shining fangs. "I want to watch the Celt's brat die."

He began to pace around the globe, staring at Smoke with coldly speculative orange eyes. Smoke stared back, panting in a combination of exhaustion, pain, and rage.

There had to be some way to beat the bastard, some weakness he could use. Something. Otherwise Logan, Giada, and the children had no chance at all.

As he glowered, the werewolf gave his hands another absent shake.

And in a flash of inspiration, Smoke realized how he could escape the monster's trap.

But the price—Gods and devils, the price would be high . . . It might be better to die. But no, dead he was no

good to those who needed him. Alive, there was still a chance to get back what had been stolen.

And make the bastard pay.

The widow looked like a Katrina survivor, as if she'd seen her entire world washed away and was wading chest-deep in the filthy remains. Lori Davis's brown eyes were swollen pits of dazed suffering that defeated the makeup she'd so painstakingly applied. She wore a simple black dress and a string of pearls, and she leaned on the stool someone had brought her, half sitting, half standing. The sheriff stood protectively behind her, his expression grim, looking as if he'd been aged ten years by the weight of sheer guilt.

When Logan and Giada stepped up, Lori's tired eyes brightened, and she managed a smile, though her lips trembled. "Lieutenant MacRoy—I'm glad you could make it."

Logan shook her extended hand, his smile warm and kind, despite the pain Giada could feel reverberating through the Truebond. "I wouldn't have missed it. Mark was a hell of a cop, a great bomb tech, and a good friend."

"He thought a lot of you, too. He told me there was nobody he'd rather go through a door with."

This was high cop praise, Giada knew. It meant you knew the other officer had your back, regardless of the danger.

Logan drew in a breath as his smile faltered, and Giada winced at the stab of guilt and grief in his mind. "I'm . . . so sorry. More than I can say. If there's anything you and Tara need—anything at all—just let me know."

She gave him a sad, tired smile. "Thank you, Lieutenant." She thought his offer was rote, but Giada knew otherwise. The department had started a fund for Lori and her daughter; Logan had put fifty thousand dollars in it, funds from investments and savings, plus the nest egg his parents had given him when he went out on his own. An anonymous donation Lori probably wasn't even aware of yet. Knowing Logan, he'd probably add to it as soon as he could.

Giada murmured her own sympathies, even as the

momentary animation drained from Lori's features, leaving her eyes dull with grief.

The line carried them onward after that, toward the casket covered in roses and star lilies and great puffs of baby's breath. Mounds of floral arrangements surrounded the gleaming oak box, in baskets or vases filled with flowers Giada didn't even know the name of.

Normally at events like this, the casket was left open so the mourners could view the deceased. Not this time.

There wasn't enough of him to view.

Giada could feel Logan's rage grow as they stared at the casket, a fury so intense, his hands started to shake. *I'm going to kill those bastards.*

I'll help, Giada thought back.

He shot her a faint smile and rested a hand on the small of her back as they started to turn away.

Their attention fell on a uniformed deputy winding his way toward the sheriff. Heather and Andy followed him, both dressed oddly in Windbreakers zipped all the way up. The jackets hung on their bodies, as though somebody had put them in coats intended for adults.

Giada stiffened. Both children's faces were bruised, blood trailing from Andy's nose and Heather's split lip. "What the hell!" the sheriff said, alarmed. "What happened?"

The deputy leaned over to whisper in his ear. His eyes widened, and he went pale as he jerked as if someone had Tased him as he stared at his grandchildren in horror. "Evacuate the building." Sheriff Jones's voice rang with command, sure, steady, though Giada could sense his fear. "MacRoy, you're with me. Where's Billings?"

"Probably standing in line. I'll get him." Logan pulled his department-issued cell off his belt and called the last surviving member of the bomb squad. Meanwhile, a flurry of voices rose around them as the deputies began herding the civilians out of the room.

"What?" Lori asked in bewilderment as the sheriff gently urged her to her feet and handed her off to a deputy. "What's happening? *What about Mark?*" That last was a wail.

Giada and Logan exchanged a single tense look. They'd be lucky if Mark was the only one in a closed casket when this was over.

Smoke glared through the wall of his magical prison. His captor smirked at him before stepping closer.

That's right, you bastard, Smoke thought. *Come on. Let's finish it.*

"Such eyes . . ." The Dire Wolf laughed, but if he was going for confidence, he didn't entirely succeed. "You look as if you'd love nothing better than to rip me open."

Smoke smiled with bared teeth. "I like to eat the heart first."

Warlock jolted, then recovered enough to snarl. "We will see who eats what, *pussy*." He plunged his ringed hands into the globe and sent his power rolling.

Just as Smoke had intended.

The pain was vicious, clawing, but he ignored it. It was going to get worse. Besides, he damned well wasn't going to let it stop him, so it was irrelevant. He hadn't lived this long without learning to deal with a little pain.

Or even a lot of pain.

He knew he had to act fast before Warlock realized what he was doing. Reaching down deep into his spirit, Smoke did something he hadn't done in centuries: allowed the whole of his immortal life to flood his mind. All of it, all the crushing weight of millennia, of thousands of years of grief and pain and power. The failures and the triumphs, the loves and the hates.

Everything.

And then he drove it right into Warlock's siphoning spell.

The Dire Wolf was pulling hard, sucking like a thirsty leech, expecting him to fight the draining of his mind and powers.

He obviously did not expect Smoke to shove the lot of it right down his throat.

Millennia of magic and memory hit the werewolf in a

thundering cataract that tumbled him off his feet. In that instant, he lost his mental hold on the spell that held Smoke captive. Deprived of Warlock's magic, it popped like a soap bubble.

Smoke hit the ground hard enough to rattle every tooth in his head. He rolled to his feet with one thought blazing in his mind. *Run!* He had to get as far away as he could before Warlock had time to recover his senses.

He'd had to give the Dire Wolf the full package—all the power, all the memories. Otherwise, the fucker would simply have taken it all anyway and killed him, and he would have had no chance to help those he loved.

And he couldn't—*wouldn't*—fail them again.

So Smoke ran, bare feet flying over the grass, armor and clothing having vanished with his sacrificed powers, knowing only that he had to get away.

He raced for the woods by pure instinct. There was safety in the darkness deep beneath the trees. But with every step he took, his memories grew fainter. As if he was leaving them behind.

In Warlock's skull.

Warlock was fifteen hundred years old, and he'd thought he understood how much centuries weighed. But the weight of the demigod's memories was immeasurably more.

And the bastard's power *burned*.

Worse, emotions Warlock had never felt raged in his mind—guilt, love, loss. He, who had always existed in a clean bubble of pure purpose, suddenly felt the weight of the emotions mortals spoke of.

He'd always felt such contempt for mortal weakness. He'd had no idea.

Sick, aching, Warlock rolled onto his belly, fighting the poison that damned demigod had infected him with.

Vulnerable. *He was vulnerable. Anyone* could kill him now. Even that damned Smoke, stripped of his powers and memories as the demigod was.

Warlock knew he had to return to his sanctum. Heal himself in the belly of his magic and get control of these alien powers. It would mean he could play no part in helping George Devon and his daughter kill the Celt's son, but that was a minor concern at best. If they died, he would simply recruit new followers. His survival was all-important.

He was, after all, Merlin's Heir.

The sheriff blocked Giada's path as she started to follow Logan and the children into the room across the hall. "You need to evacuate, Ms. Shepherd. You've risked your butt enough for a training placement."

She met his gaze and cast a quick spell. "I can help keep the children calm, Sheriff."

His face relaxed as the spell took hold. "I'd appreciate that. The kids are pretty scared."

"And I'm sure their parents are, too. Why don't you go out with the others and help keep them calm? We've got everything under control. The children will be fine."

A smile of pure relief spread over the sheriff's face as her magic gave him complete confidence in the bomb team. "I'll just go take care of Jeff and Amy. They're probably out of their heads with worry."

He turned and strode off, determination in every step.

Watching him go, Giada blew out a breath. She just hoped the bombs would yield to her magic half that well.

Opening the door, she slipped inside the room.

It was the kind of sitting room designed to give mourners a place to chat, with two hunter green couches against the opposite wall and a pair of straight-backed chairs in the corners. Heavy gold curtains draped the two windows.

Heather and Andy stood in the middle of the room. Logan and Lieutenant Billings had unzipped the kids' engulfing jackets. Now, crouched in front of the two children, both men wore sick expressions. "Oh, fuuu . . ." Tom glanced at Andy and bit the curse off.

"What have we got?" Giada crossed the room to join

them. Tom frowned at her and opened his mouth to throw her out. She shot him a look and a spell. *"I can help."*

He closed his mouth, looking confused. He was evidently a little more magic-resistant than the sheriff, but not, thank God, by much.

Logan glanced up at her, his expression grim. Getting a good look at the bombs, she knew why.

The kids wore thick black vests punched with holes. The right front of each featured a bulging pocket painted with some kind of runes she'd never seen before. A square of fabric was cut away from each vest, revealing an LED timer ticking down the minutes. Both timers read 36:03:02, with fractions of a second ticking away in a blur of red.

Thirty-six minutes. Holy God, they only have thirty-six minutes.

A second pocket lay between the kids' shoulder blades, holding something the approximate size and shape of a brick. Both children were wrapped with loops of black wire that crossed and re-crossed, dipping in and out of the pockets.

"What the hell is this?" Giada demanded in horror.

"Every bomb tech's worst nightmare," Tom told her grimly as he crouched to dig through a duffel of bomb disposal tools. He must have had the gear in his car. "We can't use any of the usual techniques we'd use with an in situ bomb. No bomb suit because we need all the fine motor control we can get. And we can't disrupt them with a water shot because we'd blow holes in the kids."

"The bomb guy told us if we fall down or try to run, they'll blow up," Andy said. His hazel eyes looked dazed and shocky, and his voice sounded dull, as if he'd given up hope. "If you try to take them off us, they'll blow up. If we get too far apart, they'll blow up. If you disable one bomb, the other one will blow up. And if one bomb goes, the other will, too." His voice dropped into a defeated mutter. "I think we're just gonna blow up."

TWENTY

Logan laid a comforting hand on the boy's shoulder. "We're not going to let you blow up, Andy."

"You know what I don't get?" Tom stared grimly at the bulging back of the child's vest. "Two pounds of C4 on each kid. Where the hell did the bastard get that much military-grade explosive?"

"Somebody's got a lot of nasty connections." Giada scrubbed her fingers over her temples. She was getting a bitch of a headache.

"And a very nasty imagination. He's put at least three detonators on these things." Logan shot her a look she didn't need the Truebond to understand. *Disable these fucking things so we can get them off these kids.*

Giada took a deep breath and called her magic, sending the spell into Heather's vest.

It felt as though she'd grabbed a live electrical wire. She yelped in pained surprise and dropped the spell.

What? Logan demanded through the Truebond.

Don't know. Cautiously, Giada tried again, sending a thinner tendril of power to investigate.

The runes written on the vest pouches were apparently

some kind of spell she'd never encountered before, thus the shock. What's worse, they blocked her magic from reaching the contents of the pouches.

We need more witches. Closing her eyes, she sent a communication spell to Guinevere. But the message hit a crackling wall of energy and fizzled out before it could punch through into the alternate universe. *What the—Logan, I think the vests are producing a jamming spell.*

Shit. Should I try the cell Mom gave me?

Worth a try.

He flipped it open and murmured into it. The resulting feedback squeal made even Tom jump.

Fuck. At least the Truebond is still working. Disgusted, he slid the phone back onto its clip on his belt.

We're close enough to be inside the radius of the jamming spell. The spell couldn't block all magic, because it would block itself.

Bastards are playing with us, Giada said grimly.

They've been doing that from the beginning. They don't just want to kill me—they want to make me suffer by terrorizing these kids. He clenched a fist in rage.

Heather had been watching Giada's face as she worked. Apparently something she'd seen made her decide to take a chance. "Dr. Shepherd?"

She looked up, met the girl's one good eye; the other was swollen shut. "Yes, Heather?"

"This is gonna sound crazy, but it's true, I swear." She glanced at Tom and Logan, then leaned closer. "There are . . . things in the building. Hiding." She swallowed. "Dogs. Or something."

The kid's expression was so conflicted, it was obvious she'd wanted to say something she'd considered far more unbelievable. "Dogs?" Giada said softly. "Or wolves?"

The girl nodded.

"Werewolves?" She murmured it in a voice too low for Tom to hear.

The kid nodded. "I know it sounds crazy, but I swear . . ."

"How many?"

"Two," Andy said. "And maybe another one. They bit a guy. He's supposed to . . . um. Change. Into one of them."

Tom frowned at the boy. "What are you *talking* about?"

"Later, Tom," Giada interrupted. She put out a hand and touched Heather's swollen face with gentle fingers. "Now, listen to me, sweetheart. Everything's going to be fine. You don't have anything to worry about."

For a moment, disbelief flashed over Heather's face. Then her pupils dilated and her lips parted in a sigh.

Giada looked up at Logan and nodded. "You can do what you have to now. She'll be calm for you."

Turning toward Andy, she dropped a hand on the little boy's shoulder and let the spell drift over his mind. The child blinked once, slowly, and went still, his eyes slipping out of focus.

Tom's brows flew up. "What did you do?"

"I studied applied hypnotism for hostage situations," Giada lied glibly. "I got to be pretty good at it."

"Oh." The lieutenant blinked. "That's handy."

Giada and Logan exchanged another look. *I'd better go look for those werewolves.*

Fear chilled Logan's mind like a wave of ice Giada could feel as if it were her own. *I really don't think that's a good idea. Those things are resistant to magic. How the hell can you fight something your magic can't affect?*

I have no intention of throwing around spell blasts. There's more than one way to use magic in a fight.

He saw what she intended, and his alarm faded slightly. *I'd still rather you waited for me. You'll be outnumbered.*

Yeah, but I don't think we've got much choice. If I don't distract the Dire Wolves, one of the furry creeps may detonate these bombs before you finish disabling them.

He muttered a curse under his breath as he examined her logic. Finally he sighed in defeat. *Point taken. Just . . . be careful. Please.*

She gave him a smile. *It'll be fine.*

Logan snorted. *Save it for the mortals.*

Giada opened the door and started to step outside.

"Where are you going?" Tom demanded.

She looked back at him, frowning. Better take care of him before she left. "Don't worry about it. Just ignore anything you hear and concentrate on saving the kids." A thought struck her, and she met his gaze, adding another jolt of power. "And do whatever Logan tells you to do."

The spell did its work, and he instantly lost interest in her. Turning to Logan, he said, "So what the fuck are we dealing with here?"

"From what the kids said, I figure radio transmitters to tell one bomb if we disable the other. Probably motion sensors and a dissolving switch, too . . ."

Giada slipped through the door and closed it behind her.

The hallway was deserted and eerily quiet—apparently the sheriff had succeeded in evacuating the building.

Except for the werewolves.

And where the hell were *they*? Her gut coiled another fraction tighter, and she rubbed her stomach anxiously. What if she fought the wolves and lost?

Worse, what if Logan and Billings couldn't disable the bombs? They'd all die, including Giada. The shock of the severed Truebond would kill her on the spot. Which was probably just as well, because without Logan, her life would be . . .

Giada? Logan said in the bond. *Wait. Let us take care of these damned bombs, and then you and I can hunt the Dire Wolves.*

She straightened her shoulders with a jerk. *No. Too risky. The wolves are a complication we don't need right now.*

But . . .

Giada clamped down on the Truebond, blocking him out—and, hopefully, keeping him from sensing her fear any longer. Fear that might distract him when he could least afford distraction.

She really wasn't up to this, a voice gibbered in her mind. Fighting werewolves? She was going to end up like that Maja who'd gotten her throat ripped open at Sam's house . . .

Shut up, Giada told herself savagely. *Quit being such a relentless pussy. Logan's depending on you. Those kids are depending on you.*

And she was damned if she'd fail them.

Reaching for her power, Giada let magic roll across her body, flashing like a swarm of fireflies. Armor appeared in a gleaming steel wave—breastplate and greaves and pauldrons, gauntlets and mail and helmet.

And finally, the sword. Its hilt filled her gloved hand, four feet of steel engraved along its length with words of power. It seemed to weigh nothing at all in her hands, but when she hit a target, it would acquire the mass of a battle-axe. She'd spent so many months training with this kind of blade that both it and the armor felt a part of her. Just having them on made her a little more confident.

I can handle this. I will handle this.

She moved down the corridor on soundless feet, her armor a comforting weight on her shoulders.

Logan growled a curse. Giada had blocked her end of the Truebond so he could no longer sense her thoughts. All he got was the faint echo of her emotions—fear, determination, fury, and a nagging worry that she wasn't good enough.

None of which you can help her with right now. Get your mind back on business, or you're going to get everybody killed—including Giada.

"Logan?" Tom was staring at him, brown eyes sharp with concern. "We can't afford to waste any more time, buddy."

"I know." He looked down at the pouch he'd opened in Heather's vest. It was a deliberately confusing snarl of wiring and dummy parts, designed to keep a tech from correctly identifying the real parts of the bomb so he could disable it. If he clipped the wrong wire, he wouldn't even have time to realize he'd made a mistake before four pounds of C4 blew them all to hell.

The two children stood shoulder to shoulder so that Logan and Tom could work in concert. The only way to defeat the bombs was for the techs to do the exact same thing at the exact same time. Otherwise, if one tech disabled his device before the other did, the active bomb's radio would trigger a

blast. With the four standing so close together, none of them would have a prayer.

There were a whole lot of ways the two bombs could kill their victims. Logan wasn't interested in discovering any of them.

Luckily, he had one advantage the bomber hadn't anticipated: his vampire nose. As he examined the open pouch, he could clearly smell the bastard's scent on the tangle of wiring and parts.

Leaning closer, he ignored Tom's lifted eyebrows and gave the bomb a deeper sniff. There were definitely parts of the device that carried that scent more strongly, as if they'd been handled more. Logically, the ones the bomber had handled the most were probably the ones that blew up.

"I think this is the motion sensor," Logan said, his finger hovering over a small tube filled with mercury. A long black wire snaked away from the sensor into the rat's nest of wiring wound around Heather's body, eventually leading to the pouch on her back and the brick of C4.

The lieutenant craned his neck to look over Logan's arm. "How can you tell? There are at least four sensors in here, and three of them are probably dummies."

"I just know." He leaned down to examine Andy's pouch, quickly identified the sensor with the strongest scent, and pointed it out to Tom.

The lieutenant eyed him, brows lifted. "How in the name of little green apples can you tell?"

"Tom—trust me."

"What the hell." Sighing, Tom shook his head and lifted his wire cutters. "You've never steered me wrong before."

The two men simultaneously clipped the leads to the two sensors. And waited, tense as drawn crossbows. Heather and Andy, deep under Giada's spell, didn't so much as twitch.

Nothing happened.

Tom blew out a breath and nodded. "I think that's got it. What next?"

"Now we go after the dissolving switches . . ."

* * *

Giada eased around the corner and through a pair of double doors. The room beyond evidently served as a chapel, judging by the big gold cross that gleamed in recessed lighting on the wall. The pews were built of a dark, somber wood, with burgundy upholstery on the seats and backs. The thick carpeting was the same shade of burgundy, and the walls were painted off-white. Arched stained glass windows in abstract patterns lined the room, the colors dull because the sun was down.

She padded silently down the carpeted aisle, scanning for magic, her sword lifted warily in her hands. A spell opened a second set of double doors at the opposite end of the chapel. Giada stepped through . . .

The werewolf hit her like a bullet train, smashing her off her feet and back through the swinging doors. She hit the floor hard on her back in a hail of broken wood, the impact jarring her head in her helmet.

Amanda Devon crashed down on top of her, a crushing, snarling weight, claws raking at her armored head. A gaping mouth full of teeth opened wide and lunged for her throat.

Giada stuffed her armored left arm between the werewolf's jaws and swung her sword at the creature's brawny side. Blood flew, and Amanda twisted away with a startled yelp. The beast cleared five feet in a single leap and landed, a rumbling growl of fury peeling the lips off her teeth. "Bitch! You'll pay for that!"

"Bitch?" Giada rolled to her feet, despite the stabbing ache she suspected was a broken rib. "I'm not the one with fur and a tail—Mandy."

"Don't call me that!" The werewolf sprang at her, one long arm swinging. Before Giada could even bring up her blade, metal shrieked as claws raked across her breastplate. She backpedaled, and Amanda lunged after her, fangs snapping.

Damn, the wolf was fast—so fast Giada couldn't even get in a shot before the creature ripped at her and darted

away. When she dared a look down, blood rolled along her gauntleted arm.

"Very nice," a rumbling male voice said. "You're doing well, my dear. Show me what you're capable of."

"I'm capable of *anything*," Amanda snarled, her feral gaze locked on Giada's face. "I'm not some weakling like this one. I am Chosen."

"What you are," Giada spat, "is a hairy lunatic."

From the corner of one eye, she saw a big, lean black werewolf enter the room. Had to be George Devon, pater-familias of serial killers and furry sociopaths. The bomber limped at his heels, cradling one bloody arm. More blood covered the mortal's face, and his expression was contorted with pain. Evidently he'd been bitten.

Oh, sweet Merlin's Cup. Andy was right—they'd gone and made the psychotic bastard a werewolf.

"What the hell do you think you're doing, George?" Giada growled, knowing she was wasting her time. You couldn't reason with fanatics. "Murdering mortals, Latents, *and* Majac—putting bombs on children, for God's sake! Have you completely turned your back on Merlin?"

She didn't really expect the werewolf to answer, but his lip curled. "Arthur is the one who failed Merlin. How many millions have died because he didn't have the courage to control mortal leaders? He's permitted a reign of chaos out of sheer cowardice!"

With a roar, Amanda sprang eight feet through the air in an impossible rush. Giada jumped back and swung her sword. The Dire Wolf twisted with a cat's grace, but the blade caught one thick shoulder. Blood flew. Amanda flashed out a clawed hand as she landed, raking Giada's braced thigh. Steel curled under her claws like wood shavings as the leg erupted in pain.

Knowing she didn't dare stop, Giada jerked into a spin, whipping her blade around as fast as she could manage. The werewolf threw herself backward, somersaulting like a gymnast to avoid the strike. One clawed foot slammed into Giada's jaw with an explosion of pain. She went flying like

a bean bag to plow headfirst into the side of a pew. Barely conscious, she went down in a stunned heap.

Get the hell up, Giada! If you die, Logan dies, too!

The thought jolted her like an electric shock, and she tried to stand. But the room rotated like a merry-go-round, and she lost her balance, tumbling across the back of the pew.

Before she could try again, a huge furry hand grabbed her arm and hauled her to her feet. She glimpsed a snarling lupine face before Amanda backhanded her so hard, the helmet flew from her head.

Another vicious slap sent Giada slamming into the opposite row of pews. Even with her breastplate, she felt something snap.

The pain made her want to throw up.

"You fight far better than I expected, daughter." George sounded pleased, damn him.

"She isn't much of an opponent," Amanda said dismissively. "If you will permit me to kill MacRoy, it will give you a better demonstration of my abilities."

Giada braced both hands on the seat of the pew and pushed up with a bitter, wrenching effort. "Kiss . . ." She gasped. ". . . my armored ass . . . *Mandy*!"

Before the Dire Wolf could snarl a reply, the bomber reeled to his feet. Apparently he'd been sitting on one of the pews watching, the asshole. "Something's happening," he said, voice trembling as he shook like a plague victim. He reeled down the aisle toward them. "I feel like I'm burning everywhere."

"You're about to transform, you fool," Amanda told him contemptuously. "That, or die. The way you whine, I think I'd rather watch you cook in your own magic than listen to you."

He stared at her, sweating and wild-eyed. "But I don't *want* to die!"

"Join the crowd," Giada muttered. Her broken ribs made a nauseating grinding sound as she breathed, and the claw wounds on her thigh and forearm burned as if dipped in acid.

And she'd lost her freaking sword, dammit.

She started to scan the room for it . . .

Amanda was on her, one big fist swinging in a vicious haymaker that caught her in the jaw. Giada's skull detonated in an explosion of light and agony. She was only dimly aware of hitting the carpeted floor in an armored heap.

The pain was like nothing she'd ever felt. When she tried to scream, it felt as if she had an axe buried in her face. *She broke my jaw!*

Giada lay staring up at the ceiling, the room swinging dizzily around her. *Concussion*, she realized. *I'm done. No way I can fight like this.*

Through a haze of throbbing pain, she watched the red Dire Wolf approach to lean over her. One big hand grabbed her left arm and picked her up as if she weighed no more than a rag doll.

Giada's jaw fell open, spilling blood down her throat, and she gurgled a howl at the sharp pain.

"Pussy," Amanda sneered in her face. "Arthur will lose because his warriors are all cowards." She raised a hand, claws glittering as she braced to take Giada's head off her shoulders.

No! Logan will die, too! The thought sliced through her pain like a bucket of ice water hitting a drunk. *I can't let them kill me or Logan's a dead man.* But what the hell could she do? She met Amanda's vicious yellow gaze . . .

Before the Dire Wolf could strike, the bomber staggered into her, almost knocking them both to the ground. "Oh, God! Help me! *I'm burning!*"

He was right.

With a howl of agony, the bomber burst into a blue-white blaze of magic bright enough to light up the entire chapel. Startled, Amanda swung around toward him, still holding Giada by her left arm.

Giada reacted without thought, conjuring her missing sword into her right hand. Despite the savage pain of her broken jaw and shattered ribs, she swung the blade with every ounce of strength she had.

It hit bone and flesh with a solid *thunk*, magical inertia carrying it right through its target.

The Dire Wolf's red-furred head flew off her shoulders. Giada barely managed to keep her feet as the body fell. Grabbing her shattered jaw, she tried to hold it in place and fought to keep her feet. *Damn, I wish I had time to heal this frickin' thing.* Unfortunately, she could tell the break was too complicated. It would take more concentration than she could afford to give it.

"Amanda!" George Devon's bellow sent Giada reeling back a cautious step. He stared from Amanda's headless body to her, his yellow gaze first incredulous, then going dark with bloody rage. *"You killed my daughter, you bitch!"*

Giada glared at him and managed to gurgle, "Oh, fuck *you*, George."

Then the crazed fury in his eyes penetrated her anger, and she began backing away.

He started toward her, flexing his clawed hands.

"Hey!" a deep, rumbling voice said happily. "I'm alive!"

A third werewolf stood in the aisle over the shewolf's body, wearing a very toothy grin.

The bomber.

Great. Just freaking great.

Acting simultaneously, Logan and Tom clipped the wires that led to the devices' radios. Both men froze, sweat standing on their foreheads.

And nothing happened. They'd successfully disarmed both bombs.

"Thank you, Jesus," Tom muttered, and sat back on his heels with a sigh of relief.

"Amen," Logan said. But the smile vanished from his face as he remembered the danger Giada had courted by taking on the werewolves. He reached out through the Truebond—and found he was able to punch through to Giada's thoughts, as if her blocking spell had grown weak.

Pain instantly rammed through his body in an echo of Giada's injuries. Horrific, life-threatening injuries.

The werewolves were killing her.

His knees buckled, and he gasped at the combination of agony and the stark terror for her it inspired. "Shit!"

"Logan!" Tom yelped, staring at him in alarm. "What's wrong?"

"Giada . . ." he gasped, and forced himself back to his feet. What the hell happened? And how the *fuck* was he going to save her? His mind raced desperately—until a desperate idea popped into it.

Oh, Sweet Merlin's Cup. If this goes wrong . . .

But it was the only game in town. Throwing aside his doubts, he strode to the nearest window, picking up a straight-backed chair on the way. Setting his feet, he swung the chair hard. Shards of glass seemed to explode as the window broke, flying out into the cool spring night.

"What are you doing?" Tom demanded, staring at him in astonishment.

"Getting you three out of here." Logan ripped down the thick gold curtain and wrapped it around his forearm so he could finish breaking out the glass. *I hope to hell Giada's spell on Tom is still working, or I'm screwed.*

George Devon snarled as he dug his claws into Giada's breastplate, peeling the steel away from her body as if he were a can opener. The werewolf who'd been the bomber laughed like a hyena and slammed a big fist into her left leg. Something crunched.

Devon had hit her in a frenzy of rage she'd had no hope of defending herself against. He was too damn fast, too damn big.

Too damn crazy.

She should have been dead in the first twenty seconds of the werewolves' attack, but George hadn't wanted to let her die that quickly.

No, he meant for her to suffer.

He'd raked furrows in her armor, digging his claws into vulnerable flesh, spilling blood, ripping muscle, breaking bone.

And then he'd let her heal the worst of the damage. Just enough that she didn't bleed out too fast.

But they were getting tired of playing with her now, and she'd lost too much blood. She was beginning to float, the pain and terror becoming distant things.

It would not be much longer.

The only problem was Logan. She could feel him reaching for her, trying to draw her back. She was afraid she'd pull him with her when she went.

But surviving meant plunging back into that hell of blood and suffering, and she didn't think she had the strength.

Just let me go. Block me off. Don't go with me.

A thought shot back at her, powered by will and cool determination, cutting through the seductive fog of death. *No, Giada. Dammit, don't leave me!*

I can't take any more. And I'm tired of dying.

Logan raced down the hallway, following her fading life force. *Giada, I'm going to stop him. I swear, it's almost over.* He dove into the Truebond, grabbing for her consciousness with everything he had. *Hold on! Baby, please, please, just hold on! I need you . . .*

He's too strong. He'll kill you too. Don't die . . . God, her mental voice was so faint. *I don't want you to die trying to save me.*

He's not going to kill me. But by Merlin's balls, I am going to kill him. *You need to cast a shield over yourself, honey.*

Can't. She seemed to retreat. *Too weak. Go 'way. Don't want . . . you to die. Thought . . . I'd blocked you. True-bond's . . . new enough. I can . . . keep you out . . .*

No! No, dammit—But he could feel her floating away, willing herself farther behind her mental barriers. Trying to shield him from the death that hovered too damned close. *Giada, please!* He played his last card. *Giada, I love you!*

Love . . . me? She stopped retreating. At least he had her attention.

Unfortunately, he was running out of time to convince

her. He jolted to a stop outside the chapel and dropped to one knee to make frantic use of the tools he pulled from a pocket as he worked on the bundle he held.

Even as he finished the job, he gathered all his mental strength and drove it into her mind. *If you die, I swear to Merlin, I'll follow you. I'll die, too. I don't want to live without you. I can't live without you.*

With that, he dropped every mental barrier he'd ever raised against her—including those he'd used to hide the truth from himself. He showed them both his utter sincerity even as his fingers flew, putting together his weapon. *I love you, Giada.* Tears stung his eyes. *For Merlin's sake, don't leave me! Even if the Truebond doesn't kill me, losing you will.*

Agonizing seconds ticked by. *What do . . . you need me to do?*

Can you put up a shield?

I . . . Maybe. I'm weak. Lost too much blood. He felt her force herself back to consciousness, letting the full pain of her injuries hit her again. He heard her cry out, a faint, hoarse scream.

And then he felt her magic rise, powered by the very last of her strength.

Logan shoved the chapel doors open and stormed through. "Hey, assholes!"

The two Dire Wolves looked up at him in surprise as they crouched over Giada's sprawled body. Neither noticed the glitter of a magical shield waver into existence over her bloody form.

"Don't forget your toys!" Logan hefted the two bomb vests he'd wired together and hurled them overhand right at the Dire Wolves. Even as the bombs flew through the air, he dove for shelter between the pews.

The black wolf bellowed something. Logan didn't have time to recognize the word before the C4 detonated in a thunderous explosion that shook the floor. A pew slammed hard into Logan's head, and he saw sparks almost as bright as the flame that rolled across the room. Flaming chunks of wood and ceiling tile—and wet bits he didn't want to think

about—rained down around him. He curled into a tight ball, sheltering his bleeding head with both arms.

An endless moment later, the fall of debris stopped. His arm stung, and he looked up to see that his uniform shirt was on fire. He slapped the flame out and scrambled to his feet.

"Giada?"

There was a crater in the middle of the room, surrounded by tumbled, blasted pews, some of them burning merrily. Something small lay in the exact center of the blasted space.

"Shit! Giada!" He raced toward it. The air was so thick with dust and smoke, it was hard to see a damn thing. He was too busy listening for Giada's psychic spark to care.

He found her in the middle of a circle of seared and blackened flooring. The floor outside the circle was soaked with blood. Chunks of meat, bone, and seared body parts littered the floor all around.

A circle of undamaged carpet lay beneath her body; it had been protected by the magical shield she'd cast.

Dropping to his knees beside her, Logan hesitated, afraid to touch her. Bruises, claw marks, and bites marred her pale skin, and her face was so swollen he barely recognized her. He ached to jerk her into his arms, but he didn't dare.

"Oh, baby," he whispered. "I wish I could bring those bastards back from the dead so I could kill them all over again."

She needed help. Badly. And not mortal medical aid, either; he doubted a hospital could save her.

Unfortunately, she couldn't call the Mageverse for help. The Truebond told him she was out like a light, which was probably a good thing.

Luckily, he had an alternative, now that the jamming spell had been destroyed with the bombs.

Fumbling with one of the phone clips on his belt, Logan pulled out the magical cell Guinevere had given him. He knew he'd better act fast; he could hear voices in the distance. The deputies were beginning their search for bodies.

"Mom?"

An instant later, his mother answered. "Logan?"

He sagged in relief.

TWENTY-ONE

Logan's eyes opened as the sun slipped below the horizon. For a moment, he blinked up at the ceiling, disoriented by the mists of nightmares—blood, fire, explosions. And Giada, in pain. Dying beneath the claws and fangs of werewolves.

His head jolted off the pillow . . .

. . . to feel the delicate touch of Giada's mind a moment before she rolled over and draped herself across his chest. "Shhhhhh. It's okay." She looked blessedly healthy again, her beautiful face clean of blood and bruises, the body they'd broken healthy again.

Joy surged through him, so intense he wrapped his arms around her and hugged her fiercely. "Oh, God, girl, you scared me stupid."

"Yeah, well, it didn't do much for me either." Folding her long, lovely hands on his breastbone, Giada propped her chin on them and gave him a dazzling smile.

Logan stroked a strand of silky blond hair back from her face with his fingers. "What were you up to while I was in the Daysleep?"

She grimaced. "Mostly healing. It was all the other

witches who were working their brooms off. A team gated in as Gwen gated us out, and it still took half the night and all day to clean up the mess."

"I'm not surprised. There were probably three hundred witnesses to influence, most of 'em cops."

"And that's not even counting the ones with camera phones," she said wryly. "Anyway, as far as the mortals are concerned, nothing blew up. Morgana and her team repaired the damage to the funeral home and got rid of the bodies, then made everybody believe they never heard any kind of blast. They even re-created the damned vests you took off Andy and Heather."

Logan frowned. "What about the kids?"

"According to your mother, that was the tough part," Giada admitted. "Andy and Heather were heading for one hell of a case of post-traumatic stress—and that's without the memory of all those damned werewolves. Morgana had to do a lot of touchy psychic editing to make them remember the kidnappers as regular humans."

He cupped her arms, enjoying the warmth of her silky skin against his. He was starting to get hungry. "So if nothing blew up and the kidnappers were human, where did they go?"

Giada sighed. "Yeah, that was the rub. The gang supposedly slipped away while the funeral home was being evacuated."

"Hell." Logan glowered. "That means Lori and Tara don't get closure. And the sheriff takes the heat for losing the bad guys."

She shrugged. "It was that or give them pieces of dead werewolf. Which would have opened a can of worms the size of anacondas."

"What about Smoke? Is he okay? He was guarding those kids. I know he didn't let the bastards just waltz off with them."

"That's the biggest issue." Worry rolled through Giada, so intense across the Truebond that Logan stiffened in dread. "He vanished. The last the kids saw him, he was

fighting a white Dire Wolf who sounded a lot like Mrs. Devon's description of Warlock. As they drove away, he'd been imprisoned in some kind of energy globe. Guinevere did a scan for his magic, but she found nothing."

He stared at her in pain. "They're afraid he's dead."

"Yes," she admitted. "I'm sorry, Logan, but they don't think he made it. If he had, he would have returned to Avalon by now."

Logan's eyes narrowed. "Fuck that. We're going to go look."

They searched for three days, combing the area around the Jones home as well as every Mageverse haunt of Smoke's Logan could think of. They even checked out the animal shelter, in case the cat had been rendered powerless and picked up by Animal Control.

Like the Majae, they found nothing. It was as if he'd vanished off the face of the earth, magic and all.

"He's not dead," Logan told Giada as they returned to her house after yet another frustrating night. "He disappears like this all the time. He probably got hurt and holed up somewhere to heal. He'll turn up when he gets good and damned ready."

But she could feel the worry in the depths of his mind, vibrating a low, pained note through the Truebond.

As Giada watched, he dropped onto the couch and slumped, letting his dark head fall against the back. Despite his optimistic words, a mood of gloom hung around him.

Giada suspected at least part of his depression was born of handing his badge in.

This time Sheriff Jones had accepted Logan's resignation. Since he'd risked his life to save Heather and Andy, no one thought Logan had been involved in the bombings in any way whatsoever.

"I think you need cheering up," Giada announced,

reaching for the hem of her top. "And I know just how to do it."

He lifted his head and started to open his mouth, probably to tell her he wasn't really up for making love.

Then she peeled the loose cotton shirt off over her head, leaving her breasts cupped in delicate pink lace.

Logan's eyes heated. "You know, I think I'm feeling a little better already."

"Good." She reached for the zipper of her jeans and pulled it down as she gave her hips a slow, deliberate roll. Turning her back on him, she stripped them down her legs, making sure to bend deep to give him a good look at her ass. The hot purr that rolled through the Truebond told her just how much he enjoyed the view.

The panties went next. She kicked the scrap of pink silk across the room with a flick of one foot, then, still bending, reached back to unfasten her bra.

When Giada turned around, very thoroughly naked, she found Logan had gotten rid of his own knit shirt, displaying his broad, muscular chest for her enjoyment.

His socks soared across the room as she approached him in a hip-swaying stalk. He grinned as she bent and reached for his zipper, her eyes locked with his dark and hungry gaze. Yet beneath the hunger, she could still feel his pain.

The zipper hissed as Giada went after his belt, making the buckle ring as she unfastened it. Looking through the open fly, she found the head of his cock peeking over the waistband of his boxers, a drop of arousal beading its heart-shaped curve.

When Giada went to her knees, he growled, a soft, hungry vampire rumble. *Oooh, yeah*, she thought in the Truebond. *Your mood is definitely lifting.*

It's not the only thing. He caught his breath as she leaned down and licked the bead away with a flick of her pointed pink tongue. His cock reared against the soft cotton of his underwear with an eager jerk. She tugged the fabric lower, catching it under his balls, so she could trace a long nail down the length of his shaft. It was delightfully hard, with

a single fat vein snaking along its blood-darkened length. Giada gently traced her nails back up that vein, and grinned as he shuddered.

She hooked her hands in the waistband of his jeans and began to pull. He'd gotten rid of his shoes during her impromptu striptease, so she was able to peel them off and toss them aside without any pause in the delightful action.

Rising to her feet, Giada looked down at Logan as he sprawled in the dim light of the living room lamp. The light cast intriguing shadows over the muscled ridges and hollows of his big body. An intriguing ruff of soft hair rolled down his chest to fluff around his tight testicles, inviting her fingers.

Giada went to her knees and leaned forward to take his big shaft in hand. Through the Truebond, she felt pleasure jolt up his spine at her touch, and she grinned.

Then she lowered her head and gave him a long, slow lick from the base of his shaft to the head of his cock. He sucked in a breath and arched his back hard as he gasped, "That's . . . God!"

She purred at him and gave the head a slow swirling lick, as though his cock were a particularly delicious ice cream cone. The feral hunger that rolled through the bond in reply made her own arousal spike. Enjoying it thoroughly, she started licking—little flicks, long strokes, fluttering kisses.

From the corner of one eye, she watched his fingers dig into the arm of the couch in a ferocious bid for control. She hummed in satisfaction and swooped her mouth down over his cock.

The suckle she gave him made Logan's back arch like a drawn bow. "That's . . . enough!" he managed. "I want to . . ."

She dragged her mouth up until his cock escaped from her with a loud, deliberate pop. "Nope." Swirling her tongue thoughtfully over the head, she added after a moment, "I'm not finished."

"Yeah, well, unless you want *me* to finish . . ."

She lifted her head and raised a taunting brow. "I suggest you try to develop a little self-control."

But before she could pounce on his dick again, Logan reared up and grabbed her around the waist. Before she knew what hit her, he picked her up off the floor and draped her belly-down across the thickly padded arm of the chair.

"Hey!" Giada protested, trying to rear up again.

He planted one hand between her shoulder blades, holding her down as he picked up his belt.

This time her "Hey!" had considerably more emphasis, though he still didn't let her up. "I am *not* into spanking!"

Logan's chuckle sounded more than a little wicked. "Actually, I've got another kink in mind. Remember that first dream we shared?"

Intrigued, Giada subsided to stare over her shoulder at him. "The one where you . . . ?"

"Tied you up and screwed your brains out?" He wrapped the belt around her wrists and buckled it. "Yep, that's the one."

"Didn't that turn into a nightmare?" she said as he crawled onto the couch behind her.

"Yeah, well, I thought we'd give it a rewrite." He pushed her over farther and parted her cheeks so he could get at her sex. He rumbled approval when he found out how wet she was.

Hanging head-down over the couch arm, Giada moaned in delight as his tongue scooped between her nether lips, licking and swirling delicious little patterns. "Oooh," she whimpered. "That's . . . incredible. And more than a little evil."

"Just wait." He laughed wickedly. "I've barely gotten started."

Hands tied behind her back, she could only quiver in response.

Logan was merciless, licking and nibbling at her as if she were a particularly juicy peach, pressing his face close so he could get at every inch of her. Giada squirmed at the

little jolts of pleasure that arrowed from his busy tongue. Threw back her head when he slid one arm around her left leg so he could cup her hanging breast. Rolling and squeezing her nipple with delicate ruthlessness, he went on driving her slowly insane.

Her orgasm hit in a storm of heat and light, roaring through the Truebond with maddening intensity. With a growl, Logan released her, straightened, and grabbed his cock.

Giada screamed in delight as he drove into her right to his balls. Growling, he started thrusting, driving hard, grinding deep. Each deep lunge added another crazed sensation to her ferocious climax. She writhed, yelling her delight without an ounce of self-consciousness.

He came, bellowing right back at her, flooding the Truebond with the incredible erotic feedback of a shared orgasm. When the blaze finally winked out, he clung to her back, both of them sweating and half-stunned.

When he finally spoke, his voice sounded hoarse. "Marry me, Giada. I love you. I don't want to live without you."

She could feel the utter truth of that statement in their bond, just as he could feel her own love for him. "Yes, Logan. God, yes!"

With a soft, triumphant growl, he took her throat, drinking deep.

Giada moaned in delight—both his, and her own.

Together at last.

Turn the page for a special preview of
Angela Knight's next novel

MASTER OF SMOKE

Coming soon from Berkley Sensation!

CHAPTER ONE

A werewolf was killing a man. But not with claws.

With magic.

Beth Roman watched in horror from the concealment of the woods. Thick brush screened her hiding place even as branches scratched her arms. She ignored the sting, too wired to care. Next to her, Rhett Butler whined at her distress, while Scarlett licked her face. Beth gently pushed the Irish Setter's muzzle away, her eyes locked on the scene as her pack pressed close around her, the four dogs whimpering softly.

The armored man writhed almost five feet off the ground, suspended in a glowing globe of energy. An enormous werewolf watched him, a vicious grin on his fanged muzzle, eyes glowing feral and orange with greed.

The creature looked even bigger than the monster that had attacked Beth, easily eight feet tall, as brawny as a polar bear. Like the bear, his fur was a snowy white, though flecked with dark splatters—the man's blood.

I've got to do something. Beth flexed her hands as cold anxiety drew her muscles into quivering knots. As soon

as the werewolf got tired of torturing his victim with . . . whatever it was he was doing, he was going to start using fangs and claws. And the man would have no more chance than she'd had.

She had to save the poor bastard. She couldn't just sit here and watch the monster rip him apart.

Beth's stomach roiled in icy nausea at the thought of fighting another werewolf. Memories flashed through her mind, blood-soaked and echoing with screams. *Claws ripping flesh, fangs sinking into her belly, the spreading cold of death as her life drained away* . . . She swallowed hard, trying to keep from tossing the burger she'd had for dinner.

Sucking in a hard breath, Beth started to call her magic. *No*, cried a shrill little mental voice. *He'll sense me change. He'll come after me* . . .

But if she did nothing, the armored man would die. And she didn't want to live with that kind of guilt. What if someone could have saved *her*, and done nothing because of cowardice?

And that's what it was. Cowardice.

Beth breathed deep again, shoving aside her howling terror and stuffing the memory of pain and blood back into its scarred psychic box.

But just as she reached for the magic, the armored man did . . . *something*. Magic began to surge and swirl, hotter, brighter inside the energy globe, streaming into the clawed fingers the werewolf had shoved into the shimmering blue field.

What the hell is he . . .

Before she could even finish the thought, the magic detonated like a bomb. The blast was eye-searing, yet utterly silent except for the psychic rumble it sent rolling through her brain.

Gasping, Beth threw up a hand to shield her tearing eyes. The dogs howled in alarm.

When she could see again, the werewolf lay on his back, smoke rising from his singed claws, from his muzzle, even from his closed eyes.

And both the energy globe and the man were gone.

Had he blown himself up?

No, wait—there he was, running for the woods. Actually, more staggering than running, his face white and blank, stunned, as if he was moving on blind instinct.

And good grief, he was naked. Beth blinked. What had happened to his armor?

Not that it mattered. He was hurt. She had to help him.

Beth scrambled to her feet, the dogs whining in excitement as she plunged after the staggering man. Her pack galloped at her heels—the black German shepherd she called Rhett, Irish Setter Scarlett, Rocky the pit bull, and Marty the fox terrier.

Even as she ran, she threw a quick look back at the werewolf. He hadn't moved, apparently out cold on his back in the driveway of the middle-class house, curls of smoke still wafting from his body into the spring night.

Why the hell hadn't the neighbors called the cops? Could be the monster had cast some kind of spell to keep them from noticing while he tried to commit murder next door.

Though the idea of a magic-using werewolf was just *wrong*. Wasn't it enough being a seven-foot tall fanged, furry sociopath? *I mean, come* on, *Cujo. Isn't that a little over the top?*

Beth glanced around. Cujo's former victim wasn't letting any grass grow under his bare feet. He reeled through the woods as if he could see in the dark, every step shouting of a grim determination to put as much distance as possible between himself and Cujo. Not that Beth could blame him.

Hell, *she* was feeling a little better at leaving the bastard behind, and he hadn't been trying to kill her.

Though he probably would have gotten around to it sooner or later. He had that sort of charming personality. Kind of like a furry Komodo dragon.

So Beth didn't blame Naked Guy a bit for beating feet. Especially since he had a really nice ass. She could see it, showing pale and muscular through the darkness as it bobbed up and down with his determined strides.

Then he stumbled over a root, slammed a shoulder into a tree trunk, and fell on his face in the leaves.

Shit. Beth raced toward him, the dogs yipping in excitement as they paced her. Reaching the man, she slid to her knees.

"Hey, are you okay?" She took him by one brawny shoulder and rolled him over. He was heavy, massive with bone and muscle. Back in her human days, she probably wouldn't have been able to budge him at all. He stared at her, dazed. She tried again, enunciating. "Are you hurt?"

"Don't . . . know." Swallowing, he blinked up at her. "Who're you?"

"Beth Roman." She scanned his face. Damn, he was handsome, even with scratches marring his face. "What's your name?"

He opened his mouth, only to close it again. The expression of puzzlement grew in his striking blue eyes. They were pale as crystal in the moonlight. "I . . . don't know."

Beth frowned down at him, then raised a hand before his eyes. "How many fingers am I holding up?"

He didn't even hesitate. "Two."

Okay, not seeing double or anything, which was a good sign. Still . . . She bit her lip. "You probably have a concussion." Her first instinct was to tell him to stay put while she dug out her cell and called 911. Unfortunately, they were still way too close to Cujo.

If the werewolf came to before the ambulance arrived, they'd have serious trouble. And they wouldn't be the only ones, either, because Cujo might decide to eat the ambulance crew. Which was why she hadn't called the cops earlier. "Do you think you can walk?"

He considered the question, frowning deeply. "I . . . believe so. I think I'd better."

"I think you're right." She reached to help him up, sliding one arm around his bare waist and grabbing his hand in her own. He reeled to his feet and almost fell again.

"Whoa! Hey, not so fast, big guy." Beth tightened her

grip and braced him against her hip, pulling one of his arms around her shoulders by the hand.

She was abruptly aware of the feel of his body, tall and warm, his waist solid under her palm, his arm heavy with muscle. *Cut it out*, she told herself savagely.

Beth could generally ignore men, no matter how handsome—and this guy was definitely handsome, his features as sharply sculpted as a male model's. Her gaze lingered on his profile, on the full curve of lips that seemed to invite . . .

Stop it.

Just her luck to run into a guy like him this time of year, when all she could think about was sex. She badly wanted to get the heck away from him, but she strongly suspected he'd fall on his face if she let him go. *The man is hurt. Quit acting like a nympho.*

Gritting her teeth, Beth concentrated on steering him deeper into the woods.

"Where are we going?" He had a great voice, too, a deep masculine rumble that she could feel way down low in her . . .

Stop it.

"My apartment. But first we've got to make sure he can't follow your scent."

"Who?" He frowned. Even that looked good on him.

"The werewolf who attacked you just now. Don't you remember?"

He hesitated, as if searching his memory. "No." His mouth drew into a grim line. Strangely, he didn't question the "werewolf" bit at all. Must be used to weirdness. Which made sense, considering the way he threw magic around.

She was suddenly far too aware of his hair, which spilled over his shoulders halfway down his back. The ends of it tickled the back of her hand where she gripped his waist. It was a deep black, except for silvery stripes that ran horizontally across the length of it, rather than vertically. She wondered how he'd achieved the effect. It couldn't be natural.

Then again, how did she know what was natural for him? It was a sure bet he was no more normal than she was.

He jolted against her and looked down, his expression startled.

"Rocky, get your cold nose away from there," she told the pit bull, feeling a blush heat her face. "That's just plain rude."

The man shielded himself from the dog's sniffing muzzle with one hand. Big as his palm was, it didn't quite cover the territory. "Does he bite?" He sounded more than a little nervous.

"No," Beth said, then added more honestly, "not unless I tell him to. Which I wouldn't."

He looked up at her, the corner of his lips lifting in a dry smile. "I can't tell you how that relieves my mind."

"Any idea what your name is yet?" Somehow "hey, you" didn't seem appropriate, what with the nakedness and all . . .

He considered the question for a little too long. Dark brows drew down over his remarkable eyes as a muscle jerked in his jaw. "No." That growl would have done Rhett proud.

Her gaze lingered on that chiseled profile. "How does David sound? Just until you remember."

His lips shaped the name, seemed to consider the taste. "All right." He met her gaze and smiled. "David. Yes, that will do."

Oh, my God, that smile. Beth blinked, feeling as if he'd hit her with a board.

She was in such trouble.

His rescuer was beautiful. Her body curved against his, surprisingly strong considering the top of her head barely came to his shoulder. Her hair was a short, dark cap of intriguing curls, though he couldn't tell the color in this light. Her eyes were dark under straight brows, her jaw delicately angular, features elegant. She looked as if she should be

peeking between forest leaves, wings shimmering between her shoulder blades.

Memory flashed through his mind—a small face peering at him just that way, eyes bright with magic . . .

The image vanished before he could capture it, gone like smoke whisping between his fingers.

Frustration whipped through him. Why couldn't he remember? What in the name of all the gods and demons had happened to his mind?

He felt so empty. So helpless. As if something that should be there was missing. Whatever it was ached like a phantom limb, like something vital that had been amputated.

The girl was right about one thing: He'd been in a fight. He hurt, and bruises shadowed his ribs. There were cuts, too, slashing across his arms and legs. And his head ached as if he was being pounded by a fiend from hell.

Why can't I remember?

It was obvious that whatever had happened in the fight had resulted in both his vanished memories and the . . . amputation of whatever the hell it was he'd lost.

He strained to remember as they walked, ignoring the dogs that trotted beside them like bodyguards. Trying to ignore the warmth of the girl's slim body under his arm, the way she nestled against his side.

Which was much more difficult than ignoring her pets.

She smelled . . . delicious. Like deep forest and oranges. Odd combination, yet strangely seductive. Her body felt soft and strong at once, slim and solid and warm against his.

Feeling his sex begin to stir, he straightened hastily away from her supporting grip. Naked as he was, getting an erection just now would be acutely embarrassing. "I can walk on my own now."

"You sure? If you've got a concussion, you don't want to fall again." Her eyes searched his face, dark with concern. And lovely. So lovely.

"I'm fine." A lie, but necessary to his pride. He straightened his shoulders and stalked along grimly, ignoring the leaves and sticks that prickled his bare feet and the ache of

his abused body. One of the dogs pressed a big, broad head up under his hand, and he stroked the beast absently as he walked.

He was acutely conscious of the girl—Beth, her name is Beth—watching him anxiously.

It hit him suddenly that if this werewolf enemy of his came after him again, she'd be in danger.

Then I'll protect her, he thought grimly. *And I'll make the bastard pay.*

Memory or no memory.

FROM *NEW YORK TIMES* BESTSELLING AUTHOR

Angela Knight

WARRIOR

First in the Time Hunters series

In the twenty-third century, anyone can leap through time at will. Galar Arvid is a genetically altered warlord and Temporal Enforcement police agent who's been sent back to 2008 to save a pretty Atlanta artist from a Xeran time traveler who intends to kill her for profit. What Galar doesn't count on is the powerful desire Jessica Kelly ignites in him. Can their romance work with a three-hundred-year chasm between them and a maniacal killer on their tails?

penguin.com

M389T1208

MASTER OF THE NIGHT

"Her novels are spicy, extremely sexy, and truly fabulous . . . Complex and intriguing . . . Loads of possibilities for future sensual adventures."
—*Romantic Times*

"A terrific paranormal romantic suspense thriller that never slows down until the final confrontation between good and evil. The action-packed story line moves at a fast clip."
—*Midwest Book Review*

Further praise for the novels of Angela Knight

"Nicely written, quickly paced, and definitely on the erotic side."
—*Library Journal*

"The sex scenes were explosive and should have come with a warning for the reader to have a fire extinguisher handy during reading."
—*Euro-Reviews*

"Delicious . . . Wonderfully crafted . . . Angela Knight brings such life to her characters and to the world she's created for them that readers can't help but believe in magic."
—*Romance Reviews Today*

"If you like alpha heroes, wild rides, and pages that sizzle in your hand, you're going to love [Angela Knight]!"
—*New York Times* bestselling author J. R. Ward

"From the first page Ms. Knight has me hook, line, and sinker . . . Titillating and action-packed."
—*A Romance Review*

"Exceptionally written, refreshing." —*Fallen Angel Reviews*

JANE'S WARLORD

continued . . .